GLIMPSES
GLIMPSES

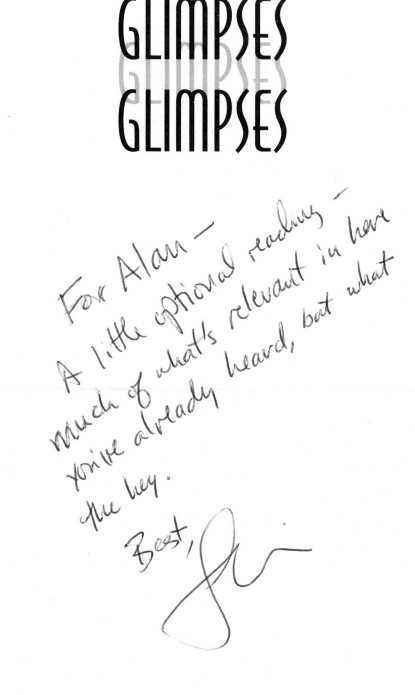

For Alan —
A little optional reading —
much of what's relevant in here
you've already heard, but what
the hey.

Best,

Also by Lewis Shiner

SLAM

DESERTED CITIES OF THE HEART

FRONTERA

WHEN THE MUSIC'S OVER (Editor)

Lewis Shiner

GLIMPSES
GLIMPSES
GLIMPSES

A Novel

Carrboro NC - Jan 5, 2001

WILLIAM MORROW AND COMPANY, INC.
New York

Library of Congress Cataloging-in-Publication Data

Shiner, Lewis.
  Glimpses / Lewis Shiner.
    p.   cm.
  ISBN 0-688-12411-9
  I. Title.
PS3569.H496G57   1993
813'.54—dc20   93-33
                            CIP

Printed in the United States of America

First Edition

1 2 3 4 5 6 7 8 9 10

BOOK DESIGN BY KATHRYN PARISE

For Mary K.,
who showed me how to end this,
with all my love

This book owes its existence to the gracious help of more people than I can mention. Special thanks are due to my mother, Maxine Shiner, to Paul Bradshaw, and to Mary K. Alberts. My gratitude also to Mike Autrey, Edith Beumer, Jim Blaylock, Viki Blaylock, Zorina Bolton, Harold Bronson, Richard Butner, Darell Clingman, Anne Cook, Marianne Faithfull, Karen Joy Fowler, William Gibson, Patrick Goldstein, James "Al" Hendrix, Tricia Jumonville, Howard Kaylan, Patricia Kennealy, Rick Klaw, Timothy Leary, Dan Levy, Bill Lightner, Martha Millard, Charles Shaar Murray, Domenic Priore, Bud Simons, Tom Smith, Joe Stefko, Roger Trilling, Elissa Turner, Mark Volman, Denise Weinberg, Bob Welch, Glen Wheeler, and Adrian Zackheim.

This book is a work of fiction, although it also deals with historical events. Those segments of the work that are historical in nature are based on extensive research and interviews. Some real persons, both deceased and alive, are mentioned in the work. However, to the extent those persons are depicted as interacting with the narrator of the novel, their actions, motivations, and conversations are entirely fictitious and should not be considered real or factual.

GLIMPSES

CHAPTER 1

CHAPTER 1
CHAPTER 1

Get Back

Once upon a time there was going to be a Beatles album called *Get Back*. They tried to record it in January of 1969, first at Twickenham Film Studios, then in the basement of Apple Corps at 3 Savile Row. Their own overpriced twenty-four-track dream studio wasn't finished and they had to bring in a mobile unit. So there they were, under bright lights, using rented gear, with cameras filming every move they made.

Paul had this idea he could turn things around. He wanted to get back to the kind of material the band did in '61 and '62, at the Kaiserkeller in Hamburg and the Cavern Club in Liverpool. It must have seemed like another century to them, looking back. They tried to warm up with Chuck Berry standards and "One After 909," something of John's from when he was seventeen. But it was winter and snowy and cold. The soundstage echoed and the basement was cramped. It just wasn't happening.

That summer they would try again, and this time it would work, and they would come away with *Abbey Road*. The tapes from the other sessions would end up with Phil Spector, who would overproduce the living Jesus out of them to make them sound alive and finally they would come out as *Let It Be*.

The new title pretty much says it all. Between winter and summer everything changed. Paul married Linda, John married Yoko, and Allen Klien took over Apple. By then it was too late to get back, ever again.

———

My father died not quite two weeks ago. I can say the words but they don't seem to mean anything or even matter much. My mind goes blank. So I think about other things. I put *Let It Be* on the stereo and wonder what it would sound like if things had been different.

Music is easy. It isn't even that important what the words say. The real meaning is in the guitars and drums, the way a record *sounds*. It's a feeling that's bigger than words could ever be. A guy named Paul Williams said that, or something close to it, and I believe it's true.

I've been in Dallas with my mother, straightening out the VA insurance, helping her write a form letter to use instead of a Christmas card, answering the phone, getting Dad's name off the bank account, a million little things that can bleed you dry. Now I'm home again in Austin trying to make sense of it.

It's November of 1988. The old man died the week before Thanksgiving, a hell of a thing. He was scuba diving in Cozumel, which he was too old for, with my mother along for the ride. He used to teach anthropology at SMU but since he retired all he wanted to do was dive. My wife and I flew up to Dallas to meet my mother's plane as she came back alone, looking about a hundred years old. She'd had him burned down there in Mexico, brought a handful of ashes with her in a Ziploc bag. Elizabeth came home that weekend and I stayed up there ten days, all I could stand. Then I drove back here in his white GMC pickup truck, my inheritance. The inside still smells like him, sweat and polyester and old Fritos.

Anyway, it's 1988 and it was just last year that they finally released all the Beatles' albums on CD, making a big deal out of how it was the twentieth anniversary of *Sgt. Pepper*. It was like everybody had forgotten about the sixties until we had this nationwide fit of nostalgia. Suddenly every station on the radio has gone to some kind of oldies format, and they play the same stuff over and over again that you haven't heard in twenty years, and now you're sick to death of "Spirit in the Sky" and "The Year 2525" all over again. Tie-dyed shirts are back and bands that should never have been together in the first place have reunion tours and everybody shakes their heads over how dumb and idealistic they used to be.

I run a stereo repair business out of the house. Most of the upstairs is my shop. The north wall is my workbench, covered with tools, an oscilloscope and a digital multimeter, a couple of my clients' boxes with their insides spread out. The wall above it is cork and there are a million pieces of junk pinned to it: circuit diagrams, pictures of me and Elizabeth and the cat, phone messages, business cards from my parts people, a big black-and-white poster of Jimi Hendrix that I've had since college. The west wall is windows, partly covered by corn plants, palms, and dieffenbachia that Elizabeth fixed me up with, all rugged stuff that even I haven't been able to kill. The south side is shelves, over and under a countertop. That's where I keep the boxes I'm not currently working on, as well as my own system. Harmon Kardon amp, Nakamichi Dragon cassette deck, four Boston Acoustics A70 speakers, linear tracking turntable, CD player, graphic equalizer, monster cables all around. There's something almost spiritual about it, all that matte black, with graphs and numbers glowing cool yellow and white and green, like a quiet voice that tells you everything is going the way it should. It's just hardware, metal and silicon and plastic, but at the same time it has the power to turn empty air into music. That never ceases to amaze me.

I only have *Let It Be* on vinyl. The second side was playing, halfway in, and "The Long and Winding Road" came on, full of crackles and pops. I was running on automatic, my hair tied back, house shoes on, resoldering a couple of cold joints. The song is just Paul on the piano, a McCartney solo track really, with a huge orchestra and chorus that Phil Spector dubbed on afterward. A decent tune, though, even John admitted that.

I don't remember the first time I heard it, but I remember the one that stuck. It takes me back to Nashville, early June of 1970. I remember it was a Sunday. I heard this announcement on the radio that my band, the Duotones, was supposed to play that afternoon in Centennial Park. It was news to me. I showed up and sure enough, there they were, sounding a little hollow and tinny inside the big concrete band shell, and there in the middle was their new drummer. Scott, the lead player, came out in the audience during the break and said, "We were going to tell you. That promoter we hooked up with, he had his own drummer."

I remember being able to see the individual pebbles in the pinkish concrete under the bench. The bench, I think, was green. There wasn't a lot for me to say. My bridges were burned. I'd spent the last month flunking out of Vanderbilt, too busy with band practice or protests over the shootings at Kent and Jackson State to go to class. I hadn't managed to stop the war, and now I didn't have a band either.

I hung around until they closed my dorm and then I hit the road. I'd already told my parents I wasn't coming home for the summer, so I just drove on through Dallas, headed for Austin, where Alex was. She wasn't my girlfriend anymore. We'd broken up the fall before. But then we'd broken up a million times and if I was there, staying at her house, maybe she would change her mind.

All I had was AM radio in my car and it seemed like they only played two songs that whole trip. One was Joe Cocker's cover of "The Letter," with Leon Russell's piano sharp as an ice pick, making me push the gas to the floor and feel the hot wind through the open windows. The other was "The Long and Winding Road." It had been a pretty long road for me and Alex. I'd known her since sophomore year in high school, since we were all in drama club together. I'd seen her long hair go from red to brown to black, listened to her rave about everything from astrology to Bob Dylan to BMW motorcycles. I'd spent the last half of my senior year and the summer after helplessly in love with her. It was my first real love affair, full of jealousy and tears, the unendurable pain of an unanswered phone, long drives back from her mother's apartment at two in the morning, dozing off at the wheel. But mostly it was making love: in the car, on the floor of her mother's den, at friends' houses, in my bed with my parents watching TV in the next room.

The Beatles didn't get it together for *Get Back* and Alex and I didn't get it together in the summer of 1970. I moved off her couch after a week or so and rented a room up on Castle Hill. Before I left I got this letter, care of her, from my father. It was always my mother who wrote me, I guess that's true in most families. This time it was him, on a sheet of yellow legal paper, printed in block capitals. "GO AHEAD AND PLAY IN THE TRAFFIC," it said. Then, at the bottom, "ONE THING YOU FORGOT: LOVE." I can't remember him ever using the word before. It looked like a lie. He signed it "DAD." I didn't tear it up, bad as I wanted to. Maybe I just wanted to keep hating him the way I did right that minute.

During those long summer days in Austin I looked for work. Everything turned out to be door-to-door sales. At night I tried to put a band together with a guy who'd just learned to play guitar and an organist who'd done nothing but classical. One day the bass player disappeared in his ice-cream truck en route to Houston, and that was the last straw. I ended up back in Dallas in spite of myself, getting a degree in electrical engineering from DeVry Institute. That got me my first decent job, printed circuit design for the late lamented Warrex Computer Corporation.

There's magic, see, and there's science. Science is what I learned at DeVry and it bought me this nice two-story house off 290 in East Austin. Magic says if maybe the Beatles could have hacked it, then maybe Alex and me could have hacked it.

If the Beatles had hacked it, "The Long and Winding Road" would have sounded a lot different. Paul always hated what Spector did to it, wanted it to be a simple piano ballad. John might have written a new middle eight for it, something with an edge to cut the syrupy romanticism. George could have played some of the string parts on the guitar, and Ringo could have punched the thing up, given it more of a push.

It could have happened. Say Paul had realized the movie was a stupid idea. Say they'd given up on recording at Apple and gone back to Abbey Road where they belonged, let George Martin actually produce instead of sitting around listening to them bicker. I'd seen enough pictures of the studio. I could see it in my head.

Here's George Martin, tall, craggy-looking, big forehead, easy smile. Light brown hair slicked back tight. He's got on his usual white dress shirt and tie, sitting near the window of the control room which looks down on Studio 2. Studio 2 is the size of a warehouse, thirty-foot ceiling, quilted moving blankets thrown over everything, microphones of every shape and size from the slim German condensers to the old-fashioned oblong ribbon types, miles of cable, music stands like small metal trees. Here's John, his beard just starting to come in, hair down to here, Yoko growing out of his armpit. Paul's beard is already there, George Harrison and Ringo have mustaches. Paul is in a long-sleeved shirt and sleeveless sweater, John and Yoko are in matching black turtlenecks, George has a bandanna tied cowboy-style around his neck. The tape is on a quarter-inch reel, not the inch-wide stuff they use now. It's been less than twenty years, after all, since the studio stopped recording directly onto wax disks. Everything about the mixers and faders is oversized, big ceramic handles, big needles on the VU meters, everything painted battleship gray. The air smells of hair oil and cigarette smoke. Everyone bums Everest cigarettes off of Geoff Emerick, who is in a white lab coat like all the other EMI engineers.

They're listening to the playback. Here's Ringo's deadened toms, four quick chord changes on John's sunburst Strat at the end of each line . . .

And there it was. Coming out of the speakers in my workshop. For half a minute it didn't even seem weird. I put down my soldering gun and listened, feeling all the emotion that had been buried under the strings rise to the surface.

Then it hit me, really hit me, what I was listening to. As soon as it did the music slowed and went back to the way it always has been.

———

I was light-headed and there was a sound like tape hiss in my ears. I cut the stereo off and sat on the old brown leather couch by the windows, thinking, what the hell just happened? The cat, who is this big black-and-gray tabby named Dude, jumped up in my lap like he always does when I sit on his couch. I started to pet him and then the fatigue washed up over me. I let myself doze off for a few minutes and when I woke up my head was going like a bass drum.

It was three o'clock. Elizabeth would be home any minute. I went down to the kitchen and ate a couple of cookies to get my blood sugar up. I felt weird, tapped out, like I'd just come down with something. I wondered if maybe I had. Maybe I'd hallucinated the whole thing.

I heard Elizabeth's car in the driveway.

I never know what kind of mood she'll be in. Sometimes it's been kids yelling at her all day and she just wants silence or the TV. I put the cookies away and rinsed out my milk glass. The door opened with a kind of squeak and pop. I heard her toss her purse on the table by the door, walk into the living room, and collapse on the couch. "Any mail?" she said.

I came out of the kitchen, drying my hands on a dish towel. I could only see her blonde hair where it hung over the back of the couch, all those different shades, gold and light brown and honey and yellow and white. "Not yet."

I thought, if she asks how my day went, I'll say something. She picked up the remote control and turned the TV on to CNN. Somebody was talking about president-elect Bush and the antidrug hysteria the whole campaign had caused.

"What a day," she said. "This one kid, Mikey?"

I walked over and sat on the stairs. "You told me about Mikey before."

"Yeah. Well, today he herded about six of the girls under the slide and charged the boys a quarter apiece to go under there with them. Of course his father's the stockbroker, so I guess I shouldn't be surprised that it breeds true."

I was too woozy to manage a laugh. "You want a drink?"

"Not right now. I need a new job, is what I need." She's talked about quitting since her first year in the school system and I don't take her seriously anymore. I went back to the kitchen and cracked a Bud, my first of the day. It didn't do much for the headache right away, but these things take time.

=====

That night I had another nightmare about my father. I go to this huge shed to rent scuba gear for him. The floor is like the deck of a ship and rolls under my weight. I don't see anything but these weird, bell-shaped tanks and I tell the guy I need the big aluminum ones. I'm pleased that I wasn't taken in by such obviously bogus tanks. He goes to get the right kind and I follow. The floor starts to really roll and then sinks. The suction of the sinking floor pulls me under. My shoes and wet clothes are too heavy. I can't get to the surface and I start to panic. I know that I know how to swim and this should be all okay, only it isn't. I start yelling.

I was still yelling when Elizabeth managed to wake me up. She made sure I was okay and then she turned over and went back to sleep. It's a talent she has. I myself lay there for a long time, trying to clear all the shit and nonsense out of my head. It's like the Zen business where you're supposed to not think about a white horse, only it's impossible, you can't *not* think about something. My father used to tell me that story, now it's my father I can't get rid of. He's right there, floating facedown in the blue-green water, the regulator hanging out of his mouth and leaking a thin stream of bubbles.

I tried to think about the thing that happened with the Beatles song. That was just as scary. So I finally pictured a wiring diagram for an amplifier and made myself an electron, and I followed my way through the gates and resistors and capacitors like I was walking a garden maze and that finally did the trick.

———

The last time I talked to my father we got in an argument over cameras. You'd think after thirty-some-odd years I would have learned to keep it from happening. Not a chance. He could always find some way, if he kept at me long enough, to get me to fight back. It was my mom that called, of course. At the end she made him get on the phone with me, and somehow he ended up telling me that no camera in the world had an f-stop larger than f-4. "I'm looking at my camera right here," I said. "I have it in my hands. It goes f-4, then f-2.8, then f-1.8."

"It must be some kind of Russian camera."

"Dad, it's a fucking Nikon."

"Well, it's the only one like it ever made."

By that point even I could sense that it was time to cut my losses. Like the guy that goes to the doctor and says, "It hurts when I bend over," and the doctor says, "Don't bend over." For the first time in my life I knew, I could see without question, that my old man would never change.

Elizabeth has this friend named Sandra that we see at parties. She's in Al-Anon, for people with alcoholic parents. The whole co-dependent twelve-step thing. They tell her you have to quit trying to change them. It's not your fault. Change yourself to where you can get clear of it.

So that was what I did. I said, "Yeah, Dad, right Dad, good-bye Dad." That was in August, the last words I ever said to him, and in November he was dead.

It was hard to walk away from an argument with him, to not try to win. Sometimes not doing something is the hardest thing there is. Not thinking about that damned white horse. Not taking that one last drink that you know will make you throw up. Not making a pass at the divorcée with the antique eight-track who would happily pay with something other than cash.

So when I got this letter from my mother in October that told me how disappointed she was that I wouldn't talk to my father, that I wouldn't even apologize, I lost my temper. I was so mad it was like shock. I sat for an hour or so trying to work and couldn't even move my hands. So I wrote her back, told her everything I could remember that he'd done to piss me off or fuck me up. I didn't hold back on the cheap shots or the whining or the guilt.

Elizabeth came home while I was reading it over and for some reason I handed her my mother's letter, and then mine. I told her, "I'm not going to send it, of course."

She read both of them and said, "No, you're right. You shouldn't send this." I felt weirdly let down for half a second, then she said, "You should make it stronger. She said she doesn't feel welcome in our house. Tell her the truth. Tell her she's welcome, but he's not. Tell her he doesn't know how to behave around decent people. Tell her the way he treats you. Go ahead and tell her."

"I thought . . ."

"What?"

"I always thought you blamed me. For the way things are between us. That you wanted me to somehow make up with him."

"I never said that. I didn't say anything like that. What I wanted was for you to write a letter like this, but I didn't want to push." She stood there with her arms folded, cold and solid, like an iceberg. I liked having that chill directed at somebody else for a change.

So I wrote the letter. I told my mother how, when he played games with me as a kid, he would tear up the cards if I started to win. How whenever Elizabeth or I cooked for him, he would look at the plate and say, "What is this shit?" like it was supposed to be funny. How when I was in high school and he couldn't find anything to punish me for, he would ground me for my "attitude." It ran to four pages. I mailed it before I could change my mind.

I got this apologetic letter back from my mother. Eventually she talked to my father about some of the things I said and he told her, "He'll get over it."

That was the week before they went to Cozumel.

━━━━━

So my father is dead, and Alex is married with two kids somewhere in Austin. But there is this other lost thing, this Beatles song, and maybe I can have that back.

Elizabeth was off to work by 7:30 the next morning. I did the breakfast dishes and went upstairs. I had a couple of easy jobs that I was supposed to get out by lunch—new belts on a turntable, an amp with a short in the power supply. I couldn't make myself look at them. Instead I got out a new Maxell XLII60 and put it in the Nakamichi. I powered it up and fast-forwarded the tape all the way through, then rewound it to get the tension right. I cued it up past the leader. Then I sat down on the couch with the remote.

I laid it all out in my head like before. The control booth, the four Beatles, the soundstage outside the window. George Martin with his chin in his hand, Geoff Emerick rewinding the tape. Martin nods to Emerick. I turned on the Nakamichi.

The song played through to the final "yeah yeah yeah yeah." After that was the squeak of the piano stool, the click of the intercom, and Martin's voice from the tape saying, "Come on up, fellows, let's listen to that one." Then silence.

My hands and my forehead were sweating. I pried my eyes open. November sunshine, digital readouts on the stereo, the spools of the cassette still turning. I rewound the tape and dropped the remote on the couch next to me.

I was exhausted. I went downstairs and washed my face, poured a fresh cup of coffee. Either there was something on the tape or there wasn't. Either way I didn't know what to do about it.

I fought my way through the two repair jobs and called the customers. Then I took a nap for an hour. I was still tired when I woke up, but my nerves wouldn't let me sleep any longer. I went upstairs and played the tape.

━━━━━

I was waiting for Elizabeth when she got home. She stopped in her tracks when she saw me. "What's wrong?"

I said, "I want you to come upstairs and listen to something."

"Right now?"

"I think so, yeah."

She dumped her purse and her books and sighed theatrically as she climbed the stairs. She sat on the couch and listened to the tape all the way through. "The Beatles, right?"

"Did you notice anything different about it?"

"I guess. It sounded faster maybe."

"It's a totally different version."

"One of those bootlegs or something?"

"Uh-uh. It's not like that at all." I got up and went over to the deck and shut it down. "I made it," I said.

"I don't understand."

"I don't either." I turned around and faced her, leaning back against the countertop. "I know this sounds completely crazy. I was trying to imagine the song, I mean the Beatles playing it this way, and it started to come out of the speakers. So I, like, did it again, with the recorder on, and I got a tape of it."

Elizabeth sat there for a long time, looking at me. The sun behind her made it hard to read her expression. She was perched on the very edge of the sofa, like she didn't mean to stay. A half smile on her face came and went, like a rheostat dimming and raising the lights. Finally she said, "This is some kind of joke, right?"

"It's not a joke."

"I don't understand. What is it you want me to say?"

"You heard the tape. It *is* something different."

"I can't authenticate a Beatles record for you. I mean, come on. I can tell you that yes, you sound pretty crazy."

"I can do it again."

"Ray, listen to yourself. Do you really expect me to believe this is some kind of, I don't know, psychic phenomenon? I'm worried about you. I know this business with your father has been hard. You're not sleeping, you're having all these nightmares. Maybe you ought to get some help."

"I can do it again. I'll show you." I was dead tired, and it was hard to concentrate with her in the room. But I did, and a few seconds of music came out of the speakers.

Elizabeth stood up. "It's not funny, Ray. If you want to tell me what's really going on, fine, I'll be downstairs. I can't handle this right now. I need a hot shower and a little peace and quiet."

She went downstairs. I lay down on the couch in a band of warm sunlight and went to sleep.

That night I had another dream. My father is kneeling in front of me. He says something, daring me, I think, and I start to hit him in the face. I hit him until my arms get tired and then I realize out of nowhere that I might be hurting him. I start to put my arms around him, to apologize. He takes it the same way he took the beating, deadpan, no emotion, doesn't say a word.

When I woke up I wondered if Elizabeth was right. Maybe I was playing tricks on myself, maybe I was worse off than I realized. The house was cool and I felt like I was a million miles away from anybody. Elizabeth slept on the far side of the queen-size bed, her back to me, a mound of covers over her and Dude on top of the covers, staring at me with eyes that glowed like LEDs.

Elizabeth is thirty-one to my thirty-seven, six years younger than me. We met when she was waitressing, before she went back to school and got her teacher's certificate. Fall of 1978. I'd gone into the Lemmon Avenue Bar and Grill on crutches, ankle sprained from Sunday's full-contact racquetball game. I used to hang out there because of a sort of house policy where the waitresses would sit across from you and talk to you when they took your order. The food was good too. I didn't remember seeing Elizabeth before that night: medium height, slightly on the heavy side of average, that multicolored golden hair, a smile that made me wish she'd let me in on the joke. She made me put my sunglasses on before she would show me my prime rib, which she thought was too rare. She brought me a second beer without asking and forgot to charge me for it. When I pointed it out she looked at me like I was a complete idiot, which I guess I was.

I didn't ask her out for another two weeks. By then I was eating there almost every night and always asking for her station. When I finally did she said, "I wondered when you'd get around to it." It took

me years to realize that there was big difference between expecting it
and actually looking forward to it.

The thing I liked best was the way I was around her. I always wore
a sports coat when I went over to her place, always brought a bottle of
wine or some flowers. We went to plays and museums and French
movies with subtitles. It was romantic. I was playing way over my
head. She had a roommate who thought I was terrific and said so to
Elizabeth all the time. Maybe too much. It made Elizabeth dig her
heels in, refuse to be impressed.

Still she must have felt something, even from the first. The first
time I asked her name she said, "Elizabeth" right off, though I found
out later she'd always gone by Beth up till then. It was what her
roommate and all her friends still called her. I think both of us had the
idea we could pull ourselves by our bootstraps into a Hollywood love
affair, with violins in the sex scenes.

Instead it was an uphill fight. She was so young, only twenty-one
when we started dating. She was nervous about sex and put me off for
weeks. We kissed some, and that was awkward too. She finally admitted she'd never been crazy about kissing. I still can't believe I married
a woman who doesn't like to kiss. When she finally gave in and went
to bed with me I was all over her, waking her up in the night for more.

I think about that more than anything. That first couple of months
when you walk around with the smell of sex ground permanently into
your hands and crotch and face. It never lasts. Why is that? The times
I've come close to having an affair, that was what I thought about,
how it would be to feel that way again, even if it was only for a while.

I ask myself why we're still together, and I never get a good answer.
She can always make me laugh if she wants to. This August, before
school started, we spent the weekend at my friend Pete's lake house
and it had started off like a second honeymoon. We made love twice
the first day, held hands in the restaurant, walked by the lake that
night. As I went to sleep I thought, this is the reason. I made a stand
to keep my marriage together and now it's working again. But by
Sunday afternoon she had a stack of magazines in front of the TV and
I was icing down another six-pack.

Now there are entire months again where we don't make love at
all, days where we don't even talk except the menial household min-
imum, times when I know she's ready to kill me and I'm ready to kill

her and we sit and suffer in separate rooms so we don't have to look at each other.

━━━━━

Most of my friends are record collectors or dealers. On weekends we hit a few stores, a couple of times a year we'll go out of town for a big convention.

It's like men and women have their own languages. There are some of the same words in both of them, but they still come out differently. Some things men don't really have words for. I know my friends worry about me, and I even know why. They know how it was between my father and me, they know I should be feeling something. Only they don't have the words to ask and I wouldn't have the words to answer if they did.

So we talk around it. Like my friend Pete called on some pretext or other and then asked about Beth. I know he has a bit of a thing for her and suddenly I wanted to know why.

"Well, she has a lot of good qualities. She's smart, she's funny, she's attractive . . ."

"Yeah, yeah."

". . . and underneath that icy exterior I think there's a genuinely caring and concerned human being who's simply scared out of her mind."

"By what?"

"By life, old buddy. By you."

"Me?"

"Look at you. Not even forty, and you retired to start your own business. And you made it work from day one. You drink all the time, and yet I've never seen you drunk. You just handle it. Shit happens, and you handle it. Your father dies, and what happened?"

"I handled it."

"You handled it. Don't you think that's a little scary?"

"I'd think it would be comforting."

"Then you don't know women very well."

"Hey, fuck you." Women share secrets, men insult each other. It's how we know we're friends. There was a moment where I could have said something about the Beatles tape, could have asked him to listen to it and tell me if I was crazy. Only I didn't have the words.

I thought about it the rest of the day. The thing is, if there's something wrong with me, I'm not sure I want it to get better.

Pete's right about the way I handle things. Back in 1979, when I was burned out on Dallas and Elizabeth wanted to go to UT for her teacher's certificate, I made sure I had a design job in Austin before I quit Warrex. And I kept that job even after I started the repair business, worked nights until I was sure I could make a go of it full-time.

Elizabeth calls me Captain Sensible. Which is really the name of the bass player from the Damned, not that she cares. She says it in a way that is supposed to make me understand that she admires it and even counts on it, but it pisses her off too.

It was almost nine. Elizabeth and Dude were watching *Dynasty*. I went upstairs and thought maybe I was a little tired of being Captain Sensible myself. That I could either erase this Beatles tape and let the whole thing go, or I could keep pushing and see where it led.

I called Southwest Airlines, who said they could put me on a plane to L.A. the next day, round trip, for $198. Then I called a woman named Peggy who I used to work with at Warrex. She quit the same time as me, moved to New York, and went to work for Marvel Comics. I knew she sent comics to Graham Hudson at Carnival Dog Records and he sent her CDs. Hudson is the guy that does their remastering, the brains behind those sixties compilations, *Glimpses*. I had all three volumes: great lost and overlooked cuts by major bands, by national acts that died on the vine, by local acts that never made it big. "Desiree" by the Left Banke, "William Jr." by the Novas, "Go Back" by Crabby Appleton, "Think About It" by the Yardbirds.

Peggy said she'd call him for me and get me an appointment. It was only seven o'clock on the West Coast. She wanted to know what this was about and I told her she wouldn't believe me.

"Did you start another band or something? Didn't you use to play drums?"

"Not for a long time," I said.

I sat by the phone for half an hour. I promised myself that if I couldn't get through to Hudson I would forget the whole thing. Then

Peggy called back and said Hudson would see me at three P.M. Friday afternoon, the day after tomorrow.

———

They say bees can't see the color red. It was that way when I told Elizabeth I was flying to Los Angeles. It seemed to roll right off her, like she didn't accept it as real. When she asked me why, I told her it was because of the tape. She couldn't quite see the tape either.

"Can we afford this?" she asked.

"VISA's clear. I can charge everything."

After a second or two she said, "Do I get any say in this?"

"Sure. If you don't want me to go, I won't."

I thought it was what she wanted to hear but I had only pissed her off. I saw it go straight up her spine. She turned back to the TV in a terribly final kind of way. "In that case, by all means, go ahead, go."

"Look," I said. "I'm sorry. It's just something I have to do."

She held up her left hand, palm toward me, and cocked it in a short wave. I understood it to mean, "Right, fine, conversation over." The odds were she would say good-bye to me at the airport, and nothing else until then.

I called Pete to cancel Saturday. "Take some advice," he said. "Try to have fun out there. And if some little beach bunny wants to fuck your brains out, don't let your conscience stand in your way. Wear a rubber, but don't hesitate."

"I don't think I'm the beach bunny type."

"All I'm saying is, keep an open mind."

After that I called my mother. I call every two or three days because I know it means a lot to her. I still dread it every time. I see her rattling around in that big house by herself, either in her robe or the jogging suits she's started to wear the last few years. Her hair is dyed this sandy color that is nothing like the brown it used to be. She's medium height, her posture's still okay, though she has this little pot belly that no amount of sit-ups can get rid of. I don't have anything to say to her, and all she has to tell me are the tiniest details of her life—what was in the salad she had for lunch, the few percentile points she gains in interest when she moves her savings around from bank to bank. This time she replayed her conversation with an American Airlines ticket clerk, word for word, about the refund on my father's return ticket from Mexico. She corrected herself every time she got a detail out of place. Finally she gave up when she couldn't remember the last two digits of the amount, whether it was eighty-three cents or thirty-eight, and broke down in tears.

———

I thought about a lot of things that night. One of them was the way Peggy asked about my playing drums. I haven't touched them in almost twenty years, since I left Austin with my tail between my legs and went to DeVry. I still dream about it, though, those frustration dreams where you can't ever get where you need to be. I have a gig with, say, the Jefferson Airplane, only the drums never show up. Or I can't get past the guards to the stage. Or we get set up and there are these endless delays that keep me from getting to play until I wake up.

I never wanted to play drums in the first place. I wanted to be a guitarist. I got a gut-string Silvertone acoustic guitar for Christmas of my sophomore year in high school, and I practiced all the time, with that hormone-fueled obsession that is the only card you really have to play when you're fifteen. Then that summer, in this high school theater company, I ran my left hand into a Skil saw. After they put me back together I couldn't unbend my index finger anymore. Either I learned to play all over again on a left-handed guitar or I took up something else. My best friends all played guitar and they needed a drummer, so I volunteered, just to be able to play something, to be part of it.

I don't remember ever mentioning it to Peggy. It must be more on my mind than I realized.

———

I'd never been to L.A. before. The plane flies over the middle of Palm Springs and right away you start to see the swimming pools, little spots of blue in the endless tan of the desert. Then you cross the San Bernardino Mountains into L.A. itself and the air turns darker and the horizon disappears in brownish-yellow haze.

I rented a Pontiac Sunbird at the airport. It was the first time I ever had to rent a car and I felt like an idiot having to have everything spelled out for me while guys in suits shifted their weight impatiently behind me. It didn't have a tape deck, so I got my little hand-held cassette player and some tapes out of my suitcase. By the time I got onto the street it was almost dark. I was afraid of the expressways, so I took Lincoln Boulevard all the way north to Santa Monica, looking for a cheap motel.

Things in L.A. are smaller and older than I thought they'd be, lots of low Spanish buildings from the forties and fifties, nothing much over two stories until you get downtown. I kept the windows open for a while, but without the sun the air got cool and I rolled them back up. I saw people on roller skates and skateboards everywhere, lots of convertibles, kids in leather and spiked hairdos. There were a few token Christmas decorations that couldn't quite compete with the neon pinks and greens and yellows that everybody wore. There was music everywhere, mostly rap, played at unbelievable volume. It was like being in high school with my parents out of town, and me with the car all weekend. Everything was new and exciting and at the same time I felt more grown up and on my own than I had in years.

I turned right on Colorado Avenue and drove past Carnival Dog records, to make sure I could find it in the morning. It's just a two-story box, next to the Department of Motor Vehicles. Then I headed north again, toward San Vicente Boulevard.

My parents lived here from the summer of 1946 to the fall of 1949, in half of a four-bedroom house on Sixteenth Street. It's still there, tan stucco, red tile roof, palm trees and porticoes, only a few blocks from the beach. My father's aunt owned it and rented out the other half. My father had come here in the summers before the war, before he married, and he used to talk about those years as the best of his life, dancing on the pier every night, playing tennis every day. There were tennis courts down the street and he said that for the rest of his life just the sound of tennis, that distant clop of a well-hit ball, filled him with unbearable longing. The pier was different then, he said, all elegance and romance. When he talked I saw this long California sunset out over the water, heard a big band play "Moonlight Serenade," heavy on the clarinets. The air was clean and smelled of orange blossoms and the railings were lined with beautiful women in dresses that came just past their knees, their long hair piled high with silver combs.

I drove to the pier and parked above it on Ocean Avenue. The wind was cold and I zipped up my jacket and stuck my hands in my pockets. Fourth Street goes straight out onto the pier, arching out over the Pacific Coast Highway below. There's a big curved sign that says SANTA MONICA YACHT HARBOR * SPORT FISHING * BOATING * CAFES. At the closest end of the pier is the carousel, enclosed in a reconstructed Victorian-looking building. To the left some steps lead down to the sand and a small playground.

I went into the carousel building and watched the crowds lined up to ride. There are three concentric rows of horses, all brightly painted, with lots of silver and gold. Along the walls are antique-type vending machines, including a fortune-teller called Estrella's Prophecies. I bought my fortune, which turned out to be a small black-and-white card with some old-fashioned clip art on it.

"Yes my friend your greatest fault is that you talk too much. Learn to keep a secret." Did she mean the "Long and Winding Road" tape? "However your other golden qualities make up for your talkativeness. Your anxiety to help others, and your consideration of other people's wishes has earned you many friends.

"A friend will urge you to take a trip. Don't do it. Your best interest lies in remaining at home. I'm depending on your good sense to lead you on the right path." For anther coin, she promised to tell more. Thanks, Estrella.

Outside, all I could see of the water was the white of the waves as they broke. I pushed through the crowds and onto the pier proper, which is a long line of T-shirt shops and fast-food franchises: the Crown and Anchor, Seaview Seafood. People line up on both sides of the pier fishing, mostly Oriental and Chicano. Signs say NO COMER LOS "WHITE CROAKERS." At the far end there are bumper cars, showered with blue sparks from the grid of wires overhead.

Whatever my father loved here is long gone. He'd told me that. I bought myself a Venice Beach T-shirt and a pretzel and a beer and watched the waves roll in.

=====

In the morning I cruised through Hollywood and saw the sign on the hill and Grauman's Chinese. A few blocks in any direction from the Walk of Fame and things get very gray and businesslike. The sun was up there somewhere, behind a smog thick enough to wash out the city's color. I looked up at the Griffith Park Observatory from ground

level, saw UCLA, and ate a hamburger in Westwood. By three o'clock
I was in the waiting room at Carnival Dog Records.

The place is done up in African kitsch. There's a thatched straw
roof over the receptionist's desk, hard wooden chairs painted purple
with yellow polka dots, zebra stripes on the walls and on the steel-
and-concrete staircase that goes up to the second floor. There were a
few copies of the latest L.A. *Weekly* stacked by the front door. There
are these dog heads—framed prints and paintings, plaster casts,
wooden carvings—all over the place.

The receptionist had short dark hair and lots of eyeliner. She wore
a T-shirt with neon colors and a black vinyl miniskirt. She had a
buzzer that unlocked the doors on either side of her desk. While I sat
there she buzzed a long stream of people through: a tall, skinny guy in
a Twilight Zone black satin tour jacket, a heavyset guy with a black
beard and a Hawaiian shirt, a woman in a short red dress and fishnet
hose. I had on my good corduroy pants and a checked shirt with a knit
tie. I'd even put aside my Converse All-Stars for hard shoes. The idea
was to look like somebody Hudson could take seriously, and I was
starting to think I'd gone the wrong way.

At three-fifteen her intercom buzzed and she curled a finger at me
and smiled. She led me up the stairs and down a gray-carpeted hallway, past a second receptionist. In one corner was a plastic statue of
the RCA dog, Nipper, that they'd dressed up in sunglasses, a Hawaiian
shirt, and a conical party hat. She knocked on an office door, then
opened it and stepped aside.

A voice said, "Come on in." It was deep, a little hoarse, and had
a bit of a Southern accent. A man behind a desk stretched his hand
out toward me. "Pardon me if I don't get up."

I saw that he was in a wheelchair. "Ray Shackleford," I said. I
shook his hand and sat down across from him. The office has shelves
on all four walls that only go shoulder-high. From there to the ceiling
there are framed certificates and album covers and gold records and a
pennant for the Arkansas Razorbacks. The shelves are so full of albums and books and magazines, stacks of greenbar paper and unla-
beled cassettes, that the leftovers are stacked on the floor. There's just
enough room between the stacks for a clear plastic runner over the
carpet, the width of Hudson's wheels. In one corner a miniature
basketball hoop is nailed to the shelves above a wastebasket. There

wasn't much on the desk. A phone, a single Regal-Tip drumstick, a stack of paper, a few wooden pencils.

Hudson himself looks to be not much older than me. His hair is whitish-blonde, stiff, and combed ineffectively to one side. It looks like the exhaust from a rocket. He wore an L.A. Lakers T-shirt and a pair of checked Kmart pants with the left leg folded under, just behind where the knee would have been.

"So," he said. "You're a friend of Peggy's. Is she as cute in person as she sounds on the phone?"

I was shaky, but he had a quality that kept me from going over the edge into panic. "She was last time I saw her. Of course that was before she started dating this huge Italian guy. After which time it ceased to make any difference."

Hudson laughed. "What can I do for you, Ray?"

"I guess you hear this all the time. It's not what it sounds like. I want you—I want you to listen to a tape."

"We don't really do new artists on Carnival Dog. We're strictly reissue."

"I know all that. Give me ten seconds. It'll be a lot easier than trying to explain."

Hudson shrugged and smiled and held out his hand. I gave him the tape, wondering if I should offer to cue it up for him. He rolled himself back from the desk with a quick spin of the wheel rim and then shot himself over to an expensive boom box half-buried on one of the shelves. He put the tape in and started it. I didn't know what would happen next. Maybe I was crazy. Maybe I'd unconsciously taped some bootleg cut that Hudson would recognize immediately.

The volume was up high enough to hear some hiss on the beginning of the tape. Then McCartney's voice, the a cappella first line of the song. Hudson turned to look at me, obviously wondering what the hell. Then Ringo and George came in and his head jerked back to the machine. He turned up the volume and watched the little wheels turn inside the cassette.

"Holy shit," he said.

He didn't say anything else until the song was over, and the intercom dialogue. Then he said, "Is that it?"

I nodded.

"Where in hell did it come from?"

"I can't tell you that. Not right now. I want to know what you heard."

"Something that can't exist. I've read all the books, I know they never—" He went to the machine, rewound it part way, listened again, his left ear right up against one speaker and then the other. There was an equalizer built into the box and he isolated the tom-toms, then the guitar. He shook his head. "If this is a fake, it's the best I've ever heard."

I felt the muscles across my chest relax. "It's not a fake."

"Is there more?"

"Not yet."

"But there could be?"

"I think so."

"All Beatles stuff?"

"I don't know."

His intercom buzzed. "Howard Kaylan on line one for you," the receptionist said.

"Never mind," Hudson said. I understood suddenly that there wasn't really a call, it was just an excuse for him to get me out of the office if he needed to. "Hold my calls, okay?"

Hudson looked at me. "You've got my attention. You brought this here for some reason. Let's hear it."

"I'll tell you," I said, "but you won't believe it."

"After hearing that tape . . . I'd believe anything."

So I told him. About my father, about the repair business, about how I made the tape. I watched his face, waiting for his eyes to glaze or his shoulders to pull back. What I saw was intent interest.

"So you're saying you could do it again," he said. "Like maybe on a digital master tape."

"I could try."

"Then, hey, let's do it."

"You mean now?" I felt my heart turn upside down.

"I'm game if you are."

I let him lead, uncertain if I should offer to push. We went back out to the upstairs reception area where there was a small elevator. It let us out into a big room partitioned into cubicles. There were little pieces of paper pinned up everywhere: Scrawled notes, dummy artwork for CD longboxes, computer printouts. Beyond that was a long hallway which ended at a door with an unlit red bulb above it.

Hudson wheeled in and started turning things on. I realized I was looking at the lab where he does all the Carnival Dog digital transfers. I couldn't help feeling excited, even if it doesn't look like the control room at Abbey Road. For one thing it faces a curtained wall instead of a studio. The floor is parquet and there's a beat-up office chair with duct tape holding one of the rollers on. As you face the curtain there's an Ampex quarter-inch open-reel deck on the left, then a big two-track mixing console with digital readouts in the middle, then a Studer quarter-inch deck. Next to it is the Sony 1630, which I know about from trade magazines. It looks like an entire rack mount stereo system. It turns an analog signal into two tracks of digital and puts it on three-quarter-inch JVC format videotape. I wanted to take it apart, but it was not the time to ask.

To the left is a rack with a turntable on top and a couple of Tascam cassette decks. On another rack are Mitsubishi amps and preamps, the big kind with the vertical handles mounted on the face. There are three-foot JBL speakers mounted above the curtains and, above the mixing deck, a pair of Aurotone sound cubes, which I'd heard about but never seen before. They are supposed to emulate car speakers, so you can check what your mix would sound like over the radio. Hudson put a fresh videocassette into the 1630 and said, "Okay. Tell me what you need."

"Monitors," I said, "so I can hear it. And a couple seconds to like calm down and everything."

"Nod when you're ready."

I settled in the office chair and closed my eyes. The air was cool and the only sounds were the hiss of the air conditioner and a faint preamp buzz in the speakers. In the back of my head I knew I had to pull this off. I wasn't worried. I was in love with all the hardware in that room and I wanted to hear it perform. I knew the 1630 could pick up nuances that my Nakamichi never could, the scrape of the guitar pick on the strings, the tiniest variation in the cymbal strokes, the whisper of the pedals on the piano. I was up for it.

I got all the pieces together in my head. I could see Paul's face, hear John nervously tapping one booted foot. Ringo putting out a cigarette and laughing at something. It was all there. I nodded and Hudson started the tape. I closed my eyes. Geoff Emerick said, "Long and Winding Road. Take four." I heard Hudson shift in his chair, like I'd scared him. Then Paul started singing.

I opened my eyes. The needles on the mixing board VU meters were moving. Hudson stared at them but didn't touch any of the controls. He never looked at me. The song played through to the end and there was a bit more I hadn't heard before. Ringo stamping on the bass drum, a woman's voice that must have been Yoko's. Then nothing. "That's all," I said.

Hudson rewound it in silence, except for the hum of the transport mechanism. He stopped it in the middle and listened. I could hear the space between the musicians, hear each note decay separately. I wasn't as tired as I had been before. Finding it, I guess, is the really hard part.

Hudson stopped the tape in the middle of a verse.

"Well?" I said.

He still wouldn't look at me.

"Give me a minute," he said. "I don't think I can talk right now."

———

He rewound the tape, then took his time about writing my name and the date on the label. We took it to the room next door, a fireproof vault the size of a small closet. It had a lock on the door and steel shelves inside. He locked the tape inside and said, "How about a beer?"

"I would deeply appreciate that."

We went out to the parking lot and he said, "We can take my car." He wheeled himself up to a maroon Volvo and opened the door.

"Uh, listen, can I help?"

"It's no problem," he said. "You get used to it."

He parked the chair parallel to the open door and lifted his right leg into the car with both hands. Then he put one hand on the seat and the other on the door and hoisted himself inside. He folded the chair and then scooted to his right until he could pull the driver's seat forward and stash the chair behind it. Then he unlocked the passenger door and I got in. "Are you hungry at all?" he said.

"I could eat."

"We're going to have to talk about this. We can talk about it in some noisy bar, or we can go to my house. Don't worry, I'm not gay or anything. It's just I've got a case of Raffo in the icebox, and . . . you ever had Raffo?"

"Yeah. It's good beer."

We headed down Lincoln toward Venice.

"You know there's nothing we can legally do with a tape like that," Hudson said. I felt myself sink. "I believe what I saw today. Capitol Records would never believe it. They would tie you up in lawsuits until you couldn't take a leak without a court order."

"But the music . . ."

"We're talking record executives here. If they cared about music, they wouldn't be in that end of the business. You know what they used to call the Capitol executives? The Coors Club. Because at five P.M. sharp, they had a little icebox there in the office, at five o'clock everything stops and whoosh, it's pop-top time. No matter who's there to see them, no matter what band is hung up somewhere needing help."

We turned uphill into a neighborhood of one-story stucco houses and small lawns. "So what are you saying?"

He pulled into one of the driveways and turned the car off. "I'm saying we can't do anything legally. But this still needs to get out there."

"You're talking bootleg?"

"I'm just talking, you understand. It could be done. If you had forty-five minutes to an hour's worth of material, high-quality CD, full-color booklet, distributed through a network of collectors with the right connections. If it was something people really wanted, you could name your own price. A hundred dollars a unit wouldn't be out of line."

We sat there a minute or two in silence. It was late afternoon, warm enough that I could feel the sunlight on my right arm. The wind rustled palm trees next door and I could smell cut grass and flowers.

"Something to think about," Hudson said, and opened his door.

The inside of his house is open and low, flagstone floors, rough plaster walls, lots of plants. There are skylights in the roof and shelves full of stacked-up magazines. There's a wicker couch and one other chair, a coffee table, and lots of space to maneuver around them.

Hudson pointed me toward the couch and wheeled off into the kitchen. He brought back two bottles of beer and drank his off in one long swallow. Then he sighed, eyes closed, head back. It looked like he and I would get along.

I said, "What sort of thing would be worth a hundred dollars a shot?"

"Well, that's the question, isn't it? There's Beatle boots out there now, those *Ultra Rare Trax*? So the Beatles might not be the best place to start. There's a million lost albums that collectors have talked about for years. The second Derek and the Dominos, *Smile*, the Bob Dylan and Johnny Cash album. There's the Buffalo Springfield's *Stampede*. Lee Perry was supposed to do a Wailers album for Island in the mid-seventies . . . I need to think about this."

"While you're thinking, is there a phone I could use?"

He pointed. "In the hall there. Just dial one for long distance."

"I've got a card . . ."

"Hey. You're in the business now. You're tax deductible. Get used to it."

Elizabeth was home. She sounded tired. "I'm okay," she said. "I miss you. The house is all empty and echoing. Dude keeps walking around crying. Hey, Dude, c'mere, it's your dad on the phone."

"It looks like I have to be out here another day or two."

"Oh."

"I played the tape for this record guy and it really shook him up."

"The one you played for me?"

"Yeah."

There was a long silence. I could hear her think about asking again where the tape came from, hear her decide she didn't want to know. "Where are you staying?" she finally said.

I gave her the number of the motel.

"Is it nice?"

"It's seedy, in a nice kind of way."

"I love you," Elizabeth said. "I wish you were here."

"I love you too. I'll call you tomorrow."

After I put the phone down I stood in the hallway for a minute. When I'm actually in Austin she can't say the things she does on the phone, the simple intimacies, the unforced affection. It leaves me hung up in this neverland, wanting to be home in a place that doesn't really exist.

I went back to the living room. Graham Hudson had a big smile all over his face. "The Doors," he said. *"Celebration of the Lizard."*

CHAPTER 2

CHAPTER 2

The Celebration of the Lizard

The first two Doors albums end with long, complex theater pieces: "The End" and "When the Music's Over." For the third album Jim Morrison had saved the longest, most complicated yet, "The Celebration of the Lizard." Like the other two, it had evolved over the long months onstage at L.A.'s London Fog Club, and, eventually, at the Whiskey a Go Go, the top club on the strip. The album was supposed to be called *Celebration of the Lizard* too, and the song would have filled most, if not all, of the second side. It was in the punch line of this song that Morrison announced himself as the Lizard King.

It's fashionable now to blame drugs for everything. In fact the Doors recorded two brilliant albums with Morrison completely twisted on LSD. It was the booze that did him in. The recording sessions for *Celebration* were drunken orgies, with Morrison so out of control that the vocal tracks had to done over and over again. Some nights he ran amuck in the studio, punching the walls, and they had to drag him out onto the street. Other nights he simply passed out in the corner.

Paul Rothchild, their young, hip producer, patched together a version of "Celebration" from various takes. He hated the result, and so did the rest of the band. They thought it was dull, lifeless, meandering. Morrison was outvoted when he wanted to keep it. Only one short section, "Not to Touch the Earth," made it onto the finished album, now retitled *Waiting for the Sun*. They filled up the rest of the record with sentimental junk like "Hello, I Love You," resurrected from the band's early days, and "Love Street," a simplistic, piano bar ballad.

I still remember how disappointed I was when I first heard it. It came out in the summer of 1968, still early on for Alex and me. My parents spent a lot of weekends out of town and my friends would bring dates over and there would be beer and maybe a joint or two. The main thing I remember is the cold. Nobody thought about an energy crisis then and I kept the air conditioner down to the low sixties. Late at night, in the cold, we would listen to the first two Doors albums back-to-back and dare ourselves to go crazy from the sheer intensity of it.

Then *Waiting for the Sun* came out and Morrison looked less like a crazed visionary than a sad alcoholic. Alex and I saw him that June, just before the album was released. He seemed oddly restrained, despite what looked like an Italian sausage that hung down the leg of his black leather jeans. Now I realize he was simply drunk. It was pretty much the end of the Doors. The intellectual, mystical lyrics from Morrison's first white heat of inspiration were all used up. The band had to put songs together in the studio and Morrison was reduced to simpleminded dog-without-a-bone nursery rhymes. They'd hit some kind of wall.

———

Graham picked me up at my motel around noon and took me out for a tour of the city. I'd told him the night before that I needed details, had to be able to see everything in my head.

Santa Monica Boulevard, even with bumper-to-bumper traffic, felt different to me than rush hour in Dallas or Houston. Everybody seemed to be headed toward something glamorous or fun, the beach or the back lot at Universal. Half the women looked like starlets, or maybe it was just me, far from home, involved in the closest thing to an adventure I'd ever had.

We turned off onto Wilshire in the middle of Beverly Hills. The north side of the street is all red tile roofs and green lawns and high walls, sprinklers that run all through December. The south side is business district that fades gradually into the generic high rise of downtown L.A. We turned north on La Cienega and drove past the Beverly Center, which looms over fifties-era furniture and carpet stores and the occasional eighties strip center.

I could look straight ahead and see the Hollywood Hills less than a mile away, catch glimpses of high-dollar houses behind the trees. As La Cienega started to climb uphill, Graham reached across me to point at a tan stucco building with a red-tiled mansard roof. "That's where Elektra Records was. There was a studio on the second floor where they did *Soft Parade.*"

He turned right at the next corner, which put us back on Santa Monica Boulevard. We actually found a parking spot and I stood nervously in the street, watching cars swerve around Graham while he unloaded his chair and got settled. We crossed over to Barney's Beanery, more of a Texas-style burger joint than something that belonged in West Hollywood. The front of the place was painted dark green and had a painted metal menu with over two hundred brands of beer on it. The inside was dark and smoky, and there was a sign behind the bar that said FAGOTS STAY OUT.

"Friendly place," I said.

"It's part of the history," Graham said. "We won't leave a tip."

We got a table where we could look out at the street. Graham talked about Jim Morrison while we ate. "Back in sixty-eight he didn't have a car half the time, or the cops had pulled his ticket for drunk driving. He stayed at the Alta Cienega Motel, just on the other side of La Cienega. Back then West Hollywood wasn't incorporated, it was a slum, with strip joints and prostitution and lots of crime. The name Sunset Strip came from County Strip, meaning it wasn't legally part of L.A. at all. What little law enforcement there was came out of the Sheriff's Department, which is why it drew so many hustlers and nightclubs and all that. That changed after the riots on Sunset in sixty-six, but not that much.

"So in the late sixties you had this incredible scene here. Kids from all over the country were out on the streets in droves. The music pulled them in, and they stayed because nobody tried very hard to kick them out. So Morrison had everything he needed within walking distance." Graham took one of the napkins and drew a cross on it. "The Alta Cienega here, on the northwest corner. Across Santa Monica was the Phone Booth, a strip joint where he used to hang out. The Doors' offices were next door at 8512. A little farther west was the Palms Bar, where he went to drink, and across the street from that was Duke's Coffee Shop. Duke's was in the Tropicana Motel, where lots of bands would stay when they were in town. Elektra right here on La Cienega, and his girlfriend Pam's apartment, around the corner on Norton. He would eat at the Garden District or Duke's. And he came here to shoot pool. So did Janis, who went from here to the Troubadour and then back to the Franklin Hotel the night she died.

"Everybody talks about the Haight, and the Fillmore, and Golden Gate Park and all that. But I'm telling you, man, there is no rock and roll town like L.A. I mean, the R & B scene on Central Avenue, Spector's Wall of Sound, the Byrds, the whole Eagles/Ronstadt thing, Dick Dale and surf music, X and Black Flag and the Go-Go's, right up to Guns 'n Roses and Van Halen and Tone-Lōc. This is the place. There isn't a block in this part of town that isn't crawling with history."

He finished his beer and held up the empty bottle for another. "Most of it gone, of course. They knocked the Tropicana down a few months ago. The Phone Booth, the Elektra offices, the Garden District, all gone. Sunset Sound, where the Doors cut the first two albums, is gone. They made *Waiting for the Sun* at TTG down on McCadden Place, near Sunset and Highland. Hendrix recorded 'Look Over Yonder' there, but it's gone too, all gone, gone the way of Western Recorders and Gold Star. Jesus, man, you think of the sounds that came out of those places. The studios themselves were integral. Phil Spector got the sound he got because of Gold Star Studios, and nobody will ever get that sound again."

The waiter brought Graham's beer. He looked at it and said, "And another mini-mall slouches toward L.A. to be born."

I looked around, tried to take twenty years off the wood-paneled walls, the tucked-and-rolled rainbow-colored vinyl booths, the scratched Formica with the sparkles in it. I could see Jim and Janis take turns with a bottle of Southern Comfort at the pool tables, surrounded by guys in bell-bottoms and long sideburns, industry types in Madras and penny loafers, aspiring starlets in hip-huggers and tank tops.

"But you're not from L.A.," I said.

"Pine Bluff, Arkansas."

"So how do you know all this stuff?"

"The total absorption method. It's all I do. Listen to the records and read the album covers. I subscribe to all the trades and buy all the biographies. I watch the talk shows and MTV."

"What got you started?"

"You mean when I was a kid? I don't know. I always loved music. It took me away from my real life. I didn't get along with my parents—my dad and my stepmother, I should say. My real mother died when I was three. Liver cancer. From the time they found it to the time she died was two days. That's what they tell me, I don't remember her at all. Anyway, I was there in Arkansas, dirt poor, couldn't afford to buy records new, not even singles. But you could go down to the jukebox shop and buy used jukebox records ten for a dollar. They had machines where you could listen to them, too. Pine Bluff was about fifty percent black, so I got to hear all the race records—Marv Johnson, 'You Got What It Takes,' that was always one of my favorites. The Coasters—another great L.A. group, they started out as the West Coasters, did you know that?—James Brown, Chuck Berry. And of course I loved Elvis and Ricky Nelson and all that. Ricky and Elvis used to play football over in De Neve Park. Ricky had a bunch of pro players and Elvis had his Memphis Mafia. Shit. Once I get started, I can't stop until I bore everybody to death." He pushed away from the table. "Let's get some exercise."

He let me push his chair up to La Cienega. The Alta Cienega is just north of the intersection, pale yellow, two stories, with red trim and Spanish-style wrought-iron bars over the windows. The driveway that leads to the office is a kind of tunnel, with rooms on both sides and above it. "Morrison stayed in room thirty-two, on the second floor," Graham said. "You can see the building Elektra was in down the street there, with the red tile roof. It was stucco originally, then Judy Collins became their big ticket. So they had it redone in natural wood, with wrought-iron stairs up the side. A look Judy would be happy with. It's back to stucco now, and Elektra's in a high rise downtown. When Bob Krasnow came in five years ago they turned over most of the management. So that whole era is gone."

I hunkered down on the sidewalk to fix everything in my mind. "If you could find any pictures of the inside of that studio—"

"TTG?"

"Yeah. Especially of the Doors during a session, that would really help."

"Okay. Anything else?"

I shook my head. "I guess tomorrow I go home and start work on it."

"And tonight?"

I shrugged.

"How about we sneak a case of beer up to Griffith Park and watch the sun go down?"

―――――――

"When were you over there?" I asked Graham.

The lights of L.A. were spread out below us, and it was impossible to imagine an energy shortage, not with all that dazzling brilliance spread from one horizon to the other. We sat under a tree with a case of Tecate, smelling the fallen juniper needles, listening to the wind. It sounded colder than it was.

"Vietnam?" he said. "Never."

"You said something about being in the service, I just assumed . . ."

"No, man, I was in the Navy. Never left the States."

". . . I mean, with your legs and all . . ."

"No, I didn't get shot or anything. It's a lot dumber than that."

"You want to talk about it?"

"Sure. But it's a long, weird story."

"I'm not going anywhere."

"Well, you know that old line about for want of a nail a shoe was lost, and so on?"

"Yeah, I know it. Rundgren made a song out of it."

"So he did. It's kind of like that, or like the way you came up with 'Long and Winding Road.' Change one little thing and you change the whole world."

"So what happened?"

"I was eighteen years old. This was back in sixty-two, in Pine Bluff. It was my second day back from boot camp. I was scheduled to report to Navy OCS—you know, Officer Candidate School—in thirty days. I'd already passed the exams and everything. This old boy that I enlisted with called me up and we went out for a spin in his daddy's new Nash Rambler. Some clown ran a stop sign and hit us. I mean, it wasn't even our fault. This is pathetic, not tragic. Well, I hit the dashboard, which was of course not padded back in sixty-two. I wasn't too bad hurt, but my teeth and lower jaw got kind of messed up. We didn't have the money to send me to a real hospital, so I went to Millington Naval Hospital over in Memphis. After two days when the doc came around and offered passes I took one. So me and this other guy went and bought a fifth of Bacardi—nobody checked my ID or anything—and we went over to the Cotton Club. Of course that would have to be the night that the place got raided. Me and four other guys got busted for drinking under age. We spent the night in jail, and the next day the Navy chief comes around and everybody pays twenty-five bucks and gets out. Only I didn't have twenty-five bucks. The chief wouldn't give me an advance, and there wasn't anybody I could borrow from, so I had to stay in jail."

"What about your family?"

"I'll tell you about my family sometime. Just take my word, I wasn't about to call my father. Not to be asking favors of him, especially money favors. So the chief leaves me half a pack of Pall Malls and takes off. I come up for sentencing and the judge decides he's going to make an example out of me. Thirty days on the penal farm."

"Jesus Christ."

"Wait. As soon as I got there I knew I was in big-time trouble, but the sooner I got back to Millington the better. I knew I was going to have to bite the bullet and write my dad. But the mail only went out once a week, and I just missed it. So it was nine days before I could get the money to pay the fine and get sprung out of there."

"What did your dad do, when he got the letter?"

"Nothing. He just sent it, he sent me the money. It was only a matter of, by that time, twenty bucks or something. A lot of money to us in those days, but not anything that was going to break him. I don't recall him ever saying much about it, surprisingly."

"My family was pretty good when it was an absolute crisis. We just weren't very good the rest of the time."

"Yeah. Same with my dad. I never could harbor much of a grudge against him, though. I feel like he's always been abused by the job that he had, doing shift work for twenty-five years, where he had to be on day shift one week, swing shift the next, graveyard the next, and never had any kind of rhythm to his life."

"Jesus. That's rough."

"Yeah, really. Well, you know, eighth-grade education."

"So what happened when you got the money?"

"By that time the Navy charged me with 'unauthorized leave,' which was at least better than AWOL or desertion. They put me in restriction barracks from six in the evening to six in the morning, and the rest of the day I just hung around the geedunk, you know, the PX. I had to face a Captain's Mast, where I got yelled at by the base admiral, then I had a summary court martial where I got busted down to E1 from E2 and had to do sixty days in restriction.

"That was where I got upset, because I was supposed to report to OCS in about two weeks from then. And that was when they told me. No OCS until my record cleared, and my record wouldn't clear for two fucking years. All because of twenty-five bucks, all because some ya-hoo ran a stop sign, all because I went for a ride in some guy's father's Nash.

"Well, in two years my hitch was pretty much going to be over anyway. So I took the best job I could find, the easiest path to make rank. At the time that was Aviation Structural Mechanic—that's as opposed to the guys that actually work on the engines. I was in Emergency Egress Equipment."

"Like ejection seats."

"Ejections seats, explosive canopies, drogue chutes. It was kind of a joke because every test I ever took, my mechanical aptitude was the worst. But there I was, in the Navy, working as a mechanic, Patuxent River, Maryland, the Pax River TPS. There's only two test pilot schools in the country, Pax River and Edwards Air Force Base out in California. Everything we did was planes. We didn't believe the Navy really had any ships until one day we saw an experimental destroyer out in Chesapeake Bay. We all just stood around and stared at it. All that time in the Navy and it was our first ship.

"I used to go into Washington, when I could afford it, and go to the clubs. This was sixty-three. The Beatles were in *Newsweek* or someplace and I saw their hair and thought, hey, that looks neat. But life around the base was all this chickenshit stuff, they would lay for me and drag me into the base barbershop and cut all my hair off.

"Then one day these two bright red World War II vintage bombers arrive. They're full of these hotshots from Cornell Aeronautical Labs, and they're here to look at our jets. At the time we had the Phantom, which nobody else had. We hadn't even sold it to the Marines."

Graham crushed his empty can and tossed it into a paper sack next to me. "Two points," he said, and belched. I handed him another.

"There's three safety precautions," he said, "on all emergency egress equipment. This is so some jet jockey doesn't eject while he's in the hangar and splatter his brains all over the ceiling. First you pop the circuit breaker so there's no power to the explosives. Second you turn the detonator a half turn on all charges, so there's no contact. Third, each button or handle has a hole or flange, and you twist a copper wire through it so it won't move accidentally. You got all that?"

"I got it."

"I was just back from this big Italian lunch. One of those Cornell hotshots pulled a jet into the TPS hangar. I don't know what he did to fuck up all the safety precautions."

"The *three*," I said, "safety precautions on all emergency egress equipment." I was definitely starting to feel the beer.

"You got it. I was standing there talking to a couple of guys, digesting that Italian lunch. I didn't even hear the explosion."

He was quiet for a couple of seconds. "Graham?" I said.

"Those jets have one big door on the lower side that blows off. That's what hit me. Then this kind of laundry chute comes out and the crew is supposed to slide out. It hit the L1 and L2 vertebrae, you know, lumbar vertebrae. It crushed them together, and bone splinters went into my spine. That's what did the job on me, taking those splinters out, all the nerve damage from that.

"I woke up once in the ambulance. I knew I was on the road to Washington, 'cause we used to drive it so much. We were stopped for a red light. I remember seeing the red light reflected off the car next to me."

"Graham, look, I . . ."

"Shoot, I can talk about it. It's my life. I've been living with it twenty-five years. Anyway, as soon as I woke up after the operation there was this guy standing over me, they were expecting me to be nauseous. I mean, you're not supposed to eat anything before surgery so that you don't throw up under the anesthetic and asphyxiate yourself. And I'd had that big lunch and all. He was a hospital corpsman there at Bethesda, dressed completely in white, with a little emesis basin, one of those little kidney-shaped things that you brush your teeth with. And he says, 'Do you feel sick?' and I went eughhhhh and just barfed that bright orange Italian lunch all over his nice white uniform."

"Jesus, Graham, I'm trying to drink here."

He was ready for another beer. I passed one over and he said, "It's just weird, that's all. So many things had to happen just right. You know, a year after the accident, the Supreme Court decided you can't try somebody in a military court for the results of something that happened in a civilian court. It's double jeopardy."

"We used to watch *Jeopardy* in the VA hospital. It was so boring we used to bet on who would win. Sheeeit. Is it getting drunk out here?"

"It is," I said. "Isn't there a curfew or something? Maybe we should get out of here."

"In a minute. In a minute."

"Sure," I said. "No hurry."

The L.A. lights blazed on below us.

———

I lost two hours when I came back to Texas. It's the price for living on borrowed time. A hangover and all that dry airplane air didn't help. It was after nine at night when we landed. Elizabeth hates to wait around airports and the house is only ten minutes away, so I waited to call until I got in.

She sounded okay on the phone. When I go out of town it's always a crapshoot. Will I get the silent treatment, or will she actually be glad to see me?

Eventually I saw her white Honda, one of a hundred other small white Japanese cars, come around the wide curve in front of Mueller Airport. I got in and got a quick, dry kiss from Elizabeth.

"You look like you haven't been sleeping," I said.

"Thanks."

"I didn't . . . I was worried, that's all."

She shrugged. She shrugs a lot when something's my fault.

"What is it?"

"I don't know," she said. "I don't understand this thing you're doing." She dodged through the traffic and swung back toward Manor Road.

"Well, maybe you could understand this." I took Graham's check out of my jacket pocket and held it in front of her.

"What's that?"

"It's two thousand dollars. This guy Hudson is going to put the song out as a CD single, a bootleg."

"Isn't that illegal?"

"Moderately. He's the one taking the risk."

"Where did you tell him you got it from?"

"I didn't just tell him. I showed him."

She shook her head. "This is beyond me. Aren't you happy with your shop? I thought that was what you wanted."

"I don't know what I want anymore." The words seemed suddenly ominous.

"Where do I fit into this? Am I one more thing you don't know if you want anymore?"

"Of course not." I didn't sound convinced. "Of course I want you."

In the sudden silence the radio was too bright and artificial. I switched it off and waited for her to ask me about L.A. or the plane trip, or anything at all. She had both hands tight on the wheel, staring straight ahead, like if she tried hard enough she could make me disappear.

Our friends have all told us we have the perfect marriage. Elizabeth puts up a good show of affection, and I always go along with it. I guess I don't want to air our problems in public any more than she does. It's true we never fight. Sometimes we start to, like in the car. Then she goes quiet, holds it in, and I have to admit I feel relieved. It's one more crisis I don't have to deal with.

———

I waited until the next morning to call my mother. She didn't seem to want to hear about L.A. either. She's trying to decide if she should put her home phone number in her want ad for the funeral plot she no longer needs, since my father was cremated and she wants to be cremated too. She's afraid it's like a sign that says WIDOW.

"Sometimes," she said. "I get so . . . damned . . . *mad* at him. For leaving all this *mess* behind. I don't think I'll ever get to the end of it. I think of all the time he used to spend in that lounge chair in front of the TV when he could have been helping me organize . . ."

But then later she said, "I moved all of my things into the closet in your room. I hope that's okay."

"Of course it is." I didn't insist again that it isn't my room, has never been my room, it's just the guest room I stay in when I'm there. I was already in college when they had the place built.

"Next time you're up here you can take all his clothes to the Salvation Army. I can't go in that closet right now. It still smells like him."

There is only so much I can do for her. On those rare occasions when she actually does talk about her feelings, if I try to draw her out, she immediately changes the subject. The rest of the time it's just reportage, endless physical detail. Worse yet, she's gotten into the habit of calling me Jack, my father's name, and calling him Ray. Sometimes she refers to me as her husband and him as her son. It makes me feel creepy and furious. I remind her every time but she can't seem to stop.

Their house is on a slope above a creek that flows into White Rock Lake. There's this fishpond in their back yard, a real monstrosity, ten feet long and six feet wide, four feet deep at the deep end, paved with flagstones around the edges. I helped my father build it, every Sunday while I was at DeVry. One of the engineers there had me tell him about an additive to mix with the concrete so it wouldn't leak. My father decided it was too expensive, so the fishpond leaked for the rest of his life.

The week I spent with my mother, after he died, I was knotted up inside the whole time. Maybe just to get me out of the house, maybe because she really couldn't stand to look at it anymore, she sent me out there with a sledgehammer. I spent a couple of hours at it every day, a couple hours where I didn't have to offer consoling words, or worse yet have to listen to any, where there was nothing but the steady thump of the hammer and every once in a while the sound of something cracking and giving way.

There is nothing I can say to her about my father. I know she misses him. I don't have the heart to tell her I'm glad he's dead. It's a relief not to feel his lurking, disapproving presence anymore. At the same time there is this awful finality about it. I always hate it when people keep secrets from me. My father left me with questions I'll never be able to answer, not as long as I live. Was he trying to kill himself? Did he forget where he was? Was he in some kind of awful pain? Was he angry? Then the really hard questions, that I can never say out loud: Did it have anything to do with that letter I wrote? Or did he even think of me, at all?

I have a copy of the official police report written by a guy named Adkisson, who was my father's dive partner. "When he was about 15′ past me, he accelerated as if he was chasing something I could not see . . . he kept accelerating and was swimming down at approx. a 30 degree angle . . . I caught him at 93′ (I didn't know the depth at the time, I read this later on the surface). I grabbed him by the leg, turned him around, gave him the up signal and asked if he was OK. He acknowledged the OK signal & we started up . . . I came to the surface and was going to call for the Zodiac. However the Zodiac was already coming. I turned around and saw him about 40 ft from me on the surface. As I swam toward him I saw his regulator hanging down, the camera electric cord entangled in his vest. The Zodiac reached him when I was 10 ft away. I helped them pull him in the boat. He was on the surface approx 1-2 min. We arrived & CPR was initiated immediately. I don't know why he exhibited this conduct. This is the way it happened to the best of my memory."

At the end of that week in Dallas, my last night before I came home to Austin, before this whole business started with "The Long and Winding Road," my mother had a memorial service there in the living room of the house. She called it "A Toast to Life." I guess there were a dozen people there in a circle, what passed for my father's closest friends. They all loved him, that was never the problem. It's just that at one time or another I'd heard him say something cruel and dismissive about every one of them, like he had to prove that he didn't need any friends, that none of them were quite good enough for him. Bill Wyndham, who used to be his department chairman, talked about how much his students loved him. A couple from the local anthropology club talked about how much time he'd spent working with them on typology. Joe Hastings, who ran the field school in New Mexico, remembered how my father always used to kid around about adopting some good-looking eighteen-year-old female student. Donna from next door was the only one who seemed to talk about the father that I knew, and even so she soft-pedaled it, went on about the warm heart under his gruff exterior. My mother talked about how he'd died doing exactly what he wanted to do, and how lucky that made him. At the end they all shook my hand and hugged me and told me how proud he'd always been of me.

I wanted to say, "Prove it." I wanted them to tell me why, if he cared so much, he never said it to me. I wanted to take Bill Wyndham by his expensive lapels and ask where my real father was, the one who thought Wyndham was nothing but a politician and bitched about his tight-assed parties. I wanted to throw Joe Hastings against a wall and tell him that my father didn't need to adopt anybody. That he already had a son. That his bullshit macho posturing had always pissed me off as much as it insulted my mother, that I was sick of people bringing it up like it was supposed to be funny.

Then I looked at my mother as she sat there with this radiant, sad smile on her face, her eyes full of tears, her champagne glass unnoticed in her hand, and I didn't say anything at all.

Saturday, a week after I got back from L.A., was Elizabeth's birthday. Once, when I asked her why we hardly made love anymore, she told me I wasn't romantic enough. That I was too wrapped up in my work, that I didn't make her feel special or attractive, that I needed to create a mood for her. There's been no sex since my father died, almost a month ago, and I needed some physical contact.

I took her to a movie in the afternoon and out to dinner that night. I even wore a tie. When we got home I had her come out in the back yard with me to look at the stars, which were in fact very beautiful. I tried to put my arms around her and she said, "It's cold. Let's go in."

She fell asleep lying next to me on the couch, watching *It's a Wonderful Life* on TV. She started to move in her sleep. I looked over and saw her with one hand between her legs, pushing against it. She moaned and then sighed without waking up.

I felt like I was watching from a long way away. She hasn't lost her desire, obviously. She's just lost her desire for me. I remembered the way she sounded on the phone when I was in L.A., that love and loneliness in her voice. Where did it go now that I'm back?

I went to the kitchen for some Jack Daniel's and a couple of beers to help it go down. By the time I finished she'd rolled over with her back to the TV, fast asleep.

On Monday I heard a voice inside say, "Let's go." Graham had set me up with an L.A. book dealer named Mike Autrey, who'd diligently shipped me everything he could find on the Doors and L.A. in the sixties. I'd spent a week reading and studying and it had started to come together.

The first thing I did was a work tape, with the first two albums as models and a list of the songs we thought were available. Side one opens with "Waiting for the Sun," which didn't get released until *Morrison Hotel* in February of 1970. Then "The Unknown Soldier," the first single. Followed by "Hello, I Love You," the second single, and "Summer's Almost Gone." Graham and I both liked putting "My Wild Love" into the "Horse Latitudes" slot, next to last on the side. The song was an afterthought, recorded hastily after they decided to scrap "Celebration," but it fit perfectly. Then the usual long song to close the side, "Five to One." Graham thought side two might have opened with a blues, like the first album's "Back Door Man," if there was room. I used "Roadhouse Blues" from *Morrison Hotel*. The rest of the side was the only available version of "Celebration of the Lizard," from *Absolutely Live*. I could hear the edits that Rothchild had to make, even in midsong, to get something salvageable.

It wasn't all I heard. I heard why Graham wanted me to make my own tape, not just dub a copy of the one he had at home. Something in the experience of putting the songs together got inside me. It's the feeling of setting right a twenty-year-old injustice. A feeling I'd made an album that was not just better, it was more correct, closer to some kind of absolute truth.

I canceled my ad in the *Chronicle* so I'd have fewer stereos to fix and more time for the Doors. I gradually got into a routine: a few hours' work in the morning while I listen to the tape or else to the first two Doors albums, both of which I have on CD. When Elizabeth gets home it's my cue for the first beer of the day, which I take from the little half-sized refrigerator under the workbench. She kisses me on the cheek and goes downstairs. I hate the empty gesture of that kiss. If she doesn't want to kiss my mouth then she should leave me the hell alone.

Afternoons and nights I study. I have Morrison radio interviews, a British concert video called *The Doors Are Open*, and the documentary Morrison was involved in, *Feast of Friends.* He's taking shape in my mind: the sleepy, silky voice that could suddenly crack or turn vicious; the hooded eyes, the hands folded over the mike stand, the slumped shoulders, seeming drunk or narcoleptic; the sudden madman who would explode a moment later and race around the stage, windmilling his arms, screaming, sometimes throwing himself headlong into the floor or the audience.

Elizabeth is asleep by the time I get to bed. Some nights I lie awake and think about leaving her. I don't have the words to ask her to go, so it would have to be me. I would lose the house, the shop, every material thing I care about. Some nights it seems possible. Other nights I just feel trapped.

I switched to Coors, Morrison's favorite brand, despite the watery taste and the brewery's politics. It's all part of the Morrison experience. Ride the snake. Late Friday night, with ten of them under my belt, I went upstairs to give it a shot.

The idea was that I would put together a tape here at home, then go to L.A. and redo it in digital. The hardest part was getting to the album. I can't explain it better than that. It's like the new archeology, that my father always talked about, how you're supposed to decide what you're going to find before you start digging. You make your model and then you dig for it.

To make my model I had to find a way that the album could have been made. To get the album I needed the title song. The rest would follow.

The song starts with hissing maracas and tambourine and a few muttered lines of poetry. Then Morrison screams, "Wake up!" The band comes in, Manzarek mashing a handful of random keys, Krieger lifting one corner of his amp and dropping it on the stage with the reverb full on, a noise like a building collapsing. More recitation against a background of noise. We're well into the song before Morrison actually starts to sing and the band starts to play something with a melody. From there things build nicely, through the "Not to Touch the Earth" section and a big climax, then back to the tambourine and a few last lines of poetry.

The first decision I made was that it had to happen live in the studio, the way they'd recorded "The End." If I had to, I would settle for a couple of different versions that could be spliced together. But that give and take between Morrison and the band was essential. Which meant I needed Morrison in the kind of condition where he could perform a twenty-minute song.

February of 1968. A long, long time ago. If Morrison is out of control, so is the world. We're in the middle of the Tet offensive in Vietnam, a month-long all-out Communist assault that leaves hundreds of Americans killed or wounded, and at least five thousand Vietcong dead. At the end of March President Johnson will throw in the towel and refuse to run for a second term, shattered by the rising death toll of the war and the rising tide of protest at home. In May, French students will paint "Never Work" on the walls of the city and riot in the streets. Martin Luther King will be murdered in April, Bobby Kennedy in June.

February of 1968. In Dallas it's cold and windy and I've just been to see Jimi Hendrix at the State Fair Music Hall. Kevin, the lead player of my band, is up front with his steady girlfriend, driving her home. I'm in the back seat of Kevin's station wagon with Alex. I've kissed her before, at parties, but this is our first real date, this is serious, and when I kiss her she kisses back. My nose is full of her perfume and I can taste the heat of her breath. We're all four seniors in high school and for the moment everything seems full of enormous possibility. I haven't seen the things that Morrison has seen, and I can't predict the future that's almost upon us: the riots in Chicago, the election of Nixon and Agnew, the deaths of Brian Jones and Joplin and Hendrix and Morrison. Feuding with my father that will end in a couple of abortive attempts to run away from home, anguished breakups and reunions with Alex, my dropping out of college and losing the band, the growing realization of how limited the possibilities were for any of us.

February of 1968. We were helpless, but none of us knew it yet. Except for Jim Morrison.

Mike Autrey had somehow found me photos of the *Celebration* sessions. The walls are cheap wooden panels, the kind with the precut vertical grooves. Ray Manzarek sits behind his Vox Continental organ with its red and black body and its white and black keys reversed. His glasses and sunglasses and a light-gray patch cord sit on top of it. He hunches completely over the keys when he plays, a big sweep of dark blond hair falling across his eyes. From the side all you can see is the hair and the big muttonchop sideburns. He's wearing a striped shirt and jeans and a wide leather belt. It's early evening, dark and cool outside, timeless and air-conditioned in here.

Robbie Krieger, always a little spaced and awkward-looking, is wearing striped seersucker shorts and a denim jacket and sandals. He's got tinted glasses and his hair is a haphazard frizz. His red Gibson SG is on his lap, and he's finger-picking flamenco style.

Behind a wall of gobos, chest-high padded partitions, are Douglas Lubahn and John Densmore. Lubahn played bass for Clear Light, an underrated band that never got past their first album. He's strictly a session man for the Doors, since Manzarek does the bass parts with his left hand in the stage shows. He's got receding black hair and a black fringe beard. He's left-handed and plays a regular Fender bass upside down. He's on a stool in the corner, looking like he really doesn't know what the hell is going on.

Densmore is in black, hung with pounds of beads and chains. He's got a helmet of black hair and long, sculptured sideburns. He's got some stuff taped to the head of his snare drum to kill the overtones. I used to use a wad of newspaper, held down with duct tape, the drummer's friend. I know from experience that Densmore spends most of his time on his drummer's throne, his back stiff and uncomfortable, waiting, because that's what drummers do most of in the studio. At one point during these sessions he will throw his sticks across the room and yell that he's had it, he's quitting. He's sick of Morrison's drunkenness, of the hangers-on, of the lack of communication, the endless retakes—one hundred and thirty on "The Unknown Soldier" alone—robbing the songs of any vitality they ever had.

Morrison is wandering around the studio, trying to get in the mood to shut himself in the vocal booth and actually record something. Let's say for argument that he is not yet terribly drunk. Let's say this so we can take a shot at "Celebration of the Lizard." He's in his standard black leather pants, today with a brown cashmere sweater over them. He's still fairly lean and his dark hair curls past his shoulders, loose and sexy. He's shaved clean to show off his sensuous mouth, the heavy lower lip, the upper lip curled to reveal a hint of teeth. When he walks, even on a wide level surface like the floor of the studio, there's a sense that he's balanced precariously, like he's on a wall around the roof of a building, a dozen stories above Sunset Boulevard.

What the pictures don't show are three girls passing a joint on the leather couch in the corner behind Manzarek. Morrison keeps coming back to pet one of them, a pretty strawberry blonde in brown hip-huggers and a white tank top. She might be all of sixteen. Let's say that just tonight Morrison's drinking buddies, Tom Baker and Bobby Neuwirth, are off drinking somewhere else.

Rothchild and his engineer, Bruce Botnick, are in the booth and they are tired of waiting too. Rothchild is in his early thirties, high forehead, kinky blond hair slowly getting long again after a pot bust two years before. Botnick is darker, with a broad face and five-o'clock shadow.

Manzarek walks over to Densmore and Lubahn, and Krieger listens in. Manzarek talks them through the arrangement and the others all nod. Morrison takes a tambourine and maracas into the vocal booth. "Wake up!" he screams into the microphone.

Rothchild gets on the intercom and says, "Don't overblow, Jim, you've got a long way to go."

Morrison says, "Why not?" and he sounds plaintive, like a spoiled child.

Rothchild says, "Okay, Jim, let's try it."

I had the remote for my cassette player in my hand. I let off the PAUSE and lay down on the couch in darkness.

"Jim, come on, let's go." The voice was coming through the speakers now, the ones in the studio and mine as well.

"Yeah, yeah, all right." There's a pause, then Morrison says, "Hey, Paul? Paul, man, there's some chick passed out in here." He giggles. "She ain't got no clothes on, man." Rothchild comes out to investigate. Morrison's words are still coming over the speakers in the studio. "She's ugly, too."

The three other girls help their friend out of the vocal booth, drape some clothes on her, and take her away. Densmore says, very quietly, "Good. Now maybe we can get some work done." Krieger, who has been playing some meandering Far Eastern line on the guitar, stops to tune up. Everything is ready again.

"Rolling," Botnick says.

Rothchild says, " 'Celebration of the Lizard,' take—what is this?"

"Eighteen."

"Take eighteen."

Silence. It goes on long enough that Densmore and Krieger look at each other. Densmore shrugs. Finally there is a rattle of tambourine and maraca. Densmore touches his cymbals gently with the points of his sticks. "Lions in the street," Morrison says, and we're off. He gets through the opening recitation. The words are a little slurred but dramatic nonetheless, that same walking-the-edge-of-the-abyss drama that's in everything he does. Another long pause, then he screams, "Wake up!" The band crashes and growls, but Morrison is laughing. "Wake up the fat chick!" he says, and the music lurches into silence. "Get the bitch back in here! I'm so horny I could fuck a snake!" That gets him laughing even harder. "I am the Lizard King!" he shouts. "I can fuck anything!"

I sat up on the couch. It was not happening. I could see the studio, smell it, sweat and dope and cigarettes and perfume, the camphor smell of the drums, the burning rosin smell of hot electronics. I could hear the music, hear Krieger's fingers slide on the strings, the squeak of Densmore's bass drum pedal. But I couldn't get inside. Morrison is too strong. He won't let me in.

———

I didn't get up until after noon Saturday. Elizabeth reminded me that we had a Christmas party that night at Sondra and Gary's, then she went shopping. I shuffled around the house in jeans and socks and a sweater, watching the rain through the sliding glass doors at the back of the house.

It's a contest of wills with Morrison. He wants to drink; I want him to make the album. To get what I want I have to be stronger than him.

Or I have to break him.

He's not easy to push around. His father is career Navy, the kind of guy people just naturally call "the Commander." Jim grew up resenting uniforms and authority of any kind. He was compulsively belligerent to cops, even when a little diplomacy could have kept him out of trouble. His friends talked about how his eyes would go out of focus and some demon would take over. Nobody ever saw him hurt anyone else, but he would bring violence down on himself like it was some kind of retribution. The more the cops beat him the more he taunted and cursed them until finally someone else had to break it up. They said he didn't know when to back off.

I sat on the couch, my heart pounding. I remembered the times I had taunted my father in the same way, daring him, needling him. Knowing he was mad, watching it build up, being sacred and still I couldn't back down, because I was so little and he was so powerful and made me feel so helpless. Until he finally broke down and hit me, his big open hand across my face. I remembered how it felt, shame at having fucked up, at being bad, and at the same time pride that I could push him so far. The pain didn't matter as long as I could be the one in charge and him out of control.

Was it that way for Morrison? Did he have to keep pushing because the only alternative is to give in to the fear, to let it overwhelm and destroy you?

I went into the kitchen and opened a Coors. "Roadhouse Blues" played in my head: "Well I woke up this morning and I got myself a beer." It tasted terrible. I drank it down and looked at my reflection in the rain-smeared window. Yes, I thought. This is how it is.

Morrison's father was gone for months at a time, either at sea or on some top-secret project. I don't know how it was with the Morrison family, but I know how it was with mine. My father was in the National Park Service, where he did ruin stabilization, rebuilding national monuments. He helped restore Jamestown, and Fort Fredrica on the Georgia coast, and the Anasazi ruins in Chaco Canyon, New Mexico. We moved all over the country, just like the Morrisons did. If we were in one place for more than a year my parents would lose their lease or for some other reason have to move to the other side of town, which put me in a different school and took me away from whatever friends I'd managed to make. From early spring to late fall, eight or nine months a year, my father would be in the field. When he was home, or when school was out and we went to live in the trailer with him where he was stationed, he had to make up for lost time, prove all over again that he was the boss. My mother used to hang me up for weeks, saying, "Wait till I tell your father." Jim Morrison's mother did the same thing.

Supposedly all that moving around as a kid leads to three things: alcoholism, broken marriages, and resentment of authority. So far I'm two for three, and the marriage does not look good.

We left for the party a little before nine. I was at the apex of a nice high, due to careful application of beer all afternoon. I was loose and very tuned in to the inanimate world. The reflected lights in the rain-slick streets, "Riders on the Storm" inevitably, unavoidably on the car radio, my hair down and still damp from the shower, the comfortable textures of an old flannel shirt and my leather jacket. Elizabeth's silence fit me the same way, snug and familiar.

At Sondra's house Elizabeth headed for the kitchen, where most of the women had already settled. The men were mostly in the computer room with the kids and Gary's flight-simulator program. The stereo in the front room was on, just below the threshold of attention. I went through the tapes and put on *Morrison Hotel*, easing the volume up just enough that nobody would notice.

I threaded my way into the kitchen through the women's conversations: kids, politics, TV. When we first started coming to parties with this crowd, I swear the women and men talked to each other, or at least played games together. We're all college-educated, liberal people, but now when we hit some critical mass we split into two cultures, like our parents did.

I stood in the cool air of the refrigerator for a minute, liking the way it felt. I still had the leather jacket on, though it was warm enough inside to do without. I took two beers and headed back into the living room, suddenly conscious of the way I moved, feeling the beer and yet feeling very graceful, very animal, at the same time. Maybe it was my imagination, but I was sure Sondra was watching me. We'd flirted now and then, and I wasn't the worst-looking guy at the party. A bit thick around the waist, maybe, but plenty of hair, an okay smile, and something extra tonight. Confidence, or maybe recklessness.

Morrison was in the middle of "You Make Me Real" as Larry and Diane Olsen arrived with their two kids in tow. Diane looked like she'd had electroshock. Gary helped her out of her coat and Larry said, "Sorry we're late. We've just had a *bad* day." Larry is tall and blond and finishes his sentences with an involuntary chuckle, even when he isn't remotely amused. "Diane hit a kid on her way home from work."

"What?" Gary said.

"She was barely hurt, thank God," Diane said. "She just bounced off the side of the car and skinned her hands and knees. She ran right out in front of me as I was coming home. With all that rain and everything I didn't see her. I can't help but think what could have happened if I wasn't already slowing down to turn in the driveway . . . oh God, it was just awful."

Larry put his arm around her and took her to get a drink. I was suddenly aware of the Doors tape again, the very end of the guitar solo, then the clean break where Morrison says, "Indians scattered on dawn's highway bleeding . . ."

And there it was, fully formed, in my head. I was shocked and ashamed that I had even thought of it. Still I knew from that first flash that I was going to do it.

—————

When Jim was four years old, so the legend goes, the Morrison family moved from Washington, D.C., to Albuquerque. I knew all too well what the trip was like: no interstates then, just winding two-lane blacktop crowded with trucks and farm equipment. The Morrisons hit the last stretch, Santa Fe to Albuquerque, as the sun came up. A truck full of Indians had overturned and the dead and dying lay all over the road. Jim went crazy at the sight of them, screaming at his parents to stop and help. His father drove on by.

Later Morrison said it was the single most important moment in his life. He came back to the image again and again, most obviously in "Peace Frog." Death on the highway. Blood on the streets.

—————

I came home too wired to sleep. I washed my face and slicked back my hair and went upstairs.

I know Morrison liked American cars. Tonight I see him in an Impala convertible, top down of course. He's wearing brown leathers and a white cotton shirt. It's three in the morning. Earlier he staggered out of a session at TTG where they had once again been unable to get anything done. He and Bobby Neuwirth and Tom Baker had driven over to Barney's and played pool, until Tom wandered off with this teenage boy and girl, slipping Morrison a wink as he went out the door. God only knew what depravity the three of them were up to, even now.

"Are we, like, going anywhere?" Bobby says.

"Going anywhere?" Morrison says. They're headed south on La Cienega, which is totally deserted at this hour, and Morrison floors it and cranks the wheel with his index finger. The car fishtails and careens around in a U-turn, tires screaming, and leaves a cloud of black burned-rubber smoke in the air. "Are we?" Morrison says, and guns it and spins again. "Going anywhere?" He looks totally calm, he sounds calm, but there's something about his stare, he's not looking at anything, his eyes might as well be rolled all the way back in his head, because Bobby has apparently pissed him off or made him feel self-conscious or insufficiently entertaining and now the demon has taken over. "Going, going, anywhere, anywhere?"

Then Morrison calmly says, "Bat turn," and does another U-turn, and the smell of burning tires hangs over them in a cloud. They're headed north again, fast enough that both of them are shoved down in the seat, much, much too fast.

There is a gray blur off to the right. Then Morrison lunges at the brakes with his foot, his mouth open in astonishment even before the thud of impact, almost lost in the scream of the brakes, and just after it, even quieter, a sound like a hard-boiled egg cracking against a countertop. The Impala skids across the southbound traffic lanes, over the curb and into a coin box for the L.A. *Times*.

Steam hisses out of the radiator. Morrison and Neuwirth stumble out of the car, turn, see the body lying there on the pavement. "Oh shit," Neuwirth says. "Oh shit, Jim. This is bad. I got to call the cops."

Neuwirth staggers off toward a phone booth. Morrison walks out into the street, not looking in either direction, eyes fixed on the body.

It's an old man, a wino, fifty years old, but he looks much older. He's wearing a heavy tan corduroy coat despite the mild night. There is a pool of blood and yellow-gray brain tissue all around his head, which is cracked and slightly flattened where it hit the bumper.

Morrison is still standing there when the cops come. Neuwirth sits on the curb nearby, head between his knees. Two other cars have stopped and Morrison is now pinned in their headlights, head cocked at an angle, eyes puzzled and amazed at the same time.

The cops have their nightsticks out. They poke and prod Morrison into the back of the squad car. He is so stunned that he doesn't resist them. Neuwirth gets in with him voluntarily. The first cop says, "Who was driving?"

Bobby looks at his feet. Morrison says, "It was a hitchhiker. We picked him up over in Hollywood. He split after he hit the guy, just took off running, man. We tried to stop him."

"Bullshit," the other cop says. "It was one of you two queers and I'm going to find out which one."

Morrison sneers. It's not convincing. If you kill somebody while you're driving drunk in California it's murder. He's facing hard time. His hands are cuffed behind him, so he has to slide forward to keep his knees from shaking.

"Okay, fine," the first cop says. "We'll go down to the station." He reads them both their rights from a small card.

The station is linoleum and plate glass, the walls painted two shades of green. Even the prostitutes and drunks stare at Morrison's long hair with open contempt. The face in his mug shot is bewildered, withdrawn. The cop who arrested him has by this time seen all the DUIs on his record. "Make a habit of this, don't you, pretty boy?" he says. "My shift is over at six. I got us a private room booked. Just you and me, sweetie."

At five forty-five, Doors manager Bill Siddons arrives, lawyers in tow, to swing a quick arraignment and bailout. Siddons is tall and blond and long-haired, wearing a motorcycle jacket and no shirt. He has never seen Morrison look so afraid.

"Get me out of here, man," is all he says.

For two days Morrison holes up in the Alta Cienega Motel. Bobby Neuwirth and Tom Baker both come looking for him and Morrison sends them away. He's not drinking anything stronger than Coors, no more than a six-pack or two a night, which his nervous system burns off as soon as he swallows it. When he comes into the studio again he is wired, pale, in the same leathers and white shirt he's had on since the accident. "Let's do it," he says.

They start "Celebration of the Lizard." Morrison moves through the recitation much faster. His words are crisp. There is an urgency to them that everyone in the studio can feel. He breaks off during the "run to the mirror" section and says, "I don't like it, Robbie, can you play something like," and hums a guitar part. It's somewhere between a police siren and a cry for help.

Robbie says, "Yeah," smiling.

Ray says, "How about this against it?" and plays a riff. Order forms in the chaos.

"I dig it," Morrison says. "Let's do it again. Harder, faster."

They take it from the top. Instead of a dead president, Morrison sings about a "dead derelict's corpse on the side of the road," and then goes on about "bloodstained cement like a terrible sunrise." Rothchild sits hypnotized, like he did during "The End," unaware that he's even in the studio, riveted by Morrison's performance. It lasts seventeen minutes and thirty-two seconds. There are a couple of mistakes that can be edited out. Everyone looks at everyone else.

Morrison leans against the window of the vocal booth, his face pushed up and distorted against the glass. It's dead quiet for maybe a minute, then the girls on the couch start to applaud. Morrison slowly straightens up. He starts a smile, then it goes away. "I want to do another one. Can we do another song?"

"Sure, Jim," Rothchild says. "Anything you want."

There was more that I was too tired to hang on for. The remote fell out of my hand and the room went quiet.

======

I only got up once on Sunday, then only long enough to make sure the song was really on tape, that it was as good as I remembered it. It was. I told Elizabeth I was sick. It's something she can understand, a way for her to deal with me that doesn't involve sex or power games. A little of what I felt was triumph. I'd beaten Morrison and gotten what

I wanted. I felt somewhat creepy about the way I'd done it, about the dead wino and the cops, but in the end it didn't matter because none of it was real.

Mostly I was exhausted.

Elizabeth brought me chicken noodle soup for dinner. It was set out nicely on a tray with a place mat and a linen napkin in a holder and a Coke in a glass with ice and a flexi-straw.

"Ever thought of becoming a waitress?" I asked her.

"Ever wonder what it would feel like to have an entire Coke poured on your stomach?" She sat on the edge of the bed and smiled and pushed the hair away from my face. "I know what's wrong with you."

"You do?"

"Your mother's coming Tuesday."

"You don't have to remind me."

She'll stay with us through the end of the week, then we'll all drive to Houston for Christmas, exactly a week away. That's where Elizabeth's mother and father are, Edna and Willard Dean. For the last ten years, both sets of parents had insisted on having us for the holidays. We'd always spent Christmas Eve in Dallas and then driven all night to get to Houston for Christmas morning. If nothing else, this year promises lower mileage on the car.

Even though Willard is retired Navy, like Morrison's dad, Elizabeth never turned rebellious. Part of it may be her older brother and sister, who helped spoil her outrageously. Just the same, there is a lot of tension there, a lot of love-hate, especially between Elizabeth and her mother.

Edna's father, Elizabeth's grandfather, was a fisherman in Cape Cod, but Edna brought Elizabeth up to be Queen of England. Literally. She taught her everything she would need to know in case Prince Charles happened to pop the question. Still Edna seems to like me fine. I think she understands better than Elizabeth that it's okay to be working-class.

I don't know what it will do to add my mother to the mix. The Deans insist she's welcome but I know she's going to humiliate me somehow. Cry the entire time, or tell embarrassing stories from my childhood.

"You need to talk to her, Ray. I mean about your father and everything. The way you feel."

"She knows how I feel. That's one of the things she keeps apologizing for."

"I thought it might help to actually say the words. To get them out there."

"How would that help? It's Christmas, her first Christmas without him. It would only make things tougher on her."

She stood up. It was only a couple of feet but she was suddenly a long way away. "It wasn't her I was worried about."

"You still think I'm crazy, don't you? Because of all this music stuff."

"It's not the music. Nobody's saying you're crazy. It's just you've got all this resentment and anger and I think you need to figure out who it is you're really angry at." She closed the door on her way out.

I looked at the food and couldn't eat it. Me not talking? Me keeping things bottled up? I couldn't believe she had the nerve to say it. I put the tray on the floor with the napkin still in its ring and watched the ice melt and the soup turn cold.

———

I meant to work on the album Monday. Instead I went through my videotapes, watching *The Compleat Beatles* and Jeff Beck at the ARMS Show and finally *Enter the Dragon*. A wasted day. I couldn't face Morrison again, not yet.

I hadn't had any beer all day Sunday. By Monday afternoon I was overdue. I skipped lunch and ate popcorn and drank Coors in front of the tube.

Tuesday was the twentieth. My mother arrived and that was the end of the Doors for now. I fixed us grilled cheese sandwiches when we got home from the airport, and my mother prowled uneasily around the kitchen. There was a paper sack of Coors empties that I hadn't yet taken out to the garage. She made sure I saw her look at them even though she didn't actually say anything.

After lunch she came upstairs with me and sat on the couch while I worked. Mostly she read or did needlepoint, and the rest of the time she sorted through her paperwork and copied one list onto another. I already wanted a beer but I didn't want a lecture. I waited another hour then went downstairs on some excuse or other and chugged one while she wasn't looking.

Morrison told the Elektra publicity people that his parents were dead. In fact both his parents outlived him, but once he was in the band, once he had the power to cut them off, he did. He told his management not to take their calls or let them backstage, and he never set eyes on either of them again.

I crushed the empty can in my hand and looked at the stairs to my shop. "Be gone," I whispered. "Go away."

When Elizabeth got home it went from bad to worse. Elizabeth makes my mother nervous. She still isn't convinced that Elizabeth likes her. I can sympathize. After eleven years I'm not entirely sure Elizabeth likes *me*. Loves me, depends on me, whatever those things mean, sure. But you have to know somebody to like them, have to be willing to take them pretty much as they are.

When she's around my mother apologizes for everything. "I'm sorry, but I have to go to the bathroom." "I'm sorry, but I'm going to go ahead and have breakfast. I can't help it, I'm hungry." Worst of all, she drops into baby talk: "We gonna have us dinner now?" Her voice goes up an octave or two, she squints and shows her teeth, sometimes she grabs the thighs of her sweatpants and tugs at them like a shy five-year-old. Apparently this behavior was some kind of turn-on for my father but now it seems so desperately out of place that it knots me up with rage.

When my father died he was involved in an underwater site in the San Marcos River. PBS did a documentary about the river and my father was in it for fifteen minutes or so. My mother has a copy of the tape but no VCR, so she brought it with her to Austin. We all sat and watched it Tuesday night.

It was disorienting to see my father and hear his voice. Mostly he seemed pompous and artificial. I couldn't get past my annoyance to feel anything else.

Even worse was a tape she brought from one of the other divers on Cozumel. My father is just in the background of a couple of shots—sitting in a taxi with my mother, suiting up with a couple of other people on deck. He looks old, used up, his eyes too wide, like he has to strain to keep them open at all. Most of the tape is underwater footage but there are shots of the hotel, the divemaster, the boat, some women in swimsuits, and it all seems kind of sexy. Maybe it's just the idea of the tropics, what with the weather so cold and gray outside. Maybe it's memories of my honeymoon with Elizabeth, which we spent there nine years ago.

Elizabeth took my hand as we sat there, and rested her head on my shoulder. It was a comfort, though I doubted it would lead to anything more. Sure enough, by the time we got to bed, the mood had passed and she went right to sleep.

Wednesday morning my mother had me show her how to work the VCR. She watched both tapes again while I worked upstairs. First I turned the stereo up so I wouldn't hear her. That made me feel self-conscious, so I turned it off and found myself listening to every creak of the furniture.

Friday, on the drive to Houston, she rode in the back seat so she could lie down if her back started to hurt. She talked continuously, reading the highway signs and billboards out loud, like she would disappear if she couldn't hear the sound of her own voice. We stopped for gas in LaGrange and while Elizabeth was in the rest room I took her aside. "Look, Mom, you don't have to talk all the time. We can listen to the tape deck or look at the scenery." Her face was numb. "We love you." I put my arm around her, which was like hugging a marble statue. "You don't have to entertain us or anything. You don't have to apologize all the time. We want you here. Just your being here is enough."

We never touched each other much. She didn't seem to know how to react. "I'm sorry," she said, and went back out to the car.

I paid for the gas and Elizabeth came out of the bathroom. "I talked to her," I said.

"And?"

I shrugged. We got in the car and a few miles outside LaGrange my mother started to cry. I was driving and there wasn't much I could do except reach back and take her hand. She squeezed it hard, and used her other hand to fumble through her purse for a Kleenex to blow her nose. Elizabeth looked at me, then stared out the windshield.

As soon as we got to Houston, Edna took my mother to the kitchen for coffee. Elizabeth's brother and his longtime lover were there, with a pitcher of vodka tonics already mixed. They gave me hugs and a couple of drinks to get me through until Elizabeth's sister and her husband pulled in from New Orleans. They put *Wheel of Fortune* on the TV and I begged off to study a manual I'd brought with me on CD lasers.

I went upstairs and lay down. I could hear them shouting happily down in the den as I closed my eyes. I was wiped out from the drive, from my mother's constant pain, from the effort of keeping up a show of holiday spirits.

This is not my favorite time of year. When I was a kid it seems like we were always on the road for Christmas. My birthday is the week after and what I remember most is waking up in some antiseptic motel in nowhere I'd ever been before, being told "Happy Birthday" as I climbed back into the car.

As far as I could tell, Christmas was one long imposition on my father, to the point where he actually walked around saying "Humbug" all the time. I never understood the problem. The only person he actually had to shop for was my mother, since she took care of everybody else. As soon as I was old enough he delegated that to me. One year after I'd refused to help anymore, all he gave her was some money—which was pretty meaningless since they had a joint account and she didn't work—and a chocolate bar. Practical gifts were always big around our house: silverfish packets, nose hair clippers, toilet seat covers.

I didn't have the energy to take the manual out of my suitcase. Instead I went to sleep and dreamed about my father.

He looks about thirty. I must be a kid, then, because he still looks old to me. He's wearing a pair of really long Bermuda shorts. We're at this swimming hole which I vaguely recognize as being in Kansas, where my mother grew up. We chase each other around on these rocks. My father seems to get younger and younger. He's about sixteen now. Suddenly he stops, like he's heard something. Then he turns around. I can't see the look on his face. He dives into the water, a perfect swan dive, and disappears. The water is green and I can't see anything below the surface. I stand there, waiting, holding my breath. I'm not going to breathe, apparently, until he comes back up. Only he's not coming up.

I fought my way out of sleep like it was deep water, panting for breath. I had a lead weight in my head and the conviction that something was hideously wrong. I slowly put together where I was and why but it didn't help. So I washed my face and brushed my teeth and went downstairs for another drink.

———

Saturday morning, Christmas Eve, somebody knocked while I was getting dressed. Elizabeth was still in bed, waiting for the bathroom. I opened the door to find my mother in her turquoise sweatsuit, lightly made up, brittle smile in place. "I'm sorry," she said, "but I'm not going to apologize for the way I look," and walked away.

Elizabeth bit her pillow to keep from laughing. I sat on the edge of the bed with my head in my hands. "Is she getting better? Or worse?"

———

That night around eleven o'clock I shut myself in Edna's bedroom to call Graham. Because of all the company, Willard is back in the same bedroom with her, and I saw the signs of his temporary occupancy: a robe on a chair, his book and reading glasses on the floor by the right-hand side of the bed.

It was only nine o'clock in L.A. Graham answered the phone on the third ring, his voice muffled. " 'Lo?"

"Graham? It's Ray."

"Mmmmmmmm?"

"Ray Shackleford, man, I just called to wish you a Merry Christmas."

"Yeah. Ray. Yeah, right. Hang on a second." I leaned back against the headboard and watched the clock on Edna's bedside table tick off thirty seconds. "Yeah, Ray. How you doing?"

"Okay. Did I wake you up or something?"

"No, no, just watching a little tube."

"You got anybody there with you?"

"No, man. But hey, it's cool. I was never big on holidays anyway."

"I got a surprise for you. Kind of a Christmas present. I got 'Celebration of the Lizard.' "

"No shit?"

"Just the one song for now, but the rest is coming."

"Man, that's fantastic. You really got it?"

We talked for another minute or two, and then I broke it off, embarrassed for having caught him at such a bad time, thinking I shouldn't have called at all. I wished him a Merry Christmas and he said, "Yeah. Right."

Elizabeth's family opens presents on Christmas morning, not on Christmas Eve like we always did. Everybody was in bed by twelve-thirty. I couldn't sleep. Finally I went downstairs and sat in the den with one of Willard's Budweisers. Half the room, where the glass-topped table and chairs normally were, has been cleared out to make room for the eight-foot tree and the mounds of presents. In the morning everyone would set on them like sharks, all opening at once, hurling paper, shouting thank-yous in passing and moving on. There are occasional minor injuries, sometimes people end up with the wrong presents, things get lost or broken or thrown away in the madness, and nobody seems to mind. My first time there, after years of twenty questions and numbered presents and lists, it seemed like the end of the world.

Edna has sisters and in-laws all around Massachusetts, and the Dean family is big in Indiana and Florida. It's the exact opposite of mine, which is the narrow end of an inverted pyramid. Both my mother's parents are dead. Before I married Elizabeth the two of us went to Laredo so she could meet my grandmother on my father's side. That was when I found out my father had a sister. She died before I was born, but still. My father never mentioned her. When I confronted my parents with it, my mother said, "No, I'm sure we must have talked about her sometime."

Her name was Janet, same as my grandmother's. She was two years older than my father, blonde and clever. She always got my father in trouble. He was convinced his mother loved Janet and not him. Finally he ran away and lived with his father; his parents had divorced when he was just a baby. Janet grew up wild, ran around with lots of men, and died young in a motorcycle accident. My father never forgave her for being his mother's favorite. He wrote her out of the family history, like she'd never lived.

I'm the last Shackleford I know. Unless something drastic happens, the line stops with me.

I stood up and looked out the window, rolling my shoulders to feel them move under my shirt. No weather out there at all, really. It was too warm for December, and the lights of the city had turned the cloudy skies to dull red.

My father's Nikonos underwater camera was sitting on the coffee table. My mother brought it down for Elizabeth's brother-in-law, who dives. It's smaller than my Nikon SLR, sleek and black and compact. And, I saw, the lens doesn't open up any wider than f-4. Which explained our last argument.

He'd been a pretty good underwater photographer. He kept framed blowups of his favorite pictures in the living room where he could see them from his recliner: a black-and-electric-yellow angelfish, an anemone like a cluster of pink jelly fingers, a clown-faced puffer fish, a single nurse shark. Never any other divers. He spent his last two years in that chair or in bed, dozing off during the day, unable to sleep at night.

My mother had brought four rolls of film back from Mexico, his last pictures. It was stupid of me to think they would tell me anything. Still I had to know. I took them into the camera shop the day after she got back. They were ready that Friday afternoon. Slides, of course. There's a certain kind of person that has to make other people sit through a slide show.

My mother set up the projector and stacked the first boxful in the feeder. There were three shots taken from the bow of the boat, underexposed. It made the clear blue waters off Cozumel look dark and foreboding. There was one cockeyed shot of my father, taken by somebody else, not quite in focus.

The rest of the slides, four boxes' worth, were completely dark.

———

We drove back to Austin on the twenty-sixth. That night I woke up and went into the living room to find my mother watching the videotapes of my father again and crying. I wanted to scream and throw furniture. If she couldn't get over it, why did she have to make me watch? To jerk my guilt over something I didn't feel?

I was cornered. If I went into the kitchen for a beer my mother would make a big deal about it. If I went upstairs she would follow me and talk about trivia. So it was back to bed, to Elizabeth's soft snores and Dude's accusing stare.

My mother flew home the next day. Elizabeth had assigned herself a stack of books over the holidays and was holed up in the bedroom. I wanted to finish *Celebration*. It had gotten tangled up in my mind with the whole sad, frustrating holiday and I wanted it over with. I knocked out a couple of quick repair jobs and went to work.

In the end, the best I could manage was a couple of songs a day. Elizabeth tried to get me to stay in bed, telling me I was having a relapse of whatever I'd had before Christmas. I promised to take it easy, and then I went upstairs for a couple more.

Friday was my thirty-eighth birthday. Elizabeth bought me some new clothes and my mother sent money. Pete gave me a new CD from Carnival Dog called *Soul Carnival* that has great stuff like "But It's Alright" by J. J. Jackson and "My Pledge of Love" by the Joe Jeffrey Group. That night Elizabeth and I went to Louis B's downtown, her favorite restaurant, and she had a few glasses of wine. I wore a coat and tie. She was decked out in an antique silk blouse and Chanel sweater. She imitated some of her kids on the way home and cracked me up. I thought that once we were inside I would just put my arms around her and kiss her, like when we first went out. Then maybe one thing would lead to another.

I unlocked the door and opened it for her. She went straight into the bathroom. I stood by the stairs to wait. She came out and fed the cat and sat on the couch and turned on the TV. "It's *Dallas*. You don't want to watch, do you?"

"I guess not," I said.

The next night was New Year's Eve, and a party at Elizabeth's school. I'd found an old pair of jeans so tight they fit me like Morrison's leathers. Over them I wore a loose cotton shirt from India and my leather jacket. Elizabeth, as usual, was dressed to the teeth. "You're not actually wearing that, are you?" she asked me.

It was my cue to sigh dramatically and change clothes. But they felt right and I knew I looked good. Appropriate, no, but good. I heard myself say, "Yeah. I think I am."

It was Elizabeth's friends at the party. These are people who watch PBS and read biographies and take politics seriously. They seem to still be depressed over George Bush being elected and the party never quite caught fire. It was in the school cafeteria, which still smelled of institutional food, despite the overlays of booze and cigarettes and perfume. The stereo was too weak for the room and too many people had brought music from the seventies.

I felt a little crazy. My friends were either down on Sixth Street getting shitfaced or stuck like me at semiofficial parties that weren't any fun. Sondra and Gary were there, and another teacher friend of Elizabeth's named Frances. Frances was too tall for me, and moussed her black hair straight back into a ponytail that seemed too severe. Tonight, though, she was wearing the same perfume that Alex had worn in high school, floral and strong, and I orbited around her like a lost moon.

At midnight I kissed Elizabeth and said, "Rabbit rabbit rabbit." It's supposed to bring you luck if it's the first thing you say in the new year. I don't remember where I got it, but I can't stop now. Superstitions will hook you that way. Alex and I used to hold our breath whenever we crossed a bridge so we wouldn't ever lose each other. There's that long, long overpass on Loop 12 between Dallas and Arlington that used to give us fits. I could always hold my breath longer and sometimes I would slow down near the end.

Elizabeth and I danced to an echoing "Auld Lang Syne" and then there was a lot of kissing. I kissed Frances and then Sondra and then I kissed Frances again, maybe longer than strictly necessary.

About twelve-thirty Elizabeth started to cry.

"What's wrong?" I said.

She put her hands on my shoulders and dried her tears on my neck. "I don't know," she whispered. She was still crying and people had started to notice. I could hear rumors about to fly. "It's been a long year. Can we go home?"

When we got to the car she said, "I'm losing you. And I don't know what to do about it."

I stood there in the street and held her while she cried some more. Finally she pulled away. "It's the white wine. I should stay away from it." She handed me her keys. "Drive, will you?"

I walked her around to the passenger door. I didn't know what to do about it either.

―――――――――

I finished my cassette version of *Celebration of the Lizard* on January 10. It's different than I expected, raw and lean, more physical and less intellectual than the first two albums. It opens with "Unknown Soldier" and "Waiting for the Sun." Taking off from the line "Now that spring has come," they go into "Summer's Almost Gone" and "Wintertime Love," all three cut tightly together to make a kind of Three Seasons Suite. Then, like we figured, they close with "My Wild Love" and "Five to One." It was too late to keep "Hello, I Love You"/"Love Street" from being released as a single, but Morrison insisted neither of them belonged on the album and Rothchild backed him up.

The tighter, shorter "Celebration of the Lizard" left room for two additional songs to start side two. First a blues, like Graham predicted, a hard-rocking version of "Crawling King Snake." Then "L'America," which Morrison pulled out of one of his notebooks. It has the same basic melody as the version that appeared on *L.A. Woman,* only tighter, with a different bridge.

If the work tape I started with was somehow in touch with the absolute, then this was another order of perfection. It's the Doors' best album. It breathes fire and blood and semen. It scares the living shit out of me.

———

Graham brought me straight to his house from the airport. I put *Celebration* on and we sat there and listened to it in silence. At the end of side one he was in tears. At the end of side two he was speechless.

I went into the kitchen and got some beers. I hadn't even thought about drinking while the tape was on. I'd been totally caught up in the moment, hearing new things in the mix. When I came back into the living room, Graham had the tape in his hands, just holding on to it. When I was a kid and got a new comic, after I read it once and paged through it again to set the pictures in my mind, then I'd sit and hold it that same way.

"I guess I didn't really believe you could do it," he said. "I guess I thought it was too much to ask."

"Well, I did," I said, "and it wasn't. Wait till we get it on a digital master."

"When?"

"I don't care." I felt electrified. "Right now if you want."

So we did. I got the finished mix of "Celebration" that afternoon, while I was fresh. At the end we were both pretty wrung out. He offered to put me up, but I wanted to stay at the Alta Cienega.

It was after dark when we drove out to West Hollywood. The night was so incredibly warm that it felt like spring to me. Even stranger is this conviction that L.A. is home. The palm trees and seedy stucco motels, everybody in shorts with their overbred, highly strung animals, all of it is just right. These are the very things I want to see when I look around.

"This is on the company, you know," Graham said. "The motel, your food and beer, a rent car if you want it."

"How are you going to swing that?"

Graham looked over at me. "Hey, man, don't you know?"

"Know what?"

"Did you think I was just the engineer or something? I *own* Carnival Dog Records. The U.S. government bought it for me out of my disability checks."

I should have guessed. The phrase "carnival dog" comes out of a Doors song, "My Eyes Have Seen You," on *Strange Days*. And here I thought all this time they picked it because it had the same initials as "compact disc." "No," I said. "I didn't know."

"I write you off as development. If I have to, I can pump some of the profits back in as seed money. I shouldn't have to."

"Okay," I said. "I'm impressed."

We stopped for a case of Coors and then drove to the motel. I left Graham in the car and went to check in. The office was tiny, cramped, and deserted. After a few seconds a door opened behind the counter and I saw another, smaller room, barely the size of a closet. A Vietnamese woman in her fifties was angrily washing dishes. "What?" she said.

"Do you have any rooms?"

She turned off the water and grudgingly moved behind the counter. "Jus' you?" She handed me a registration card.

"That's right."

She looked out the glass door at Graham's car, saw Graham, and said, "Dirty dick."

"What?"

She sighed, jerked the card out of my hand, and wrote "36" in the little box for the nightly rate. I gave her two twenties and said, "Can I, uh, have room thirty-two? Is it available?"

She looked at me and shook her head and banged around under the counter for a key. I felt like a total asshole. How many people must come in here, bugging her for that room? She slapped the key on the counter. Room 32.

I carried the beer in, then came back to help Graham up the stairs. Tired as I was, I couldn't sit down. From the window I could see the cars crawl past on La Cienega, see the girls in neon halter tops and short skirts. I wanted to put my head on their naked stomachs and listen to their hearts beat.

"What's eating you, man?" Graham asked.

"Restless," I said. "Horny. Insufficiently drunk." I'd chugged the first beer and was most of the way through a second. I used to drink a lot, but never like this. It's like there's a hole inside that I'm trying to fill with beer. Beer is supposed to be a depressant, only it cheers me up, makes the world seem rich and full of possibilities. The ones that interested me most had to do with my getting laid.

Right then I could see leaving Elizabeth. Nothing to it. My own apartment, the basic tools to do my work. A portable CD player, a refrigerator full of Coors, and a long parade of wanton, willing women.

"It's Morrison," Graham said. "He's got inside you."

"Maybe. Maybe he has." I belched and cracked another Coors. "How'd you end up owning a record company?"

"It was the best I could do. As close to music as I could get. I wanted to be a guitar player but it wasn't in the cards. When I was first in the hospital they had a guitar there, some twelve-dollar Harmony piece of shit. They kept it with the wallet-making stuff, the crafts, you know. I started playing again, and when I got out I got myself a Gretch Country Gentleman, the Chet Atkins model, hollow body with the Bigsby bar. Same as George Harrison used. Nobody plays them any more, of course, but that was *the* guitar back then. I got in a band called Burger and the Buns. The lead singer's nickname was Burger, don't you see. We did fifty percent British invasion, fifty percent Ray Charles/James Brown kind of thing."

"My college band was called the Duotones. We had a black lead singer, a black sax player, a black guy on bass. The rest of us were just honky college boys. Keyboard player had his own Hammond B-3, pain in the ass to move, but boy did it sound sweet. We did all that Motown and Stax/Volt stuff."

"Oh yeah," Graham said. "Oh yeah. The problem was I wasn't any good." He held up his hand. "Those are butcher's fingers. Short and thick. I've got a good ear, but the hands are just meat. So I took the hint, eventually. Went to school on the GI bill, learned electronics and recording and production. I bought and sold records out of my house, dealing in cash whenever I could, socking away the disability checks, not paying any more tax than I had to. Started Carnival Dog with Howard Kaylan of the Turtles, then bought him out bit by bit over the years, God bless him. Now I own it free and clear."

"Here's to free enterprise," I said, and chugged the rest of the can.

"Amen to that."

After he left I walked up to Sunset and went in the first place that served liquor. A strip joint would have suited me perfectly, except all of Morrison's favorites were gone. Instead I got potted plants and stained glass and waitresses in tuxedo shirts and black pants. Crosby, Stills & Nash came out of the ceiling, not very loud. There were a couple of young women with piña coladas at the bar when I came in. One of them looked me over—ponytail, T-shirt, no Porsche keys dangling from my hand—and looked away again. I sat at a table and ate a chicken breast sandwich on seven-grain bread. Morrison had sung, "I eat more chicken any man ever seen." Yeah, right.

I went back to the motel and slept the sleep of the drunken.

━━━━━

We finished the digital version the following Tuesday. Being as it was me and Graham, we chose to celebrate with a case of beer. We sat in a patch of park by the Santa Monica Pier, and I helped Graham out of his chair so he could sit in the grass.

"People are not going to believe this album," he said.

"They'll have to. It's there. It's real."

A cop car drove slowly past. There was a Latin motto on the door: *Populus Felix in Urbe Felici.* "Happy people in a happy town." For a while we sat and listened to the traffic and the voices in the distance.

"We can't stop now, you know," Graham said.

"I don't even want to think about another record."

"I know you're bled dry right now. You can't blame me for dreaming. I feel like a kid in a candy store."

I drank a beer. " 'The future's uncertain,' " I said, quoting Morrison, " 'and the end is always near.' " Coors cans are so thin they crush with the slightest pressure.

"I know you have to get back to Austin. To see your wife and everything. I wish you could stay longer."

"Me too."

"I really don't have much idea what your life there is like. What does she think of all this?"

"Elizabeth? She doesn't, not if she can help it. You know, of all the women I've known in my life there's been maybe one or two who came even close to feeling about music the way you and I do. The way most of my male friends do. Suffice to say Elizabeth isn't one of them."

"Yeah, it's true. Sometimes I wonder about that, devoting my life to something most women don't really give a damn about."

We were inches from a lot of unasked questions I had about Graham and women. I wanted to keep him going. "Elizabeth always says she saves her emotions for stuff that's real, and music is just the background."

"And yet, if you go out with a bunch of married couples, it's always the women that want to dance. It makes me think sometimes that I've forgotten what rock and roll is all about. It's not about who played on what label, it's about feeling that nasty rhythm."

"Sure," I said, "but the more you know, the more you can control it, so you can re-create that feeling anytime you want."

"That's it, isn't it? We have to control everything. We can't just let it happen and, you know, dance to it." He looked at his chair, then at his beer. "In a manner of speaking. Hell, what am I going on about? Look what we did today. We created a fucking masterpiece! Give me a beer."

And then somehow we were talking about other things. Solid-state versus tube amps, microphone placement in the studio, DooTone Records and all the great groups they recorded in the fifties.

We finished the case. Graham must not have done his share because about two o'clock, right over a sign that said DANGER DO NOT GO BEYOND THIS FENCE, I heaved my guts out onto the ice plant and the

eroded cliff that looked down on the Pacific Coast Highway, while
Graham sat in his chair and held on to my belt. For a moment I
thought it would all come out of me: Lizard Kings and dead winos and
naked groupies passed out in the vocal booth.

I was wrong. We drove down to the ocean and I waded into it to
wash my mouth with salt water, soaking my shoes and pants cuffs,
nearly falling down in the freezing water. As I came back up the
concrete steps to the road I could feel him still there, coiled inside me
like a snake.

CHAPTER 3
CHAPTER 3
CHAPTER 3

Smile

Brian Wilson started work on *Smile* in the summer of 1966. *Pet Sounds* had just come out; it was big in England and had a cult following in the U.S., but it hadn't gone through the roof like the Beatles' *Rubber Soul*. Brian had this competition thing about the Beatles and it was like they had beaten him again. Mere greatness was not enough. He had to produce an authentic work of genius.

Of all the albums Graham and I talked about, over breakfast and on our way to LAX, *Smile* was the one that most intrigued me. What if Brian had gotten it out for Christmas of 1966 like he promised? The only track the Beatles had finished for *Sgt. Pepper* was "When I'm Sixty Four." McCartney made no secret of his admiration for *Pet Sounds* and *Smile* would have blown him away. Then there was the effect on Brian himself, to have produced the first rock and roll record universally acclaimed as high art.

At this point Brian lived in a house on Laurel Way at the top of Beverly Hills, a couple of miles of winding streets and switchbacks from Sunset Boulevard. He'd dropped acid and smoked a lot of hash and things had started to get weird. He built a big sandbox around his grand piano so he could feel sand under his feet while he played. He put up a sultan's tent that filled an entire room and then never went in it. It was hard for him to get out of bed, and harder still to get dressed. Then, in the grip of an idea he could barely articulate, he would rush out to Western or Gold Star Studios to put down some tracks, even if it was three in the morning.

He'd started to put on weight, too. He talked about vegetables and health food and ate hamburgers and hashish brownies. His moods swung from rage to hysterical laughter to tears. There was all this stuff in his head, ideas and music and sounds, and every scrap had intense emotions tied up in it, every note *meant* something.

———

I had mixed feelings about the Beach Boys. Sure, "Good Vibrations" is a classic, and the early car and surf songs have great hooks and harmonies. But what about those concerts on the White House lawn, and all the patriotic "Be True to Your School" attitude?

Graham tried to set me straight. I had to make a distinction, he said, between the records, which were Brian, and the touring band. It's Mike Love who keeps the band on the road, who likes nothing better in the world than to be in front of an audience, the bigger the better. He works them tirelessly, pumps them up, gets them singing along or even screaming at him, anything for a reaction. He's the Republican of the group, the flag-waver, as conservative musically as he is polit-ically. The car and surf songs were good enough for the early sixties and that's good enough for him.

Brian dropped out of the touring band in 1964, replaced briefly by Glen Campbell and then more or less permanently by Bruce Johnston. By that point the rest of the band was making only minimal contri-butions to the albums anyway. Carl played a little guitar, everybody sang what Brian told them to, and the rest was done by studio mu-sicians. Brian wrote all the songs, did all the arrangements and pro-duction.

The story is that it started with "Surfer Girl." Studio guys played the instruments, Brian and some of his friends did the vocals, and the first the rest of the band knew about it was when Brian took a finished acetate home and played it for them. Suddenly Brian didn't need them anymore.

On *Pet Sounds* Brian let the other guys come in and rerecord some of the vocals he already had on tape. If they didn't sing what he wanted, or he wasn't happy with the take, he would wait until they left and do it again by himself. He didn't start *Smile* until the touring band was away on the road.

I said to Graham, "What you're telling me is that everything I like about the Beach Boys is Brian, and everything I hate is Mike Love?"

"You said it, not me."

We'd been by Mike Autrey's store and he put me on the plane with a stack of books and cassettes, some by or about the Beach Boys, others about everybody from Sam Cooke to Bob Dylan to Prince. "Think it over," he said, "and give me a call sometime."

Inside David Leaf's *Beach Boys and the California Myth* was a check for ten thousand dollars.

———

Elizabeth was in a good mood when I called from the airport. Instead of being relieved I felt myself slipping backward into the marriage. She seemed to know every time I was angry enough or distant enough to leave her. It was like it flipped some kind of switch and she would turn seductive, break down the walls I'd built up, work just hard enough to keep me hanging on.

When I got in the car she gave me a real kiss, her tongue darting into my mouth. "I missed you," she said. We went straight out to Little Italy for dinner and killed a carafe and a half of wine. At home she stopped inside the door and kissed me again and I followed her into the bedroom.

We sat on the edge of the bed. I pulled her sweater off and she unhooked her bra. I could smell Halston and the warmth of her body. Her nipples were stiff with desire. My good intentions counted for nothing. I wanted her and I told myself it wouldn't make any difference, we could still talk about what was eating me up, only not now, let's not miss this chance.

"Ray," she said.

"Mmmmm."

"Ray." She put her hands around my neck and gently pulled my face up to her eye level. "Maybe this isn't the best time to bring this up. But if we wait much longer it'll be too late."

"What are you talking about?"

"You know I've been off the pill for six months." Her doctor took her off occasionally, per label instructions. We'd used condoms or a diaphragm the few times we'd actually done anything lately. "I was thinking. C'mere. That's better. I was thinking maybe we should take advantage of that."

"Advantage?"

"Don't be difficult. I want a baby. You know that. We've talked about it."

"Not recently."

"It's not something that's just going to go away."

I rolled onto my back, felt my erection start to fade. "You're right, this is not a real good time."

"Is it your father?"

"That's a lot of it."

"You're not like your father. You know that."

"I want to believe it. That doesn't make it true."

"You don't have to be a saint to be a father. God, you should see some of the parents at school. There's only one thing you absolutely have to do with a kid. You have to let them know that you love them, no matter what they do. That's all. Everything beyond that is gravy."

My eyes stung unexpectedly. If it was so easy, why hadn't my parents done it?

"Besides," Elizabeth said. "It might, you know, bring us closer. Closer together."

"I thought we couldn't afford a kid." Which was a shitty thing to say, considering the check for ten grand in my luggage. It was just that I'd been thinking about using that money to set myself up on my own.

"I'm going to get the vice principal's job. Martha told me today."

I rolled over to face her. "That's fantastic. I'm really proud of you."

"So money's not a problem." She reached over and unzipped me. "I mean, we don't even know if we *can* have a kid." She tugged at my pants and I helped her pull them off. She peeled off my underwear and sure enough, the erection was back, oblivious to consequences. "I mean, if it did happen tonight," she said, "it would be like fate, wouldn't it? Like it was meant to happen."

I didn't have to say anything. All I had to do was lie there and let it happen. Which is what I did.

Elizabeth never did put on a nightgown and I was aware of her naked skin all night. In the morning when I touched her waist she turned to me and we made love again. When she left for school I was still in bed and she was all smiles and kisses.

I lay there a long time. On one level I'd been manipulated. The problem was that I felt good, more relaxed than I'd been in weeks. I couldn't summon up the anger I'd felt in L.A.

I did a little work and thought about what it would mean if she was actually pregnant. Not just what kind of father I'd be, but how Elizabeth would be as a mother. Our own mothers and fathers had spent years in silence, she and I hardly talked to each other, what chance did a kid have?

And the kid would change us. After Larry and Diane had their first kid, Larry said their sex life dried up to nothing. Diane wanted back rubs instead—not that this would be anything new for me. I'd heard it over and over. If the presence of the kids isn't enough, crawling in bed between you, they change the way you see each other, not as lovers any more but as Mommy and Daddy.

That gave me a sudden vision of my father, who had to share my mother with me. Maybe it even hurt him to share me with my mother. Either way, him jealous and without the words to say why. It felt weird to suddenly see things through his eyes, weird and uncomfortable. I can see that happening a lot if the kid becomes a reality. Good or bad, it's what Elizabeth wants. If I back out now, I don't think the marriage will survive it. A couple of days ago that would have been fine. Today I don't know.

The jobs in front of me were both CD players, both with intermittent problems. Sometimes one wouldn't load the disk unless the guy slapped it on top of the box at exactly the right moment. It amazes me how people discover these arcane methods of getting things to work. This other player would hang up and let out that awful digital echo, but only sometimes, and only on the first track.

I needed a distraction so I put on my scratched LP of *Pet Sounds*. I didn't see the big deal. A lot of the songs sound alike and some of them border on elevator music. I took it off and put on *Glimpses* volume three, the one with "Codine" by Quicksilver Messenger Service and "Tallyman" by Jeff Beck.

By late afternoon I had both CD players together and running tests. It was all I could do not to open the refrigerator and start pouring beers down myself. The gray, cold day ate at my resolve to put on the brakes. At that point I was ready to talk myself out of the Beach Boys. I picked up one of Mike Autrey's books to make sure and the next thing I knew I was hooked.

Brian is the oldest of three brothers. He was the genius, Dennis was the troublemaker, and little Carl, overweight for most of his adolescence, was the spiritual one. They grew up in what was then the white, middle-class suburb of Hawthorne in South Central L.A.

Brian seemed normal enough in high school. He was six three and handsome, with soulful eyes and neatly cut brown hair. He dressed like everybody else, in blue jeans and white T-shirts. He played center field and quarterback. He had plenty of friends, he liked girls and cars and junk food.

It was his father, Murry, the would-be songwriter, that drove him crazy. Nothing Brian did was ever good enough for him. Not his performance on the football field, not his grades, especially not the songs he wrote. Murry's message was simple: Brian was worthless without him, without his coaching in sports, without his production and PR work in music.

Legend has it the Wilson parents went to Mexico for the weekend and left the boys a hundred bucks for food and emergencies. The boys used it to rent instruments instead and spent the whole time writing songs. "Surfin' " was Dennis's idea, since he was the only one of them who actually did surf. It was less of a sport at that point than something tough kids like Dennis did between beers and girls.

Brian thought Murry would be proud of him for following in his footsteps. In fact Murry was pissed off. Since he couldn't talk the boys out of it, he took over. He got them a recording session, which he produced, then he took the tapes around until Candix records agreed to put out a single, "Surfin' " b/w "Luau." When the song took off they did another demo tape that included "409" and "Surfer Girl." Murry took it to Capitol and the rest, more or less, is history. In all the years that he managed the band, though, he never told Brian that his songs were anything but junk, and he never forgave Brian for recording his own songs instead of Murry's Lawrence Welk–style numbers.

I remember how my father came home from the hospital the summer after my junior year in high school, still wobbly from his first heart attack, and told me he could still kick my ass. I remember how I knocked myself out over the next year trying to be the perfect kid, and him grounding me for my "attitude." One night in the spring of 1968 I tried to sleep out under a bridge and got picked up by the cops around two A.M. When I hadn't come home after school, my father had taken to bed with pains in his chest. I tried to explain to my mother that I had to get away, had to prove that I was a real person, capable of independent action, even if the action was stupid and pointless. My father never quit competing, never quit trying to hog the spotlight, not even at the end.

Neither did Murry.

———

You don't get pregnant, Elizabeth tells me, from repeated efforts. That lowers the sperm count. Better to save it up and take your best shot.

Apparently we've taken ours, and time will now tell. No further efforts are required on my part.

———

Brian's father could never get over Brian's success. It ate at him all his life. My father could never understand why I didn't want to be a teacher, just like him. It comes down to the same thing. What Brian or I did was only important to the extent that it reflected on our fathers. Whether we were happy or not never counted.

Sunday afternoon I put down my book and went upstairs. I loaded up a Beach Boys CD compilation called *Made in the USA* and punched up track number ten, "Don't Worry Baby." Dude got up on my legs and butted my hand until I scratched him under the collar. "Don't Worry Baby" is cowritten with Roger Christian, Brian's car expert. I'd always lumped it with "Little Deuce Coupe" and "Shut Down" and all the other simpleminded songs full of racing buzzwords and sec-ondhand Chuck Berry riffs.

That afternoon it was a whole new song. Brian sings lead, which he didn't often do in the early days, and the longing in his voice is so raw and powerful I can't believe I never heard it before. In the story line of the song it's his girlfriend who tells him not to worry, that everything will be okay. Listen to the song and you can hear how badly Brian wanted to be told those words by somebody. A girlfriend would do, but I know what he really wanted. He wanted to hear it from his father. He never would. Murry would die in 1973 after holing up in his bedroom for years, at the same time that Brian was holed up in his own bedroom on the other side of town.

I looked up and saw Elizabeth on the stairs. "Ray? Are you okay?"

"Yeah, I'm fine."

"What's wrong? You're crying."

I couldn't explain. She stood next to me and I leaned my head against her leg. She ran one hand through my hair and petted Dude with the other. I could feel how uncomfortable she was, how she wanted to do the right thing if she could only figure it out. The right thing would have been to sit down and hold me. She would never let me do that for her and I knew she would never think to offer. I couldn't ask because then she would do it out of obligation. Obligation wasn't enough. After a minute or so she squeezed my neck and went downstairs.

That night, after Elizabeth was asleep, I tried *Pet Sounds* again. It wasn't the same album I'd listened to just a few days ago. Suddenly I could see exactly what Brian wanted to do. It was like his feelings came straight out through the sound of his voice. No holding back, no second thoughts, no coyness, just up-front emotion.

I went back to the early stuff and saw it had been there all along. When Brian sings about his heart coming all undone in "Surfer Girl," or lets out that high, wordless moan at the end of "Dance, Dance, Dance," it sails out over the melody, transcendent, joyous, and infinitely sad at the same time.

Pet Sounds isn't out on a domestic CD yet. I went out the next day and paid twenty bucks for a Japanese import. I listened to it twice, then I called Graham in L.A.

======

"I want to do *Smile*," I said.

"Attaboy. I knew you'd come around. By the way, I got a couple of test pressings from our last effort."

"How's it sound?"

"Fucking unbelievable. I've got my art director in on it now. Get this—we're doing an embossed cover on the CD booklet. It's a takeoff on the cover art inside *Waiting for the Sun*, with the gila monster, and we're embossing the scales. It is just so bitchen."

"Great." I couldn't get excited about the Doors right then. It's hard to describe. I'd been there, and now I was excited about something new. "You sound really good, Graham."

"I'm stoked about this. I've already let the word out a little. It's going to be a monster."

The word "monster" hit me funny. "I hope not," I said.

"What?"

"Nothing, man, don't listen to me. There was some ugly shit in my head during all that. I'm not totally over it."

"*Smile* will fix you up. I guarantee it. Go have a beer or something."

"Yeah," I said. "Good idea."

———

Smile was going to be Brian's humor album. The critics had called *Pet Sounds* gloomy, when all Brian really wanted was to give people some comfort. So he decided to pull out the stops. Everybody around him—and there were a lot of hangers-on—thought he was crazy when he talked about sounds having emotions. I don't. The train and the barking dogs at the end of *Pet Sounds* are the loneliest things I've ever heard.

During that fall and winter people thought all of Brian's ideas were crazy. He went through with most of them anyway, and most of the time people came around. Even if it took years.

For *Smile* he drove all over L.A. and out into the hills to tape sound effects. He had his dinner guests roll around on the floor and make animal noises, or play their dishes with their silverware. He couldn't put into words what he wanted but he could play it, or tape it, and when he played it back it was there.

Capitol records insisted that he put "Good Vibrations" on the album to help sales. They weren't happy with *Pet Sounds*, despite the fact that it eventually cracked the top ten and sold half a million copies, despite the fact that they'd torpedoed it when they released a

Best Of compilation within two months of it. They didn't like the hundreds of hours of expensive studio time he was burning with no visible result. "Good Vibrations" alone took seven months and sixty studio hours and ten thousand dollars to record.

The second single was supposed to be "Heroes and Villains" and it too started to take forever. In fact it didn't get released until July of 1967, after Brian had clearly given up on *Smile,* and when it came out it was a pale, three-and-a-half minute shadow of the seven-minute musical comedy it had, according to witnesses, once been. Or maybe "Vegetables" would have been the second single. When the Beach Boys didn't release it a band called Laughing Gravy did, using Brian's backing tracks.

The rest of the album would have been slices of Western Americana (like "Cabinessence" and "Surf's Up" and "Heroes and Villains"), silliness (laughing horns in "George Fell into His French Horn"), pure harmony ("Our Prayer"), and maybe a love song or two ("Wonderful"). There was a recurring theme, the "bicycle rider" theme, that shows up in "Heroes and Villains" where they sing "come and see what you've done" barbershop-quartet style. A Four Elements Suite was supposed to consist of "Vegetables" (Earth), "Wind Chimes" (Air), "Mrs. O'Leary's Cow" (Fire), and "Love to Say Da-Da" (Water). The whole record would be intercut with sound effects and even spoken comedy.

All six months before *Sgt. Pepper.*

———

I couldn't talk to Elizabeth about it. She was bored by things I found unbelievably fascinating, like the way Brian used a bicycle bell as an instrument on "You Still Believe in Me." As soon as she sensed this was to do with the other weirdness, the "Long and Winding Road" and the Doors weirdness, she got a panicked look in her eye and froze up. Afterward she reacted to the very mention of Brian like it was a physical blow.

She stopped drinking once she decided to get pregnant, and now we don't even have that to do together. Once the sex part was over I took to spending my nights in the workshop, reading and listening to the Beach Boys, coming to bed after she was already asleep. So maybe it's as much me as it is her.

All the while *Smile* has been getting under my skin. It says something that an album that was never released, that's never been heard except in distorted fragments, has inspired so much passion over more than twenty years. There is at least one full-length book about nothing but *Smile*, there are four different bootleg versions, there are fanzines and an entire underground network of disciples who watch Brian's every step.

On the last Monday in January I got a FedEx from Graham. Inside was a copy of *Celebration of the Lizard,* the cover black and ominous, with an embossed pink-and-gold gila monster looking over its shoulder at me. I took it upstairs and put it on. It sounded timeless, no fattened bass or big drum sound, clean and eerie and violent. I couldn't listen all the way through. I went downstairs and cleaned up the kitchen and let it play on without me. The Doors were then, I thought. This is now.

I was still downstairs when Elizabeth came home. She didn't even yell hello, just went to the liquor cabinet and poured herself a stiff shot of vodka while Dude rubbed against her legs.

"Hi," I said.

"Hi." She turned on the TV, flopped on the couch, and took a big hit of the vodka.

"You okay?" I said.

"Fine."

I stood there for a minute. For some reason Elizabeth always thinks she can convince me she's not in a bad mood, when every twitch of her muscles screams it. "Something happen at school?"

"No. Why?"

"You look tired, that's all."

"Thanks."

I started up the stairs.

"I'm sorry," she said. "I'm getting my period and I'm a little cranky."

I came back and sat down next to her. "I'm sorry," I said.

"It's just a period. It's no big deal."

Sometimes I wish she would break down, smash the furniture, yell and blubber and completely lose it. "Okay," I said. "So it's no big deal."

She nodded, staring at the TV like it was about to tell her the secret of life. I went upstairs and listened to *Pet Sounds* on headphones.

At the end of November 1966 the Beach Boys returned from their European tour and listened to what Brian had done on *Smile*. Mike Love hated it. He called a meeting with Van Dyke Parks, who wrote the lyrics, and demanded to know what the songs meant. What did all this bizarre Americana and obscure wordplay have to do with the Beach Boys? Van Dyke quit.

Brian, meanwhile, was already freaked. Fires broke out all over Los Angeles after he recorded "Mrs. O'Leary's Cow," including one across the street from the studio. Brian thought it was his fault, and supposedly tried to burn the tapes. He got obsessive about the moral content of his work, about the kind of vibes it put out. He meant to record a new "Fire" segment based on the idea of a candle rather than a raging inferno. He never got around to it.

There were so many songs. A couple dozen, anyway, most no more than fragments. Before he could finish one he would have another idea and lay down basic tracks for it. Then Mike Love stepped in to throw his disapproval around. Capitol wanted an album right away, only not this album, and suddenly it was June of 1967 and *Sgt. Pepper* was on the stands. Why break up the band, the only family he had left since he and Murry quit talking, just so he could come in second to the Beatles again?

That was the end of *Smile*. Brian threw together a neutered version of "Heroes and Villains" so Capitol could have a single. He'd left the house on Laurel Way in April and moved to a mansion in Bel Air with its own recording studio. He took two weeks out of the summer to whip out a replacement album called *Smiley Smile* where he let the other guys play their own instruments and sing whatever they wanted. He took his name off as producer. He gave up.

It was the start of a long, slow, downhill slide for Brian, and the beginning of the end for the Beach Boys.

Elizabeth and I made another try in February. I cut down on the booze, ate a lot of seafood, took her temperature, and fucked her enthusiastically when the thermometer told me to. I didn't care anymore. If she got pregnant I would deal with it. I guess deep down I didn't think it would happen.

I'd been at work on *Smile* for a month and hadn't tried to get anything on tape. I was intimidated. Brian's vision was too overwhelming, too much to get into my head at one time.

I called Graham.

"Don't feel like the Lone Ranger," he said. "When the Beach Boys signed with Reprise in 1970, *Smile* was part of the deal. Carl even announced it for seventy-two. It never happened. Capitol said they would put it out last year, when Brian did his solo album. It all sounds so easy in theory, the tapes are all there, only once you start wading through them, all the different bits and pieces and outtakes and miles and miles of tape, everybody just gets . . . dragged . . . down."

"I don't think that's it. I can't, I mean, I don't think this album was meant to be."

"Ray, you've come to me with some crazy-sounding ideas. Most people would say this whole thing has been crazy. But this 'meant to be' shit is the first totally crazy thing you've said. It's like some fifties movie with giant insects. 'General, there are some things man was not meant to know.' "

"Look at it from Brian's point of view. It's a no-win situation. There's no way Mike Love and Capitol Records could live with what Brian wanted to do. So he has to choose between his music and his family. If he was the kind of guy who could blow off his family, he wouldn't be the kind of guy that could make *Smile*."

"Don't be so sure. I heard Brian kept working on the tapes for years after *Smiley Smile* came out. Just for himself. He could have finished it."

"He was too close to it. He needed somebody there with enough perspective to keep him on track. And there wasn't anybody. Even David Anderle thought most of the stuff he did was crazy. Until he heard it played back."

"Come out here. We'll drive around, we'll talk about it."

"I don't know."

"Why not? Is this a money thing? I told you I don't care about money."

"No, it's just . . . personal stuff." I hadn't talked to my mother in a week. Elizabeth was now officially one day late. I'd turned down a

couple of referrals from old customers, which really hurt. I felt like I'd broken a trust, like my obsession with a nonexistent album from 1966 was keeping people from having any music at all.

"I'll think about it," I told Graham. "I promise."

That was Monday. Wednesday afternoon, three days late, Elizabeth got her period. She acted like there was nothing to talk about.

—————

I didn't sleep much that night. Songs from *Smile* played through my head, and at the same time I couldn't stop thinking about Elizabeth, sleeping quietly away with her back to me. For a minute I felt like I was in the Alta Cienega Motel again, dressed in black leathers and roaring drunk. I wanted to throw her out of the room and then smash the furniture to bits. Instead I went upstairs and booked a morning flight to L.A.

I guess my chest had been tight for weeks. I never noticed the pressure until it was gone. It happened after I changed planes at DFW, the first time the flight attendant mentioned our arrival time at LAX. Graham was at the gate to meet me and I felt this huge grin spread across my face.

We had a beer there at the airport, at ten in the morning, then picked up a couple of six-packs for the road. Graham had an address for the Wilson family home in Hawthorne, 3701 West 119th Street. I'd seen a picture of it in one of my books: dark-wood siding, an evergreen shrub by the front door, a lawn of that fine-bladed California grass, three brothers standing arm in arm and squinting into the sun.

Hawthorne is virtually in the flight path of the airport. The land there is totally flat, and things have gone downhill since Brian's day. It's mostly poor Chicano now, the houses that aren't boarded-up and covered with graffiti.

119th Street stops and starts again and turns into 119th Place. We drove around for fifteen minutes and couldn't find the house. The street curved where it shouldn't, before we could get to 3701, and on our third pass I noticed the asphalt looked brand-new where the street went funny. Graham got out his Thomas Bros. guide and we looked at page fifty-seven. The Century Freeway, Interstate 105, was a dotted line across the block where we sat.

"That's it, then," Graham said, pointing. On the other side of the curving street was a chain-link fence and raw yellow earth. "Brian's house would have been . . . right where that bulldozer is." He handed me a fresh beer. "That's L.A. for you. In a nutshell."

He got on the San Diego Freeway, headed north toward Beverly Hills. It was not quite noon and traffic was light. Missing Brian's house seemed trivial compared to the fact that it was March 2 and spring had arrived. I could smell orange blossoms, jasmine, and honeysuckle, even from the freeway. The sky was the same blue as shallow ocean water over a sandy bottom. The sun made everything glisten and at the same time the air was so cool and sweet I wanted to put it in a glass and drink it down.

"God, I love it here," I said.

"It's the negative ions. They make people want to let go. That's one theory. California's always been this way, even in the nineteenth century, all the nut cults ended up out here. The rest of the country thought California was crazy even then."

"I wonder if Brian's music would have been the same if he'd lived somewhere else."

"No way. He might never have made music at all."

"It's like you can really see the American Dream from here. It's so close you can almost touch it. But not quite. You just get that glimpse of it, and then it's gone again. I never heard anybody else show that sadness inside the dream before."

"They tell me this is nothing compared to the early sixties, back when Brian was first writing. Orange groves and open spaces, still plenty of money and water to go around. Disneyland when it was new, and Pacific Ocean Park. You ever heard of POP?" I shook my head. "It's kind of an obsession of mine. I always wanted to write a book about it. Used to be just down the coast from the pier at Santa Monica, like a little Disneyland. All kinds of corny rides and concessions and like that. It closed at the end of the sixties and people still talk about it. It pisses me off that I never got to see it. It was so perfectly California. Just this cornball innocence. When it went under, everybody said it was the end of an era. And I guess they were right."

We got off on Sunset and wound through the residential district of Beverly Hills. The houses on Sunset are big enough, but they're crowded together on tiny lots and hidden behind high walls. We took a left on Beverly Drive and headed uphill. I noticed that the street is lined with alternating fat and skinny palm trees. Each cross street seems to have its own distinctive tree—ponderosa pines, scrub oaks. It's screwy but very California that you can find your way home if you remember the right sequence of trees along the side of the road. Laurel Way has ficus: no bark, no protection from the world. Just like Brian.

We made our narrow and winding way toward the top of the Hollywood Hills. Finally we came to a cul de sac lined with houses that face back toward the city. Graham pulled over and parked in front of the first house on the right. "This is it," he said.

It's a white stucco box, flat-roofed, built into the side of the hill, so the level that faces the street is the second floor in back. I could see the garage and the front door but the rest was submerged in junipers, palms, bamboo, and ivy.

"You want to get out?" I asked him.

"I'm okay here. You go on."

I walked out into the middle of the circle. The rear of the house faces downtown L.A. and the view has to be pretty spectacular at night. I could see the skyline from where I stood. There was no other traffic, no other sound but birds and a distant lawn mower.

I wanted more. I wanted to knock on the door and see if they'd let me look around. Sure they would. Me smelling like beer and wearing the kind of clothes they wouldn't wear to work in the garden. If they ever worked in their own gardens.

I got back in the car. Graham held up his hands and said, "Listen." He closed his eyes, so I did too. "Can you hear it?"

"Hear what?"

"The music. All that music. He sat at a grand piano in that house and wrote all the songs for *Pet Sounds*, everything on *Smile*, right there."

"With his feet in a sandbox."

"Forget the sandbox. Just listen."

I listened. I could hear it. Brian playing the grand piano and singing "Surf's Up," like he had on the CBS *Inside Pop* special in the summer of 1966.

"I hear it," I said. "Do you hear it?"

"I hear it."

"What is it? What do you hear?" I opened my eyes.

Graham tilted his head. "It's . . ."

"Yeah?" I could still hear "Surf's Up," plain as day, as if it was coming out of the car radio, just Brian and the piano.

"It's . . . 'Good Vibrations.' The high part near the end, before the theremin and the fade-out."

I felt totally let down. "C'mon, let's get out of here."

———

We took a case of Raffo to Graham's house and he nuked some frozen lasagnas for dinner. Afterward I couldn't seem to sit down. I looked out Graham's front window at a row of streetlights that trailed off into the sunset.

"What was your family like?" I asked him. "You said something before about how you didn't get along."

"That was kind of an understatement."

"Is your dad still alive?"

"Yeah, he and my stepmother moved out here five years ago. I wish they hadn't. I came out here to get away from the sons of bitches in the first place."

"But at Christmas . . ."

"I was here by myself. I know. I told them I had people over so they wouldn't hang around, make things worse than they already were."

"That bad?"

"Hell, if you want to hear the story I can put up with telling it."

"If you can put up with telling it I want to hear it."

"I told you about my mother dying and all, when I was three. Well, her parents were just grief-stricken. I guess they wanted to hold on to something of her, and they tried to get me away from my dad. Of course they didn't have any case at all, he got a lawyer and won me back, and turned me over to his own mother. She lived near Hot Springs, and, man, I loved it there. I would get up every day and go over to the nearest kid's house, which was a mile away, and then we would go *miles* out into the Hot Springs National Forest, playing all day long by ourselves, no supervision, coming home and eating, and nobody ever thinking a thing about it.

"It was two weeks before first grade when my dad showed up with my new mother, my stepmother, and took me back to Pine Bluff. Now, up to then I hadn't seen much of religion. This woman was Church of Christ, which means she wasn't just a fire-breathing fundamentalist, she went to a church that hasn't even got *music* in it.

"I remember the first day I was in Pine Bluff. I saw some kids playing down the street and I started to run off and play with them. My stepmother leaned out the kitchen window and yelled at me, 'Stay in your own yard!' That was so crazy, with me having been out in the National Forest every day up to then, well, it didn't even register. I just kept on going. She came out of that house like a cavalry division and dragged me back in the house. That started a war that lasted until the day I finished high school and went into the Navy."

"Did she make you go to church too?"

"Three times a week until I got out of high school."

"I can't feature you in church. Were you into it?"

"My first memory of it was resentment. Because my stepmother had this thing where I had to go home in the afternoons, instead of playing, like the other kids, I had to go home and memorize Bible verses. It was bad enough to miss play, but then to have to do something I hated doing, memorizing those verses. Then I caught on to the fact that she never did any memorizing herself, she just sat there with the Bible open, reading, while I was the one that was doing the memorization. When I realized that, I ran away from home. That was the first time I ran away. I was in the fourth grade. I decided I was going to be a cowboy."

"How far did you get?"

"About ten miles out of town. It got dark and some country people took me in, and slowly but surely they got the story out of me and called my parents and they came and picked me up. It was not very well organized. I was pretty stupid."

"Hey, man, you were just a kid."

"I got better. I don't remember when the third time was, but I was gone for three or four days and I had them really worried."

I said, "I ran away twice, senior year. Never got far. My mom promised she was going to make things better and all she did was end up taking up for my dad."

"That sounds familiar. I've told people this before and they couldn't believe I would run away from home. They said it was incomprehensible."

"I comprehend it all right. Sometimes I wonder why it took me so long. My father never let up, you know? No matter how good I was."

"Well, I wasn't perfect, but I wasn't, you know, a criminal or anything. It was just horseplay. What got me was the punishment for accidental stuff. Like reaching for something on the table and knocking over a glass of milk and getting your ass beaten for that. My father kept this three-foot tree branch. He called it 'The Stick' and it sat on top of the refrigerator for no other reason than to beat my ass. I got so used to it that I thought it was normal. Then one time I was over at my friend's house, and his little sister got up on this cabinet and pulled an entire cabinet full of glass over on top of her. And her mother screamed and ran over and grabbed her up and I thought she was going to pop the hell out of her, which is what my dad or my stepmother would have done, and she started shaking her, to get the broken glass off, and saying, 'Are you all right? Are you all right?' and I almost started crying. I was so amazed that she wasn't *mad* . . .'"

It was quiet for a long time. I watched a couple of cars drive by in the darkness, shadowy figures behind the wheel. "You did some college on the GI Bill, right? Did you ever think about going straight to school instead of the Navy? You're smart. You could maybe have gotten a scholarship or something."

"I took the SATs and did real good. I had a teacher at the high school that was going to do what he could for me. But my father said no. He said, 'You're not smart enough to go to college.' And that was that."

"You're kidding."

"Fuck no, I'm not kidding. He never could find a good word to say to me. Or to anybody. Love is the one word you never heard in our house."

"Sounds like Brian's dad."

"Or Morrison's. Morrison's dad was Navy, same as mine."

"Was your dad the one made you join up?"

"No, that was my idea. If I wasn't going to college I had to do *something*."

"Or maybe . . . maybe you thought by going in the Navy he would finally be proud of you."

After a minute Graham said, "Maybe so. Pretty stupid, huh?"

I came up behind him and put my hands on his shoulders. "No. Just human."

He held onto one wrist for a couple of seconds, then he reached for his beer again.

=====

I slept in Graham's guest room, on a foldout bed that was too short for me. He gave me a scrapbook he'd put together on Pacific Ocean Park and I sat up for a while with it. I can see why it has such a hold on him. It wasn't just a lot of rides, it was an entire magical world you could escape to, a world where all the restaurants served hot dogs and pizza, where kids could drive miniature freeways or pretend to live under water.

I couldn't calm down enough to sleep. I kept hearing music in my head, "Surf's Up" and this other *Smile* song called "Child Is Father of the Man." The title is the only lyric, repeated over and over against a simple melody. One of Mike Autrey's books pointed out that it's the Bicycle Rider theme backward, ascending instead of descending. I couldn't make it stop. It made me think of a cartoon from when I was a kid, a guy kneeling in front of a chopping block, saying to the headsman, "Ever have a song go around in your head and you can't get rid of it?"

I slept for a while. In the dream I'm in bed with Alex, we're both naked, we both want each other, only my father keeps coming in the room for stuff. He doesn't really look at us, he just comes in and gets a stamp album or a clay pot or a box of Kleenex.

I woke up horny and sad and still drunk. What I wanted was to feel clean and fit and sober and rested. Outside, the sky had started to turn pink. A dog barked down the street. I wanted to look forward to a brand-new day, not pray for a few more hours of sleep.

I didn't need Estrella the gypsy lady to tell me that sleep was not in my future. I put on last night's clothes and washed my face and brushed my teeth, then I looked in on Graham. He was sprawled out on his stomach, one arm hanging off the bed. Go, man. Saw that wood.

I left him a note and called a taxi and went outside to wait for it. I had my little cassette recorder with me, and a couple of tapes that

I wasn't ready to listen to yet. The day was coming up raw and bloody, like I felt. A salt breeze rattled in the palms and sea gulls fought over a torn bag of garbage down the street.

I felt like the last human being alive on the planet. Everybody else had died in their sleep—Elizabeth and all her smug friends, my mother and her memories of a saintly father I'd never known. Died, all of them, and left me here in this damp red morning.

I wondered what Brian would make of all this. What music he would find that exactly conveyed the color of the sunrise, the hollowness in my chest. I could see him at his grand piano, eyes out of focus, bare-chested, feet in his sandbox, playing it.

The taxi finally arrived, driven by some kid with thick glasses, acne, and greasy hair. He didn't say anything, just nodded when I told him I wanted the nearest place I could rent a car. After that I stopped at Jim's Do-Nuts for a half dozen glazed and two cups of coffee. It left me wide-eyed and eggshell-thin all over.

I got in the car and drove. With *Glimpses* Volume One in the tape player I slipped into a caffeine and sugar fugue state, wired, edgy, and at the same time barely tuned into the real world. I sat at a green light staring at a beautiful blonde in a string bikini top and cutoffs until the cars behind me started to honk. Then I missed the shift to second and ground the gears loud enough to hear a mile away.

I'd devolved to some pre-Alex high school mentality where beautiful women were my enemies. They had what I needed to be happy, and they wouldn't give it to me. I hated them for it. It was my lizard brain talking. Worse yet, it was the Lizard King himself.

The Doors were on and I hadn't noticed, a B-side called "Who Scared You?" It's snake music, sinuous, cocky, threatening. Once I saw what was happening to me I felt a desperate need to cool out. I pointed the car toward the ocean, waiting for the Doors to finish, and finally they did. I found my way onto the Promenade as the next song came on: "Beat the Clock" by the McCoys. I had to pull up at the curb and let it all roll over me, May of 1967, the end of my junior year. The song would still be on the charts when my father had his first heart attack. Suddenly I thought I was about to break into a million pieces, that all the different people inside of me were about to crawl out and walk away in a million different directions. They were all so real that I could feel them crowding me, bouncing off the walls inside me.

"Beat the Clock" is the next to last song on the tape. I knew what was next and I wasn't ready for it, so I switched the player off as the refrain started to fade. I put the car in gear again and drove to Brian's house. I knew exactly how to get there. Traffic seemed to part for me. When I turned onto the last stretch of Laurel Way I started the tape again and turned it up.

It was the title track for the series, an obscure Yardbirds cut called "Glimpses." A hypnotic bass line, washes of guitar noise, finally the band singing harmony with no words, just ahhhh ah ah ahhhh. The first time I heard it it scared the shit out of me, it was so otherworldly. Lost-sounding, somehow.

I drove around the circle and parked across the street from Brian's house.

After a while this voice comes on. Some old British guy, sounds like a physics professor, voice distorted like it's coming out of a radio tuned between stations. He talks about energy radiating from a source, some other stuff that is too distorted for me to make out. The last thing he says always makes my blood run cold, with the eerie chanting and the distorted guitars all around it: "Time is just a cumular image—which but one glimpse—can overcome." The last two words repeat over and over, "Can overcome. Can overcome."

I sat there in the rented Sunbird with bright sunshine all around me, shaking, crying, all sense of time and placed destroyed. I got out of the car. I could still hear the song. It speeds up at the end and McCarty is hammering this bolero kind of thing on drums and Page is playing ascending chords faster and faster.

The music was inside me, pushing, it was pushing at right angles to any kind of direction there is. I staggered into the street. I had tears in my eyes and everything was blurred, a wash of color, and I heard something that might be a car and I tried to run and suddenly I was falling, reaching out for something to take my weight.

When I opened my eyes it was nighttime and I was crouched on the sidewalk in front of Brian's house and it wasn't 1989 anymore.

CHAPTER 4
CHAPTER 4

Brian

Music came out of the house, and over that, voices and splashing from the pool in back. The rest of the block was dark and quiet. It was cool enough to bring up goose bumps on my arms. The garage was open and well-lit; inside I saw a Stingray, a Jaguar XKE, and a Rolls. What really got me were the license plates, black with orange letters instead of blue on white.

I sat down on the curb and waited for the hallucination to pass. Except I knew it wasn't a hallucination and it wasn't going anywhere. If I was where I thought I was, I was a hundred feet away from Brian and the *Smile* tapes. It was the chance of a lifetime.

I got carefully to my feet. I felt light-headed but apparently I wasn't going to float away. I was wearing the same clothes I'd put on that morning: slightly faded blue jeans, a green polo shirt, black All-Stars. Except for my hair I could have passed for a Californian from any time since the fifties. All I needed was a story.

I walked up to the gray double front doors and rang the bell. I felt like I was in a movie, that I wasn't responsible for anything I did. The door opened on a good-looking guy in his twenties, with short, neatly combed dark hair, dark slacks, and a white shirt.

I took a chance. "David Anderle?"

"That's right. Do I know you?"

"Ray Shackleford," I said. "RCA records." I held out my hand. "This is really a pleasure. I understand we might not have gotten to hear 'Good Vibrations' if it wasn't for you." Brian had been on the verge of selling the song to an R&B group when Anderle heard it and went crazy for it. His enthusiasm got Brian fired up enough to finish it and release it. If this was the winter of 1966, as I was sure it was, Anderle didn't have an official status with the Beach Boys yet. He was just one of Brian's friends. Within a few months, though, they would start Brother Records and Anderle would be named president.

"Where in the world did you hear that?" He seemed more flattered than alarmed.

"It's my job to keep my ear to the ground. Um . . . I was hoping to talk to Brian. Can I come in?"

"I was just leaving . . . but sure, why not, come on. Brian's back in the pool."

Then I was inside. I had to tell myself it was really happening, I was really in the house on Laurel Way. Exactly where I most wanted to be, doing exactly what I most wanted to do in all the world. There was the den, there was the jukebox full of Phil Spector singles and acetates of the new songs. Down at the end of the hall was Brian's office, with the grand piano and the sandbox. There were new-looking magazines on the coffee table, and I sneaked a look at the dates. *Time* for December 2, 1966, *Newsweek* for December 5.

Things hadn't yet gone too far. Not yet.

Brian's beagle, one of the dogs that barks at the end of "Caroline, No," clicked across the kitchen linoleum to check me out. I bent down and he waddled over to be petted. "This one's Banana, right?"

Anderle said, "You've really done your homework."

"I'm interested in Brian. I might be able to help him."

"Are you talking about the Capitol thing?" At this point Anderle had sued Capitol for $275,000 worth of producer's royalties that Brian had supposedly never been paid. Things had turned ugly and the Beach Boys were threatening to break their contract and go elsewhere.

I was about to make a pitch on behalf of RCA when my conscience kicked in. I'd made it inside the house, no point in lying any more than I had to. "I can't offer you a record deal on the spot or anything. But there's lots of different kinds of help."

The decor was schizophrenic: plaid drapes and pole lamps and heavy Spanish furniture, mixed with Lava Lites and orange-and-blue wallpaper and campy religious icons. It was all I could do not to rub the curtains between my thumb and forefinger, or pocket an ashtray for a souvenir.

Downstairs there were glass doors that led to the pool. A slide curved down to it from the roof of the house. In the steam from the pool I smelled chlorine, perfume, cut grass. Of the four people who splashed around in the shallow end my attention went to Brian right off. First because he was so big, six four and really starting to put on weight. There in his baggy trunks, as he straddled a child's inflatable horse and almost sank it, he seemed larger than life.

Especially next to Van Dyke Parks and his wife, Durry, who could have been a couple of elves. Both had their glasses on, both still had dry hair. The fourth person in the pool was Diane Rovell, Brian's sister-in-law, wearing a blue bikini with a huge white T-shirt, probably one of Brian's, over it. Brian's wife, Marilyn—Diane's sister—sat in a lounge chair. She wore a purple one-piece bathing suit with a built-in skirt. Her hair, which was blonde at the moment, hung down around her shoulders from inside a loose white cap. She was in a bit of a heavy phase herself.

Anderle walked me up to the edge of the pool and Brian looked over at us. He was laughing at something. My first impression was exactly the one I'd expected from his photographs, only stronger. It wasn't his musical genius that came out, or the sensitivity that sometimes went over the line into neurosis. It was his niceness. I wanted him to be my friend.

"Brian, this is Ray. He says he's with RCA. But I don't want you to talk any business tonight, okay?"

"Okay."

"Promise?"

"Yeah, sure, I promise." He paddled over and we shook hands. "Hey, Ray. You want to put on a suit and join us?"

"Uh . . . yeah. Yeah, I'd love to."

"David, could you . . .?"

"Sure, Brian." He showed me where to change and waited for me to come out. I put on a madras suit that made me suck in my gut and wonder where I got the nerve to talk about other people's weight problems.

Back at the pool Anderele said, "This time it's good-night for real." He looked really tired. I was afraid to ask how late it was.

Brian sang "Good-night, Sweetheart" as he waved good-bye, leaning backward on his inflatable horse until the last few words came out as a gurgle. With a tremendous splash he went completely over on his back, his legs stuck out of the water and kicking. Diane laughed and Van Dyke and Durry smiled nervously. I got in at the shallow end and shook hands with all three of them and said hello to Marilyn. She had a bemused look on her face like this happened all the time, which I guess it did. Finally Brian came up like a sounding whale. He splashed water all over the yard and sent Louie, the weimaraner, into a barking fit.

It made me giddy, like being in love or suddenly rich, like my inside was too big for the outside. I leaned over and made this trumpeting noise, blowing a lungful of air out over my tightened lips. If you do it with your mouth just touching the water it echoes like crazy.

Brian stopped and stared at me. "Wow, man, how did you do that?"

"I don't know. It's something my old man used to do."

"Do it again."

I did and Brian laughed like a little kid. His face was angelic. "This is far-out," he said. Then he leaned over and did it himself, same pitch, everything.

"Okay," he said, suddenly serious. "Van Dyke, you do this." He clapped his hands with water between them.

"Come on, Brian," Van Dyke said. His voice was nasal and high, like it came from high in his throat. "Do we have to get into another whole production thing?"

"You'll love it. Just try it."

Van Dyke reluctantly started to clap his hands.

"Slower," Brian said, moving his hands like a conductor. "Okay, Ray, do your thing." I did my walrus noise and Brian came in on top of me, in a higher key, somehow making the sounds reverberate together.

"Jesus Christ," I said. "That sounds like . . . have you ever heard whales sing?" It was 1966, the *Songs of the Humpback Whale* album was still years away as a pop event.

"Singing whales?" Durry said.

"Whales!" Brian said. "That's it! It's perfect, man, we can get whale noises for the water thing in the 'Elements.' "

"Brian, you're crazy," Van Dyke said.

Brian said, "If everybody was crazy"—and Van Dyke and Marilyn and Diane all joined in as he said—"then maybe we'd have world peace." And Van Dyke said, "Yeah, yeah, yeah."

"You'll see," Brian said. "I'll do it and it'll be great."

It all felt real. I just felt like any minute somebody was going to turn and point at me and scream that I didn't belong.

Durry whispered to Van Dyke and he said, "Brian, it's three o'clock. We've got to go home."

"Don't you want some more hash? We've got some more hash. Mare, go get some hash for these people."

Marilyn said, "They want to go home, Brian. Let them go home and get some sleep."

"Yeah, okay." He looked at me and his eyes lit up. "How about you, Ray? You want some hash?"

"Sure," I said. "Why not?"

Brian hoisted himself up the ladder and padded into the house. I got out and looked around for a towel. Marilyn, still bemused, pointed to a pile of them on one of the lawn chairs. Durry grabbed a towel and started in. Van Dyke shook my hand and said, "Nice to meet you."

"You too," I said. I stopped myself before I told him how much I liked his *Song Cycle* album, which hadn't been recorded yet.

They headed for the front door and I followed Brian into the den. He stood in the dark in front of the jukebox, his baggy swimsuit dripping onto the carpet. I wrapped my towel around my shoulders, cold now that I was out of the heated pool.

I thought Brian had simply spaced out. Then he said, "Have you heard anything from *Smile*?" He was still staring at the jukebox.

"Just 'Good Vibrations.' " I wasn't sure what was recorded at that point, what I could safely claim to have heard.

"That was Capitol's idea, to put the single on there. If it was up to me, I'd do the whole album new." He punched a couple of buttons on the machine. "Listen to this."

The record was an acetate, a demo cut right in the studio. It was scratchy and distorted from all the times Brian had played it. I heard his voice count off, then there was a high piano, a French horn, a bass, then a wall of pianos, Spector style. By the time the drums came in I had recognized "Child Is Father of the Man," the song that had been playing over and over in my head. There were four or five vocal parts on the demo already, chugging along on the word "child." It was no different from the version on the bootlegs, but to hear it there, in Brian's house, gave it incredible power.

Then Brian started singing, a high falsetto that wove in and out of the other parts. The song was totally transformed, filled with sadness and triumph. My eyes started to tear up there in front of him. Brian didn't seem to notice. When the take broke down on record Brian kept at it for another few seconds, still with that lost look on his face.

"Wow," I said, eventually.

"I just thought of that. Pretty neat, huh?"

"It's great."

"I got to remember that part." He went over to a mahogany coffee table next to the couch and rummaged around in a drawer. "I've got this really groovy pipe, I think it was in here . . . yeah, here it is."

The pipe was clay and looked like a kazoo with a couple of bluejay feathers hanging off it. Brian opened a crumpled piece of foil and rolled up an oily green pellet of hashish.

"So," he said, "RCA records, huh?" He took some matches from a dish on the tabletop and fired up the pipe. "You think you might want to do *Smile?*"

"David said he didn't want you to talk business." Brian handed me the pipe and I took a small toke. Easy, Ray, for Christ's sake, you'll get stoned and God knows what'll happen.

Brian shrugged. "So we don't say anything to David."

I gave the pipe back and breathed out smoke. I'd never actually had hash before, only marijuana. The smell made me dizzy and my heart beat like crazy. I could see perfectly in the dark.

"Look Brian . . ." He sat crossed-legged, eyes closed, holding a lit match over the ball of hash. His eyes opened in slow motion and he took the pipe away. I said, "I have to tell you the truth. I'm not with RCA. But I can help you just the same."

His eyes got jumpy. "What are you saying, man?"

"You don't know me, but I know you, because of your music. I know more about you than you can imagine. I would never do anything to hurt you. You have to believe me."

"What do you mean you know things? What kind of things?"

"I know Mike Love doesn't understand what you're trying to do. He hasn't heard any of the *Smile* stuff, has he?"

"No. The guys just got back from London."

"When he hears it, he's going to freak."

"Yeah, probably. He hated *Pet Sounds*. He said 'Good Vibrations' was 'avant-garde crap.'"

"I know what's happening here. Everybody thinks you're crazy. You took acid and it was this incredible religious experience, only nobody else wants to know about it. Every time you try something new, every time you hear some new sound in your head, everybody fights with you. You're growing and opening out and nobody can keep up with you. Am I right?"

His eyes were wide. It took him a long time to nod.

I said, "Sooner or later, everybody realizes you were right. But the next time they still fight you all over again."

"How do you know all this?"

"I just know it. You're moving so fast now, there isn't anybody in the world who can keep up. The thing is, if you're not careful, they're going to drag you down. Between Mike Love and Capitol Records they'll drag you down and wear you out and the record will never get made."

Brian lit another match and fired up the hash. He took a huge hit into his lungs and held it. "No way, man," he said through clenched teeth. "This is going to be the greatest fucking album ever. Better than Spector, better than the Beatles." He blew a cloud of smoke around his head.

"Being good is not enough," I said. He held the pipe out to me and I shook my head. "Timing, Brian. You got to have timing. How many songs have you got for this record? Fifteen? Twenty?"

"Something like that."

"Pick a dozen and finish them. Finish them now. Before you play it for anybody else. Get the whole album finished and turned in."

"I can't do that, man. Carl has to sing 'Wonderful.' I need Dennis's harmonies. Besides, I can't go around Mike. He's always been part of the group. He's family. They all are."

"If you wait for them you're going to lose it."

"How do you know that?"

"I just do. If I told you how I know you wouldn't believe me."

Brian toked up another huge lungful of hash. It would have brought a horse to its knees. "Try me."

I sat for a while wondering what I should tell him, and then it just started to come out. "For the sake of argument, let's say I was from the future. Let's say I know everything that's going to happen if you wait for Dennis and Carl and Mike."

Brian was so huge. He was like some kind of bear or something, looming over me. I could see his eyes, bloodshot from the pool and the drugs, glow in the dark. "Tell me," he said.

"You play the tapes for them. Mike hates it. He says, 'You're blowing it, Brian. Don't fuck with the formula. Surfing and cars, Brian.' He calls Van Dyke in and demands to know what 'crow cries uncover the cornfield' means. Van Dyke refuses to explain himself and quits in a huff. Capitol demands to hear what you've got and they hate it too. You lose momentum. You know the album is brilliant, but your confidence is shaken. It's so hard to keep pushing. You fool around, start more new songs and don't finish them. You think if you get it perfect enough, everybody will have to like it. Suddenly it's June and there's a new Beatles album out. It's called *Sgt. Pepper's Lonely Hearts Club Band.*"

"You're joking."

"No. It's got songs that run together and repeated themes and sound effects. It's not as good as *Smile,* but it is really good, and it takes the world by storm. It's acknowledged as rock's first masterpiece. It takes the heart right out of you and you never finish *Smile.* Never."

The first emotion across his face was disbelief. Then he said, "This is too weird. You couldn't be making this up." He got up and shambled around the room. "Fucking hell." He walked all the way around the room four times and sat down again. "Sergeant what?"

I told him.

He closed his eyes and sat that way for a long time. Finally he shook his head once, slowly, in a big arc, and stood up again. "Are you hungry at all? I am totally starved."

"Sure," I said. "Why not?"

We changed clothes and went out to the garage, which was still open to the night. Brian got in the right side of the Rolls and for a second I thought he meant me to take the wheel. Then I realized it was probably still set up for right-hand drive.

I fumbled for a shoulder harness that wasn't there, and Brian said, "You like it?" I nodded. He hadn't started the engine yet. He just sat there in the garage, turning the wheel. It occurred to me that Brian was really stoned and the steering wheel was on the wrong side of the car. Maybe this was not a good idea.

Brian suddenly leaned forward, his eyes shining, and started to make engine noises. He ran through the gears, squealed the brakes, even missed a shift and shrugged apologetically. With my eyes shut I would have thought I was on a racetrack. Then Brian pretended to throw the car into a huge, screaming skid that ended in a crash. He rocked back in his seat and sat there in silence for a while.

"Wow," he said at last. "Great ride. So why am I still hungry?"

I started to laugh and then Brian did too. We must have rolled around in those leather seats for five minutes, laughing. Finally Brian said, "C'mon, we can get something to eat inside."

It turned out to be chocolate ice cream in the black-and-white kitchen. I made him stop after he put a couple of scoops in my bowl. He put half the carton into his. "You live in L.A. or what?" he asked.

"No." I could feel the ice cream where it had stuck halfway down my throat, a cold, hard pellet. I was all alone, a hell of a long way from home. I had maybe a hundred dollars in my wallet, which would be okay as long as nobody thought to look at the dates on the bills. "I guess you could say I just got here. I don't even know what day it is."

Brian was really going through that ice cream. He was even child-like in the way he ate, giving it his undivided enthusiasm. A hank of brown hair fell across his face and he kept pushing it back between bites. He didn't look up when he said, "It's Monday. November twenty-eighth. I guess actually it's Tuesday morning now. Have you got someplace to stay?"

"Well, no actually. Not really."

"You can stay here if you want."

"That's . . . that would be great. Thanks."

He stood up. "I better get to bed. There should be a couple of bedrooms with nobody in them."

I put both our dishes in the sink and ran some water in them. Brian led me to an empty room and switched on the light by the bed. With his big hands it was like he was playing with dollhouse furniture. "Okay?" he said.

"Perfect. Thanks."

Brian shrugged and started to turn away. I was exhausted and I knew I wouldn't be able to stay awake much longer. I didn't know where I would be when I woke up. What the hell. If this was all I got, it was still great.

"Brian? Think about what I said, okay? About *Smile*. The world needs that record."

"Then we'd have world peace, right? I'll think about it. Night, Ray."

"Good-night."

The room was done up in chintz curtains and matching white-painted furniture. There were stuffed toys and green-and-blue flowered sheets on the bed. There was a private bathroom, where I showered off the chlorine from the pool and used the guest toothbrush.

As I got in bed I thought again, I am truly happy. However this happened, I don't care. I'm happy.

———

When I woke up it was noon. I was still in Brian's house, still in 1966. "Thank you," I said, to nobody in particular. I got dressed and set my watch by the bedside Westclox. If I'd known I was coming I would have packed a bag. No way Brian's clothes were going to fit me.

I found Diane and Marilyn at the kitchen table with a guy who looked instantly familiar. He had long black hair, massive sideburns, and intense eyes. "Good morning," Marilyn said. "Do you want some coffee?"

"I'd love some. Thanks."

"Ray, this is Danny Hutton."

"Of course." I knew him from Three Dog Night, which was still a few years away. He'd had a couple regional records by 1966 and David

Anderle was managing him. " 'Roses and Rainbows Are You.' Great song."

"Not exactly 'Good Vibrations.' But it's a living."

I sat down between Danny and Diane. Marilyn had her back to me, pouring coffee. She said, "I talked to RCA this morning. They say they don't have anybody named Ray Shackleford who works for them." She brought the cup over to me and then walked away like she didn't expect an answer.

The cup had four-petaled flowers on it, green with blue centers. I wrapped my hand around it, felt the heat sting my palm. "I told Brian the truth last night. He knows what's going on."

"What exactly *is* going on?" Marilyn said. Danny and Diane stared at the tabletop. "What did you tell Brian?"

"Personal stuff. I'm here to help him. I wouldn't hurt him, you have to believe that."

Marilyn sat down at the other end of the table from me. "You have to understand. Brian is like a little kid. He's a wonderful musician and singer but he's not exactly Mr. Capable. We have to watch out for him. We have to be very careful that people don't . . . .take advantage of him."

"Believe me, I don't care about his money. I just want to see this record get made."

"You and everybody else," Danny said.

Diane said, "Is Ray Shackleford your real name?"

I nodded. "I'm from Austin, Texas. I . . . fix stereos. Right now I don't really have a fixed address." Jesus, in a couple of years Charlie Manson would walk in from the desert and ask Brian's brother Dennis to trust him in pretty much the same way. Manson came complete with his harem of hippie chicks who would fuck anyone he told them to, which Dennis couldn't resist. I didn't have anything to offer Marilyn except empty assurances.

"I'm not crazy about this," Marilyn said.

"Why don't you let Brian decide?" I said. "If Brian wants me to go, then I'm gone."

"Yeah, Mare," said Brian from the doorway. "Why'ncha let Brian decide?" He said it in a goofy kind of gangster voice. He was wearing white shorts and nothing else, scratching the pale expanse of his stomach.

Marilyn got up. She look resigned. "Morning, Brian," she said. She moved skillets and dishes around. "I'll fix you some breakfast."

That was all for the moment. Brian and Danny talked about Danny's career. Brian told Danny how much he liked his voice, that he wanted a chance to produce him. Eventually Brian would, a prototype version of Three Dog Night that he would christen Redwood, but Mike Love would refuse to let Brian sign them to Brother Records.

Marilyn brought Brian's breakfast, which consisted of bacon, scrambled eggs, and an entire avocado. I ate a couple of pieces of toast. When Brian was done he stifled a theatrical belch and said, "It's a gray day. I hate gray days. What can we do to save it?" Everybody ignored him, like they knew what was coming. "I know!" Brian said, holding up a finger. The gesture looked false and well-worn. "What about a trip to . . . Pacific Ocean Park!"

"Oh, Brian," Marilyn said.

He looked around the table for support. Danny and Diane were watching the tabletop again. I shrugged and looked interested, feeling like I owed it to Graham, at least.

"Maybe me and Ray'll go," he said.

Marilyn took away his empty plate. "Fine, Brian."

He went to change clothes and I followed him as far as the den. I stood and looked at the jukebox until he came back, dressed in wheat jeans and a football jersey.

The Rolls sat running in the driveway, a uniformed driver behind the wheel. It was hazy and cool, around sixty degrees, with rain a real possibility. Eventually Brian took a step toward the car and the driver got out and opened the doors for us.

The back of the Rolls was tricked out like a limo, with a small bar and an eight-track player and a radio tuned to KHJ Boss Radio. They played "Sugartown" by Nancy Sinatra and "I'm Losing You" by the Temptations and "Good Vibrations," which was hovering at number two, then they played "Born Free" by Roger Williams to take them into the news. I'd forgotten what it's like to hear so many different kinds of music on one station, how it used to be that the same person could like different kinds of music, pop and Motown and psychedelic too.

We drove west on Sunset toward to the ocean. I'd taken the same trip with Graham and the difference was astonishing. There were long stretches of open countryside, followed by pockets of civilization that were more like individual country towns than segments of one mono-lithic city. Cars whipped around us through oncoming traffic and made me think of Jan and Dean's "Deadman's Curve."

We turned south on the coast highway. The Rolls was so smooth and quiet it was like watching it on a movie screen. Half the cars on the road seemed to be trailing smoke and I realized that they didn't have emission controls yet, that the air outside was worse than in the eighties.

When the news came on it was full of a big drug bust at Santa Monica High. Nine kids had been arrested for smoking pot, and the city was in shock. A police psychologist said they were using marijuana to "overcome the insecurities of being a teenager." That made Brian laugh. Up in Berkeley, Mario Savio was leading protests against Navy recruitment on campus. The sportscast was about the first-ever Super Bowl coming up in January at the L.A. Coliseum.

"If you're from the future," Brian said, during a Pepsi ad, "who's going to win the Super Bowl?"

I shook my head. "That's more than twenty years ago for me. I'm not that big a sports fan, anyway."

"You're not convincing me, here. What about 'Good Vibrations'? Does it ever make it to number one?"

"Week of December tenth," I said. "That one I know. It's my wife's birthday."

"The December tenth *Billboard*'ll be out this Friday. We can check up on you." After a couple of seconds he said, "So your wife's Sagittarius. What about you?"

"Capricorn. December thirtieth."

"Uh-oh. You guys ever had your charts done? I mean they do still do charts in the future, right?"

"It's a little late for charts." There was something in my throat. I cleared it out and said, "I don't really think we're going to make it." It was the first time I'd said it out loud. Having the words actually out there scared me.

"How long you guys been together?"

"Together for eleven years. Married for ten."

"That seems like such a long time. I've only known Marilyn four years and it seems like forever sometimes."

It shocked me too. I'd forgotten that Marilyn was only eighteen. From the way she acted, she could have passed for a seasoned thirty. Being a full-time mother to Brian had done it.

"It's so intense," Brian said. "It's like . . . I don't know. I can't say it. I really admire guys like Van Dyke, that are so articulate. It's like the time per se, I mean the years, they don't really mean anything. Only the emotions. Maybe there isn't anything else in the whole universe. Just emotions. The only thing that's real is how we feel about something, not the thing itself."

We passed the pier at Santa Monica. POP was just ahead. If my feelings were the only things that were real, I was in trouble. My feelings were all over the map. They could fly out of my hands and I would wind up back in 1989. "We don't have to do this," I said. "We could go back to the studio and you could do some work."

"It's too cloudy to work. Maybe tonight."

"It's all so fragile," I said. "The littlest thing can just . . ."

"Relax," Brian said. "Smile."

The DJ said, "Here's something from last year by the Kinks." I recognized the opening chords of "Something Better Beginning."

Brian turned the radio up. "Just listen," he said.

Ray Davies sang about dancing the last dance with some girl he'd just met, wondering what lay ahead. Heartbreak, or the start of something big. The song was about more than just a boy and a girl. Sitting there in the mist and drizzle, the dusty, comforting smell of the heater filling the back seat, it seemed to tell me everything I would ever need to know.

Brian said, "It's the whole world, see? It's like we're just waking up. New music, new ideas. It's only the start of something, something incredible." He looked over at me. "But you've seen it, right? You know where it's all headed."

"It's going to be big," I said. "The next three or four years are going to be so intense some people will never get over them. They'll be talking about them for the rest of their lives." Like me, I thought.

Brian wrote "HELP ME" in backward letters in the mist on his window. "What would you do?" he said. "If somebody could tell you the future? Would you want to know? I mean, sometimes all you have is hope, and if you knew, it would take that away."

"In the first place, I don't want to tell you. Besides, if you make your album maybe it'll come out different."

How could I tell him? Even if I wanted to? The next summer would be the Summer of Love, and fifty thousand kids would descend on San Francisco in their tribal colors. I would smoke my first joint in the garden shed behind my parents' house. All over the country, vague notions of change would clarify, as they already had in California. The problem was greed and hatred. The answer was peace and love. The way to get there was music and drugs. We knew we could change the world.

Then came 1968. While Morrison turned into the Lizard King in L.A., one step ahead, as always, the rest of us found out it wasn't going to be easy. Martin Luther King and Bobby Kennedy were shot down and the Democratic National Convention in Chicago showed us how futile and empty our dreams of political power were.

Then came Manson and Altamont and the dream was over. Brian Jones was the first to die, then Hendrix and Joplin and Blind Owl Wilson of Canned Heat, all by the end of 1970. It was hope and promise turned to ashes, grass and LSD turned to coke and heroin, heavy music and acid rock come to mean songs that weighed you down and burned to the touch.

It was the question that haunted my generation. What happened to us? Where did we go wrong? Drugs were a symptom, not a cause. Maybe we couldn't change the American political system overnight. We could have gone outside and around it. It was more like something was wrong in the initial conditions, some built-in flaw that meant the structure would never hold.

Morrison had understood it better than anyone. He knew that "no limits" meant sooner or later you would end up looking over the edge of a cliff. Morrison didn't even slow down, just sailed right off. He knew we were all doomed and he didn't want to be the last one at the party. His girlfriend, Pamela, said when she found him dead in that bathtub in Paris he was smiling off into space. Not lost, like Cream sang in "Mother's Lament," but gone before.

When I was trying to find the *Smile* album, back in 1989, I'd started to feel the same way. Like there was some kind of curse built into it, the same curse that had ruined the sixties. That if you tried to make music with no limits it would fall apart. Even so I had to try. I had to get into the studio with Brian, add my will to his, see if together we couldn't make it happen.

=====

The driver let us off in front of the park. There was a six-legged arch over the ticket booth that looked like the 1950's idea of the future, where everything was triangular or kidney-shaped. It took me a minute to figure out it was supposed to be a starfish. A pole came out of the top with plastic bubbles all up and down it and sea horses at the top. Even the walls of the booth were curved, and it would have all been wonderfully modern-looking if the plastic hadn't been pitted and cloudy from the salt air and the stucco hadn't started to crack.

"Have you been here before?" Brian asked.

"No," I said. "Just heard a lot about it."

Brian bought two tickets and we went through into a courtyard of concrete pools and fountains. At the end was an elevator with a clear tube through the middle. The doors closed behind us, the tube filled with water, and gurgling sound effects came through hidden speakers. Brian grinned like a lunatic.

When we came out it was like one of my dreams of swimming without scuba gear, of being able to breathe underwater, like in the Hendrix song. Windows opened up on fish tanks with sharks and rays and all kinds of other fish. The walls were sea-green and white, with peeling murals of waves and fish and seaweed. Sunlight came faintly through yellow-green skylights overhead. Seedy as it was, I could see that Brian loved it. Memories, maybe. I was getting into it myself, maybe only because it was such a perfect artifact of its time, a time when the future was someplace I really wanted to go, full of sleek machines and flights to Mars.

After that was a midway with the usual hot dog stands and skill games. There weren't more than twenty other people on the whole length of it. Behind the popcorn and frying grease I could smell the real ocean, salt and fog and decay.

We rode miniature cars on the Ocean Freeway and I went along with him on the cable car, despite my fear of heights. It took us out over the ocean and all the way out to Mystery Island, a pocket Adventureland with thatched huts and palm trees and a miniature train. Then I stupidly agreed to try Mr. Dolphin, a ninety-foot-high tower with enclosed cars on the end of rotating arms that spun out over the park. I knew right away it was a mistake when I felt my stomach lurch and my vision close down and my head start to pound. There was nothing to do except ride it out and when it was over I had to sit on a bench for a while.

"Hey, man, are you okay?" Brian asked.

"Not really. I never could handle rides like that. Christ, I used to get carsick when I was a kid, every time the road started to curve."

"You should have said something."

"I haven't been on one since I was a kid. I didn't know it would get to me this bad. Now I've screwed up your day. I really feel lousy." I wanted to cry.

"It doesn't matter."

"Yeah it does. I feel like such a sissy."

Brian was quiet for a minute, and then he said. "Your dad used to yell at you for it, didn't he? Even though you couldn't help it."

"Yeah. At least twice I threw up down the back of his neck while he was driving." Brian thought that was really funny. "I don't know why I couldn't just throw up on the back seat," I said. "I would feel it coming and I would stand up and try to say something and then it was too late."

"Is your dad still around?"

"He died a few months ago."

"Wow, man, I'm really sorry."

"Don't be. If I'm not, you shouldn't be."

"You shouldn't talk like that about your old man. I mean, he was your father."

"Come on, Brian. Everybody knows your father treats you like shit."

Brian got up. "You think you could eat something?"

I could see I'd gone too far. I didn't know how to apologize. "I could try."

We got pizza and beer from Joseph Primavera's stand, the guy who claimed to have single-handedly started the pizza craze in the States. We sat down at a table and Brian looked at his paper cup full of beer and said, "To this day, I can't stand to drink out of a glass. A paper cup like this is okay, that you can't see through, you know, but out of a bottle would be better. A clear glass, it just, it makes me want to puke.

It's because when I was a kid I went in the bedroom and saw my old man's glass eye, he had it in a water glass next to the bed while he was sleeping. He used to terrorize me with the goddamn thing."

After a while he said, "Marilyn and I want to have kids. I guess you already know if we do or not, right?" I didn't say anything. "I'm scared. I'm worried about what kind of father I would be. You know, that whole 'When I Grow Up to Be a Man' thing."

"You don't have to be like your father," I said, though Brian would eventually admit he had failed his kids, would go for years without talking to them. The only consolation was, I'd heard the grown-up Brian Wilson was genuinely proud of their musical careers and was able to say it in public. "Your dad didn't like *Pet Sounds*, did he?"

"Hated it. Said I still didn't know how to write a popular song. But I didn't write *Pet Sounds* to be popular, I wrote it to, you know, find a way to touch people."

"And if you could just get *Smile* completely perfect, then he'd have to see, right? He'd have to admit you know what you're doing."

Brian looked down at his pizza. "Pretty stupid, huh? I guess I do feel like that."

"You can't change him, Brian. You're beating your head against a wall."

"That's easy to say. He's still my old man. He's not going to disappear." He suddenly stopped and turned his good ear, the left one, toward me. "You hear that?"

"What?"

"The sea gulls. That's what I'm talking about, don't you see? All the emotion in that sound. It sounds so lonely all by itself you don't have to say anything else. You see what I mean? The lyrics can be about anything at all, but if you put that sound in there, everybody will know what you really mean. If I could only . . ." He made a fist with his right hand and rocked, almost imperceptibly, back and forth.

I said, "I don't know how long I can stay here. I just sort of appeared in front of your house. I could lose it any minute. I would really like, before that happens, to see you in the studio."

"You mean, like, put a session together? Get the Wrecking Crew in there?" The Wrecking Crew was what the top L.A. session musicians called themselves: Hal Blaine on drums, Tommy Tedesco and Glen Campbell on guitars, Carol Kaye or Ray Pohlman on bass, Leon

Russell and Larry Knechtel on piano. The older session players hated them for doing rock and roll, said they were wrecking the business.

"You've got basic tracks. I want to hear you finish something." Do it for me, I wanted to say. In 1966 Brian's father would have been forty-nine, just ten years older than me. Let me be your father just for today, let me give you the chance to hear somebody tell you how good this stuff is.

Brian finished his beer and wiped his mouth with the back of his hand. "Okay, you want to see the studio, we can go by there. I'll play you some of the tracks. But I can't work if I don't feel it, you understand?"

═══════

The driver took us back to Sunset through light rain. The radio played "Ain't Gonna Lie" by Keith and "Coming On Strong" by Brenda Lee. I'd started to feel shaky. I couldn't tell if I'd actually heard those songs before or if they just sounded familiar, the way any good pop record is supposed to sound the first time you hear it.

We parked in a driveway next to Western Studios. I followed Brian through the smoked-glass front doors into a reception area that was closed down. "Where is everybody?" I said.

"There's another studio down the street, United, same people own both of them. They've got a receptionist and everything there."

We turned right, then left down a long hallway. There was a young guy there in a white shirt and dark slacks, carrying a clipboard. "Hey, Brian," he said nervously. "You didn't, like, have Studio Three booked or anything did you?"

"No, it was just an impulse kind of thing."

"Okay, well, because Bones has the Turtles in there, and, you know, I guess I could . . ."

"I just wanted to listen to some stuff."

"You could have Studio Four."

Brian looked like he was about to have a temper tantrum. I couldn't tell if he was kidding, or it really made him that mad not to have the studio he wanted any time he wanted it. Maybe Brian wasn't sure if he was really mad himself.

The guy with the clipboard unlocked the vault, which was just an air-conditioned room lined with steel shelves. There were labels on the shelves with the names of record companies. Over the Capitol label was a big stack of Scotch quarter-inch tape boxes. Lettering ran vertically down the side of the box: a three-digit number, then a one-digit number, then BEACH BOYS, then sometimes an album title. Some were labeled SMILE and some DUMB ANGEL. Brian grabbed a handful of boxes and carried them into the control room of Studio 4.

I could see the studio itself through the glass: walnut paneling, a carpet stained from years of beer and Coca-Cola. A couple of people at most could squeeze in there for vocals or overdubs. There was a music stand, and a guitar baffle covered in ugly light-green fabric. There were quilted movers' blankets on the floor and more of them thrown in the corner.

Brian put on a pair of black-framed reading glasses and threaded one of the tapes. It was "George Fell into His French Horn." As the liner notes on one of my bootlegs say, it's the answer to a trivia question: what Beach Boys song contains the lyric "stick your horn up your ass and shove it"? It also features laughing brass and session musicians talking through their mouthpieces, sounding like muffled Stan Freberg. It was definitely the single weirdest thing I'd heard from the *Smile* sessions.

As soon as it was finished Brian was going to ask what I thought. I remembered all the stories I'd heard about how he'd scrap entire songs when people weren't enthusiastic enough. Why couldn't he have played me "Wonderful" or "Surf's Up"? Why did he have to play the one song that was genuinely crazy?

It went on for more than five minutes. Finally the tape ran out and Brian said, "Well?"

"I really like the part with the horns laughing. I mean, it does just what you said, it makes you smile."

"And the rest of it?"

He didn't seem to be freaking out. "I'm not sure exactly. It's hard to see where it fits into the whole album."

"That's the thing, see." He spun around in his chair. The glasses somehow made him look younger instead of older, like they were only for pretend. "I don't know where it fits in. You know what Desputols are? They're speed. I've been taking handfuls of them. I get all these great ideas, only they don't really fit together. One day I think I've got it, the next day I've got a better idea. The ideas just come so *fast*." He stopped spinning and his eyes went out of focus. "Sometimes the whole thing feels like it's out of control."

"Maybe you could split it up," I said. "Like the horns are an audience for the rest of the album."

"Oh wow," Brian said. "That's really cool."

Sure it is, I thought, realizing I'd stolen the idea from *Sgt. Pepper*.

Brian said, "Let's nip outside for a smoke."

I recognized two of the guys in the hallway. They were Howard Kaylan and Mark Volman, lead singers of the Turtles, who would later tour with Zappa, and on their own, as Flo and Eddie. Howard would end up as Graham's silent partner in Carnival Dog Records. His hair was still black and he was fairly slim and clean-shaven. Mark's hair was all over the place and he was heavy, though not like he would be in a few years. They were both in Hawaiian shirts and jeans. Howard shook his finger at Brian. "Naughty naughty, Mr. Wilson. I know that fiendish look in your eye. You're headed for the alley with some of that mind-altering substance. You shouldn't be doing that, you know. Not without us you shouldn't."

We slipped out to the alley and everybody got stoned. Mark talked about the mixdown they'd just done for "Can I Get to Know You Better," which they hoped to hell would be a hit. "Everything since 'You Baby' has stiffed. It's desperate, man, we got to do something."

Brian said, "I don't care about hits anymore. I want to do albums."

"Easy for you to say," Mark said. " 'Good Vibrations' is number two in the fucking country.

"Number one come Friday," Brian said. He looked at me and winked. "Wait and see. Right, Ray?"

"Anything you say, Brian." It was true. I would have done anything for him at that moment, jumped off a cliff if he'd asked me to. It could have been the hash but I don't think so.

We ended up at a party in Bel Air that Mark knew about. Lou Adler was there, and John and Michelle Phillips. I wandered into a paneled den where joints were going around. It felt like high school again, me out of place and a little desperate, too self-conscious to do anything but nod and smile to the beautiful blonde with the ironed hair ahead of me in the circle. At one point she took my left hand and flirtatiously pretended to look at my wedding ring. "Married," she said. "Too bad."

"Not really," I said. I took the ring off and put it in my pocket. Elizabeth was somewhere else, in another reality, and it had been a long, long time. "I was just keeping it for somebody."

She laughed and shook her head. "Nice try. Married guys will say anything to score. When it comes down to it, you always end up protecting your marriage."

Jim Morrison would have known what to do. He would have swaggered and smoldered until he got his way, then he would have gone cold and pulled his leathers on and walked off into the night. Me, I said, "But I'm not married. Not really."

"Right," she said, and laughed and turned away.

The dope was weak, compared to what would be around in twenty years. I remember thinking it wasn't doing anything to me, shortly before I passed out in one of the bedrooms under a pile of coats.

When I came to it was four in the morning. The house was dead quiet. It occurred to me that Brian could have gone home without me. No reason not to, he didn't owe me anything. I wandered down a long shag-carpeted hall to the living room, with its plaid Early American furniture, its console TV with the nearly circular picture tube, its rows of empty beer cans and overflowing ashtrays. There was only a single lamp lit. I didn't recognize the woman asleep on the couch, though she was pretty enough to have been an actress. Abandoned here like the other empties.

I went back down the hall. Three of the four bedrooms were occupied, one by a couple thrashing drunkenly under the covers. None of them had bothered to close the door. I didn't see Brian.

I found my way outside. There was a moon, and a few stars had burned their way through the haze. The grass had gone white with tiny droplets of mist. Somewhere in the distance a big diesel rig sounded its air horn as it passed. I wondered what I was going to do. Go back into the bedroom with the coats, maybe, sleep it off. Walk or hitch to Brian's in the morning and hope Marilyn would let me in.

I felt impossibly far from home. I wondered what was happening in 1989, if my body was still there, if the police were searching for me. I wondered what I would do if I never made it back. I wondered if I woke up the woman on the couch if she would let me hold her for a while, just until the sun came up. I started to shiver and I thought I might be close to coming apart.

There was a hand on my shoulder. I turned around and it was Brian. "Hey, Ray," he said. His eyes shone. "I been trying to find you, man, where'd you go?"

I shrugged. Even though he was tripping like a bastard he'd still been looking for me. I was so glad to see him it made my throat tight and my eyes hurt.

"I been thinking about all the stuff you said to me," Brian said. "About my father and the album and all. And it's like . . . it's all so clear. It all fits together so perfect. God is in the music, man, and God *is* the Father, you see? It's so fucking simple, so beautiful, man."

"Anything you say, Brian. I think the car is over this way."

He left his hand on my shoulder and we staggered off together.

At one the next afternoon I was wandering around Brian's house, needing to borrow some clothes or at least get a ride into town to buy some. I was about to walk into the kitchen when I heard voices and held up.

The first one belonged to David Anderle. ". . . is this guy? I mean, what does he want?"

Brian said, "He wants me to finish the album. Same as everybody else does. Only he's got good ideas and he doesn't think I'm crazy."

"That's great," Anderle said. "Some nut case walks in off the street and as long as he tells you what you want to hear, you trust him totally."

"I've got a good feeling about him."

"Shit, Brian."

"Give me till Friday. Wait and see if 'Good Vibrations' goes number one."

"Of course it's going to go number one. It doesn't take a psychic to figure that out. It's a brilliant goddamn song."

I knocked quietly on the doorframe. Anderle and Brian were sitting at the table with Marilyn and a guy I thought might be Jules Siegel, the music critic for the *Saturday Evening Post* who had come to interview Brian and become part of the entourage. Anderle turned, saw me, and looked away.

"Come on in," Brian said. He had a can of Reddi Wip and every few seconds he would uneasily squirt a dab onto his tongue. I sat down at the kitchen table, not knowing what to do. Marilyn brought me a cup of coffee and I smiled at her with spaniel-like gratitude. I felt guilty because Anderle didn't trust me, as if his opinion was more important than my own.

Anderle said, "I think you need to get the rest of the guys in tonight, listen to the tapes, talk about finishing them up. What do you think?"

Brian looked at me. I looked at the coffee cup. Brian said, "There's still some stuff I want to . . ."

"There's always going to be stuff you want to do." He clearly didn't like the way that sounded. "This isn't anything final, just a kind of strategy session, a chance to get everybody rolling behind the album."

"I don't know . . ."

"Brian, you've got to do it sometime. Sooner or later they've got to hear what you're up to."

I wanted Brian to stop looking at me. "He's right," I said. "You can't keep them away forever. You might as well get it over with."

"Okay," Brian said.

"About eight? Here?"

"Okay."

"I'll stop by the studio and get the rough mixes."

"I'll do it. You'd never figure out what was what."

"Brian . . ."

"I swear, I'll do it."

"Let's go now, then. Both of us."

Brian nodded. "Okay."

I felt Anderle's weariness. He'd been pushing Brian uphill much longer than me, had sat through every kind of craziness along the way, had rolled around on the floor of the studio grunting like an animal, had played his dinner plate with his silverware. He turned to me and said, "Can I talk to you for a minute?"

"Sure."

I followed him out to the front driveway.

"I don't know what you're up to," he said, "or what you want from Brian. But if you hurt him, I . . ." He shrugged and looked like he wanted to cry. "He's just a big kid, for God's sake. He's a genius, a sweet, generous, crazy genius and the world needs the music he's got inside him. I can't threaten you, I don't do that kind of thing. All I can do is beg you, don't fuck this up."

"I don't want to fuck it up. I want the record as much as you do. I know that's hard for you to believe, but it's true."

"Will you tell me who you are?"

"My name is Ray Shackleford. I come from Austin, Texas. I fix stereos."

Anderle walked away. He had both hands in the air, turning them, like he wanted to find something to hold on to. "Jesus Christ," he said. "Jesus Christ."

He got something out of the trunk of his car and came back up the sidewalk. It was a fancy shopping bag from the Broadway department store. "Brian said to bring you some clothes, said you were about my size. I hope they fit."

"Thanks," I said, stunned.

"Don't mention it." He started back toward his car. "Please. Don't ever mention it. And if you see Brian, tell him to hurry up."

<hr>

I showered and put on clean clothes for the first time in days. I sat in my room and looked out at the city until Brian got back, and then we played pinball all afternoon. He wouldn't talk about the album. I could see how nervous he was by how much he ate. At seven he sent Marilyn off in the Rolls to get hamburgers from Dolores' Drive-In. Mike Love showed up at seven-thirty.

I had always pictured him as small because Brian was so much taller, but he was my height, over six feet. He and Brian hugged and it was obvious that whatever else was wrong between them, they were still family and Mike really cared about him. Marilyn came in with the food and we all ate at the kitchen table. Mike and Brian made stupid puns through the entire meal and ended up throwing french fries at each other.

Al Jardine and Carl showed up together just before eight, with

Anderle right behind. Carl was baby-faced and heavy, only nineteen and a year out of high school. Bruce Johnston, who replaced Brian in the touring band, rang the doorbell at eight o'clock sharp, ever the professional. By eight-fifteen Van Dyke and Durry Parks were there and everybody decided not to wait for Dennis.

Brian herded us all into the dining room. There was a massive Spanish table there, big enough to seat twenty. He'd had headphone jacks installed into the edge of the table and there were headphones like place settings in front of ten of the chairs. Marilyn brought out beer and cokes and coffee.

Once we were settled Brian started the tape. First it was "Do Ya Dig Worms" with the chant, "Rock, rock, roll, Plymouth Rock roll over." It went from that into the bicycle rider theme, then a weird kind of Hawaiian chant, punctuated with kettledrums. I started to feel like I did in the studio when I listened to "George Fell into His French Horn," only worse. The album seemed totally crazy. There was no way it would work. I looked at Mike Love. His face was completely rigid, expressionless.

Brian put on "Cabinessence" which, at least, had a more obvious melody. Not that it mattered. I already knew what was about to happen. Mike took a ballpoint pen out of his shirt pocket and made notes on a napkin. By halfway through "Surf's Up" he was shaking his head. Brian saw it and jumped up and shut off the tape.

We all took off our headphones.

"Mike?" Brian said. "Is something wrong?"

Mike took a second or two to get cranked up, then he let fly. "What is this shit? It's crazy. Why can't you write songs like you used to?"

Brian said, "Cars and girls and surfing."

"What's wrong with that? It's what people want to hear. You don't need other people to write lyrics for you that nobody can understand." I saw Van Dyke flinch; Mike acted like he wasn't there. "You're going to blow it, Brian. Stick to the old stuff. Don't fuck with the formula."

"I like those lyrics," Brian said. He said it with a hesitant defiance, like he expected Mike to jump over the table and hit him for it. I suddenly thought of Jim Morrison and police nightsticks, of me facing my father.

Mike looked down at his napkin. " 'Crow cries uncover the cornfield'? Those are the lyrics you like? What the hell is 'crow cries uncover the cornfield' supposed to mean?"

He looked up at Brian, who didn't answer him, then back at the napkin. "How about this one? 'Colonnaded ruins domino.' You want to tell me what you love about that line?"

"Columnated," Van Dyke said.

He finally looked at Van Dyke. " 'Columnated'? What the hell kind of word is 'columnated'? Would you care to explain this song to me?"

"I have no excuse, sir," Van Dyke said.

"Just tell me what the hell the song is supposed to be about."

"I don't know what the songs are about. They're about whatever you feel when you listen to them." Over by the tape machine Brian nodded.

"What I feel is a headache. How am I supposed to sing lyrics nobody understands? This is gibberish, and it's going to destroy the group."

Van Dyke stood up. Durry looked at him with alarm. At that point Dennis strolled in with a lit joint in one hand and an open beer in the other. His hair was past his collar and his eyes were bloodshot. He wore a pink T-shirt, jeans, and no shoes. From what I'd read I'd expected him to be damaged goods, mindless and out of control. Instead he projected a kind of innocence and vulnerability. Which was maybe why women found him so hard to resist. "Hey everybody," he said. "What's happening?"

Van Dyke said, "I guess I'm just leaving." He stood behind Durry's chair while she got up. He looked at Brian and Brian wouldn't meet his eyes. Van Dyke and Durry went out and I heard the front door slam.

Dennis looked confused. "Something wrong?" He nodded to Brian. "Hey, Bri. This the new record?"

Brian nodded. Dennis took a chair and said, "What are we waiting for? Let's hear the goddamned thing." He put the headphones on and Brian restarted the tape. Nobody else made a move for their headphones. We all just looked at each other. Dennis bobbed his head to the music, completely unselfconscious. Then he leaned back in the chair and closed his eyes. After a minute or so I saw a tear run down his face.

The tape ran out and clattered around the end of the reel. Dennis took his headphones off and said, "It's fucking brilliant, Bri. No shit."

Mike looked at him with disgust, then turned on Brian again. "Have you played any of this garbage for Capitol?"

Anderle cleared his throat. "We've got that lawsuit with Capitol. They don't get to hear anything until that's settled."

Mike gave Anderle a look. It said Anderle was not family and his contribution was not desired. Back to Brian. "Capitol won't like it any better than I do. I'll fucking guarantee it. You can't put any of this shit on the radio." He sighed, tried to look reasonable. "Look, I'm the one out front that has to sell this to an audience. I know what those kids want to hear. I know it because I'm actually out there, day after day, while you're cooped up here with your dope and your weird ideas. The kids love those old songs, cars and girls and surfing and good times. Nobody else can give that to them the way we can. Haven't you got anything for *them*? Another 'Good Vibrations,' even?"

Brian flipped the hair out of his eyes. He looked like a schoolkid in the principal's office: scared, hurt, defiant. "I guess not."

Mike got up. "I guess not," he repeated. He started out the door.

"Hey, Mike," Dennis said.

Mike turned around.

Dennis held up his middle finger. "Fuck you, man."

Mike started for him. Al Jardine jumped up and grabbed him around the waist. It slowed him down long enough for Bruce Johnston to step in and help. "Come on, man," Al said. "Leave it."

I looked at Anderle. His head rested in his right hand, fatigue and despair all over his face.

———

It was just me and Brian in the swimming pool at midnight. Everybody else was afraid to talk to him. I was a little worried myself. I'd seen him pout but I hadn't had the full-fledged temper tantrum yet.

It turned out he got calm as soon as he was in the water. "It was just like you told me it would be," he said. "Like, word for word."

"I didn't want to see this happen."

"I know. I know." Brian held up his right hand. It was shaking. "I'm really scared, man. You're from the future, right? In the future there is no *Smile* album, because of all the shit that went down tonight."

"Yeah, basically."

I could see him struggle with the ideas. "So what you want is for me to change the future, which has to mean that you don't like it the way it is. If I change the future, then what happens? Anything could happen. Anything. Nuclear war. The end of the world. I might die. Or Carl, or Dennis."

I didn't say that Dennis was already doomed. He would drown in the Marina Del Rey harbor, December 1983, seventeen years away. "You have to take that chance."

"You're saying make the album anyway. Not a Beach Boys album, a Brian Wilson album."

"Like 'Caroline, No.' You put that out as a Brian Wilson record."

"Yeah, and it died. I'm scared, man. You're telling me to give up my family."

"You don't have to give up Carl and Dennis. They love you. I think they'll stick with you."

"Even if it breaks up the band?"

"It wouldn't have to. The band can go on without you. Carl can produce. They can use outside songwriters. They'll manage."

"IdontknowIdontknowIdontknowIdontknowIdontknow." He leaned forward and fell face first into the water, arms straight against his sides. The force of it took him down a foot or so, then he floated back to the surface and just lay there.

"Brian?" He wasn't moving. I knew he was only kidding around but that image, the body facedown in the water, burned holes in my guts. "Brian?" I grabbed his arm and yanked it hard.

He pulled his head up and shook the water out of his hair. "Easy, man, I was just fooling."

I went over to lean against the side of the pool. "It's . . . my father drowned. That's how he died."

"Hey, man, I'm really sorry."

"It's okay. It's not your fault. It's not anybody's fault." I thought about that for a second, then I said, "That's not true. It's our fathers' faults. They've got us both fucked up. This whole thing tonight, this is about your father, not about the Beach Boys."

Brian looked at me.

"Your father has you convinced that nothing you do will ever be good enough. So when Mike tells you *Smile* is no good, you believe him. You're afraid to leave the band because the band is all the family you've got. It would be like leaving your father. You have to get out from under that. You have to believe in your own talent."

"That whole 'Brian is a genius' thing? That's hard to live up to, you know? You start asking yourself, everything you do, is this up to snuff? Is this genius-level work, here? I don't know if I can handle that."

He had the spoiled, whiny kid look on his face again. I saw then that it was just another way for him to hide. "Cut the shit, Brian," I said, while part of me stood back thinking, you just told Brian Wilson to what? "You know what I'm saying. You know how important *Smile* is. You can't just let it die."

"I'm cold," Brian said. "I want to go inside."

"Fine. Let's go for a ride. I'll tell you about the future."

━━━━━

Brian drove the XKE over the hills into the San Fernando Valley. The Valley reminds me of central Arizona, where I spent third through sixth grade playing in brush-covered hills like these. The moon was out, and a few of the brighter stars.

"They'll close POP inside two years," I told Brian, remembering the stuff from Graham's scrapbook. "Then they won't have the money to knock it down. Winos and junkies will move in. There'll be a fire. The place turns into a public eyesore. It's 1974 before they ever tear it down."

"Why are you telling me this?"

"They don't make many records anymore. Everything is either cassettes or these new things called compact discs, or CDs. They're about this big around and you play them on a kind of computer. It's perfect reproduction. In 1989 Capitol will finally release their entire Beach Boys catalog on CD. They're making a really big deal out of *Pet Sounds*, your masterpiece. Because after that the Beach Boys went to shit. There's some okay albums and the occasional good song, mostly a lot of aimless crap. No more masterpieces. Not ever. Because you decided to go with your family instead of your music and you knew it was wrong, and knowing it was wrong made you crazy and you couldn't work at all anymore.

"In 1989 there's a kind of sexually contagious cancer called AIDS. That was the last straw for free love. All the rest of the stuff that seemed like a good idea in the sixties, like feeding the world and loving your brothers and sisters, has gone out the window because it costs too much money. We got out of Vietnam but we still have wars because they're good for the economy. Money is all anybody cares about. There's a revolution happening in Eastern Europe, not over idealism but because people there think it will get them cars and TV sets and the good life. For twenty years kids have been listening to this music they call heavy metal, this real ponderous stuff with lots of distorted guitars and posturing and black leather and lyrics about death."

Brian pulled over to the curb. I didn't look at him. I was on a roll. "There's a hole in the ozone layer that lets in ultraviolet radiation. You can't lie in the sun unprotected anymore without getting skin cancer. Oil tankers are spilling oil all over the world's beaches anyway, and nobody stops them because we don't want to give up our cars. Which create so much pollution that the carbon dioxide in the air is holding in heat, turning the whole planet into a greenhouse. The polar ice caps are starting to melt—"

"Stop it," Brian said.

I finally looked over at him. He was crying now, not some put-on, spoiled child act, really crying, in complete silence, tears running down his face.

"Why are you doing this to me? What do you want from me?"

"The album, Brian. I want you to make the goddamned album."

———

He woke me at eleven the next morning. "Capitol Records just called. Somebody at *Billboard* told them 'Good Vibrations' will be number one tomorrow."

"Congratulations," I said sleepily.

"So what are you waiting for? Get up, get dressed. The studio's booked, I've got everybody on their way. Let's go."

He stood there, shifting his not inconsiderable weight from foot to foot while I dressed and brushed my teeth. He was humming something I'd never heard before.

The driver was waiting with the Rolls to take us down to Western Studios. "What should I do today?" Brian asked me.

"It has to be your album, not mine."

"I don't know what I want. I've got feels for a bunch of things I haven't done much with." "Feels" were what Brian called his basic musical ideas for songs, scraps of melody or chord progressions. "There's 'Look,' 'You're Welcome,' 'I Ran,' 'I Don't Know' . . ."

"What was that you were whistling this morning?"

" 'I'm in Great Shape.' "

I tried not to show any reaction. It's a song that's listed on the album jackets that Capitol printed for *Smile*; otherwise there's no remaining evidence of it. I hadn't even heard of the titles of the other songs he'd just rattled off at me.

"Okay," Brian said. "I've got basics for it somewhere, but who cares? We'll do it fresh."

The Wrecking Crew was already in Studio 3, Brian's favorite. Marilyn's sister Diane, who did the hiring and the booking, met us in the hall wearing a short knit dress, her dark hair tied back in pigtails with orange yarn. "We've got everybody here," she said.

She reached out to fuss with a loose thread on Brian's sweater. It was a wifely, almost a motherly, thing to do.

We went in. There were maybe a dozen people already packed into a studio that could barely hold all of their equipment. Most of them seemed to have cigarettes lit. I recognized Hal Blaine, one of my all time heroes, and Tommy Tedesco who would go on to write a lot of guitar columns in the eighties. Blaine was the first drummer I learned to identify by ear, back when I was in high school. I saw his trap set in the corner and I have to say it made my heart beat a little fast.

They were all happy to see Brian. It was sincere, not like the boss had just walked in. Within ten minutes he had them all in their places and learning the song. He would either sing them their parts or play them on the piano. Tommy Tedesco had a tough time with the guitar part, shaking his head, even when he finally got it the way Brian wanted it.

"Brian, that sounds like shit," he said.

"Trust me, you'll see."

They did a take. Sitting there in the studio the balance of the instruments was all wrong and I could hear too many overtones on the drums. But the playback sounded wonderful, all but the guitar.

"Did you hear that, Brian?" Tedesco said.

"Perfect," Brian said.

"It sounds like shit."

"Trust me," Brian said.

It's like he had on a Walkman and was trying to get the band to play along with what he heard. He knew where every note was supposed to go without writing anything down. He could sing what any given instrument was supposed to play at any given part of the song without having to think about it. While the tape was running he conducted with both hands, as if he could sculpt the music while it hung in the air.

I can't remember ever being happier in my life than I was there, watching Hal Blaine and listening to the rest of the band play a brand-new Brian Wilson song. Everything Blaine did was surgically precise: timing, tonality, dynamics, everything. The whole time he was making goofy faces or had a cigarette hanging out of the corner of his mouth.

Brian got a take he was happy with and went immediately into overdubs. Tedesco was still unhappy about the guitar part. They laid down the overdubs and played it back while Brian sang the melody he'd been whistling that morning. Suddenly the guitar part was perfect, inevitable. Nothing else could possibly have worked.

"See?" Brian said to Tedesco, who had his hands in the air, shaking his head and grinning. "See?" You couldn't miss the energy that sparked through Brian's entire body. It was bigger than he was. He put a rough mix of "I'm in Great Shape" on acetate and sent the Wrecking Crew home. I helped carry of couple of Blaine's tom cases and got to shake his hand. I thought Brian would be ready to go too. Instead he sat at the piano and recorded a beautiful solo piano part that almost sounded like New Age music, or Brian Eno. When it was done he told me it was the "Air" section of the Elements suite.

"What about 'Wind Chimes'?"

"How'd you know about that?"

"Everybody thought that was supposed to be 'Air.' "

He seemed to look through me for a minute, like he could see all those people in the future looking back at him. "No, man, 'Wind Chimes' is like its own song."

At two in the morning, in the back of the Rolls, he smoked a huge ball of hash to celebrate. He was still bubbling over with excitement. "I feel good about this," he said. "I can feel it coming together. The mixes Mike heard were still rough, it wasn't polished like 'Good Vibrations' was in the end."

He was back to the band, fighting to keep his hopes alive. I didn't have the heart to knock him down. "Maybe you should go ahead and get some finished mixes," I said carefully, "with all the vocals on there. Use Dennis and Carl if you want, but get everything completely done. Then if Mike wants to get involved you can always record him over the parts you have. Right?"

"Right," Brian said. "Yeah, okay."

"Listen, do we have to go straight home?"

"No, man, where do you want to go?"

I had the driver take us to Santa Monica. We took Sunset all the way, and I watched out the right-hand window as we passed the block with the Whiskey a Go Go, the London Fog, and Hamburger Hamlet. The Doors had just moved up to the Whiskey and their name was there on the marquee, second to the Buffalo Springfield. The show was over and kids were pouring out onto the already crowded Strip. I saw somebody out of the corner of my eye, on the roof of a car on Clark Street, screaming at the moon. It looked like Morrison, but I'll never know for sure.

I rolled down the window, smelling history in the air, and it smelled like dope and buckskin, incense and perfume. The Strip was drawing disaffected kids, runaways and musicians, dealers and groupies by the thousands, the way San Francisco's Haight would draw them the next summer. The sidewalks were literally teeming. For the last month there had been riots every weekend over a 10 P.M. curfew that was designed to keep the kids away and let developers take over the Strip. The focus was a coffee house called Pandora's Box, and the cops had been brought in by the busload, swinging nightsticks and firing tear gas. We'd already passed Pandora's Box back at Crescent Heights, closed and on its way to becoming a traffic island.

It was the start of something. The riots sparked Stephen Stills to write "For What It's Worth" and within a month it would be on the radio. Like the song said, the battle lines were drawn now, with the cops and developers and store owners on one side, the *Free Press* and the musicians and the kids on the other. The cops would back off and the curfew would end and the riots would die down, but from now on everyone knew this was war.

I wanted to shout at them to cool out, to love each other, not to let the lizard-things inside them run wild. Then I thought, maybe *Smile* will do that. Maybe Brian has already done it for me.

We wound our way through the foothills to Santa Monica. I got out on Ocean Avenue near the spot where, in twenty-two years and a few months, I would puke my guts out. The thing that had made me sick, the part of me that wanted to curl up with strange starlets on somebody else's couch, was calmer now.

Brian and I sat in the damp grass. There were a couple of proto-hippies out as well, a girl with long ironed hair and a boy with bangs and glasses and a black turtleneck sweater.

"It's really going to happen, isn't it?" I said.

"The album?" Brian seemed blissful. "Yeah. I guess it was kind of floundering there. Maybe I needed a kick in the ass. Now I know I can get a tape to Capitol for Christmas. With that tape at stake, man, I bet they settle that lawsuit on the spot."

Not if they don't like the tape, I thought. I couldn't understand why I wasn't happier. Brian was going to finish *Smile* and I was there to see it. Hell, it would be due to me. Maybe it actually would change the world. Maybe, if and when I ever got back to 1989, the world would be a better place. Maybe Elizabeth and I would be in love the way we were at first. Maybe Alex and I never broke up.

I was blindsided by a sudden rush of emotion. I lay on my back and crushed blades of grass between my fingertips. Waves of change ran out from me in all directions, shifting the universe, and I was suddenly terrified. I didn't want to be responsible. If Elizabeth had never existed, if I had Alex back, would it make any difference?

"You doing okay, man?" Brian asked.

"Sure," I said. My throat was closed up and it was all I could get out.

"Listen, I was thinking. Are you tired?"

"No." He didn't seem to hear anything wrong with my voice. I opened my eyes wide and let the night air burn into them. Brian was carried away with the heat of his creation. I loved him anyway. I remembered his hand on my shoulder outside the party, bringing me back.

"Maybe we could like get a burger or something and go back to the studio. I'm really in the mood to work. I could do some vocals, do some mixes. What do you think?"

Say yes, I told myself. I got up on my elbows and nodded. "Great," I said.

"Are you sure you're okay?"

"Allergies," I said. "Let's go."

———

In the car I told Brian the joke about the guy who gets a flat tire in front of the insane asylum. While he's changing the tire, see, all the lug nuts roll away and fall into the storm drain. So the guy is standing there, trying to figure out what to do, when one of the inmates leans over the fence and says, "Why don't you take one lug off each of the other wheels and use them to hold the spare on till you can get to a garage?"

So the guy says, "Wow, that's really a great idea, I mean, for a guy who's, well, you know . . ."

And the inmate says, "I may be crazy, mister, but I'm not stupid."

I like the punch line even better in Spanish, the way I first heard it: "*Estoy aquí por loco, no por pendejo.*"

Brian loved it, especially the Spanish, which he made me repeat three times, until he had it perfect.

———

It took Brian six days to finish *Smile*, like Jehovah in the Old Testament.

I watched it come together and I saw why nobody else could have reconstructed it from the tapes in the vaults. It was like the Tommy Tedesco guitar part. Nobody but Brian knew what the missing pieces were, and the missing pieces changed everything.

He worked all day and all night. We would sleep five or six hours in the morning and then go back to it. He delegated what he could and then put all the pieces together. I was in charge of sound effects. At four one morning I got caught holding a microphone to a fountain in somebody's front yard in Bel Air. The cops called the studio and Brian somehow kept me out of jail. I taped myself digging a hole in Brian's back yard and riding a bicycle with a playing card that rattled against the spokes. I went out for hamburgers and bags of produce. That's me biting the celery on "Vegetables," a part played by Paul McCartney in another version of history, the one that ends up with *Smiley Smile.*

The biggest thing I did was keep Brian away from Mike Love. At least fifteen times Brian wanted to play something for him, and every time I convinced him to wait just a little longer, to wait for that finished master.

He wrapped up the last vocals at 11 P.M. on December 7, a final touch-up on something called "Grand Canyon," which had ended up being the "Earth" section of the Elements suite. He mixed it down, spliced it into his test reel, then ran us out of the studio so he could listen to the whole album by himself. It was me, David Anderle, Diane Rovell, and Carl, in the hallway waiting.

"Capitol's not going to like it," Anderle said.

"Here's what you say," I told him. "You say, 'You guys may not sell a million units of this today. But you will eventually. You'll still be selling copies of this record in twenty years.' Then you should have Derek Taylor give an acetate to the Beatles. McCartney especially. Maybe he'll give you a quote you can use in publicity."

"A quote?" Anderle said. "Like on a book cover or something?"

"Why not? You have to market this as a work of genius, not a piece of disposable pop." I was wired, ecstatic. It was so close.

"It could work," Anderle said. "It might actually work."

Brian came out half an hour later. He was smiling.

═══════

We sat in the darkened studio. The fear that I'd felt that night in the park, sitting by Ocean Avenue, came back strong. I wanted the light on. I knew I couldn't ask Brian. It was his grand moment and I couldn't take that away from him.

The tape started. The sound of a pedaling bicycle (me), laughter (human), laughter (horns). A distant, tinkling foretaste of the bicycle rider theme, then into "Heroes and Villains." It's a full-blown comic opera, complete with legendary cantina scene, gunfights, and even, buried deep in the mix, Brian's voice saying *"Estoy aquí por loco, no por pendejo."*

Then into the "Barnyard" and "Do Ya Dig Worms" segment, "The Old Master Painter" and "You Are My Sunshine," on through "Cabin Essence" at the end of side one without a break. I couldn't tell if it was crazy or not. I was too close to it, somewhere deep inside the music, fitting it carefully into my head so I wouldn't lose a note of it, smiling and crying at the same time.

Brian's voice came over the intercom. "Side two," he said.

"Good Vibrations" led off. Instead of fading where the single did it went into a brief orchestral section which recapped the bicycle rider theme, slipped into a few seconds of "George Fell into His French Horn" and then segued, amid the laughter of horns, into "I'm in Great Shape." Then "Child Is Father of the Man," "Vegetables," and the Elements Suite proper: "Grand Canyon," "FreeFall," "Mrs. O'Leary's Cow," and "Love to Say Da-Da." Then, finally, "Surf's Up," complete with columnated ruins dominoing.

I knew "Surf's Up" would be the last song. It was the thing I'd been afraid of since the lights went out. With the first notes, spare and haunting, just piano and bass and Brian's voice, I started to shake. Like the version I knew, it built into a reprise of "Child Is Father of the Man" and then it went further, pulling everything in, the "ahhhs" from "Good Vibrations," the cellos from "Old Master Painter," the laughing horns, finally the "Bicycle Rider" theme and I knew it was over, all of it, not just the album but everything I'd come for.

The final notes of the harpsichord swelled instead of fading, kept getting louder and louder until they distorted, until I could feel the pressure of the sound in my ears. I didn't know if it was the tape or me. I couldn't see the lights from the booth. I thought I might have fallen onto the floor. I couldn't tell. I only knew that I'd found *Smile* and now it was me that was lost.

When I was a kid I used to have this hallucination. I would lie in the dark and see the fibers in my pillowcase getting bigger and bigger. It terrified me. I thought I was about to fall through the spaces between things, between the fibers, between the atoms. And now it had happened, I'd come loose and I was falling and there was nothing solid around me, my atoms were falling through the spaces between the atoms of the chair and the floor and everything was dark.

I wished I'd had the chance to say good-bye to Brian.

Somewhere someone said the word "Doctor."

It was dark because my eyes were closed. I opened them up.

I didn't have to say "where am I" because I was obviously in a hospital. I didn't have to ask "when" because Elizabeth and my mother were both there. I didn't have to ask if anything had changed because when Elizabeth looked at me there was relief and love but there was anger and sorrow in it too.

A nurse came in and picked up my wrist. It looked thin and there was a glucose drip stuck into it. "Welcome back," she said.

"Yeah," I said. "Right."

CHAPTER 5
CHAPTER 5
CHAPTER 5

In Transit

On the approach to Cozumel the plane comes around low to show off the reefs. The water is so clear it looks like there's something the matter with it, some kind of purple ooze on the surface. Then you blink your eyes and it clicks into place. The purple is submerged coral heads. The milky blue-green is where it's shallow over a sandy bottom. Out past the reef, where it gets sunset blue, that's the drop-off. Three or four hundred feet straight down, farther than a scuba tank can take you.

That's where my father bought it, there on the edge. I sat in the plane and looked at it, and after a couple of seconds I reached up to shut off the air-conditioning nozzle. I crossed my arms and felt goose bumps on the skin.

The guy in the next seat gave me a concerned look. I didn't want to talk about it. I've talked about it to Elizabeth and Graham, I even talked about it to Brian, and talk has gotten me nowhere.

My rent car sat on Laurel Way for two days before somebody called the cops. When they finally came to tow it off they found me sprawled across the floorboards, dehydrated, apparently in a coma. The rental papers had Graham's address on them, and he got me into a private room and sent for Elizabeth. She did the right thing and called my mother, though it meant a week of her apologies for being there. Then they both sat down to wait for me to live or die.

One doctor said alcohol poisoning. Another one thought maybe some kind of blood-sugar problem. Elizabeth was convinced it was a plain old-fashioned psychotic episode. Consequently I woke up to every test in the book, from glucose tolerance to Rorshachs and MMPI. The doctors found a guy pushing forty who drinks too much and doesn't get enough exercise or decent food. The shrinks didn't find anything at all, but then I've always been good at tests.

The first chance I got I phoned a record store and asked for *Smile*. The kid who answered was maybe sixteen and had to look it up in the *Phonolog*. "Not listed," he said.

I asked for a manager and got a woman who said, "I know the album you're looking for. I'm sorry, it never got made. It's kind of a musical holy grail."

So if I changed things, it wasn't in this world. Not yet.

As soon as the hospital let me go, Elizabeth booked us a flight to Austin. She convinced my mother that I would be okay without her. She was a little cold about it, but I let it go. I only managed a couple of minutes alone with Graham before we left, long enough to tell him that I'd found the album, that we'd do the tape when I was stronger.

When I first got home I slept twelve or fourteen hours a day. I couldn't stand the smell of beer and couldn't eat anything but eggs and turkey sandwiches and vanilla yogurt, just white food. I found myself crying a lot, not for any reason that I could understand. Nothing seemed real. It still doesn't. I've been taking long walks every day, three and four miles. I roam the neighborhood, watch the cars on 290. If the weather's nice I take my shirt off and work on my tan. Elizabeth hasn't mentioned getting pregnant again. We haven't made love, needless to say. It's like all of that never happened.

I spent a couple of late-night hours on the phone with Graham. *Celebration of the Lizard* was selling like crazy and he was hot for the follow-up. He'd got hold of one of the original insert booklets Capitol printed for *Smile* and he bootlegged the art for our CD. Everything was printed and he pushed me to come do the master tape. I tried to tell him about me and Brian, about the way Brian had changed me. All Graham could see was the music.

I keep coming back to my father. I've started to dream about him again. In one I'm trying to exercise, to do some sit-ups, and my father is standing on my chest. I hit his leg with my fist and he still won't get off. I ask my mother for a hammer so I can smash his leg with it. Then I realize this is the wrong approach and pull his sock down and try to tickle his foot, not playful at all but deadly serious. He then tries to tickle me with equal seriousness, and there is this contest of wills being fought in this totally ridiculous way.

The dream seemed obvious. Hating my father is not working and I have to find a less violent way to deal with him. That was when I started to think seriously about Cozumel.

I was an emotional basket case, and I knew the *Smile* tape would wring me out even more. One night toward the middle of April Elizabeth and I were eating in front of the TV. We had the doors and windows open and the air was full of honeysuckle and the sound of crickets. The news was about the Iran-Contra trial which had just started, and Abbie Hoffman's death which might have been suicide, and drug cult murders over the border in Matamoros. It all connected with the sixties in my mind, the way everything had gone to pieces since. Elizabeth was only eleven in 1968. How could I explain? I said, "I've been thinking about Cozumel. About us maybe going there."

Elizabeth looked at me in disbelief. "How am I supposed to find time to go to Cozumel?"

Something happened to me then. Up to that point I was a guy who wanted to work out some problems with his marriage. In the back of my mind was our honeymoon in Cozumel in 1979, right before we moved to Austin. Maybe I thought all that sun and sand could get something started again. But when Elizabeth looked at me that way I thought, this is not just another argument. This is serious and I want to be very careful. My heart started to pound. "Just for a week," I said. "We could do it next month, after school lets out." You have to try to meet me halfway on this, I thought. Just halfway.

"This is still about your father, isn't it? What are you trying to prove? What's in Cozumel that's going to change anything?"

It was like she wanted me to snap. I'd already decided this was not going to be my fault. "It's about us, too. Don't you think it would do us good to get away?"

"We can't afford it."

"I can pay for it out of Graham's money."

"I thought you'd spent that."

This wasn't about my going to L.A. to do another album. I wanted to stick to the issues. "There may be some more coming in."

She didn't move except to turn toward the TV, only it was like she was falling away, falling down the huge chasm between us. There was nothing I could say, nothing I could do to reach her. "I don't think I want to go to Mexico," she said.

"Well, that's it, then, isn't it?" And it was. Inside I was numb except for a clear, calm voice that said, as of now, this marriage is over. There's nothing left to hold on to. I should have told her then and there that I wanted a divorce but I didn't have the guts. I'd been biting my tongue too long.

I looked down at my plate of spaghetti. It had gone cold and inedible in a matter of seconds. I picked up a piece of it and put it down again. I'd cooked, so the dishes were Elizabeth's. I went upstairs and listened to *Pet Sounds* for a while, then I called the airlines and made some reservations. To L.A. first, then to Mexico. When it was done I felt giddy with relief.

———

The divemaster is named Tom Crane and he was at the airport to meet me. I recognized him from my mother's videotape. He looked perfect for the part: tan, weathered, calm. He had a beard and balding hair that were both trimmed short, thongs, white jeans, a blue *guayabera*. He pushed off from the wall and said, "Mr. Shackleford?"

Mr. Shackleford was my father, and he's dead. I said, "Just Ray. Please." We shook hands.

"I want you to know how sorry I am about . . . everything. We did all we could—"

"I know all that," I said. "I'm not down here to make trouble, I promise you."

Suddenly this thin woman in dark glasses was next to him. "Then why the hell *are* you down here? If you don't mind my asking?"

I hadn't realized they were together. "Sorry?" I said.

Crane rubbed his forehead. "This is Lori," he said. "My . . . assistant. She's worried about lawsuits and all that. I tried to tell her—"

"I've got no complaint with you guys," I said. "You were real good to my mom. I'll put it in writing if it'll make you feel better. I've got some personal stuff to work through, that's all."

I couldn't manage a smile. I was hung over from a celebration blow-out with Graham the night before. We'd finished the final mix on *Smile* and we were both pretty thrilled. I had a cassette copy in my suitcase along with my hand-held recorder, a portable CD player, and a bunch of CDs. You'd think I was down for a music convention.

She wouldn't have gone for the smile anyway. She projected this image of tough and impatient and not in the mood for my bullshit. Her clothes looked like they'd been thrown on in a hurry: a loose red cotton blouse, tucked here and there into cutoffs, and nothing else but rubber thongs. Hair reddish brown, almost to her shoulders, wavy and lighter at the ends from a perm that had grown out. She wasn't quite as tan as Crane and the sun had peeled her nose and left little lines at the ends of her mouth. I couldn't tell anything about her eyes just then because of her cheap red sunglasses.

Crane took my shoulder bag, which was full of CDs, and I asked about customs. "They don't really care," he said. "You could buy anything you want down here for half what it would cost in the States. Why smuggle it in?"

We got through the crowd into daylight. The sky was bright blue and there was a line of palm trees across the street. The breeze smelled of spice and dust and diesel, the essence of the tropics. At the curb was a red VW convertible with Cozumel Dive Surfari on the side. A kid of about seven sat on the hood. Crane gave him a dollar and he ran away without a word or a smile.

Lori said, "I'll get in back." Her red shirt fell open when she got in and I got a sudden, unexpected glimpse of her left breast, small and perfectly formed. I stood there with my hand on the door, unable to move. She obviously wished she'd never set eyes on me, and there I was, paralyzed with teenage longing.

"You coming?" Crane said.

I nodded and got in the car.

Crane has half a dozen cinder block guest rooms behind his shop which he rents out as part of the dive package. The walls are painted yellow inside and out and the bathroom floor is raw concrete with a drain in the middle. I thought it was fine. It was clean and the air conditioner blew cold when I turned it on. Crane gave me a key and told me to meet him next door when I was settled in.

I unpacked the CD player first and connected the pocket-size speakers. I put on Earth, Wind & Fire and hung up some clothes and then stretched out on the bed, which smelled faintly of mildew. I thought about taking a shower, which would leave nothing to do between dinner and bedtime. After a while I got up and put on a Hawaiian shirt to remind myself I was on vacation. I shut the music off and went outside.

The bar next door is a thatched-roof job with beat-up metal tables. Most of the paint is worn away, but you can make out the logos if you know what to look for: Tecate, Corona, Superior. The chairs are generic beige folding chairs, like the ones at Western Recording or TTG Studios, only rusted and caked with salt. I was surprised to see Lori in one of them. They had three of the tables pushed together. Tom was across from her and there were four other people in the group.

I sat down next to Tom and got introduced around. There was a young, athletic-looking couple who could have stepped out of a toothpaste ad. They are Pam and Richard and they work for Delta. He's a navigator and she's a stew. He had black-rimmed Ray Bans and an open shirt over Speedo trunks. She had long brown hair hanging down over one of those red one-piece suits that Elizabeth calls Barbie suits. Her nipples made bumps in the fabric, but not on my account.

There was a guy in his fifties with a salt-and-pepper beard, glasses, and thinning white hair. He was bare-chested and was sunburned everywhere I could see. "This is Dr. Steve Lang," Tom said, "our resident headshrinker."

"Dr. Lang," I said, shaking his hand.

"That's okay. You can call me Dr. Steve." I couldn't tell if he meant it as a joke.

"And this," Tom said, turning to the girl I assumed was Lang's daughter, "is—"

"His companion," the girl said. She looks like a *Playboy* centerfold, if they took overdeveloped sixteen-year-olds. Her breasts bulged out of the top of a green-and-pink neoprene bikini, and the mousse on her hair looked like it had melted in the intense sunlight. "Allyson. With a Y."

"Y?" I said.

"Why not?" She laughed like a kid.

Was the old man really screwing this nymphet while everybody stood around and winked? I couldn't gauge Lori's reaction because of her sunglasses.

"Interesting," Lang said to Tom. "Why did you choose to introduce me in that particular way?"

"Cut it out," Tom said.

"The first thing you mention, even before you introduce Allyson, you tell him I'm a psychiatrist. Are you trying to protect him, or . . ."

"I would try to ignore Dr. Steve's sense of humor if you can," Tom told me. "You want a beer?"

"Sure." Hair of the dog time. My stomach was still somewhere out over the Gulf and the rest of me was parched and wilted. Tom ordered Bohemias and Lori held up her empty bottle of mineral water without looking at the waiter.

I tried to be companionable. "That stuff any good?"

She said, "I'm an alcoholic."

"Oh."

"I've been sober two years." She looked at the bottle, which showed the Virgin in orange and blue robes. "It doesn't taste like much of anything."

Lang coughed and hawked up a big mouthful which he spat at his feet. "Gross," Allyson said, making a face. "I'm going to puke." She is too young to qualify as remotely sexy, but that drunken lecherous ghost of Jim Morrison is still in there. Morrison must have had dozens, maybe hundreds of precocious little girls like her. He didn't care about their ages any more than he cared about anything else.

The beer arrived. Just the smell made my headache worse. I stopped the waiter and asked for a mineral water like Lori's. Okay, maybe I wanted a rise out of her. I didn't get one.

Tom drank his beer in three pulls and started on mine. "Waste not, want not," he said.

I asked why they weren't out diving.

"We went for a look at the La Ceiba drop-off this morning," Tom said. "Got in enough bottom time for one day. The motto here is take it easy, don't push pain. We're spending the afternoon in serious pursuit of freeing up our nitrogen." He drank some more and then said, "Look, you must have a lot of questions."

"Not really. I read Adkisson's report. I talked to my mom. I don't know what there is that anybody could tell me. I just want to see where it happened, maybe it can help me . . . I don't know. Get my mind around it better."

"My father died when I was a kid," Tom said. "I'd seen dead people before and everything, but that was, I don't know, personal somehow. It's like death was suddenly real for the first time."

"Yeah. It was like that for me too." It wasn't something I expected to hear from a total stranger. I felt naked and uncomfortably sober.

"You seeing anybody about this?" Dr. Steve asked. I shook my head and he shrugged. "You might think about it."

Allyson said, "All *you* do is give people drugs."

"A lot of depression is simply chemical imbalance." He took another drink of his margarita.

Tom said, "It was a regular drift dive, out on Palancar reef. We're going out there tomorrow, if you want to see it. You are certified, right?"

"I got a Y Advanced Diver card. I haven't used it since I was down here on my honeymoon, actually. It's been ten years."

"That's okay. I'll check you out in the morning." There was an awkward silence, then he said, "Do you want to talk about it? I mean, I was there."

"Tell me," I said.

Tom hesitated, like maybe he shouldn't have started. Then he said, "I was already headed up. We were all of us out of air. He and Adkisson were waiting for the boat to circle back, just sitting around on the bottom at thirty feet, burning up the last of their air. There's a wall there that goes straight down forever. All of a sudden your father just takes off, over the drop-off. He didn't look confused or panicked or anything like that. He was swimming fast, like maybe there was something he wanted to take a picture of. Adkisson went after him and that's when I thought maybe something was wrong, so I started down too. It took Adkisson a long time to catch him. Finally he gets him by the ankle and turns him around. They give each other the okay sign and start up. By then I was totally out of air. I went up and yelled at Hector to get the boat over. By the time we got to your father he was dead."

"His mask was full of vomit," Lori said.

I already knew that my mother's line about his getting to die while doing what he loved best was a lot of self-serving crap. But this was like a punch in the gut. I guess I was startled more than anything. I had no idea what she expected me to say.

"Lori, for Christ's sake," Tom said.

"When Tom gave him mouth-to-mouth, he got your father's vomit all over his face."

Dr. Steve said, "Why do you have this compulsive desire for ugly truths? Are you substituting that for your addiction to alcohol?"

Tom said, "Will you both just shut the fuck up?" He looked at me, tried an apologetic smile.

"I just wanted you to know that," Lori said.

Tom acted like he hadn't heard her. "Is your mother okay?"

"She's holding up," I said. I was still a little stunned, my mouth on autopilot. "She's got a lot of friends. She's been traveling, she spent Christmas with my wife and me."

"She's a really brave lady. I wish she hadn't had to see it. To be on the boat when we, you know, pulled him in and everything. But she handled it and after that she just took over. Dealt with the police and funeral home and just handled it."

"At least she was there," I said.

He looked confused.

"If somebody dies in a hospital, it's like they're available, they're there, you can try to get through to them, you can maybe clear up a lot of unfinished business. With my father it was like some bull elephant, going off to the elephant graveyard all by himself, and to hell with everybody else."

"Yeah, I guess so," Tom said. "Excuse me, I got to go syphon the python, I'll be back in a sec."

Dr. Steve said, "How long ago did he die?"

"Almost six months." I hesitated, then I couldn't stop myself from saying, "Six months a week from tomorrow."

"Yes, the grief process should be . . . Were you close?"

I started to say something diplomatic, but the truth came out instead. "No. I hated his guts, actually. I just never got to tell him that."

Lori let out a one-syllable laugh, "Huh." She took the sunglasses off and rubbed at the bridge of her nose, eyes closed. "Sorry," she said. "I didn't expect that."

She looked up at me and I saw the whole of her face for the first time. Her eyes are dark blue, the color of deep water. All I wanted was to keep looking at her. I think I said the words in my mind: Don't look away. Some kind of magnetic force came out through my eyes and connected her to me. I could see it register in her face, that she felt it too. I was sure I'd been staring at her too long, that everybody else at the table had noticed. I still couldn't make myself stop.

Something moved in the distance behind her. It was Tom, walking toward us from the bathroom. When I looked at Lori again she had the sunglasses in place. It didn't matter. Everything had changed. Gravity pulled harder now from her side of the table. I knew exactly where she was, even when I looked the other way. I heard alarms go off in my head and the words "trouble," very distinct.

At six we went up the road to a seafood place. Pam and Richard were arm in arm, her hand on his ass. Maybe that's all it takes, to be young and good-looking and not think too much. Dr. Steve was drunk, holding Allyson by the shoulder. Tom and Lori kept apart. He was loose in the way he walked, flushed from the beer. She had her head down, walking hard.

The restaurant is called Mariscos Typicos. It's built out over a lagoon and you can see the water through the boards in the deck. The roof is thatched, there aren't any walls, and all the tables have plastic tablecloths with thumbtacks around the edges.

We all ordered and listened to Tom complain about his business. Apparently the tourist dollars that come in can't keep up with Mexican inflation. "What the fuck. I can always cut my losses and get out. I've got the boat, I've got the dive gear, I've got a couple hundred bucks."

"You've got me," Lori said.

"Yeah. I got you, babe."

Two waiters brought the food. One of them reached across Allyson to give Dr. Steve his steak. "Oh, gross," she said. "Red meat. I'm going to puke. How can you eat all that blood?"

Tom said, "Don't get Lori started. We'll hear about the rain forest again."

Allyson looked at Lori and said, "Are you a veggie?"

She said, "I eat fish sometimes."

"But no cows," Tom said. "Because cow farts are causing the greenhouse effect and the end of life as we know it."

My snapper came in a thick sauce of tomatoes and onions, Veracruz style. One eye stared up at me. I remembered my father's joke where at the end the halibut says, what's the matter, buddy, don't you eat across the street anymore? Our silverware clanged like picks and shovels in the tense silence.

I wondered what it would be like to change places with Richard. To get blasted and fuck my brains out all night, and have a body that could still go diving in the morning.

When I finished I put some dollars on the table and excused myself. Lori got up at the same time and said, "I'll walk with you."

I thought for a second she'd thawed. Once we were outside, though, she started down the highway in silence and I had to run to catch up to her. Eventually she said, "Women still can't walk alone after dark down here. I hate it, but what are you going to do?"

I said I didn't know. That was the extent of it. She went in the back door of the dive shop. We each said good-night. For a second I saw their bedroom framed by the doorway, sagging bed with sheets rumpled in the middle, table lamp with a yellowed shade, a shelf of battered paperbacks.

I walked to the lagoon, where a floodlight on the dock shines into the water. A dozen foot-long catfish swarmed in the shallows, eating insects drawn by the light. To my right I could see the lights of downtown; straight ahead, moonlit clouds were scattered out to the horizon. Waves slapped the concrete at my feet.

As great as travel is, sooner or later you end up someplace. If your problem is loneliness and you end up there alone, you're no better off than you were. I wondered what would have happened if I'd asked Elizabeth's friend Frances to come with me. I thought about the way she'd kissed me on New Year's and wondered if she might actually have done it, if once she got down here she might have let that tightly pulled-back hair come loose. The thought gave me my first serious hard-on in days.

I reminded myself that I was on vacation. Anything was possible. Adventure, romance, cosmic truth.

——————

Except for waking up around five and lying there for an hour, I slept okay. I would have slept better with a couple or six beers in me. I'd thought about it before I turned in and it hadn't seemed worth the trouble.

This business of waking up before dawn, though, has got to stop. It always happens when something is eating at me. When I was single and would get dumped by a girlfriend I could count on it, sure as clockwork, wide awake at five A.M., thinking about every shitty thing I've ever done.

So at five o'clock I woke up with the memory of this girl I'd gone out with freshman year at Vanderbilt, a blind date. We went to see *Blow Up* on campus and then sat around the basement of her dorm and made out for two hours. She had short brown hair and she'd been a long time between dates. Her mouth tasted a little like Salisbury steak and she let me put both hands up under her bra. I never called her again.

I got back to sleep around six and got up in time to meet Tom on the dock for my checkout. He seemed embarrassed about making me go through with it and I think he was a bit hungover besides. That was when I realized I wasn't. In fact I felt pretty decent.

It was only eight-thirty. I could feel the sun on my bare legs. I was half asleep and my body hadn't warmed up yet. I put the regulator on the tank and checked the pressure. There had been so much dream stuff in the last six months, scuba tanks, bodies floating in the water facedown. I thought about Brian in his pool and it made me smile.

Tom crouched beside me, watching everything I did and talking to make it look more casual. I told him about the stereo business, that my wife taught grade school. For a second I had a crazy urge to confide in him. It was easy to see he and Lori had problems. He would understand about Elizabeth. It could be a guy kind of thing. Except it was too early in the morning, we would need darkness and a few beers to feel natural.

I was supposed to ditch my gear near a buoy in the lagoon, surface, then go down and put it all on again. I jumped off the edge of the dock, surprised as always that sea water is so salty, at the way it stings the eyes. I swam to the buoy using just my snorkel. The tank weighed a million pounds and it took forever. Then I put the regulator in my mouth and went under.

The water was cloudy with sewage and dirt and oil from the boat traffic. Even so it was clearer than anything in Texas. I blew a little air into my vest to get my buoyancy neutral and there it was. Weightlessness. Like a dream of flying, removed of all of Dr. Steve's leering sexual connotations. It was enough to float there, to let the water touch me all over. A lone fish swam up to look me over. It was the size of my hand, colorless. It blinked at me and I blinked back. My bubbles made a ringing sound as they streamed out of the mouthpiece.

I followed the rusty chain from the buoy to the sandy bottom, ten feet down. Boat traffic had killed everything, left the entire bottom white except for the occasional red of a Coke can or brown of a beer bottle.

I ditched my gear and went up to wave at Tom. It took me two tries to get back, and in the end I had to use the chain to pull myself down. I hung there, upside down, one hand holding the air tank to keep from floating up, the other fumbling around for the regulator.

Eventually I got the tank turned on and the regulator started to bubble. I put it in my mouth and hung there, headfirst, breathing, waiting for my heart to slow down. Simple pleasures. Breathing. It's easy to forget. After a while I put on the weights and the rest of the gear, blew out my mask, and swam underwater to the dock.

When I handed Tom my fins and started up the ladder, he said, "You use the chain to get down the second time?"

I wondered if he expected me to lie. "Yeah."

He nodded. "Kids under thirty never seem to think of that."

━━━━━

Tom's assistant is named Hector. He's young and dark-skinned and he wore mirrorshades and a belt buckle in the shape of a shark. He finished off a Kahlúa and milk as we pulled out of the dock, and tried to start a conversation in halting English with Allyson. She blushed and giggled and seemed to think it was all very exciting. Dr. Steve was not amused. He kept his eye on the oversized diver's knife strapped to Hector's ankle.

We were out of sight of land and there was enough of a swell to move the boat around. Tom and I had the stern to ourselves. I said, "Is this where it happened?"

"No, it was a drift dive, like this one. Your dad . . . it happened at the end, when we picked everybody up."

We put on our tanks and hit the water, which was just cool enough to feel good on my skin. When the bubbles around me cleared my stomach lurched and the muscles in my legs started to crawl. The water was so clear my brain thought I was falling. The mountains and cliffs of coral below me looked purple because of the depth. Beyond them was a blue hole that seemed to go down forever. It was like looking down into the sky.

The current had split us up. The others looked like sky divers in slow motion. The sight of Pam and Richard fifty feet below me and a hundred yards downstream put everything into scale and made me feel tiny. I blew some air into my vest to slow my descent. Tom swam by and flashed me an OK sign. I gave it back and looked at my depth gauge. Fifty feet and counting. I figured Pam and Richard for ninety, at least. Their air wouldn't last long at that depth. It was also pushing things if they'd had a decompression dive the day before. When the water is that clear and the reef is that deep it's easy to lose track.

A school of stubby yellow fish changed direction in front of me, close enough that I could almost feel the hundreds of tiny fins brush my face. The current pulled us along the reef which rose to meet us. We drifted parallel to the drop-off and along the edge I could make out the real colors in the coral: red lacework, pale green fans, pink and electric-yellow sponges. They grew out of a base that looked like lava except that it too was alive, an aggregate of tiny animals.

Tom banged his tank with the handle of his knife and waved the others to close up ranks. The reef rose slowly toward the surface and leveled off at forty feet. The blue hole disappeared somewhere to my left. I had the rhythm of it now, my weight neutralized, arms at my sides, kicking just enough to stay level.

Tom waved me over and pointed to a patch of sand between coral heads. The top layer of sand suddenly came loose, sliding off the back of a spotted ray that was maybe three feet across. It banked in front of us and fluttered away. Despite Hector's bragging, it was the closest any of us saw to a shark. In fact there weren't many fish at all beyond a few chubby green parrot fish and an occasional school of yellow tang. My father made a big macho thing about sharks, had even hit one in the nose with his camera once. I was just as glad we hadn't run into any.

The reef brought us up to thirty-five feet. The coral slowly sank into the sand and within a few hundred yards everything turned white. The heads of gnarled brain coral had begun to crumble and the bottom was flat in all directions. Except for the clarity of water we could have been in the harbor. I looked for Tom and couldn't see him. Ahead of me, Hector swam next to Allyson, touching her arm, pointing and nodding. Dr. Steve huffed along behind them, blowing huge clouds of bubbles out of his regulator.

The cool, dry air from the mouthpiece left me parched. I took it out long enough to rinse my mouth with Caribbean water. The salt only made it worse. It was like being lost in the Sahara, trudging through endless plains of sand.

Not sand. Ashes.

Just before I ran out of air, the reef came back to life. It was like the glimpse of heaven that the revived dead are supposed to see. The sand fell away to the left and the drop-off was back. The coral turned gray and then purple again. There was a fan with an angelfish behind it who looked at me with mild contempt. There was an anemone, waving rubbery tentacles.

Dr. Steve was already headed for the surface. Another of my father's macho obsessions was to use less air than anybody else. It was supposed to prove how fearless he was, because if you're scared you use more air. Here I was empty, a disappointment to his memory. I wanted to be alone down there, to have a few minutes to sort things out, but it was already hard to breathe. I looked up and saw the boat overhead, like a knife blade slicing the dome of the sky. I pulled my reserve lever and swam to the edge of the drop-off and looked over.

There it was. X marks the spot. There was nothing to see but empty blue. I didn't feel much of anything. I turned around and Tom was behind me. He looked at my air gauge and stuck his thumb toward the surface. I signaled OK and started up.

=====

Pam and Richard broke open the cooler. I can't explain why I took a mineral water instead of a beer. The beer looked good and I felt okay after a night of abstinence. Knowing the feeling would go away once the alcohol hit my system had never stopped me before. I sat on the aft rail and drank my mineral water and wondered if I was trying to sober up, and if I was, why I'd picked this of all times to do it.

The old man driving the boat dropped anchor. He was Hector's father, if I understood right. A few seconds later Hector and Allyson came up the ladder. Allyson went first and Hector gave her the assistance of both hands on her firm, adolescent ass. I don't think Dr. Steve saw it or there might have been a knife fight there on deck. Hector stowed his gear and then came over to me, drying his black hair with a towel from the Presidente Hotel.

He pointed to a spot off the stern. "Your father come up there."

I nodded.

"He was good man, your father. Very funny guy, you know? But too old. Too old for this, I think."

"*Lo creo también*," I said. I think so too.

Tom was the last one up. He made a show of counting heads and then he came over to us. "You okay?"

"Fine. What was the deal with all that dead coral?"

"Yeah, I forgot how long that seems. It's only a few hundred yards, really. Listen, we're going into town for dinner tonight, party down a little after. Maybe go down to Scaramouche. Local disco, pretty corny. It's what passes for a good time around here. What do you say?"

Hector did a two-step on the deck, arms around an invisible partner. "Dancing . . . nice girls."

"I'm kind of beat. I better pass."

"We can talk about this if you want. I know it can be tough. Nobody should ever have to go through something like this. But everybody does."

"It's okay. I'll get to bed early, maybe look around the island some tomorrow."

"You're welcome to stay as long as you want. Seriously."

"I appreciate it."

"Okay," Tom said, and squeezed my arm. The kindness made my eyes sting. "Let me know if you change your mind about tonight."

"Think about it," Hector said. He raised his hands head-high and snapped his fingers. "*Very* nice girls."

"Forget it," I said. "I'm married."

It sounded lame even to me.

=====

Back at the room I showered and changed. I started to play the *Smile* tape and then decided I would save the magic for another time, when it might do some good. I had *Celebration of the Lizard* in with my CDs and I took it out and looked at it. Graham is selling the hell out of it, and I'm not surprised. Rumors of a Doors movie are only part of it. It's the times, crack and AIDS and global warming, something desperate and final that *Celebration* is perfect for. I can't get away from the idea that it's more than background music, that it's some- how contributing. In any case I sure as hell didn't want to listen to it. I put on *Soul Carnival* and punched up Don Covay's "Mercy Mercy."

I stretched out on the bed, pleasantly tired from the dive. My head was clearer than it had been in a while even if I didn't have any answers. I came, I saw, I didn't get a goddamn thing out of it. Give me one good reason not to change my flight and go home.

Elizabeth.

I thought about the dry peck on the cheek she'd given me when she dropped me at the airport, the long aching silences in the house whenever we were both there, like we added up to less together than either of us alone.

It was four in the afternoon. I was in Cozumel, for God's sake. It was time for a swim.

I splashed around in the lagoon for a while. I could hear the wind rustle the palm trees, hear the sea birds shout at each other. The ocean felt alive, even there in the dirty harbor, the waves picking me up like giant hands and dropping me again. I could have been a cork or a piece of seaweed. Everything around me was white or green or blue and that was all I thought about for half an hour or so.

When I came out, Lori was on the front step of the dive shop, drinking Tehuacán water. She had on a one-piece swimsuit flowered in blue and green, with one of Tom's long-sleeved shirts over it like a jacket. She had the sunglasses on, reading a paperback romance with a red cover and an oval picture in the middle. I nodded to her and she nodded back. I started to go to my room and then changed my mind and crouched next to her in the sand.

"Listen. Did I say something to piss you off? I mean, I don't want to be an asshole or anything, but I can't understand why you dislike me so much."

"I don't dislike you at all," she said. I heard a trace of an accent, Southern, that I hadn't noticed before. "*Au contraire.*"

"I guess I have to believe you. You have this thing about the truth, right?"

"Maybe that's part of the problem. I don't hide my feelings too well. It's just that most of them have nothing to do with you."

Another stunner, even when she tried to make nice. She was right, of course. Why should I be the center of her universe?

She sighed. "I think you're attractive and everything, but you're married. It's obvious you came down here looking for trouble. I don't want to be the trouble you find."

"Me? Looking for trouble?"

She studied my face, still half smiling, and said, "Maybe you don't know it. I could believe that."

"I'm down here because of my father. That's all."

"Really? How's your marriage?"

"It's fine, what's that got to do with it?" She didn't answer and after a second I said, "Okay, it's not fine, it sucks. I still don't see your point."

"I'm just saying I don't want to get involved."

"Nobody asked you to."

"Okay, okay. I'm sorry. I'm way out of line, as usual. How's this? We drop the subject, and you can come with me and see some of the island. Unless you're going into town with the others?"

I shook my head. "Aren't you?"

"I got to see everybody drunk last night. Anyway, I've got errands this afternoon. I'm headed out to the commune."

I made an interested noise and she said, "Bunch of neo-pagan kids, mostly Northamericans. The locals hate their guts. They have a pretty tough time of it—not enough food, lots of hassles with the cops. You can come along if you want."

"Sure," I said. "Why not?"

I took another shower, playing it back in my head. Looking for trouble, she said. Am I? And what was it she said about finding me attractive?

I put on khaki pants, a black T-shirt with a pocket, moccasins. Lori was loading a green plastic trash bag into the back seat of the VW. She told me they were cans from the boat, and from the bar next door. The commune kids sell them to a guy on the ferry from Playa del Carmen.

I got in and we roared away. She revved the little bug to a high squeal before she shifted, came right up on the bumper of anybody in front of her. There didn't seem to be any malice or impatience in it, she was just totally into the act of driving.

"Tom hates the way I drive."

"My dad used to tell a story about his first field trip, when he was in college. Anybody who complained about the cooking had to take it over. So whoever got stuck with it would put rocks in the eggs and cardboard in the pancakes and stuff like that."

"So you think I drive like this to piss Tom off?"

We weren't communicating. "I just meant I'm not that crazy about driving. So I try to let other people drive however they want."

"You talk a lot about your father. I mean, for supposedly not liking him."

I didn't have an answer for that. We were headed south, away from town and the airport. We passed the Chankanab Lagoon with its resort hotel and park and within a few hundred yards there was only the road and the scrub brush and the empty ocean.

"The commune's in this abandoned hotel called El Mirador. You speak Spanish?"

"It means window or something, right?"

"Right. Only there's no view there at all, you can't see the ocean from it. Which was why it went broke in no time and this brother and sister from Amsterdam were able to cash a decent-sized inheritance and buy the place. Then once they had it they invited all their Wiccan friends to move in."

"Their what friends?"

"Wiccans. Witches. Pagans, you know."

Alex had always talked about being a witch in high school. She never called it wicca, though, and I'd never taken her very seriously. "Are we talking Aleister Crowley and sacrificing animals and all that?"

"Basically they worship the Goddess and keep a low profile. They're trying to kick technology."

"What about you? Are you into all this Goddess stuff?" I had a sinking fear that this woman, who had started out so interesting, would end up having some prefab belief system.

"If you want to have a religion, it seems better than most. It reveres women, for one thing, instead of being terrified or hostile like most of Western culture. It respects life and doesn't believe in fucking up the planet. I'm not real comfortable with the supernatural parts, but the here-and-now agenda sounds okay."

I couldn't argue with it either. After a few seconds she said, "When I got sober, a lot of things changed for me. That's when I gave up meat and all that. I started to come here once a week to do yoga. And I got interested. At least interested enough to learn some more, if not to . . ."

"Commit?" I said.

"Something like that."

The Mirador is pink stucco, with thorny gray-green vines that grow up over the walls. It's a featureless square, two stories high, with the outside windows boarded up. I guess the boards keep out hostile rocks and bottles.

We parked on the side of the road. Lori took the cans and I carried a canvas tote bag with groceries in it. There's an arched entranceway that opens into a patio with haphazard landscaping: fruit trees, tomatoes, corn. A veranda runs all the way around the ground floor, with half a dozen hammocks strung between the posts. Two were occupied by dusty men in their early twenties. A woman of about the same age was weeding the garden, along with an older man with gray in his ponytail and a blond boy of maybe seven. A couple of toddlers chased each other down the veranda, one in makeshift diapers, the other naked.

We took the stuff into a kitchen near the front gates. The place was clean enough, and smelled like earth and spices. A few flies circled lazily, unable to find anything worth landing on. The refrigerator and stove were both hooked up to what looked like a propane tank. "I thought you said they were getting away from technology."

Lori saw where I was looking. "They burn methane. You can make it out of garbage, so it's renewable."

I picked up a heavy, Swiss-made butcher knife. "And steel? Just curious."

"Recyclable." She gave me a look. "You can always beat it into a plowshare."

A guy in his late thirties, black, with short dreadlocks, came in. He was bare to the waist and had that kind of hairless and glossily developed chest that, if I had one, I wouldn't wear a shirt either. "Hello, darlin'," he said to Lori, and hugged her. I could see her hesitancy, and so could he. It seemed to surprise him. He looked a question at her, which she ignored.

"Ray, this is Walker, the local shaman."

We shook hands.

"Who else is here?" Lori asked.

"Everybody. Joost and Debra are upstairs fucking or something." He pronounced Joost like it started with a Y and rhymed with ghost. Lori unloaded celery, cheese, eggs, and a tub of tofu from the tote bag.

I was grating cheese with my back to the door when Debra came in. Something made me look around. I looked back at the cheese, then turned again to see her smiling at me. She's nearly six feet tall, broad in the hips and shoulders and chest, with a narrow waist and thin ankles. She had on a black cotton skirt to midcalf and a black leotard top. Her feet were bare, the toes curled against the concrete floor. With the light behind her, her hair made a golden haze around her head. She wore round wire-rimmed glasses and a silver belt. "Hi there," she said.

I nodded. "I'm Ray."

"Hi, Ray. I'm Debra."

Lori said, "Or Moonflower, as she's sometimes known."

Debra didn't react. "That too. Are you at the dive shop, Ray?"

There's a Germanic lilt to her voice. If I looked at a photograph of her I would probably think she's overweight and kind of plain. In person she was magnetic. "That's right," I said.

"How long are you down for?"

"I don't know. I haven't decided yet."

"We'll just have to keep you amused, then, won't we?"

Whatever it was, she knew about it. She spun around theatrically and her skirt swirled up. "What are we making?"

"Enchiladas," Lori said coolly. "We could use some green onions."

"Walker knows where they are."

Walker clearly didn't want to make an issue out of it. "Right," he said, and went outside.

Debra moved next to me, close enough that I could smell her faint, musky-sweet perfume. "I'll help you chop," she said.

There were ten of us for dinner. We ate at a long table in the court-yard, under the last of the sunlight. Debra sat next to me and some-how Lori ended up across the table and down toward the far end. Joost, dark-haired, with the same magnetism as his sister, sat at the head of the table, Walker at the foot, by Lori.

There was a French couple, both dark and thin, and a broad-hipped girl from the United States with protruding eyes and a raucous laugh. There was Jeff, the guy with the gray ponytail, and an eighteen-year-old runaway from Veracruz.

Debra wanted to know "who I really was." She seemed sincere enough, so I told her about the stereo business, that I'd made a lot of money in computers but it didn't mean much compared to music.

I said, "Lori told me you guys are witches."

Her "yeah" sounded like "jah." "Pagans, witches, whatever you want to call us. We worship the Goddess, which basically is Gaia, the Earth. We see her as a living being. We try to live inside her rhythms. To be clean and peaceful and reverent."

Jeff, on the other side of her, said, "Sounds like the Boy Scouts." Then we had to explain to her what Boy Scouts are and how they're different from Hitler Youth, which turned out to be tricky.

There wasn't enough dinner to fill me up. The French boy had talked about how Americans eat three times the calories we need, so I didn't ask for more. When everybody was done I started to help clear the table. Debra grabbed my arm and said, "We cooked. We don't have to clean up."

"What do you guys do at night? What's for fun?"

"Sex is popular," she said, smiling. Okay, maybe she was flirting a little. I found myself embarrassed and erect. "Joost plays guitar, some-times there's drumming and dancing." When I looked interested she said, "We have congas, timbales, lots of kinds of drums. You look like a drummer."

"I used to be."

"You'll have to come help us out."

"I don't know. It's been a long time."

Walker and Lori were standing behind us. "It's a great high, man,"

Walker said. "People been getting fucked up behind it for hundreds of thousands of years. The drums get into a groove, people start dancing, they can dance themselves to death and never feel it."

"We need to go," Lori said. She sounded very cool. Debra looked at her with a kind of cocky smile. Bad blood under the bridge between those two, no question.

I stood up. "Thanks for dinner."

"Come back," Debra said. "Any time."

———

On the road Lori said, "I can take you back there and leave you if you want. She'd like that. Fresh meat."

"You've got me wrong."

"Do I?"

Without meaning to I saw myself in one of those crumbling stucco rooms with Debra, both of us sweating, her bare skin moving against me. "I don't understand what you've got against her. She seemed like a pretty okay person. All we did is talk."

"Why is it men find promiscuity so attractive? I used to eat myself up over it. Are men just naturally lazy, they want to save themselves the chase? That didn't seem like the whole answer somehow. Part of it, but not the whole deal. Then it came to me. It's not that women like Debra are so easy to get into bed. It's that they're so easy to leave."

"What did I do that's got you so upset?"

"Nothing. I guess I'd hoped for more from you."

"More than what?"

"Do you deny that you wanted to fuck her?"

"She's attractive. Very . . . sensual. The point is, I *didn't* fuck her. And I don't intend to. Jesus, we sound like we're married."

The idea seemed to amuse her.

"You're from the South somewhere, aren't you?" I asked.

"Was my accent showing? You can tell when I let myself get mad."

"Kentucky?"

"Tennessee. Thank you for not saying Mississippi. I come from a suburb called Murfreesboro." She pronounced it in Tennessee fashion, with about one and a half syllables.

I told her about my two years in Nashville. She's a year older than me, was away in St. Louis at college then, only home for the holidays. She wouldn't have seen the Duotones anyway, she would have been at the Grand Ole Opry, in the Ryman auditorium downtown.

"I wouldn't have figured you for a country music fan," I said.

"Why not? What does a country music fan look like?"

"I don't know. Bouffant hairdo and a polyester smock?"

"I like country music. It's music for grown-ups. At least some of it is."

"Drinkin' and cheatin' and drivin' a truck."

"Some of it. And some of it's about having to get up and go to work every day and still not having enough money, or about living with somebody who treats you like shit, or about watching your kids grow up and leave you behind . . ."

"You don't have any kids. Do you?" She shook her head. "And as jobs go, yours doesn't seem too bad." Silence then, while we both thought about the third thing.

"So what do you listen to?" she asked after a while.

"Lots of stuff. I guess my favorite is the kind of stuff the Duotones used to play, R&B, those great Stax/Volt songs from the sixties, Motown."

"Sounds like you're living in the past."

I thought of Brian, Pacific Ocean Park, the studio. "Maybe I am," I said.

We were back at the dive shop. The place was dark and quiet, though it was only ten-thirty. "They must still be at Scaramouche," Lori said. Neither of us had made a move for the doors of the VW. I didn't want to be the first.

"Are you tired?" she said. I shook my head. "Come and talk to me for a while."

She headed for the bar next door. The place was shut down, the tables empty in the moonlight. "I've got a key," she said. "You want something?"

My hormones were in a state. I didn't know what I wanted any more, I only thought that a beer might smooth me out, take some pressure off. I didn't ask because I didn't want to see the disapproval in Lori's eyes. "I'll have whatever you're having."

I sat down at a Tecate table. I could smell the ocean and hear it, but I couldn't see it because the dive shop was in the way. Lori came back with two bottles of Tehuacán water that dripped tiny granules of ice.

She'd overheard what I said about the stereo business and wanted to know more. I said I was consulting now with a record company in L.A. It wasn't a lie, exactly. We talked about music again and she went to her room for a jam box and a Rosanne Cash cassette, *King's Record Shop.*

Lori has a psych degree from Washington University and she reads a lot: biographies, pop psychology, romance novels like I'd caught her with that afternoon. I would be amazed, she said, how many women read romances. "Career women, intellectuals. It's like this Cinderella Complex thing. No matter how great your career, no matter what degrees you have or how great a physical shape you're in, women in our culture are brought up to believe they're nothing without a . . . a Grand Passion."

"What if I said I feel the same way?"

"Only not about your wife, right? Obviously not about your wife."

"I thought I did. It didn't last. I know you have to accept that, that your first blazing passion isn't going to last forever. So you think at least you'll have somebody there to share your life with. To talk about the movie you just saw or the dinner you just ate or something you just happened to think of. Only you find out that when you want to share it she doesn't want to hear about it. Or the only time she wants to share something with you is when you've just fallen asleep, and then you know it's because of that extra cup of coffee that she had after dinner that you didn't dare complain about because it would piss her off, even though you know it means she's going to toss and turn and thrash all night long and you might as well get up and go sleep on the couch right now, but if you do she won't understand and she'll be pissed off about that, and even if she's not you'll lie there on the couch and worry that she might be, so you might as well forget about sleeping at all. That's not romance, it's . . . I don't know what it is."

"Life in the real world."

I was all worked up. I hadn't seen it coming. "Well, if that's what it is, it sucks."

"You say passion never lasts. Do you believe that?"

I saw something in her eyes behind the tough talk, an empty place that I knew she would deny. A longing. "I don't know," I said. "I don't guess I've ever seen it."

"That doesn't mean it can't happen."

"No," I said. "It doesn't mean it can't."

Around midnight we heard voices up the road. Lori shut off the tape player in the middle of John Hiatt's *Slow Turning*. We sat in the dark and silence while Tom and the others shouted good-nights and staggered off to their separate rooms. When it became obvious that Lori wasn't going to let them know we were there I felt guilty, like we were getting away with something.

"I have to go in," she said, standing up. "I don't want to, but there it is."

"That's twice."

"Twice what?"

"Twice you've said something like that about Tom. If you do it again I'll have to ask."

"And if you ask I'll have to tell you, being the personality type that I am. So I should make up my mind whether I want to talk about it, shouldn't I? Instead of dropping all these hints. But before I make up my mind, are you sure you want to hear it?"

"I've got no place to go."

"Do you mean that? Oh hell, I can't ask you to . . ."

"To what?"

"Wait for me. Tom'll be asleep in half an hour and I could come back . . . ?"

"I'll wait," I said.

It was closer to an hour. I didn't mind the time. It was warm and the night was full of soothing noises: the sea, traffic on the highway, the hum of a fluorescent light at the back of the shop. I might even have dozed off for a few minutes.

When Lori came back there was something different about her. Her hair was damp, like she'd washed her face, but there was something more, in the way she held herself. I wondered if she and Tom had made love. It didn't seem possible that she could be so matter-of-fact about it. She put the tape on again, quietly.

I asked her where she met him. She told me how after college she worked temporary jobs, secretarial mostly, and used the money to travel. Sleeping on the beach in Greece, waiting tables in a small town in the Dordogne. For some reason the stories gave me a real pang, like jealousy. Not of the places she'd been, but of the experiences she'd had without me.

Slow down, I thought. It was her eyes that did it to me. I almost wished she would put the sunglasses back on. I've never seen blue eyes that dark before. They look black in the moonlight.

She met Tom in Greece. He had a sailboat then. He taught her to dive and sail. It sounded like something out of a movie, out of one of her Silhouette romances—the perfect weather, the photogenic couple, the azure water, the sun-bleached islands. It makes my life feel squalid and dull.

"So what happened?"

"It's the real world," she said. "You don't get paid to sail around and drink retsina all day. Tom heard about this shop for sale and it seemed so perfect. A little stability, a chance to know where your next meal is coming from. He traded the sailboat for the dive boat and used the difference to make a down payment on the business."

It sounded like there was more. "And?"

"And then he wasn't happy about it. Tom's the kind of guy that is always refiguring things. I mean, he makes quarterly estimated tax payments, and no two payments are ever the same."

"And you're different."

"I'm different. I'm slow to make up my mind . . . well, not always slow. But I think it out, I make up my mind, and that's it. I live with the results. When I quit drinking, that's what happened. I read a lot and thought about it and then one day I stopped. No more booze. Tom quit the same time as me and then started up again two weeks later."

There was that tone again. "You're thinking about leaving him, right? I warned you I was going to ask."

She looked away. I waited for her answer so long I almost forgot the question. Then she said, "Yeah, I think about it. I think about it a lot. But where would I go?"

"What about your family?"

"My mother's a drunk. I can't be around her. My father is remarried with teenage kids. It's like, not really my family, you know?"

The tape ran out and the machine clicked off. "Wait here for a second," I said.

I went to my room for *Smile*. This is crazy, I thought. She'll hate it. Then I thought, I have to know.

I put it in the tape deck. "What is it?" Lori said, and I shook my head. When "Heroes and Villains" came on she said, "Oh, the Beach Boys. I used to really like them." I watched her face during the cantina section. "This is different. Isn't it?"

I nodded. "Do Ya Dig Worms" started and I saw the music actually take hold of her. She stopped talking to listen, and I watched a smile start on her face.

"What *is* this?"

"It's a long story," I said.

I didn't tell her about Brian and 1966. I told her it's part of what I do in L.A., to put together lost albums from "newly discovered" master tapes. Which is all true, as far as it goes. I told her about *Smile* and Brian and the Beach Boys and she really listened. The grim stuff about Tom fell by the wayside. The snippet of "George Fell into His French Horn" made her laugh out loud. I thought how proud Brian would be to see that.

It was three o'clock before we were too tired to have anything left to say. Lori was the first to stand up. "This was really nice," she said. "Thanks for waiting for me."

"Hey. You were buying the drinks."

She smiled again. Her smile is off-center, unselfconscious. Like the monkey with the wire in its pleasure center, I wanted to push that button again. Instead I said good-night and took the tape back to my room.

I remember I said the words to myself when I got into bed. I said, "I think I'm in love." It's something I've said too many times before and I suddenly felt guilty for it.

I wasn't in love as much as I was scared. I was off the map and going much too fast.

———

Tom pounded on my door at eight. "You diving today?"

I sat up and tried to focus my eyes, which were gummed shut. "Uh, not this morning. Maybe this afternoon?"

"It's an all-day trip. Take it or leave it."

"I guess I'll pass. But thanks."

"Later, guy."

I dozed for another hour or so, then went downtown for breakfast. Afterward, sitting in the clear morning sunshine of the *zócalo*, I thought about my marriage. In eleven years I've never been unfaithful. There were a couple of opportunities when I wasn't ready, and there were more than a couple of nights when, if the opportunity had come up, I don't think I would have held out.

There was a moment last night when Lori turned to say good-night when I think she would have let me kiss her.

I wandered through some of the tourist shops, full of polyester T-shirts and onyx chess sets and brilliantly colored hammocks. I found Elizabeth a pair of seashell earrings, long and dangling, the kind she likes. On some level I was buying off my conscience. I got some postcards and stamps and then I couldn't think of anything to write.

When I got back to the dive shop Lori was in a lounge chair near the bar. I couldn't help but think that it was a good spot to watch for somebody coming in or out of any of the rooms. She was wearing shorts and a Hawaiian shirt, open over the blue-and-green flowered swimsuit. And the red sunglasses. She had a different romance from the day before.

I said good-morning and she pushed her glasses down so she could look over the top of them. I liked it that she was showing me her eyes.

"Hi," she said. "How'd you sleep?"

"Good."

"You didn't go diving." She folded over a page in her book and put it aside.

"It's not like diving is that big a deal for me. I don't take pictures like my father did. It doesn't, I don't know, *mean* anything. Maybe if I was with friends."

"Or your wife?"

"She's afraid of fish. And she wears contacts and she's afraid of losing them. I'm amazed I got her to go out at all ten years ago."

"Tom goes out there day after day and he can't seem to get enough of it. Something about being in control of all those people. He gets off because they do."

"You sound like Dr. Steve."

"I'm addicted to psychobabble. I already warned you that I'm an addictive personality. What about you?"

"Addictions? I guess I drink too much. I used to smoke but I gave it up twelve or thirteen years ago." I took a breath. "Sex. I mean, you can still be addicted to something when you're not getting it, right?"

"Definitely," she said. Neither of us looked away. "But I haven't seen you drink since you got here."

"Giving it a rest, I guess."

"You managed to keep me talking all night last night and you didn't say much at all about yourself."

"I thought I did all the talking." I shrugged. "I guess I'm just interested." The words hung in the air. "In what you were saying, I mean."

It looked like we were done. She reached for her book and pushed the sunglasses into place. I started toward my room.

"Hey, Ray," she said, still looking down at her book. "What are you doing for lunch?"

———

She knocked on my door an hour later with an honest-to-God wicker picnic basket and an ice chest. I had an awkward moment with her in the doorway, not knowing whether to ask her in. Her voice was a little too bright. The Wailers on the CD player sang "Could You Be Loved." We were both aware of the bed in the corner of the room. I switched off the music and followed her out to the VW.

We drove south past the commune and across to the eastern side of the island. We were in sight of the ocean when Lori turned right onto a badly rutted dirt road.

I asked her, "Isn't there a lighthouse down here?"

"On the Punta Celerain. We turn off before then."

She turned left on a road that was barely there at all. "Tom and I used to come here," she said, almost an apology. "It's been a long time. I hope I've got the right place."

The road, such as it is, winds between sand dunes and purple-gray lava. Small palms and thornbushes grow out of the dunes. I could smell the ocean. She put the VW into four-wheel drive as the sand got softer and she finally pulled up behind a big rock. "All ashore," she said.

She took the food and towels; I brought the ice chest and sunscreen. We came up over the rocks and there was the ocean. It frothed pale blue at the shore, turned impossibly deep and blue at the horizon. Straight ahead, unless you veer off to Cuba or Jamaica, is ocean all the way to Africa. The beach is no more than a pocket of sand between black lava hillocks, with enough room for two people at most.

"So what do you think?" Lori said.

I was thinking how jealous I'd been of her romantic youth, thinking that my life was not necessarily over after all. "It's great," I said.

She set the jam box on the rocks and then shook out the towels. Hers was a faded red with the sun in the middle and mine was a washed-out yellow green. "You don't mind the music, do you?" she asked. "I mean, if it's going to spoil the mood . . ."

"Music never spoiled anything."

She pushed the button and it was the Wailers' "Is This Love," the first cut on the *Legend* album that I'd been listening to that morning.

She said, "I heard you playing it. You had it cranked up a bit."

"Sorry."

"It sounded good. I don't just listen to country, you know. You can't live in this part of the world without hearing a lot of reggae. God help me, I even like the Rolling Stones."

I was beyond words. I lay down on my towel and felt the heat of the sand underneath. I heard Lori settle a few feet away, knew, like I had from that first afternoon, where she was by some internal radar. I could feel the grass on the slope behind me, the salt drying on my skin, the fish in the sea. I asked God to kill me where I lay, while everything was still perfect. It could only turn real from here, or not happen at all, and either way lay certain disappointment.

After a couple of minutes I sat up and rubbed sunscreen on my arms and legs. Between the hospital and the exercise I'd gotten rid of my pot belly, but I was still pale. The coconut smell of the lotion was full of images. Lori reached for the bottle and I handed it to her without speaking. Then I let the music wash over me.

Neither one of us talked until the side was over. I was nearly empty of desire, living completely in the moment, from one tick of the cymbal to the next. When she finally got up to turn the tape over she said, "Hungry?"

"Mmmmm. Sure."

I sat up and opened my eyes to a pale, sun-drenched world. Lori unpacked the basket. There were hard rolls and cheese, boiled shrimp, plantains, and oranges. "I don't really cook," she said. "I'm more of the found objects school."

"It looks great." There were purple linen napkins and real glasses for the Tehuacán water. I sat cross-legged and started on the bread. Bob Marley sang about shooting the sheriff. I said, "Have you ever actually tried to leave him?"

"I got as far as Mexico City once. I'd forgotten what it was like living alone, sleeping alone. You get . . . *unreal.* You know what I mean? Like you're not really there."

"I've been married a long time. I think I could stand to be alone. I mean, it gets unreal with her there."

"So why are you? Still married, I mean?"

"I guess I'm getting something out of it, right?"

"Some things you do because you can't see any other way. If you say some inner-city kid who dropped out of the sixth grade is selling crack because he's getting something out of it, well, that's not very compassionate, is it?"

"I guess not. I spent the night at a motel once, after one of our non-fights, when she'd told me how unromantic I was and I let it stew all day. When I came home she was hysterical. I mean, completely over the top. Convulsive weeping, screaming, swearing she couldn't live without me. It was more like a threat than anything else. Like if I ever tried to leave her again she would hunt me to the ends of the earth."

"That's a lot of emotion for somebody you say is cold."

"Or for somebody who doesn't even seem to like me anymore."

"Like and need are different things. Emotional blackmail is what it is. I've done it too. I guess every woman I know has."

"She was really scared—"

"Of what?" Suddenly Lori was furious. "What did she have to be afraid of? Did you hit her? Did you smash the furniture?"

"No, but I—"

"She was afraid you were going to leave her. Before she could leave you first." She got up and walked to the edge of the water, her back to me.

"Lori?"

After a minute she came back and sat down again. "I'm sorry," she said. "It's just . . . women think they can't live without a man. And really all it is, we can't stand for someone else to do the leaving. It makes me so fucking mad sometimes."

The suddenness and violence of her anger had unnerved me. "Are you saying I don't have any responsibility to Elizabeth?"

"Of course you do. You're a Rescuer."

"This is more of that self-help stuff, right?"

"Yeah. You're a Rescuer and I'm a Victim." She smiled. "We're made for each other."

―――――

We finished lunch. Lori put Bonnie Raitt on the jam box and we talked about music. Who we'd seen live, favorite records, like that. I remembered the drunken conversation Graham and I had in Santa Monica, about how few women there were that I could have this conversation with. It made me dizzy. When the talk wound down I asked her if she wanted to swim.

"It's dangerous. The current's fast around here."

"I'm a good swimmer." I smiled. "I'll rescue you."

"Very funny. I'll go in with you, but don't get cocky and don't get out too far. I don't want to have to tell your mother that we drowned you too."

I wondered if she would say anything at all that came into her head. She stood up to take off her shirt and shorts. I didn't make the pretense of looking away. It wasn't about sex so much as sensuality, to see her stretch and move in that particular way. It seemed to embody everything that desire was about. I waited until she was done, then got up and walked into the water.

I felt the pull of the current, strong, like she'd said. I kicked hard against it and still didn't make a lot of headway. As soon as I stopped to look I felt myself drift back. That was okay too. I was full of sexual energy, a little scared of it, and the ocean was a safe place to burn it away.

Eventually I let the current carry me back to the shallows. My hair had come halfway loose from its ponytail and I took off the elastic tie and shook it out. Lori sat in the shade of a lava outcrop, up to her neck in water. "Leave it down," she said. "I want to see."

I combed through it with my fingers as I walked toward her. "Well?" I said. "What do you think?"

"I think you should watch your step. There's a lot of sea urchins around." She showed me the crooked smile again.

I reached both hands out to her. She looked at me for a second, then took them. I pulled her onto her feet and watched her face for a sign. Apparently the swim hadn't been enough. Before I knew it I had pulled her toward me and leaned into her. Slowly, very slowly. If she started to turn away I would have time to pull back. She didn't turn, and she didn't lean toward me. She stood there and let it happen.

There was a moment when it was clear I meant to kiss her. That was when she closed her eyes. I closed mine too.

Her lips tasted of salt and summer sunshine. I smelled coconut sunscreen and a faint perfume from her hair. Her lips were soft as quicksand and I felt them move under mine. I put my arms around her and her arms went around my neck. I felt the curve of her shoulder blades, the small muscles of her back under my hands. Her fingers stretched out across the side of my head and grabbed a tangle of my hair.

I broke the kiss and started again, this time touching her lips with my tongue. Her mouth opened and her tongue flickered against mine. Something cracked inside me and a moan came out. I didn't understand for a second that it was me who made the noise, me, whose wife complained because I was so silent in bed.

It was a long kiss. When it was over I said, "And I thought you didn't like me." She smiled and her hands moved over my face, her thumbs next to my mouth, her little fingers under my chin, and she pulled me into her and kissed me with a concentration that made my knees go weak.

She took my hand and led me to the beach. She lay down on her towel, not on her back, which might have ended with us making love, but on her side, her head propped up with one hand. I pulled my towel over until it touched hers and then I lay facing her. I didn't know what she wanted so I leaned in to kiss her again. She put one hand on my chest as our mouths met, not resisting, but still holding me away.

I kissed her for a while and then I said, "What happens now?"

"I don't do things like this," she said. "I've been with Tom five years and I never . . ."

"Yeah, I know. Eleven years for me. But this is happening."

"You just . . . took me by surprise."

"Is that all it is?" I rolled her onto her back and kissed her again. Her arms went around me and held on tight. When I lifted my head we both had trouble breathing.

"No," she said. "It's not just surprise. It's trouble. I knew you were trouble the minute you got off the plane. It's why I tried to scare you away." We kissed some more and then she said, "I don't want you to stop kissing me. But I can't go any further than that now. You scare the hell out of me."

"I'm scared too."

The next time we pulled back she said, "Tell me what you're afraid of."

I rolled onto my back, leaving one hand on her waist. "A lot of things. I'm married, you live with somebody. I have a plane ticket that says I'm out of here in four days. I'm not looking for some kind of tropical quickie. I don't want it if it isn't real. I barely know you and you don't know me at all."

"I think I have a pretty good idea."

"No. You don't. I'm crazy, and there are things happening to me that I can't explain."

"Does this have anything to do with that Beach Boys tape you played me last night?"

I was stunned. "How did you know that?"

"The way you acted. Why don't you just tell me about it?"

I realized that I'd been looking for an excuse. So I told her. I told her about the Beatles song and Graham and *Celebration of the Lizard*. I told her about 1966 and how I went into the studio with Brian to finish *Smile*. "I can't say it wasn't all a hallucination. I may be completely out of my mind."

"But you don't feel crazy."

"Yeah, sometimes."

"You don't sound crazy."

"Thank you. And there's the tapes. The tapes are real. You heard *Smile* last night, and I've got a CD of *Celebration* in my room."

"If it felt real to you, then it was real."

"That sounds like Brian. Feelings are all that's real."

"He's right. Do you know how it happened? Can you do it again?"

"I don't think I want to. It was too . . . out of control. Anything could have happened." I touched the smooth soft skin of her face. "I didn't think I would be able to tell you all that."

"And now?"

"Now I'm really glad I did."

"Me too," she said. She leaned over and kissed me and we didn't talk again for a long time, just lay there kissing in the sand, and the entire world consisted of the smell of coconut oil and the sweet taste of her mouth, the heat of the sun and the gentle pressure of her body. I wanted her, the touch of her tiny, delicate hands drove me crazy, and at the same time I could have lain there and kissed her for days.

There was one moment that I will always have, like a photograph. She was lying in the hollow of my shoulder and she said, "I wonder sometimes why people can't just be happy. I know you can't be happy every minute, but most of the time. Just be happy unless there's some immediate tragedy right in front of you."

When I think about my life it doesn't seem like I've been happy that much of the time. She made it sound like the easiest thing in the world.

Something finally brought us back. The wind shifted or there was some sound below conscious recognition. Lori looked at her dive watch and said, "Christ, it's almost three. If Tom finds us gone he's going to wonder."

To hell with Tom was what I thought. The words that actually came out were, "I don't want to go."

She stopped in the middle of getting up and kissed me one last time. "Me either. We're going to do it anyway."

"We could run away," I said. "To some romantic Caribbean island."

"You're really something." She straightened up and grabbed the basket. "Shake out the towels and bring them to the car."

═══════

On the ride back I said something about Dr. Steve and Allyson, that if I was crazy I wouldn't get much help from a guy who was screwing a sixteen-year-old.

Lori laughed. "He's not screwing her. That's some weird game she's into. She's his daughter."

"Now that's really twisted."

"You get used to it. I mean, most of the people we get are like Pam and Richard, or retired people like your folks. But every once in a while we get weirdos. It's the tropics. People come all unglued."

"Tell me about it." I leaned over and kissed her on the side of the neck. This time she did physically push me away.

"We have to be careful. I mean it. Like *really* careful. Okay?" She turned to look at me.

"Okay," I said.

"If anybody asks, we had a picnic. If they ask where, say near the Naked Turtle. Which is not exactly a lie, we weren't far from there. The Naked Turtle is public and Tom wouldn't care so much about that."

"Okay."

She pulled into the driveway and was out of the car, carrying the basket, before I could react. I got out slowly. She was already at the door of the dive shop. "I'll see you tonight," she said.

"Okay."

When I got out of the shower I heard voices outside. Tom and Dr. Steve. I puttered around the room, wrote postcards to Elizabeth and my mother, tore up the one to my mother, started one to Pete. I've met somebody, I wanted to say. I wanted to tell the world.

It was an hour, all told, before my desire to see Lori overcame my nerves. I'd gotten to where I was looking at my watch every few seconds. I dried my hands on my pants legs and went out into the sunshine. They were all at the bar next door. Lori faced my way, masked by her sunglasses. She shifted in her chair as if she'd seen me, held still for a long second that made my heart beat hard, then turned to say something to Tom.

I sat in the same place as the day before, next to Tom, across from her.

"You look like you got some sun," Tom said.

I touched my forearm and the fingerprint showed white. "I had sunscreen on. I guess I needed something stronger."

"This is the tropics," Dr. Steve said. "You have to be careful."

I needed a drink. I ordered Tehuacán water instead.

"Getting a real taste for it, eh?" Tom said.

I felt like everybody there could read my guilty mind. Though Lori hadn't spoken I knew her eyes, behind her sunglasses, had never left me.

I asked about the dive. It turned out they'd seen a couple of sharks at Maracaibo. Allyson couldn't stop talking about them. "I thought I'd be so scared, and I wasn't. It was like, they didn't give a shit for me at all. It was like watching a hurricane or a forest fire or something."

Dr. Steve said, "Me, I'm scared of hurricanes and forest fires."

Tom said they were going back to the south end the next day, to the Columbia shallows. "Hector wants a couple of days off," he said to Lori. "Do you think you could help out with the boat?" She nodded and he said, "We'll do the shallows tomorrow and the drop-off on Friday." He turned to me. "What about it, are you in?"

I looked him in the eyes. There was no suspicion there, only the usual things that one man might show to another: the appearance, at least, of nothing to hide, the readiness to have another beer or tell another joke. "Sure," I said.

We all walked downtown for dinner. I don't remember much of it. I wanted to be alone with Lori, wondered if she felt the same. Tom didn't sit next to her, didn't physically assert himself. Still his attention centered on her all night, more so the more he drank. I saw Lori's submission to it, knew that if I offered to leave she wouldn't come with me.

We stayed at the restaurant until after ten. Afterward I sat in the darkness of my room for half an hour. Then I opened the door quietly and walked over to the deserted bar.

The moon was less than half full, low in the sky. What light there was came from the stars. There was a breeze off the ocean. I let my hair down and turned into the wind to feel it more. I had my eyes closed when Lori walked up, slow footsteps in the sand. Maybe, like me, she wanted to draw the pleasure out. She took forever to get there. Finally I opened my eyes. She was in cutoffs and a long-sleeved white sweater, and the loose waves of her red-brown hair were blowing too. I thought she was beautiful beyond words.

I reached one hand for her and she backed away. "No," she said. "No touching."

"Okay."

"Talking," she said. "We can do talking." She sat down across the table from me.

"What do you want to talk about?"

"I thought about what you said today. About Brian Wilson and all that. You make him sound so real, like I almost know him now. But it's like what you said about your father dying. It's hard to get your mind around it, that all that really happened to you. I know it's the truth. I know that. It's just hard."

"I could prove it to you. I can make the music come out of any kind of stereo. I could make it come out of your tape player, if you wanted me to." I heard the reluctance in my own voice.

"I believe you. I don't want a demonstration. You say it's over, and I think I like it better that way. It happened. It's in the past. I don't care about the past, I never did."

"And the future?"

"I guess I'll believe it when I see it."

"Which leaves right now."

"Yes."

"That's not so bad."

"No."

"What would you do if we were really alone? If nobody could see us?" It's not like me to take so much for granted. It had to be Lori that brought it out.

She put her arms on the table and rested her chin on them. She was halfway across the table toward me. Her dark blue eyes burned into me. "Kiss you," she said. "I thought about kissing you all through dinner."

"I want to make love to you."

"Ah, sex. Sex is more difficult."

"Sex is easy. Everybody does it. You don't even need a license."

She straightened up and her face disappeared in shadow. She was quiet so long that I said, "I'm sorry. I didn't mean to be so . . ."

"That's okay. It's not you, it's me. I don't have orgasms easily. That's what I should have said in the first place. I don't have those earth-shattering vaginal orgasms I read about in books. Books that *men* write, most of the time. In fact when I read about them it seems like some kind of cruel joke."

It was hard not to be able to touch her. "You don't come easily or you don't come at all?"

"I can come. With a lot of patience and . . . tenderness. And like that."

"Which Tom doesn't do."

"Not in a long time, no. I mean, there's sex. There's lots of sex. Tom comes. Every forty-eight hours. You could set your watch. You're tired of this, right? Of the truth all the goddamn time? It can be pretty exhausting."

"Is that what . . . last night . . ."

"Yeah. I had to excuse myself to perform my duties."

"And then you came back out here, and . . ."

"And had a perfectly lovely time with you. Yeah, that's what I did. Can you see that sex is not a big deal for me? It's like Tom has some bizarre disease and I have to give him this treatment every other day. Sort of like an insulin shot, only messier."

"I don't know what to say."

"There's nothing you *can* say. I should go."

"Wait. Don't just walk away. I want to hold you."

"No. I said no. It's too dangerous."

"I'm starting not to care who sees us."

"Well, I do. Okay?"

"Okay," I said.

She stood up. "I'll see you tomorrow."

"Lori . . ."

"Today meant a lot to me."

"Me too."

"Okay. Good. I'll see you."

She took three steps toward the dive shop and then she turned. I was already on my feet. She came into my arms and kissed me in a way that turned my brain to white light. There was nothing held back. She was completely there, her breath, her mouth, her tongue, her body, her hands, her arms.

Then, just as suddenly, I was alone in the dark.

———

Columbia Shallows is a maze of coral walls. The reefs come almost to the surface and the bottom is only at thirty or forty feet. I dove a tank in the morning and snorkled in the afternoon. In between we had a picnic lunch on the beach: fried chicken, potato salad, beer for those who wanted it. Eventually I relaxed enough to enjoy Lori's presence, even if I couldn't touch her or ask her anything more than to pass the salt.

The shallow water made for long, easy dives. The sponges were huge, all shades of incandescent reds and yellows, and starfish sunned themselves on top of the coral walls. Everybody was relaxed and joking—except for Tom, who circled Lori like a shark.

When we got back, just before sundown, he announced that everybody was on their own for dinner, and he and Lori disappeared inside the shop. Dr. Steve asked me to join him and Allyson, which I thought was pretty sensitive of him, given what I'd seen so far. He knew a place with Texas-style enchiladas, a rarity on the island.

Halfway through dinner he asked me, "Made any progress?"

I was thinking of Lori so the remark threw me. "What?"

"On this father business."

"Oh. I don't know. I don't feel like I'm really getting any answers down here."

"Of course not. This is where you have to look." He tapped the side of his head. He leaned way over his plate to fork up another bite of enchilada, and dribbled cheese into his beard. "Do you know the questions you want answers to?"

"Some of them. Part of it is purely selfish, I guess. I want to know if he was thinking of me when he died. I want to know if he killed himself, I mean, deliberately decided to die. If I could just know what he was thinking, it would tell me so much. When he died, that was the first time death was ever *real* to me. It's like his brain was a camera, and it took a picture of death. If I could get inside his brain, I could see what death looked like."

"I don't see what the big deal is," Allyson said. Her dinner was a fruit plate, a daiquiri, and a stack of corn tortillas. "Why do men worry about death all the time? I mean, the point is like to live. Live until you die, and then it's over. Am I right?"

Once I thought about it, it did seem that most of the people who rail against death and struggle for immortality are male. My mother says she's ready, whenever her time is up. "It's hard to argue with," I said.

Dr. Steve belched loudly and excused himself to go to the bathroom. He seemed lost as he wandered off through the restaurant. The conversation had lapsed without him, so I said, "Do you and your dad travel a lot?"

"My dad? You mean Steve?"

"It's okay. Lori told me he was your father."

"She told you that?" She laughed a jaded, forty-year-old laugh. "She probably believes it."

"You mean he's not . . ." My face felt hot.

"Actually I'm hurt that you could even imagine a resemblance." She grinned and rolled up another tortilla. I looked down at my plate and concentrated on my food. We were sitting that way when Dr. Steve came back.

He poured the rest of his beer into his glass and said, "You know, the Buddhists say that all unhappiness springs from desire. I don't know what made me think of that except I just had my penis in my hand. Anyway, Lacan said that desire springs from loss. The loss of your father leads to desires you can't fulfill, for knowledge maybe, or for some transformative experience. The lack of fulfillment of our desires leads to unhappiness, hmmmm? Loss is inevitable, you know, you can't change that. So maybe you should work on the desire."

It was more sense than he'd made in the entire time I'd known him and it took me by surprise. Besides which, the word "desire" only made me think about Lori more. "I'll have to mull that over."

"It's highly symbolic, you know. To lose your father to the Abyss. It's a potent symbol, like the crossroad in African mythology, the place where the spiritual and physical worlds cross. I think of Nietzsche, the business of the Abyss staring back into you. Jung had something about it also, which I can't bring to mind."

"Jesus," Allyson said. "Nietzsche and Jung. I think the poor guy just needs to get laid."

═════

We got to the dive shop around nine. I turned the corner of the yellow cinder block building and saw that Lori wasn't at the tables. My heart sank. I said good-night to Allyson and Dr. Steve and spent five minutes in my room for the sake of appearances. Then I went outside and sat at the Tecate table.

The light went out in Tom and Lori's room at nine-thirty. Waves breaking in the distance sounded like voices. I thought of them having sex there in the dark. Lori had said every forty-eight hours, and tonight was the night. It knotted me up inside.

Maybe she would tell him no. Maybe even now they were arguing, she was telling him she would leave.

Yeah, right.

I heard the tick of a slowing bicycle. I turned and saw a white shirt, starlight glinting off chrome, a face: Walker, from the commune. He propped the bike against one of the tables and sat down next to me.

"Where is everybody?"

"An early night," I said.

"You seen Lori?"

"She and Tom are holed up in there."

"Ah." He stretched his blue-jeaned legs, folded his hands behind his head, wiggled his bare toes in the sand.

"So what's happening down at the commune?"

"Everybody's having sex down there too."

"Not you."

"No, man, it's sad. I lost my taste for earnest, unwashed college girls. One of those things, I guess."

"Maybe you're a romantic."

"I see you been talking to Lori." When I didn't answer right away he said, "I had a flirtation or something with her, I guess it was last fall. Didn't come to anything. She stuck with Tom because Tom doesn't really give a shit about her."

"What do you mean?"

"I mean she gets what she needs from him. In her case, that means she gets knocked around a little. No way I'm going to play that shit. Is there any beer around?"

I was falling down toward Palancar Reef with too many weights and no buoyancy vest. "There's a bar over there but I think it's locked."

"Screw it, I don't need one."

"He really hits her?"

"I've seen the bruises, man. Gave her a black eye once. Guy's got a temper, gets wound up tighter and tighter and then boom. About once a month you see some busted up piece of furniture out by the dumpster, you know Tom's on the warpath again."

"I can't believe she'd be the type to put up with that."

"Type? There's no 'type,' man. You never know what somebody else is going to bring out in you. That's why people don't give up on sex entirely, stay home and practice self-touch. Like my daddy used to say about poker, never two hands the same. Always that thrill of the unknown."

"So," I said. "You came down to see her?"

Walker shrugged. "Okay. Maybe I am a romantic."

We were quiet for a while, just a couple of guys, sitting around the tropics, looking at the stars.

After a while I said, "Lori called you the local shaman. Is that for real?" I was thinking of Doors songs: "Shaman's Blues," "The WASP," and of course "Celebration."

"I guess. I don't want to get into a whole 'what is reality' thing. Calling me a shaman is as good as anything. Every society's got to have somebody in that slot. Weddings and divorces. Help the sick. Pray for rain. Raise the dead."

"What?"

"I'm not talking zombies or anything. I've been known to conjure up a departed spirit, if somebody really needs to talk to them. Plus I'm sort of the bandleader for the all-night drumming sessions."

The thought had sprung up against my will. "Could you raise my father?"

"I could give it a shot. You want me to?"

"What, right now?"

"No, it's a pretty involved thing. You have to fast and meditate, we have to do a lot of ceremonial shit. It pretty much takes all day. I can put it together for you if you want."

"No," I said. "No, that's okay."

We talked for another half hour. I told him about the stereo repair business. He told me about growing up middle-class in Harlem: poetry, theater, card tricks, then the step from stage magic to the real thing. "They're closer than you think. Ask anybody who does sleight of hand. When it really cooks you can feel it, the mechanics disappear and you're making it all happen through the force of your will. Which is exactly what capital-M Magick is about. The guys that do the best sleight-of-hand stuff—I'm not talking about disappearing elephants,

I'm talking like Harry Lorayne—they can do a card trick that will change the way you see the world."

"And that's what you do?"

"That's what I aspire to. Shamanism's really the same, a few tricks to change your perspective. Get you back in touch with the world."

"The Gaia thing."

"Yeah. If you can make people experience the planet as a living thing, man, that's deep. You can turn them around."

"I'd like to see the act," I said.

"Saturday night. Day after tomorrow. We're going to do a drum thing out at the beach."

"Perfect. Because I am out of here early Sunday morning."

"Cool." He stood up, put a hand on my shoulder. "Come by as early as you can. Skip breakfast and lunch if you really want to get into it. That way if you want to work on your father, we can do that too. Either way, the drums start a little before sunset."

He walked his bike out to the highway and the clink of his pedals faded into the darkness.

I looked at my watch. It was 10:30. Everything I thought I knew was slipping away. I thought about Lori and Tom fucking, Tom hitting her and breaking up the furniture. It was another tough one to get my mind around. Then I thought about Lori flirting with Walker and Lori flirting with me and wondered what the difference was, if any. After that I thought about a bunch of hippie types dancing in a big circle on the beach. In the middle of the circle was supposed to be a big fire, only it was a pile of smoking ashes, like the ones my mother brought home to Dallas. The smoke turned into a wavy cartoon ghost with my father's head, with bushy cartoon hairs coming out of his nose and ears.

My watch said 10:32. It looked like a long night.

I walked up to the highway. It was stark black against the lesser darkness of the sky. There weren't any cars. I kicked off my moccasins and started to run. I ran at the night as hard as I could, on and on, until fire crawled up my side and left me gasping on my hands and knees.

―――

The morning was cloudy and cool. I couldn't seem to get my blood moving. The boat ride took an hour. The whole time I had the sensation that Lori was trying to meet my eyes. I would look at her and she would be staring off in another direction. I told myself she hadn't really had a chance. I thought about the way she kissed me Wednesday night and told myself to be patient.

I couldn't get it out of my head that in less than two days I was supposed to be on a plane to Texas.

Images danced in my head, some of them the same as the night before. I skipped the part about my father. My father wasn't much on my mind. It was Tom and Lori, Lori and Walker. Lori and me at the beach, which already seemed as distant as a dream.

We anchored off the south end of the island. To the east were the shallows where we'd been the day before. The sun slid in and out of the clouds. Every time it went under I got a chill. I was the last one to suit up, hoping in vain that Tom would leave me alone with Lori and Hector's father, if only for a moment.

I hit the water in an explosion of bubbles. I blew air into my vest and waited for Tom, then we turned and swam together down to the reef. The sun broke through for a moment and the milky water turned clear. The towers of coral below us lit up in shades of yellow and purple and green.

I'd slept badly. I was jittery and the water felt cold. I had to consciously make myself slow down and go easy on the air. It was hard to pay attention, even to myself. It was like I wasn't entirely there, like the water flowed through me. Like I was a ghost.

We pulled up at the top of the reef and I checked my depth gauge. Seventy feet. Tom pointed at something and it took me a second to understand. It was a sponge, the biggest I've ever seen. It must have been five feet tall, neon yellow, shaped like a Greek jar. A queen angelfish hid behind it. It fluttered away from Tom's hand and shook its tail at him. I could see him get a real charge out of it.

We drifted for an hour, Tom pointing at things, me nodding. When he swam off to herd the other couples into line, he was never out of my sight. I would look up now and then and see the boat far above us, following the trail of our bubbles.

We were low on air. Tom had led us to the top of a coral tower at fifty feet. My heart was beating strangely, hard but not very fast. I could feel it shake my chest. Tom looked at Allyson and Dr. Steve's air gauges and sent them up. Then Pam and Richard waved him over.

I was on the edge of the drop-off. The Abyss, Dr. Steve called it. There were terraces, with white patches of sand between the coral heads, as it fell away into darkness. After a while I started to swim down.

It felt good to be moving. My heart beat faster and I was warm and comfortable. My air gave out and I reached back to flip the reserve lever. It was noticeably darker as I got deeper. I closed my eyes.

Something grabbed me. Shark? I thought, suddenly afraid. I turned around and a huge shadowy thing took hold of me and shook me. It was Tom. His face was inches away, rage in his eyes. He had me by the straps of my backpack. Shaking me. Shaking me.

I thought, where the hell am I?

We were ascending, keeping pace with the cloud of bubbles from our regulators. I looked up. Pam and Richard were alongside the boat. They looked like insects, skimming the surface of an upside-down ocean.

I tried to push Tom away, nodding and signaling that I was okay. He shook me again and didn't let go. His eyes, inside his mask, looked like he was going to hit me.

Holy Christ, I thought. I went over the edge.

In an instant the water leeched all the heat from my body. I couldn't look at Tom any longer. Pam and Richard, please, God, had already started up and hadn't seen it. If Tom said anything to Lori . . .

We were almost up. I had to suck hard to get any air. Tom stopped at ten feet and let me go with one hand long enough to reel in his depth gauge. It said we'd hit a maximum depth of 103 feet, not far enough to worry about decompression.

My air was gone. I touched my mouthpiece with two fingers to show I was out. Tom looked like he was trying to decide. I threw my mouthpiece over my shoulder to let him know I was serious. He waited another second or two, then gave me his. It was a hard pull. I saw he'd already tripped his reserve too. I gave it back and pushed his hand away and swam for the boat.

When I broke the surface I saw Lori by the ladder. "Everything okay?"

"Fine," I said, trying not to gasp. I heard Tom come up behind me. I handed her my fins, then undid the straps and let her pull the tank up and off. I climbed into the boat and sat down.

I didn't look at Tom. I unclamped my regulator from the tank, following routine, not letting my brain kick in. My hands shook and I had to take it slow, elbows on my thighs. You're supposed to blow air out of the tank to dry the seals on the regulator. There wasn't enough in mine to hiss.

Pam and Richard were raving about some monster piece of staghorn coral they'd seen. Tom sat down on the opposite side of the boat to strip off his vest and T-shirt and knife. The clouds had burned away. Everything was so bright it stung my eyes. I felt drunk and detached, and at the same time I felt sick and scared, mostly over what Tom would do next. I got my gear sorted out and then sat aft, arms wrapped around my knees, trying to look casual.

"Can we go to the shallows and snorkel for a while?" Allyson said. "That was cool yesterday."

Tom looked up. I didn't like his eyes. They were flat and cold and dark. "We didn't bring lunch," he said. He sounded almost normal, but not quite. Allyson got very quiet. Lori turned around from the wheel to look at him. Hector's father gathered up the empty tanks, head down, and racked them.

It was a long ride back. Long enough for the sun to finally warm me up, though my brain was still in shock. Lori parked the boat and we all carried our tanks into the shed for refills and hosed down our personal gear on the dock. I barely had the strength to carry my tank. I wanted to lie down and sleep for a million years. Mostly I wanted Tom to act like nothing had happened. But as I walked away I heard him behind me. "Your room," he said.

We went in and Tom closed the door. I got a fresh towel and dried off, then sat on the edge of the bed. I ached to stretch out and close my eyes.

"So what the fuck happened?" There was no way to pretend he wasn't mad.

"I don't know."

"What do you mean you don't know? Another ten feet and we could both be dead. Bent, embolized, drowned, anything. What the hell was going on in your head?"

"That's just it," I said.

"What's just it?" I don't think he knew he was shouting.

"I wanted to know what was in my father's head when he went over the edge. And then it happened to me, and . . . I mean, there was nothing there. My brain was empty. It was like . . . it just seemed like the right thing to do at the moment. And . . . I don't know. That's what it must have been like for him. No putting his life on the scales, no agonizing, just a stupid impulse and . . . gone."

Tom slammed the wall with one open hand. "I don't put up with this kind of shit on my tours. You understand? I want you out of here, today, this afternoon. That's number one. Number two, you need to get some professional help. I don't know what's wrong with you, but you are definitely one screwed-up son of a bitch. If I were you I would get on a plane this afternoon and go check in someplace where they would watch me around the fucking clock."

I saw then that he was more scared than anything. I didn't especially like somebody who beat up women calling me sick, but on the other hand I could see his point. My dad came from the same place. Keep your problems to yourself, and sure as hell don't let them endanger other people. And if you sit on them long enough maybe they'll go away.

I wished I was in Southern California in 1966. Brian would have understood. Brian didn't hide his feelings, Brian knew what kind of Pandora's box you open up once you treat your emotions like they're important. I was about to get misty-eyed right there, which was not what Tom needed to see.

"Okay," I said. "I'll settle up and get out. But I can't go home right now. I promise I won't go near the reef. That's over. I'll get a room downtown until Sunday."

"Shit." I watched the fear and anger drain out of him. "You might as well stay here. At least I can keep an eye on you. But no more diving. I could pull your C-card for this, and I might do it anyway."

I nodded.

He stood there awkwardly for a second, flexing his hands. "All right. You look like you need some rest. If you . . . if you start to feel crazy, come and get me. We can talk or something."

"Yeah, okay." I barely heard my own voice. "Thanks."

As soon as he shut the door I kicked off my wet swimsuit and fell into a sleep that shut out the entire world.

═══

Somebody was knocking, barely loud enough to be heard. I got into a pair of jeans and stumbled to the door.

Lori had already turned away. "I woke you up. I'm sorry."

"Don't be," I said. "I'm not." She was in a plain white T-shirt and cutoffs. The sight of her was enough to wake me up. "Come on in." I left the door open and went to wash my face and rinse the stale sleep taste out of my mouth.

I heard the door close. "Tom wouldn't tell me what happened down there today," she said.

"Thank God for small favors," I said. "At least he's not spreading it around."

She was still by the door when I came out of the bathroom, arms folded over her chest. "So what did happen?"

I sat on the bed with my back against the wall. "Apparently," I said, "I tried to kill myself."

"Oh Jesus. You mean, like your father?"

"That's what it looked like."

"You sound like you weren't even there."

"In a way I wasn't."

She sat in the bentwood chair in the corner.

"Where's Tom now?" I asked her.

"They all went into town. I'm supposed to join them. He thought my hanging around here was fishy as hell, as a matter of fact. I really can't stay."

I nodded. "I guess—"

"You guess what?"

"I guess I'm really fucked up, aren't I? I mean, that's the thing that just surprises the shit out of me. I thought I was pretty normal. And look at me."

"That's not what you sounded like the other night. When you told me about Brian Wilson? You didn't sound like you thought you were normal then."

"That was weird, but it was functional. I came out of it with a tape. This is like nonfunctional in a major way." I closed my eyes and leaned back until my head hit the cinder blocks. "My father always used to say, 'You can't complain about the way we raised you because you turned out okay.' Well, guess what, Dad?" I was crying, for Christ's sake. "I'm not okay. I'm fucked up. My marriage is in the toilet, I've been drunk for the last fifteen years, I've been in fantasyland for six months, and now I just tried to kill myself. So can I complain now?"

Lori stood up. It was like she was a toy, with one set of hands pushing her toward me and another set holding her back. The first two steps were hard, and then she was sitting on the edge of the bed. "Oh, Ray," she said. "We're *all* fucked up. We're all damaged goods. Every one of us. You have no idea. I have so many dark, ugly secrets . . ."

She put her hand on my bare chest and I felt the energy hum between us. I gripped her arm above the elbow and with my right hand I cupped her face and pulled her into a kiss. I felt her breath change, turn deep and shaky. So did mine.

"Ray? Ray, I know where this is heading. You do too. I don't know if I'm ready for it, can you understand that?"

"Yes. I don't know if I'm ready for it either."

She took my face in her hands and kissed me. "Thank you. It's so easy to be with you. I never thought it could be like this."

"Me too."

"I really, really, have to go."

"Wait."

She pushed my hands away and stood up. "I have to meet Tom. He's suspicious already."

"Something's happening between us, it's happening right now. I want to hear your secrets. I want to know everything about you. You can't walk out on that."

"Yes I can. You don't want to know, Ray. If I told you, it would change everything between us. Don't push. Please."

"I want to push. I want to know everything."

"I have to go." I saw that I'd done all I could. "I'll be here tonight.

Late. I'll meet you out at the tables. Tom's already drinking, he'll be passed out by ten."

I started toward her and she ducked outside. "Tonight," she said.

━━━━━━

I ate in town at some hole-in-the-wall. There were no tourists there, just local men in fresh *guayabera* shirts and slicked-back hair, ready for Friday night. Afterward I walked for a long time, my mind empty.

I was outside the dive shop before ten. Eventually Lori came, still in the T-shirt and cutoffs, wearing a black-and-white flannel shirt like a jacket. She led me to the water and than up along a ragged lava cliff. I took her hand, and once we were out of sight of the dive shop I kissed her.

"Talk to me," I said. "Tell me everything."

"Please don't start again."

"It's about Tom, right? Look, Walker was down here last night."

"Oh God."

"He told me Tom hits you. It's true, isn't it?"

She turned her back on me and sat on the edge of the cliff. I heard the water smash against the rocks and smelled the spicy odor of the brush behind us. The breeze played with her hair.

"What happened to honesty, Lori?"

"Okay. Yes. He hits me. Some of the time . . . I don't know, most of the time, it's my fault. I push him to it."

"Bullshit."

"You have this idea of who I am, but that's not me. I'm not a good person. Bad things happen to me. Something about me makes them happen. It's been that way all my life."

I sat down next to her. I gave her a couple of feet and didn't try to touch her.

"Okay," she said. "Okay. You want the truth? Here's the truth. I was molested by my grandfather when I was eleven years old."

I nodded. "I thought it was something like that. Can you talk about it?"

"Sure. Sure I can talk about it. I spent a lot of time on psychiatrists' couches so I could talk about it. You know what the irony is? My grandfather's name was Tom too. Everybody called him T.J., but the T was for Tom."

We listened to the waves for a minute and then she said, "My mother's family had this farm in Missouri. We used to go up there in the summer, and . . . I can't tell you what it was like. All those memories, they're just not the same anymore. But it was like . . . magic. It wasn't a real working farm, Grandpa was this sort of gentleman farmer with a lot of land and a big brick house and all these animals. I always wanted a sister, and during the summer my cousin Sara would be there, her and her brother John, and we'd swim and play all day long."

Another pause. "When I was eleven we moved to St. Louis. Daddy couldn't find a job in Tennessee and Grandpa hired him at his furniture store there. It was just for a year or so, till we could get back on our feet. We ended up moving back to Murfreesboro two years later. Anyway, it was summer, and Momma and Daddy would spend every weekend in St. Louis looking for a house, and they left me at the farm. Then we'd all be there on weekends. So during the day us kids would all go out with Grandpa on the tractor. I remember . . . we must have been pulling something, because John and Sara were riding on whatever it was we were pulling, and everybody got to take turns sitting up front on his lap and steering and shifting and stuff. And when I was up there he put his hands between my legs. I was just kind of . . . I couldn't tell if he was holding me on the seat, or what. It struck me as odd but not really serious, you know?

"Then that weekend Momma and Daddy came down. The routine for the children was that we got to play in the yard all morning, have lunch, and then go swimming. Momma had two younger sisters. One still lived in Missouri and the other brought her kids home for summers. Real close, right? The perfect family. Anyway, you had to have a nap between lunch and swimming.

"I was upstairs, and they had us in separate bedrooms, so we'd at least pretend to sleep. I was in Grandma's bedroom, which was at the top of the stairs, and he came in and put his finger to his mouth and said, 'Shhhh,' like maybe he was going to let me get up or something, I don't know.

"Then he molested me.

"He did things he shouldn't have done. He touched me between the legs, he put his finger inside me. And I was very scared and very quiet until it was all over. He had these huge hands. He was such a big man, with these great, huge hands.

"As soon as he was gone I went to the bathroom, where I could see him come out of the house and go to the barn. Then I went downstairs to Momma and told her everything that happened."

"He did it when your mother was there in the house?"

"Her and at least one of the aunts. But wait. Grandpa was bad enough, but Momma was a hundred times worse. The first thing she said was not to ever mention it to anyone. We would talk about it later. I had to promise her never, ever, to tell Daddy, because if he found out he would kill Grandpa. And she said it was up to me to just stay away from Grandpa, to not let it happen again."

"Jesus Christ."

"She wasn't even drinking much then. That came later. What was weird was that she didn't ever disagree with me, she never actually questioned me about what had happened. She just took it all in stride. I didn't figure that out until a long time later."

"You mean he'd molested her too."

"You got it. We figured it out when I was in therapy. This was later, when I was in college in St. Louis. I told my shrink all about Grandpa and he thought it was weird too, for her not to have been flabbergasted and go, 'Oh my God, no! You must have misinterpreted.' It was my shrink who first brought up the idea that maybe this was a generational thing, that Momma had herself been molested. I finally got her to admit it one night when she was drunk. I don't know about the other sisters.

"It was so important to the sisters that our family looked perfect from the outside. The same with Momma, she had to be the perfect mother, and she told me from the day I was born that I was the most important thing in her life, that we had the perfect family. She would do anything to hold the family together. Grandma was absolutely not interested at all, not in housekeeping, children, or anything else. There were cooks and maids and things, but it was Momma who ran things. And I guess she had an investment in keeping the sham alive, to prove that she'd done the right thing by her younger sisters in helping raise them. Grandma and Grandpa were always fighting and threatening to leave each other and get a divorce. Momma sure didn't want that when she was young, she had too many burdens as it was without one or the other of them being totally gone.

"It wasn't until both Grandma and Grandpa were dead and buried that this supposed closeness of the sisters came apart. First one sister was the bad guy and was excommunicated and then another. They went to court over the will and nasty, horrible things were said, and it finally fell apart. I mean, it was a farce."

"Did you ever go back there, after it happened?"

"Are you kidding? Every summer. Momma made me go back every summer, for like a month at a time. When you first got to the farm there were these big white gates and a sign saying SHANGRI-LA. Can you imagine? The land of eternal youth. Huh. Finding out no one's ever going to take care of you or protect you makes you grow up very fast."

"And your grandfather?"

"Grandpa tried to touch me again a couple of times but I got away. When I told Momma she acted like it was my fault, that I was responsible for keeping away from him.

"I tried to talk to her about it, years later, after I was grown up and out of college and everything. When she wasn't drunk, of course, I could never talk to her about anything when she was drunk. I went to her and said, 'Look, I'm really, really mad and I want to know why you did this. I was eleven years old. I was supposed to be the most important thing in your life. How could you have been more concerned with protecting your father than protecting me? How could you make me go back for all those years? How could you, how could you, how could you?'

"Well, all she would say was, 'I did the best I could at the time.' And shit like, 'Well, we didn't know back then the things we know now about sexual abuse and counseling, it never occurred to me to get counseling for an eleven-year-old child. I did the best I could and there's nothing more to talk about.' She could always shut down a conversation with just one of her looks."

"Okay," I said. "I can see why you might not be too keen on going back and staying with your mother."

"You can't imagine. By high school she was really drinking heavily. I think that led to my being real shy in school, not having a lot of friends. There was no way I could possibly bring anybody home. I'd walk in the door, Momma would be drunk, it was something I just couldn't deal with. And she would pick at Daddy, just keep nagging and picking and nagging and picking until he'd turn around and they'd have an all-out fistfight."

"Fistfight?"

She nodded. "I remember once getting up in the night, I guess I was a senior in high school. I walked in the front room in time to see Daddy throw Momma across the room. And then he turned to me and apologized for it. I mean, neither of them ever laid a hand on me, but I saw things a child should never see. I saw Daddy dunk my mother's head in the toilet to try and sober her up.

"After Daddy left her, I tried to keep up some kind of relationship. That same urge, I guess, to try and pretend we were a real family. And we'd go out shopping or something, and have a great time, and we'd come home and then she'd start getting drunk, real fast. I'd never see the liquor. To this day I don't know where she hides it. We'd just be sitting there and she would get drunker and drunker and drunker. It was so . . . heartbreaking, to get this taste of what it was like to have her back and then lose her again, in the space of maybe half an hour."

"Do you think the business with your Grandpa, I mean, do you think that was why she drank so much?"

"Who knows? I know Grandpa has haunted me all these years, maybe it was the same with her. There is a kind of epilogue to the Grandpa story. When I was in college in St. Louis and going to this shrink, he wanted me to go back out and look at the farm, see what else it might bring back. It had been sold to these other people, and I was just amazed at how wrecked the place was. It was utterly, utterly destroyed. It was so strange because now the outside was as ruined as all my memories were. Anyway, after I drove by the farm I went out to the cemetery where Grandpa is buried. On the way I stopped at the store and bought a can of black spray paint. I was going to go to his grave and black out his headstone. I thought it would be like blacking him out of my life or something, I don't know.

"When I got there I started to lose my nerve. I mean, if anybody was there they would see my car, and the Tennessee plates, and there wouldn't be any doubt about who did it. I walked around for a while and the sun started to go down, and then I walked over to Grandpa's grave. And I found it was all coming back. I mean, how truly, totally sick that man was. How that sickness destroyed everyone around him. How he ruined my childhood—retroactively—and screwed up my teen years, and how he'd ruined my momma's life in a completely different way. And I thought about his funeral, when I looked at him in the coffin and was scared that he wasn't really dead, like he was some kind of vampire or something. And I just thought, 'You . . . son . . . of . . . a . . . bitch.' And so I wrote that, just wrote S.O.B. in big drippy spray-paint letters on his tombstone.

"And I drove back to St. Louis and I felt a hell of a lot better."

The night was turning cool. She had both her hands knotted together and it seemed like a bad time to touch her. "Did you ever tell your father?"

She nodded. "Oh jeez. That's another can of worms. Haven't you had enough for one night?"

"We've come this far. I want to hear all of it."

She was quiet again for a while, gathering herself. "I told you I was seeing a psychiatrist in St. Louis, at college. The reason is I was raped, senior year. And I just went into total isolation afterwards. I wasn't leaving the house except to go to class or see the shrink, I didn't answer the phone, my finances were all screwed up and I was bouncing checks and stuff. Daddy started calling and yelling into the phone and leaving nasty messages, and finally I sat down and wrote a letter addressed to him and Momma both, telling them about the rape, and that I just couldn't cope with the world right now. And when my father got the letter he immediately got on a plane to St. Louis, and like the next thing I knew he was there at my door, carrying this bottle of Drambuie. He must have stopped on the way to the airport because he knew I liked Drambuie, like that was going to make everything all right. It was just ludicrous. And we sat there on the couch, drinking brandy, and I was crying and he was crying, and he said, 'I can't understand,' because this was literally months after it had happened, 'why you couldn't just have told your mother, if you couldn't tell me.'

"And I just snapped. This horrible, hateful, yelling and screaming anger came over me and I called him a son of a bitch and I said, 'You want to know why? Let me tell you about something really horrible.' And I told him. And I said, 'How could you have been so fucking blind that you never saw the change in me, never saw that I had no child-hood? Why did I have to watch those drunken battles, why didn't you just take me away?'

"And he just flipped. I don't think he heard anything I said against him. He started threatening to kill Momma. I stayed up with him all night, trying to calm him down, but something had snapped in him too. He went back to Murfreesboro and like the next month he served papers on her and moved out."

"Jesus."

"So you see what I'm talking about? Grandpa, my parents' screwed-up marriage, the rape, my mother's drinking, it's all my fault. I've never had a relationship with anybody where I didn't push it over the edge. You see the hurt in me but you don't see the anger. You ask about me and Tom, can't you see I belong with him? How I punish him as much as he punishes me? For not being what I want, for not being the way out from my miserable existence? He and I deserve each other, at least we're not hurting anybody else. I don't want to hurt you, I don't want to fuck up your life."

"What about your life? Isn't that worth anything? I mean, you're in physical danger here."

"You don't get it. You just don't understand. That's what being a woman means. It means you're a little bit scared all the time. With Tom at least I know where it's coming from."

"And of course, you deserve it, right?"

"Maybe. If somebody treated me like I was the heroine of one of these romance novels, I wouldn't know how to handle it. Because that's not me. I'm trouble, and I destroy everything I touch. Look at you. We spend one wonderful afternoon at the beach and a day and a half later you nearly kill yourself."

I grabbed her by the shoulders. "Stop it. That's a lot of melodramatic crap. I'm at least three quarters in love with you already. You're the most beautiful, fascinating creature I've ever seen."

The toughness melted away before my eyes. The person underneath seemed terribly young and curiously innocent and I knew it would be very easy to hurt her. It was the woman I'd seen the first time she took her dark glasses off. "Really?" she said.

"Really." I kissed her and for a few seconds she clung to me, kissing me back passionately. Then she pulled away, touching my forehead with the top of her head.

"I'm sorry," she said. "I'm just on this roller coaster. I feel all these things for you, and then, wham, there's all these images from my past again. Can you understand that at all?"

"Of course."

"I mean, with what I've been through in my life, I shouldn't let a man near me. But . . . it gets lonely. Everybody needs to be touched." She ran her hands down my arms. "You're very sweet, Ray. But it's time for you to fly back to Texas and breathe a huge sigh of relief as you leave this crazy woman far behind you."

I pulled her close and ran my fingers through her hair. "That's not till Sunday. I understand that this is not the time or the place for us to make love. I don't care about that now. I want to spend the night with you. Just talking, and kissing, and holding you. Can we do that?"

"Yes," she said, her voice very soft.

———

We stayed up until five, kissing and gently touching each other and not going any further. We were both scared and the limits made it easier. I hadn't done anything like it since high school.

We talked a lot too. About our parents, about books and music, about each other. She couldn't believe I'd seen through her tough-guy act and I couldn't believe she expected me not to.

I left her outside the dive shop. It was still dark and it was the quietest I remember the island ever being—no birds or insects, the ocean calmed to a whisper.

"Are you diving today?" she said.

I shook my head. "I'm going to see Walker."

"And Moonflower?" I heard an edge of jealousy still there. "She'll give you what I didn't."

"Just Walker. And maybe go to the drumming thing. Will you come?"

She softened again. "I'll try. You know how Tom is."

"Tonight's the night, you mean."

"Yeah. But maybe it's time to change that."

———

I slept for a few hours, then walked down the road and called a cab to take me to the commune. I was starved, but Walker had said no food. I felt weightless. It was Lori's gravity that held me, not the gravity of the world.

Inside the commune I asked for Walker and the French girl

pointed me to a room on the second floor. Concrete steps led up to a sagging walkway. I knocked on a weathered door and Walker's voice told me to come in.

There was a woman in the narrow bed with him, her face to the wall, a long expanse of pale naked back and dark hair turned toward me. She snored softly. Walker was cross-legged, the sheet over his lap, smoking dope in a pipe that reminded me of Brian's. "You're early," he said. I started to apologize and he said, "No, it's cool." He got up, casually naked, and pulled on a pair of drawstring cotton pants. "You ready to raise the dead?"

"I don't know. Is that what I'm here for?"

He picked up a dark green knapsack by the straps and we walked outside. "Well, I guess you got to tell me. You look ready for something."

I followed him to the kitchen and watched him fry up something that involved tofu, onions, mushrooms, and three or four different kinds of peppers. My stomach growled at the sight of it.

"You eaten anything today?"

I shook my head.

"What now?" I asked.

He sat at the kitchen table and I took a chair across from him. "Okay," he said. "First we have to focus you. I want you to think of a picture of your father and describe it to me."

I had to think. "There's a picture sits on my wife's dresser. My mother gave it to her because I'm in it. It's at my grandmother's house in Laredo. I'm on a kind of park bench between my mom and dad, maybe four or five years old. I can remember the shirt I'm wearing, it's this green seersucker Hawaiian shirt, all crinkled and scratchy.

"So here's my father with his wife and kid, legs crossed, left arm up on the back of the bench, lit cigarette in his right hand. He's all grown up, see, he's a man, a family man. Only this guy in the picture is younger than I am now."

"Tell me about his face."

"He's got short dark hair, combed back. His face is tanned, pretty dark, lots of squint lines from the sun."

"Is he smiling?"

I thought about it. "It's a grudging smile. A let's-get-this-over-with smile."

"Clothes?"

I closed my eyes. "Long-sleeved white shirt and clip-on bow tie. My mother's in a brown-and-gray checked cotton dress. She's self-conscious, can't relax. And nobody's actually touching anybody else. We're as close as we can get without touching."

After a few seconds Walker said, "What's your father thinking?"

I could see his eyes. They were narrow and unrelenting. It would have been my grandmother who took the picture, his mother, the one he'd run away from as a kid.

"Come on," Walker said, "throw something out."

" 'Why me?' "

"Go on."

" 'Why do I have to sit here for this photograph? How did I end up on this park bench with this woman and this child? Is this the person I thought I would be? What am I doing here? Why me?' "

Walker finished the last of his breakfast and poured a cup of coffee. "Tell me about this man. Who was he?"

"His parents got divorced when he was like seven or eight. He felt like his mother didn't love him, so he ran away and went to live with his father. He spent a lot of time out in the country, hunting rocks and arrowheads, camping out, that kind of stuff. His family tried to make him a civil engineer and sent him off to Texas A&M, which he didn't handle too well. He wanted to fly. So he took private lessons and then he joined the Air Force for World War II. That was where he met my mother, who was working for Boeing in Wichita. After the war he put himself through school and got a Ph.D. in anthropology. We spent the next ten or fifteen years moving all over the country."

"That doesn't tell me who he was."

I went with the first thing that popped into my head. "In high school, every time I brought a friend over to the house, he would get into an argument with them. Politics, music, anything to get a reaction. He would keep at it until he got under their skin. Then he'd get disgusted, and pick up a newspaper or turn on the TV. It got to where I didn't want to bring anybody home.

"He was so critical of everybody. I remember he told me about this party once where one of the guests was from China. He was very proud of the fact that he went up to her and corrected her pronunciation of Chinese. This based on his being in China for a couple of years in

World War Two. He couldn't even pronounce 'Taoism,' you know?

"So this one time he was working down south of Austin, and he came through and gave me a ride up to Dallas. He said something snotty about some supposed friend of his, and I couldn't stand it anymore. I said, 'You don't like anybody, do you?' I don't think he said two words on the rest of the trip. And a few weeks later my mother asked me how I could say such a horrible thing to him, how I could tell him he was a bitter, lonely old man without a friend in the world, that nobody gave a damn for him. So, despite their telling me all my life how important honesty is, I ended up apologizing to him for something I never said."

"It was true, though, wasn't it?"

"That nobody liked him? No, lots of people liked him. Loved him even. But none of them were good enough for him."

"Of course not. None of them was his mother."

I shook my head, the thread of the conversation lost. Walker drank the last of his coffee and said, "This is going to be interesting."

On the way out he stuffed a section of newspaper into the knapsack from a pile by the gate. "It's a five-mile walk to the beach," he said. "You up for it?"

I shrugged.

We followed the road for the first mile or two, finding the rhythm of walking together. After a while we talked about music. He was enough younger than me that he had his emotional roots in the seventies: Parliament/Funkadelic, Earth, Wind & Fire, the Ohio Players.

As we got close to the beach we gathered up whatever dead wood we saw. We carried it to a place they'd obviously used for a while. The sand had been trampled down hard and the rocks had been cleared away, except for a circle of them in the middle, a tiny Stonehenge full of charred wood and ashes. Walker built a fire there with the newspaper from his pack.

"Let me give you a little theory," he said. "You know about astral bodies, right? Everybody's got one. It's like a balloon that's the same size and shape as your body, only it's not physical. So it pretty much goes wherever your body goes. Only sometimes it comes unstuck. Like when the body is in a coma or you have an out-of-body experience. Great sex sometimes does it.

"Most of this stuff goes back to the Egyptians. They split the person into nine different 'vehicles'—body, mind, soul, spirit, shadow, heart, so forth and so on. Some of the distinctions are pretty fine. What we care about is the astral body, which is the *ka*, and the *ba*, which is the soul. The ba can live in either the physical body, the *khat*, or the ka. Am I going too fast?"

"I'm okay so far."

"When the khat dies, the ba hightails it to the ka. So now you've got the consciousness—the accumulated awareness of the person—stuck in the astral body."

"Like a ghost."

"Yeah. Sometimes the astral body hangs around for a long time after the physical body is dead. Haunting people, if you want to use that word."

"I don't believe in any of this stuff, you know. If that makes a difference. Neither did my father. He didn't believe in God, or ghosts, or anything but himself."

"That's cool. Belief isn't strictly necessary here. Think of it as a metaphor."

"For what?"

"Ghosts are just memories, right? It's the shit we can't manage to forget that haunts us."

"And it's what we feel that makes them real."

"You got it. The point is we are not raising your old man for his sake. It's for yours. Got it? It's for whatever you need."

I'd just swum off a cliff and given my heart away to somebody I might never see again. I no longer knew what I needed.

By that time the fire was roaring. The heat was like a pressure on my skin. I could smell my own sweat. It occurred to me to move away. I didn't. Walker took a handful of some kind of leaves and reached into the fire and dropped them into the center. They turned instantly to smoke. I couldn't believe that his arm hadn't burst into flames.

"What are you doing?" The sweet smell of the leaves gave me an instant and powerful image. I was in my father's lab, holding an Indian skull in my hand, hundreds of years old. It should have been treated to preserve it, and it hadn't, and now it had started to decay from the inside. The smell was sweet, almost sexual, cloying. The hollow eyes stared up at me.

Walker said, "Just a little something to open you up."

"You're not setting me up for some two-bit hallucination, are you?"

"No psychedelics here. I got nothing against them, they're fine for what they are, but we're after something different. We want to get you connected again." The sweat was pouring off him now too. "Everything's connected, see. That's what makes magic work. A rock that looks like a duck can stand in for a duck. The blood of an animal can stand in for the blood of a person. Your clothes are imprinted with your personality. If the king is getting laid, there'll be a big harvest.

"Look at the planet. The planet's being poisoned the same way we poison ourselves. It's like there really is this death wish inside everybody." I felt myself go cold, even with the fire roaring through me. "Some people go after it with booze or smack or cigarettes, some people go over the edge, like your old man. That's what demons are supposed to be, you know. A physical manifestation of that urge to self-destruction. They call you to it."

"I've been drunk for years," I said. "Maybe I was killing myself. Maybe I was medicating myself to keep from killing myself. Maybe both. Medicating myself so I can live with the idea that I'm pissing my life away. That I should be fucking all those beautiful women on MTV and not my wife, that I should ditch my two-bit job and go after the big bucks, that I need a new car and a swimming pool."

"Sure, man, we got to have all that material shit. We got to gratify those short-term desires. Take that next drink, have another McDonald's hamburger. Snort some more coke, drive around in that big car. And pretty soon your liver's turned into a piece of rock and there's oil all over your beach. Making all that shit turns the world into an ugly, dying place and owning all that shit makes us into ugly, dying people. We got no connections left to the natural world. And no magic left, because that's where the magic is, in those connections."

I was dizzy, disoriented. My eyes wouldn't focus anymore. I had no idea what time it was, when I'd last eaten. I didn't know that I could stand up until Walker pulled me to my feet.

"Let's dance," he said.

He draped my arm over his shoulders. "The grapevine," he said. "You ever do this?"

I shook my head.

He showed me. We moved sideways across the sand, one foot behind the other, to the left, kick, back to the right, slowly getting faster. Walker hummed wordlessly. I saw an ancient flatbed truck pull up at the edge of the road, full of people from the commune. They began to unload congas and timbales and shakers and bongos, hollow logs and tambourines. They started to play them as they carried them across the sand toward us, picking up our rhythm.

Walker slipped out from under my arm and his movements got more complicated. He turned and slapped the side of one foot as he kicked, then stamped his heels in the sand. "Don't stop," he said, but I had.

Debra was suddenly there. She hugged me quickly and then began to dance around me. "Like this," she said.

Everyone was either dancing or drumming. There was no one to point and stare. I let my head roll around on my neck and then I let myself move again. My thoughts of Lori took over. The passion and frustration and fear spun me around, faster and faster until I fell down. Even then I couldn't hold still. The drums had ceased to be a sound and had become a physical force that was impossible to resist. I don't remember getting up but somehow I was on my feet and dancing again.

My mind moved faster than my body. Maybe it was my astral body about to come loose. I had a sensation of flying low over water at dazzling speed. There were images of Lori, and then of the drop-off, and then of my father, first floating facedown in the blue-green water, then a hundred others, him hitting me, him shaking my hand, him in a suit, him in a T-shirt and bathing trunks, him on that park bench next to me, smoking a cigarette.

My body responded to what it heard and saw and went on without me. There was no sense of time. I remember a point where my stomach began to burn with hunger. After a while the feeling went away. Someone brought me a pitcher of water and I drank it all.

The next thing I noticed was the sunset spread like fire across the west. The sky to the south was the dark blue of the abyss, the color of a feeling that I have no words for, a feeling I've been carrying all my life. Only the feeling was in the sky now, where I could see it, and that made everything easier.

Someone put more and more wood on the fire. It was pitch-dark and I saw the headlights of cars as they pulled off the highway to watch us. I no longer cared.

Then Walker came up to me and put his hands on either side of my neck. They felt cool against my skin. My feet stopped and I stood swaying in the sand. He turned me until my back was to the fire, then he kissed me on the mouth. His lips were dry and barely brushed mine.

"Your father," he said. He lifted his right hand, the first two fingers pointing vaguely behind me, toward the fire.

I turned around. I was off-balance and the sand sucked at my feet. My heart pounded. I felt myself reel with fatigue and hunger. I blinked. "There's nothing—"

My father walked toward me from the center of the fire.

It looked like he was projected onto an invisible screen. He was the same age as the picture I described to Walker: middle thirties, dark hair slicked back, mouth set in a private smile. He didn't look at me.

"Dad?" I said.

He closed in on me, slowly, steadily.

"Dad?"

He wasn't blurry, wasn't a dream, wasn't an optical illusion. He was hyper-real, hallucinatory. The colors of the dancers' clothes were electric. The flames left hot yellow afterimages in the air. I smelled smoke and sweat and the musky salt of the sea.

"Look at me!" I shouted, my numbness gone, anger in its place.

He ignored me. When he was only a few feet away I ran at him. I had my left arm out in front of me, my right hand balled up into a fist. My left hand went into his chest with no resistance. I swung at him with my right, aiming for the thickness of his nose, and my fist slipped through empty air.

I went down on my knees in the sand. I thought the dancers would have stopped. They only got more frenzied. They looked at me and then rolled their heads back and yelled at the sky.

My father walked right through me. Not like he was a ghost.

Like I was.

———

I staggered away from the fire, through a line of tourists who scrambled out of the way. I found a sand dune and lay with my head against it, watching whitecaps flash.

Later I saw somebody walk across the beach toward me. I was a shell around emptiness. I couldn't move.

She stopped in front of me.

"Lori?" I said.

She knelt beside me and brushed the hair from my face. "Are you okay? What happened?"

"I saw my father," I said. "He was in the fire."

"Your father?"

"Yes. And he . . . and he . . ." I couldn't talk. My throat had closed up and tears ran down my face.

"Come here," she said. "Come here, baby." She pulled me against her chest and I let go of the last of my resistance. I cried till it hurt. My nose ran and my eyes ran and I drooled. Strangled noises came out of my chest. There was soot all over my face and hands and I left black marks on her clothes.

When I was able to talk I said, "He didn't care," and that started it all again.

"No," Lori said. "He didn't care. Or couldn't care—what's the difference? He let you down like my momma let me down. So did your momma and so did my daddy. In this whole round world all we have is ourselves."

The coconut smell of her skin, the touch of her tiny, delicate hands, turned the agony instantly into lust. I pulled away far enough to put my hands on her face and pull her into a kiss.

"Easy," she said, when I let her go. "Easy. You got me all maternal and now you're crossing my wires."

I fell back in the sand. "I have to be out of my mind. I've totally humiliated myself."

"No," she said. She leaned over me and kissed me, one hand on my stomach. The hand was both reassurance and promise. I knew then that we were going to make love.

She swayed back and got onto her feet. I watched with disbelief and joy as she unbuttoned the same faded red shirt she'd worn the first time I saw her. She tossed it on the sand and I watched the moonlight slide over the sleek lines of her body. She stepped out of her cutoffs and she was naked.

Everything was still clearer and brighter than life. I had to stare at her for a long, timeless moment because I had never seen anything so beautiful. I sat up and pulled my shirt over my head. A quarter of a mile down the beach the dance went on, I could smell the smoke from their fire, but they might as well have been on another planet. I got out of the rest of my clothes and reached for her. She backed toward the far side of the dune, beckoning. I scrambled to my feet and went after her and she turned to run.

I caught her by the wrist and she spun around. Her eyes blazed. I pulled her against me and kissed her, again and again, her neck, her shoulders, the front of her throat. "Oh God," she said. "Oh God." I dropped to my knees and kissed her breasts. She made a strangled noise and fell to her knees too. She sucked my lower lip into her mouth, biting it, devouring me. I pushed her onto her back and moved over her and she said, "Yes. Yes."

———

It had been so long. Everything about Lori was new. Her exotic, overlapping tan lines, a patch of freckles on one shoulder, the warm, sweet taste between her legs. The scent of her skin, the sound of her sighs and moans and cries in my ear, the feel of her fingers twisted in my hair. We were both covered with sand. When I came it never seemed to stop, only to slowly fade below some threshold of recognition.

When I rolled away she said, "Now. Touch me here." She guided my hand down between her legs, into the thick, hot fluids, showing me what to do. She moved against me, a short, convulsive roll of her hips, her whole body tied into the effort. I leaned into her, kissing her, and when she finally came I felt it too, through my hand, through her mouth into mine, like some kind of spirit escaping her body, leaving me changed where it passed through.

I remember thinking, whatever this costs, it's worth it. It's worth anything.

"Was it okay?" she said, her head buried in my shoulder. "I mean, my not being able to come and everything, was it still okay for you?"

I realized that the drums were still playing, quieter now. "You came at the end."

"Not with you inside me. Did that ruin it for you?"

I lifted her face with both hands and made her look me in the eyes.

"It was the best I ever had. I've never wanted anybody so much in my life."

"Really?"

"Really."

"Okay," she said. She put her head back on my shoulder. "You can't blame me for wanting a little reassurance." She rubbed my chest. "Ray. Ray. I want my own name for you. Something nobody else has ever called you. What's your middle name?"

"Ray. I'm actually John Raymond Shackleford Junior. You can't call me John because it's my father's name."

"I want us both to have new names. New names for everything. Our own language, so we don't have anything to do with the rest of the world."

"Or the past?"

"That's right. We'll make it all go away. It's abolished. We can both be twenty years old again, with our new names."

"If we were twenty again, how would I know you'd turn out the same as you are now?"

"Better," she said. "I'd turn out better."

"No way."

"Sweet." She kissed my neck. "But you know it's true. The real world is going to pull us apart."

"I don't want to talk about that." But it was too late. "Oh Christ. Is it Tom? Do you have to go?"

"No. I told him I was going to dance tonight. I told him I might be out all night."

"What did he say?"

"He accused me of sleeping with you. I told him I wasn't, which was the truth. At the time. He said you were crazy and told me about the drop-off."

"Oh God."

"I told him I didn't care, I wasn't interested in you anyway."

"Oh yeah?"

"Yeah," she said, laughing, and sat up. She got to her feet and used her shirt to dab between her legs. "What a mess." She looked back toward the fire. "The tourists have given up. How about a swim?"

"Not yet," I said. I walked over to her on my knees and buried my head in her stomach. "You smell like sex. I don't want you to wash it off. Not yet."

It was different the second time, slower and at the same time more urgent too. Afterward we swam and then lay together on my clothes, holding each other for warmth.

"Come away with me," I said. "Leave him and come to Austin with me."

"And what, move in with you and Elizabeth? That would be cozy."

"I can put you up in a motel until I get her out."

"And if she doesn't want to leave? Ray, think about it. I can't just sit in a motel while you sort all this out. And I've got sorting of my own to do."

"Lori. I love you."

I felt her stiffen.

"Not saying it won't make it go away," I said.

"I know."

I told myself I didn't care that she didn't say it back to me. "I can't let it end like this."

"This has been the most wonderful week. It's been like one of my novels. Don't try to make it into anything more."

"It is more than that and you know it."

"You say that now, with the waves crashing and the drums beating and the tropical moon overhead. Once you get home you'll think what a great adventure you had, and you'll get back in your routine and you'll think, she was really crazy. I'm better off without her."

"I love you."

She pulled away. "I'm freezing to death. Come on, we better go."

It really was too cold to lie around any longer. We got dressed and she started off across the sand. "Well?" she said. "Are you coming?"

We rode back to the dive shop in silence. I refused to believe this was the end, frantically tried to find an argument that would change things. When we pulled into the driveway I said, "At least come in long enough to shower and dry off."

She shrugged. "Okay."

She followed me into my room, still sullen, and went into the bathroom and shut the door. It was only two in the morning. A minute or so later I heard the toilet flush and the shower start. I knocked on the door and opened it.

"What?" I said. "What did I say? What's wrong with you?"

She hadn't gotten in the shower yet. She had hold of the cheap fiberglass shower door, as if to brace herself against an invisible storm. "What do you think?"

"I think you don't want me to go any more than I do."

"Bingo," she said. She was naked. I'd never seen her naked in the light before. God, she was beautiful. She got in the shower and I got in after her.

I held her in my arms under the hot water. "You've told me so much," I said. "Why couldn't you tell me that?"

"Because I'm tired of scaring people away."

"You can't scare me away."

Finally, finally, she smiled. "Easy for you to say."

We washed each other's backs and toweled each other off and I convinced her to stay until the last minute, until she absolutely had to go. She told me to set the alarm for five o'clock. I set it for four-thirty and she fell asleep in my arms.

I was already awake when it went off and we made love again in that fragile, sleepy darkness before dawn. When I came she had both hands full of my hair and we were staring into each other's eyes, both of us knowing this could be the last time, and when I felt it start, like a tearing loose in the exact center of my body, the beginning of the end, it made everything else come loose too and I was crying yet again, and so was she. I saw one of my tears fall thick and hot on the side of her nose and leaned down to kiss it away. Then I slid my hand down between us and brought her slowly to her own climax, me still inside and on top of her, still looking into her eyes, until she closed them in a long shudder that sent another flood of tears out of the sides.

She showered again and while she was in there I lay in the rumpled sheets and kneaded both hands into my crotch, rubbing her juices into my skin. Then I held my hands to my face and inhaled her smell deep inside me. The water stopped. She came out and dressed and sat on the edge of the bed. I started to tell her, again, that I loved her, and she put her fingers on my mouth. "Please," she said. "There are all these things we're about to say to each other and I can't bear it, I absolutely can't stand it if it happens."

"Okay," I said.

She kissed me once, lingeringly, and went out without looking back.

Four hours later I was on a plane to Austin.

CHAPTER 6
CHAPTER 6

New Rising Sun

I slept enough on the plane to feel hollow and disoriented. I must have looked like hell when I got off: hair come loose from its ponytail, clothes hopelessly wrinkled. I used the toilet on the plane, and I was sure that Lori's smell still clung to my penis, despite a long hot shower before I left.

It wasn't guilty conscience. I wanted Lori again already. I had a brief moment of gratitude that Elizabeth wasn't pregnant, that we don't already have a kid. I could see the future coming and it was going to be hard enough on both of us.

She wasn't there to meet me, no surprise, so I called home. She said she'd be there and hung up. I stood outside to wait. The sun wasn't as bright as in Cozumel, and the air was thick with humidity. When Elizabeth pulled up to the terminal she squealed the tires against the curb. I got in and she avoided my eyes. We turned left onto Manor Road and the strip centers and hills and low trees of Austin seemed both familiar and utterly strange.

After a minute or so I said, "What's wrong?"

"You didn't call. You were gone an entire week and didn't call once."

I sighed and leaned back in the seat, pissed off because she was right. Even the postcard I'd written her was still in my luggage. "I'm sorry," I said.

"You could have left a message on the machine, even. So I'd know you were okay."

"It was a pretty emotional thing for me, down there." I almost died, I wanted to say.

"I have emotions too."

I looked at her. I couldn't remember the last time she'd said something that personal. "Beth? Are you okay?"

The car weaved in the lane. "No," she said. "I'm not okay." She swung her head around, looking for a hole in the traffic, and pulled off onto the shoulder, into the rough-cut grass and fast-food bags and beer cans. Tears came up in her eyes.

"You want me to drive?"

"No, I don't want you to drive." She swallowed a sob. "I want to know what's going to happen to us."

"I don't think this is the time or place—"

"I do. I want to know now. Are we splitting up?"

I froze.

It took forever for my mind to function again, and then it instantly overloaded: Lori telling me how I was going to get back into my routine and forget her, the blonde in 1966 telling me that married men always protect their marriages, the hysterical fit Elizabeth threw when I spent that night at the motel. And there I sat, knowing that I should say yes, yes we were splitting up, that it was what I wanted, that I've wanted it for years.

It was the last thing Elizabeth was ready to hear. It would say my happiness was more important than hers. It would be the same as if I hit her or smashed up her antique furniture and her hand-blown glassware. I didn't believe I was capable of it. I said, "Are we?" and was so ashamed of my own cowardice that I couldn't look her in the eye.

"What do you want? For once, just say what you want."

I couldn't speak. I forced my lips apart and nothing came out.

"You're never here," Elizabeth said. "Even when you're here, you're somewhere else. You never give me anything to, to push against. I don't think you understand other people very well. I don't think there's anything in your world except you." She slapped the steering wheel. "You're going to make me do this myself, aren't you? You're not even going to help."

"What do you want me to say?"

"I want you to tell me what you want. Tell me if you want me to move out."

"I could go."

"No you can't. That's your workshop, it was your grandmother's money that was the down payment. I won't throw you out of your own house. But if you want me to leave you're going to have to say it."

I felt like I had a noose around my throat. Every time I opened my mouth it got tighter. "Yes," I said.

"Yes, what?"

"Yes, I want you to go."

All her visible emotions shut off. "Fine," she said. Her tears were dry and she looked hard and beautiful. I knew if I touched her she would knock my hand away. She shoved the gas pedal to the floor and we shot back onto Airport Boulevard.

———

I sat on my ancient leather couch. I could hear Elizabeth's voice as she talked on the phone downstairs but none of the words. I was too cold to move.

"Frances is going to help me find a place," she said, standing halfway up the stairs. I knew if I asked she would change her mind. It would flood her heart with happiness and relief. I had that power. She only wanted a sign.

"I want to keep Dude," she said.

I hadn't thought beyond the moment. I hadn't thought that I would lose the cat as well. "This is his place," I said carefully. "I would be glad to have him stay."

"No, I need him."

Dude had been her cat before we met. I wouldn't win this one. "Okay."

"I may need some money, too."

"I just got ten thousand from Graham. Half of that is legally yours."

"Half," she said. "Just to get me started."

We already had separate accounts. She came the rest of the way upstairs while I wrote the check. She folded it and held it nervously in both hands.

"Anything else?" I said. "I mean, can I help you look for a place, or . . ."

"No," she said, shaking her head. "No, that's it." She turned and walked back down the stairs. I closed my eyes. After a while a car pulled up outside and a few seconds later I heard the front door slam.

———

I stood in front of the open refrigerator. There were ten cans of Budweiser lined up neatly on the middle shelf. I counted them twice. I shut the refrigerator door and sat down at the kitchen table. I pictured how it would be to take a can out and set it on the table. As I opened the top it would let out a deep, liquid sigh. The first long swallow would tickle my throat and quench my thirst and make the fist in my gut relax.

I pictured Elizabeth going through the paper, calling realtors, wandering through apartment complexes. The cheap carpet, the hairline cracks in the walls, the faint smells of insecticide and latex paint.

God.

I checked the refrigerator. Still ten beers.

It didn't matter that the marriage had been over for years. It didn't matter that making love with Lori showed me what it is I really want. What I felt or wanted didn't matter at all. All I felt then was Elizabeth's anger and hurt. I couldn't see myself except through her eyes. Worse, through my imagination of how she saw me.

I stood in the hallway and looked at the phone. I had the number of the dive shop in Cozumel and it was only midafternoon. Maybe Tom was out drinking and Lori was by the phone, hoping I would call. I felt her expectations too. I couldn't tell her Elizabeth had left, not until I knew that it wasn't a false alarm.

There was my mother. I hadn't written or called her from Cozumel either. What did she think, me down there where my father died? It must feel like salt in her wounds. Yet if I told her about Elizabeth she would be on the next plane to take care of me.

Dude walked up and got in my lap. "I think this is it, big guy," I said. He leaned into my chest and pushed against me as hard as he could, with all four feet, the way he does when he knows something's wrong. He was in a fight a couple of years ago and his leg got infected. He nearly died, and I said good-bye to him then. I promised myself that if he lived, any time I had with him from then on would be bonus time, that I would take what I could get and not hold him to any more than that. "I promised," I told him, but I cried some anyway. I was about to lose all my ballast; the things that weighed me down were also the things that kept me steady. With Elizabeth and Dude both gone I wouldn't be responsible for anybody at all.

The silence in the house stretched out to infinity. When the phone shattered it I jumped and Dude rocketed off my legs. It was Graham and from the start I knew he had something on his mind. He kept to the forms, though, and asked how I was. I told him about Elizabeth and he kept asking how I felt about it. I told him I didn't know. Then I told him about Cozumel, about Lori.

"You son of a bitch! You gonna bring her up here?"

His enthusiasm seemed painfully out of place. "I tried," I said. "She wouldn't come."

"She'll change her mind. She's got to be crazy about you."

"She may just be crazy. Look, Beth only walked out a couple of hours ago. This is all premature."

As I went through the options with him—separation, divorce, reconciliation—I felt myself sink under the enormity of it. Even to think about it was oppressive.

"You need to take your mind off it," Graham said. "A hobby or something."

"A hobby?"

"Like maybe another album."

I listened to the hiss of the phone lines. "Man," I said, "this is not the right time."

"Okay, okay, forget I said anything. You're right, I was being self-ish. I know *Smile* was really hard on you. Not that this one would be anything like that."

I dragged a chair over and sat down with my head in my hands. "Ray?"

"Look, I'm not going to do it. It's not just that *Smile* was too scary and I want to put it behind me, it's that I'm really fucked up right now. Everything is falling apart and I don't know where any of the pieces are going to land."

"I can dig it, man, really. It's okay. Things are weird here too. I mean, *Celebration* was weird enough, but since *Smile* . . ." I didn't say anything, and I guess he took it as permission to push on. "I mean, I knew there would be trouble over *Celebration,* and there was, some of my front people have caught hell. Elektra's looking for somebody to sue, the trades are full of letters from pissed-off Doors fans who want to know why Elektra never released it, *Billboard* wants an inquiry, it's been nuts.

"Well, I started pressing *Smile* CDs as soon as we finished the tape. I had all the packaging done already, so I've been shipping them out all week. Yesterday, by messenger, I got a letter from a VP at Capitol. He said he knew it was me, he said he doesn't know how I managed it, and he doesn't care. He said he was a shipping clerk in 1966 and he's been waiting more than half his life for this record and he's just glad he's finally got it."

"That's great, but—"

"Great? We're talking Capitol Records here. It's beyond great. It's all the way into impossible. And for him to put it in writing? It means that the album is actually changing people. I don't mean just changing their moods, I mean it's changing them inside. Hell, I feel like it's changing me. It's making us all more like Brian."

"Graham, that's crazy."

"Not any crazier than what you went through to get it. Do you understand what I'm saying here? I'm saying that we are actually changing the world. I screwed up the first time, I should have seen that *Celebration* was a bad vibe. But we more than made up for it with *Smile.* And my God, think what we could do with one more record. With the *right* record."

"Graham . . ."

"I'm only going to say one word to you. *First Rays of the New Rising Sun.* Jimi Hendrix. That's all I'm going to say."

"Yeah, okay, you've said it. Listen, man, I really have to go."

"Shit, look, man, I'm sorry. I'm being a jerk. I got myself all stoked up over this, and I had to tell somebody. Forget about it, okay? What do you need? Are you okay for money?"

"Yeah, I'm fine. I've got a bunch of stereos here to work on and maybe that's the best idea right now, to work with my hands and not think about anything else. This has just left me . . ."

"I understand. I'm going to call and check up on you, though. And if you need anything you'll call me?"

I told him I would and we said good-bye. I still felt cold and I finally got up and shut the air conditioner off. An hour later the phone rang again and I nearly leaped into the air.

It was Elizabeth. She'd found a place up on Spicewood Springs she could afford. "I'm going to go ahead and stay with Frances tonight. I'll start moving stuff out tomorrow. We have to decide who gets what."

My head throbbed. "Okay."

"We don't . . ."

"What?"

"We don't have to go through with this, you know. I don't want to leave you. I would rather work things out."

"Why? I mean, after what you said today. That I don't understand other people. That I'm never here. Why would you want to work things out with somebody like that?"

"Because I love you."

"Do you?"

From the breaks in her voice I knew she was crying. "Yes. I do. I'd go to counseling again, if that's what you want."

We tried it five years ago. The therapist asked Elizabeth hard questions about her family, especially about her mother. She refused to go back. By that time I'd used up my anger and just wanted things back to normal. It was one more crisis that simply ran out of steam. "I don't think so," I said.

"Well," Elizabeth said. "That's it, then. Right?"

"I guess so."

I went upstairs and tore apart an Akai cassette deck. There were a few seconds at a time when I forgot who I was, when my hands became the work they did.

Sometime after midnight I even managed to sleep.

═════

I dreamed I was trying to fix the roof of this two-story house with my father. I know the house from other dreams. It doesn't have any stairs and there are no ladders, so I have to climb over windows and balance on projecting bricks and so forth to get to the roof. I fall and hurt myself somehow. My father wants me to go back up. He has this garden hose with tremendous pressure, like a fire hose. I can actually ride the flow of water upward, and I'm trying to do it, but I can't get all the way to the roof. I fall again and my father says, "I don't care, as long as somebody gets hurt." This freaks me out and the dream turns into another violence thing, with me beating him, trying to smash his nose, maim him.

I woke up angry, had to remind myself that he's dead. Still dead. Then I remembered Elizabeth was gone and I shivered, even through the covers, even as the house sweltered in the May heat.

The next afternoon Elizabeth and Frances showed up with Frances's brother and his pickup truck. The guest room had doubled as Elizabeth's sewing room. She took that bed and all the sewing stuff and her clothes. I let her have the TV and the sofa and the recliner. I helped them load the truck each time they came back. The earrings I brought her from Cozumel were in my pocket; there was never a moment to give them to her.

Between loads I worked upstairs. I had the Holland/Dozier/Holland CD from Motown on and it sounded false, out of date. So I got out my *Cry of Love* LP. This is the record Graham was talking about, or part of it. The tracks Hendrix finished for *First Rays*, which would have been a double album, had mostly been split between *Cry* and the *Rainbow Bridge* soundtrack. They were rough mixes, the best Warner Bros. could find at the time. It's hard to tell from those two records what he had in mind.

It was something to think about, like Graham said. Something other than Elizabeth's apartment, slowly filling up with things we'd accumulated over more than a decade. Something other than what her first night there would feel like, full of strange sounds in the night. I didn't want to think about Lori either, Lori and Tom, a thousand miles away.

So I thought about Jimi Hendrix.

My first real date with Alex was to the Hendrix concert in Dallas, February 16, 1968. Hendrix seemed like a god to us then. The first time I heard him was on KVIL FM, a middle-of-the-road station that was interviewing the press agent for the Monkees tour. "You won't believe the guy that's opening their shows," he said. "Listen to this," and he played the British single of "Purple Haze." I'd never heard anything like it. It was exactly what I'd been waiting for, the consummation of the need that Bob Dylan awakened in me in November of 1965 at Moody Colosseum when he came on for his second set with an electric band behind him. When Hendrix's first album finally appeared I grooved it out on my parents' sapphire-needled monophonic console hi-fi.

In concert he did everything we'd heard about: played with his teeth, humped the guitar, snaked his arm over the top of the neck between chords, produced sounds no one had ever heard before, transcendently beautiful screams and hisses and howls. None of that compared to Hendrix himself. I never saw anyone so much himself on stage, so completely alive in the moment, so full of joy and passion and a need to share it. It was contagious. When I kissed Alex that night I felt the music still burning in her.

Hendrix was the only one who ever put that West Coast psychedelic sound together with the blues and R&B flavor that spoke to my heart and made it work for me. That was where he was headed when he died, and *First Rays of the New Rising Sun* would have been a new fusion of soul and rock, blues and pop, black and white, healing music that would bring everything and everyone together. On some of what survived—"Freedom," "Dolly Dagger," "Straight Ahead"—you can hear him struggle to find that new voice.

When *Cry* was over I put on *Electric Ladyland*. I remember the first time I heard it, in my dorm room at Vanderbilt. I turned out the lights and let the music take me, that delicious noise that opens the record, the slowed-down guitar explosions and voices and phasing, circling between the speakers, finally melting into the crystalline beauty of the title song. I can hear the night in that record. It sounds like neon reflected off puddles of rain in the cool and humid darkness. The colors are brighter than anything in nature, smears of pure red and green and gold and blue that shine but never burn.

"Voodoo Chile" came on and I put down my soldering iron and closed my eyes. Summer sunlight streamed across the workbench but I was listening to the silence between the notes, the long, lonely distance between the guitar and organ. It had barely started when Elizabeth came back for her last load.

━━━

We said good-bye in the hall. It had turned dark. Dude was in his cat carrier, crying, afraid he was going to the vet, afraid, as all cats are, of change. Frances stood to one side, making a point of not watching. Elizabeth and I stood a couple of feet apart, as awkward as if it was our first date.

She gave me her address on a piece of notepaper. The paper has a cartoon of a cat on it and says, "Make a list . . . because last time you forgot the cat food." She said she'd call when she had a phone.

"In case you change your mind," she whispered, so quiet I wouldn't have understood if I wasn't watching her mouth. "If you want to try again, if you . . ." She shook her head. "You can call me." She started to cry then, hard. I put my arms tentatively around her. She put her head on my shoulder. The hot tears went through my shirt and her hands gripped my back.

I started to cry too, and then I had a moment of perfect clarity. I saw that I was crying because I was scared for her, worried for her, sad for her. It was the same reason she was crying. Which made both of us crying for Elizabeth and nobody for me. My tears stopped and I let her go.

Elizabeth straightened and said, "I'm sorry." Then she laughed and cried at the same time and said, "But I'm not going to apologize." She stepped back and kissed me once, firm and quick, on the mouth. Then she picked up Dude's cage and carried him out. Frances smiled awkwardly at me and followed her out to the truck. I stood in the doorway until they were gone and then I shut the door.

━━━

I went upstairs and shut off the stereo, then came back down. My footsteps echoed. There was a silence that wasn't just the absence of noise, it was the absence of noise to come. No more thumping as Dude scratched in his litter box. No more distant whisper of the TV or water running in another part of the house. I was exhausted. The tension that had held me together was gone. I went into the bedroom and lay down with my clothes on and fell immediately asleep.

Three or four times I came wide awake during the night, convinced that, across town, Elizabeth was awake and crying. I felt like the phone was about to ring and she would be on the other end, hysterical. I couldn't get back to sleep for the fear of it.

What finally got me up the next day was the idea of moving furniture. I had an old bed in the garage that could go in the empty guest room. I could repaint the walls, fix it up.

I spent the day at it. I'd never finished the shoe molding in there, so I put quarter-round down before I repainted the trim. Then I spackled and repainted the walls, all of it in pure white paint. I got the paint stuff cleaned up and the carpet vacuumed and the windows washed. I moved the bed in and put on clean sheets and a white bedspread. I found an old end table in the garage and put that in too, and a lamp with a red-and-black bandanna draped over the shade.

Late in the afternoon, in the grip of an impulse I didn't understand, I went out to the Door Store and bought a bookcase, the kind made out of pressed wood and covered with thin white vinyl. I put it together and set it against one of the perfect new white walls. Then I moved in all the rock and roll books I'd collected since the business with Graham started.

It was nearly dark by then. I put the light on and fried up some cheese and tortillas for dinner. When I was done I went back to the guest room and stood in the doorway. Everything was white and clean, as if it was me that moved out and not Elizabeth, and this was my new apartment. I took a spare wooden chair out of the dining room and positioned it in one corner. Then I sat down, my forearms on my legs, my hands clasped together, and marveled at how clean and white it all was.

It was Monday when Elizabeth moved out. She called Tuesday afternoon to give me her phone number. It was businesslike and we didn't talk long. My mind was still on my painting. She said she might be by the next day to get some things out of the garage.

She did come by on Wednesday, already looking different. At first I thought it was me, then I realized she'd cut her bangs. She cut them a little short and it makes her look surprised. There was a new distance to her too that made her seem foreign. I helped her carry the boxes out to her car and then we both stood there while I tried again to read her mood. In the end I hugged her and we clung together for a few seconds. It helped, even if it was Elizabeth and even if I don't want her back, to have somebody touch me.

That night I called Lori.

I'd been over it a hundred times in my mind, trying to anticipate. It rang five times before Tom answered. He sounded a couple of sheets to the wind. I couldn't help but wonder if I'd gotten him out of bed with Lori. I asked for Lori in a kind of muffled voice and he wanted to know who I was.

"Her cousin John," I said.

He put the phone down and my heart went crazy. Then Lori picked it up and said, "Hello?"

"It's Ray," I said. "I told him I was your cousin."

"Uh-huh."

"You can't talk, right?"

"Of course not." She'd put on an artificial, cheerful tone.

"First I have to know if you're okay. He didn't hurt you, did he? Because you stayed out all night with me?"

"I'm fine," she said. "Really."

I let out a long sigh. I hated the sound of myself, knew I was on the verge of being a fool. "I just wanted to tell you. Elizabeth and I split up." I told her about it as simply as I could, wishing I could gauge my words by her eyes.

"So what happens now?" she said.

"I don't know. I'm just taking it like an hour at a time."

"Same here."

"I really miss you."

"Me too. Big-time."

There was a long silence. "I guess I should go."

"That would be a good idea."

"You have my number here, right?"

"Right."

"I love you," I said.

There was another silence, and she said, "Take care of yourself."

"You too."

"Okay," she said, and there was a click as she hung up.

I sat for a long time and replayed what we'd said, trying to read in different meanings. None of them stuck. I counted the number of beers in the refrigerator, which was still ten, and went to bed.

———

I dreamed about Hendrix. I'm playing with the Duotones at the DKE house at Vanderbilt. We're playing "Fire" from Hendrix's first album when I see that Jimi is in the audience. With no transition we're not playing the song anymore and Scott is out in the audience, trying to get Jimi to come up on stage with us. Scott offers his Les Paul like a squire offering a sword to a knight. Jimi shakes his head and waves his big hands, saying, maybe later. We start some other song, which doesn't come together. Jimi seems to be having a good time, but no matter how much everybody in the band begs him, he won't come up and play, and I'm left with this powerful longing.

When I woke up it was still there.

———

Thursday night Graham called. I hadn't done much except sit in my workshop all day. I only had a couple of simple jobs left, and I couldn't get involved. I didn't have the energy to get up and change the stereo either, so most of the day went by in silence. It's like surgery. Even if what they cut out was killing you, it was still a part of you. You're in shock. You have to lie quietly for a while and figure out what's left, what you can do and what you can't. The hardest thing is to imagine the future, to think any further ahead than dinner. Dinner is hard enough.

Graham wanted me to meet him in Seattle. "It's a consulting gig," he said. "I'll pay you a thousand bucks, plus all expenses."

"What for?"

"Research. I need somebody to help me get around, take notes and pictures and all like that."

"Bullshit. You don't need anybody to help you get around. What are you researching?"

"Well, it's, uh, kind of a private deal . . ."

"Is this the Hendrix business again?"

"Look, Ray, what's the point in sitting around the house feeling sorry for yourself? That's no way to be. What harm would it do you to come to Seattle, which is beautiful this time of year, for a few days' vacation?"

"Graham, I don't want to do the record."

"I'm not pressuring you to do the record. There's no strings attached, I swear. I lined up an interview with Jimi's dad, and I thought you'd like to come along. I mean, how often do you get a chance like that?"

"Let me think about it."

"The interview is Sunday. So I need to know pretty soon."

"I'll let you know, okay? I have to think about it."

I went to the white room and stretched out on the bedspread, careful not to wrinkle it. I've never been to Seattle. I can't picture it. Somebody told me once they have the highest suicide rate in the country because of all the rain. That's all I know. Except that Jimi grew up there and is buried there.

My clothes were barely unpacked and washed from Cozumel and now Graham wanted me to leave again. But then the only reason to stay was in case Lori called.

I didn't think Lori was going to call.

I woke up in the middle of the night, still lying on top of the covers. It seemed ridiculous to fight it any longer. I got undressed and folded my clothes up and put them on the floor of the closet. Then I got under the sheets, smelling the fresh paint and seeing the white walls in the moonlight. I was asleep again in seconds.

———

There was an Avis rent car in my name at the Seattle airport. It was four in the afternoon and raining. It occurred to me as I drove into town that I was a free man, with no marriage to protect any longer. A small universe of possibility opened up before me. My heart belongs to Lori, but Lori may not be one of those possibilities, not any time soon. And Lori, as my phone call made so very clear, has her own relationship to protect, her own agenda and timetable. I am, essentially, available. I noticed on Wednesday that Elizabeth had taken her wedding ring off. Mine is still on, though I'm not sure why.

Maybe I'm scared that the separation will blow over, like so many other crises. Or maybe as a reminder that I haven't behaved very well lately. That I waited around until Elizabeth forced me into a decision that I should have made on my own, long ago. That I live in a house that she helped pay for, with furniture she helped pick out, while she is in a strange apartment. That Lori is in Mexico and I'm half a continent away from her and I don't know how I let that happen.

I was so distracted that I took the wrong exit off I-5 and ended up in a district of gray warehouses and torn-up streets. It took me ten minutes to get turned around and by that point the gloom had seeped into me.

I finally got to the Hilton, downtown on Sixth Avenue, and parked in their garage. Graham had booked us adjoining rooms with a view of Elliott Bay. The bay is gray and cold, even in summer, with low clouds hanging over it. There are mysterious green islands in the distance. Seattle Center and the Space Needle were off to my right, the Kingdome to my left. All the hills give the city a powerful presence. You can't ignore your physical surroundings when you feel them in your legs.

Graham was into his second six-pack of some darkish beer I didn't recognize. "I love this town," he said. "It's like the sixties died everywhere else, or went into hiding. Here they evolved. You been on the street yet? You need to go up on Capitol Hill, where the community college is. You'll see everything from pink hair to long hair to skinheads, skateboards and punks and hippies. And the bands. The scene here is unbelievable. Maybe we can catch Soundgarden or Green River some night while we're here. Have some of this beer."

"Not right now."

"They've got all these microbreweries here, it's fantastic." He saw something in my face and said, "Jesus Christ, you haven't quit drinking, have you?"

"I don't know."

"You don't *know?* What the hell kind of answer is that? Have you gone crazy, man? What's life without beer?"

"Different."

"And not a lot of fun, from the sound of you."

"Give me a break, okay? I just split up a ten-year marriage."

Graham turned his chair around and looked at the clouds over the bay. His voice dropped to a whisper. "Hell, man, you think I don't know that? I just want to cheer you up a little. And you won't give me a chance."

I walked up behind him and put my hands on his shoulders. "Sorry," I said. "My mom, my friends, they've all been trying. I guess I'm not ready to cheer up yet. So everybody gets pissed off at me and I feel guilty for not cooperating."

"You've got to remember you're not the Lone Ranger. We've been through a lot together, you and me. At first I thought you were one of the easiest people to get to know that I ever met. But there's part of you that's closed off and nobody can get to it."

I sat down on the bed. It felt like Pick On Ray Day. As if I hadn't given myself enough grief, now Graham had to join in. I'd told my mother where I was going, maybe she'd call up and take a few shots herself.

I said, "Closed off how? What do you mean?"

"You talk about your old man and you talk about your marriage and you never get mad. Not at them or me or anybody. Not even just now, when you told me to go to hell. You didn't get mad, you just showed me how hurt you were so that I would back off. Is that what happened with Elizabeth? Did you just keep backing her off until you backed her out the door?"

I wondered how he could say I didn't get mad. I hated his guts at the moment. At the same time I knew what he meant by the closed-off place. There was a wall there, and behind that wall I was still a cowboy, like the ones I watched on TV as a kid. I kept to myself and didn't talk much. I knew I was right and anybody who said different was wrong. At the end of the day I would ride off into the sunset. Alone.

If we were cowboys I would have called him out and we would have settled it in the street. But cowboys don't stay in high-rise hotels and drive in freeway traffic and live in neighborhoods where little kids play on the sidewalks. Cowboys don't have wives and they don't have mothers who call them two or three times a week, they don't have jobs and they don't have people trying to pick their brains apart.

I felt the tears start.

"Goddamnit, Ray, I love you, man. You can cry all you want and I'm not going to lay off. Talk to me, goddamnit. I want to know what's behind that wall."

My throat was so swollen it was hard to talk. "I don't know. It's safe in there. Nobody can hurt me."

"Hurt you how?"

"I don't know!"

I went to the bathroom and got a handful of Kleenex. I came out and sat on the bed and blew my nose. "By leaving me."

"Who left you?"

"Everybody." Then I said, "No. They didn't leave me, my parents took me away from them. Over and over.

"I used to have this doll when I was three. It was this ugly plastic boy doll. My parents hated it because they didn't think it was right for a boy to play with dolls. I called it Boy Baby. When we moved from Tucson to Virginia I threw it out the window of the car and then I screamed until my father went back for it. They told me if I did it again they wouldn't stop. So of course I did it again, and they didn't stop. They just kept going. It was supposed to be a lesson. My mother brought this up over Christmas and I couldn't figure out why."

"You tried to stop them. It was like you were yelling 'Stop!' and they wouldn't listen."

Tears burned my cheeks and I couldn't talk for the ugly noises that came out of my chest. I kept thinking about that doll lying abandoned on the side of the road, waiting, like it had feelings. Like it was me. It was the saddest thing in the world.

Graham rolled his chair over next to the bed. I put my arms around his neck and he hugged me. He smelled like beer and sweat. I felt the stubble on the underside of his chin. After a while I was able to let go and we sat there for a while, both of us a little embarrassed, I think.

Eventually I said, "Thanks."

"It's okay. Really."

I made one last pass with the Kleenex. It seemed to be over for the time being. "Are you at all hungry?" I said.

"Pretty much. Are you up to going out? We could do room service or something."

"No," I said. "Out is good. Just give me a minute."

———

The rain had let up. We went down to the waterfront, me on foot, Graham having to slow his wheels more than push because of the angle of the streets. We ended up at the take-out window of Captain

Ivar's Acres of Clams fish bar. The place is decorated with pictures of the Captain and dumb jokes like "Keep Clam."

I felt washed-out, tender around the edges. I didn't feel like I had to say anything more to Graham. I'd never felt as intimate with anyone I'd never had sex with. We both got deep-fried baby prawns and sat along the edge of the water, watching sea gulls hustle french fries. It was chilly and grim with the gray water lapping endlessly against the pier.

When we got back to the hotel I told Graham I was ready to turn in. I was asleep in seconds.

———

I dreamed about my father. He's reading a newspaper and there is some review in there of a Jimi Hendrix album. "Would I like this, do you think?" he asks me.

I mull it over for a second, then I say, "No. You're dead."

———

In the morning we went to Greenwood Memorial Park, southwest of the city. The office looks like a tract house except for the hearse in the carport. A guy in the office gave us a map where he'd circled Hendrix's grave.

It's a perpetual-care cemetery, with the headstones laid flat into the ground for the convenience of the lawnmowers. A sign warned us that no artificial flowers were allowed during mowing season. We had to go past a gazebo surrounded by immense pines into a flat, tree-less area with a marble sundial in the middle. The headstone is the size of a suitcase, carved from gray marble. There is a right-handed Strat on it, and the words "Forever in Our Hearts/James M./"Jimi" Hendrix/1942———1970." Somebody had left a red guitar pick there.

The Duotones did a couple of Hendrix numbers, the R&B tunes like "Fire" and "Come On (Part 1)." There was a guy who used to come to all our gigs and yell, "Hendrix is God." He would have driven across the country to leave his guitar pick on Hendrix's grave. I guess a lot of people would.

"Hey," Graham said. "Check this out." He was sitting by the

sundial. "Jimi's grave is the third stone from the sundial." There's a Hendrix song, see, called "Third Stone from the Sun." What do you call a coincidence that seems to mean something?

I used Graham's camera to take pictures of him by the grave, and he took a couple of me. I tore a piece off the map and wrote a line from a Brian Wilson song on it: "Love and mercy to you and your friends tonight." It was all I could think of. I folded the paper very small and dropped it into a pot of flowers on the next grave over, Jimi's grandmother Nora.

From there we went to see Al, Jimi's father. His house is in the Skyway neighborhood, south of the actual Seattle city limits. We stopped at a grocery to buy a six-pack of Michelob and a six of 7-Up so we wouldn't arrive empty-handed. It was after noon when we got there, and a crew was putting down new shingles on his roof.

We knocked on the front door and a minute later a carpenter came out and saw us. "Hey, Al," he yelled. "Somebody here to see you." He was young, maybe twenty-five, and he gave us a smile that said he knew why we were there.

Al came to the door. He's barely five feet tall, shy, with fringes of iron-gray hair on both sides of his head. His forehead is smooth and there are a lot of deep smile lines around his mouth. He had on a blue knit shirt and white pants. We introduced ourselves and he shook our hands. His hands are amazing, the hands of a man twice his size, soft and enveloping and powerful. I got the strongest feeling then of warmth and spirituality, a sense of Jimi I'd never had before. It was like touching Jimi's hands.

The house is a shrine to Jimi. There's a formal living room inside the front door with a couple of desks and a set of shelves, all of them covered with photos and trophies. A staircase leads from the den to the back yard, and all the way down are more framed paintings and photographs, and five gold records from Reprise. Al didn't want anything to drink. Graham took a beer and I took a 7-Up and we sat on the couch in the den.

Graham asked a lot of questions that I knew he already knew the answers to, about how Jimi, who was then Jimmy, used to play a broom until he got a guitar, how Al bought "an ordinary acoustic guitar" from one of his friends for five dollars and gave it to Jimmy.

About how Jimmy used to play along to B. B. King and Muddy Waters on Al's record player. It wasn't what I wanted to hear.

"How did you guys get along?" I asked when Graham slowed down. "I mean, my parents always hated me being a musician. They said it was a terrible life."

Al said, "We had a good relationship. I liked to see him play, on account of at least I knew where he was at. I mean, it kept him out of trouble, being interested in something like that. I didn't have to force him into it or anything. He just took up on it himself. I was glad that he did."

I wonder how many times he's told the story, to how many hundreds of people. I wonder how much real feeling there is left in it for him. He didn't seem to mind, though, and there was something I wanted from him if I could only figure it out.

"Did he keep in touch? After he got famous and everything?"

"When he come out of the service, well, he told me there wasn't no use in coming back this way, there was nothing here. He just traveled around and met a lot of different musicians, played different places. He always kept in touch though, he'd send postcards or phone. I remember he called me from England. I knew he'd been playing down there in New York, you know, when he was discovered by Charles Chandler. And then I got this call from him in London. I was surprised, 'cause I didn't know anybody over there. He told me at that time, he said, 'I think I'm on my way to the big time.' He said he was going to name the group the Jimi Hendrix Experience, and he told me how he was going to spell his name, Jimi. I thought it was a strange name, but there's so many of these groups got strange names." He laughed then, and for a second his voice sounded enough like Jimi's to be genuinely spooky. "The Who, the Beatles, and what have you. I told him, 'Well, you take care of yourself. Keep your nose clean.' "

"What did you think of that first record?" I asked. Graham watched me, thinking he had me hooked.

"I always told him, 'When you go into it, do your own thing, whatever it is.' The first time I heard his record, some people next door happened to have it. I hadn't heard him play as the Experience or anything. They'd just bought the record that day. They came over and gave the record to me. I thought, Oh no! I listened to it, I thought, well, I told him to do his own thing, and he sure did." Al shook his head and we all laughed. "He sure did."

Graham said, "Did he practice a lot when he was a kid?" It seemed like a dumb question and I wanted to kick Graham for asking it.

"He used to practice all the time. I mean, I didn't have to tell him, it was just something he wanted to do. He'd be watching TV, there was a program around that time on TV with the little kid Opie . . ."

"*The Andy Griffith Show,*" Graham said.

"*The Andy Griffith Show.* Jimi, he always used to be laughing about the kid walking along there and dropping the fish off the line . . . he used to be watching that, and in between, like, in the commercials he'd be plunking the guitar. He just played it all the time, carried the guitar with him, everywhere he went."

I tried to ask about Jimi's mother. I knew she and Al had divorced, that Jimi resented not getting to see her. When Al had refused to let Jimi go to her funeral, this was back in 1958, it had put a permanent barrier between them. Al was polite but evasive, insisted that none of that had been a problem.

I was out of steam. Graham asked a few more questions, got Al to give us the addresses of the houses they'd lived in while Jimi was growing up. Then Al took us into the other room and had us sign his guest book. We shook hands all around and thanked him and went outside.

The morning clouds had burned off. I could see Mt. Rainier in the south as I walked to the car. There was enough haze that it seemed to float unsupported in midair. Graham said, "Some days it's there, some days it's just gone. Some days it floats, like today. The Indians were supposed to have a legend about it, that when it disappeared it went into the spirit world. If you were on the mountain when it disappeared, it would take you with it."

We got in the car. I headed toward town, Graham checking the map for the addresses that Al had given us. "So," he said. "What did you think?"

"I don't know. I guess if my old man had outlived me, he would have told everybody that we were pals too."

"Exactly."

"He was really sweet, Al was. I mean, I liked him a lot. But there was stuff that bothered me. If he and Jimi were that tight, how come he had to get a copy of *Are You Experienced* from a neighbor?"

"Especially since there were British singles from December of sixty-six on, and the American album didn't come out until August of sixty-seven."

"None of which Jimi sent him."

"You know what got me? That stuff about *The Andy Griffith Show*. Jimi and Opie. Here's Opie, like Jimi, growing up with a single dad. Only Opie has got Aunt Bea and the world's most perfect father, and Jimi has his grandmother and, well, let's say . . . a flawed human being."

I took Yessler to Twenty-sixth, where Jimi grew up, then down Twenty-sixth to Washington. It's a quiet urban neighborhood on the south side of town, lots of low frame houses, poor but well-kept. There was some kind of family dispute that had emptied out onto the lawn, one guy yelling at another one from the yard, the second one walking away and turning back every few steps to shout something. On the porch a woman stood with a little boy held against her skirts. We kept driving. Somebody had scrawled HOMES NOT DOMES on the side of an empty building. We went around the block and drove north again on Twenty-third Avenue, past Garfield High School. Al said Jimi had "got to be a visitor up there," and then dropped out in his senior year.

Graham had asked Al where he thought Jimi was headed musically. "The last time I saw him," Al said, "when he was out here, he said that he was going to change his style, and he was going to change his mode of playing or whatever. That was July of seventy. Performed out there at Sicks Stadium, they had it outside. It rained, I got soaking wet."

———

That night I dreamed my father and I are stalking each other through this old frame house. It's a lot like the Hendrix house on Yessler. We both have pump shotguns and there is patricidal rage in my heart.

When I woke up I felt a wave of sadness. The night before it seemed really meaningful that I'd known, even asleep, that he was dead. I'd thought maybe it was a new start.

Over breakfast, Graham said, "Admit it. You're thinking about it."

"About what?"

"The album. *First Rays.* Hell, your *name* is Ray. It's like fate or something."

"Graham, if I started to want to do this album, it would mean . . ." I shook my head. "It's just a bad idea, okay?"

"It's a bad idea now. Maybe it'll turn into a good idea later." He held up both hands. "That's all I'm going to say. Not another word from me, I promise."

I left for Austin that morning and it was night by the time a taxi dropped me off at the house. I was surprised at how little I wanted to be there. I left my suitcase in the hall and slept in the white room.

The next day I couldn't face the rest of the house. All my music books were there in the white room, so I got down what I had on Hendrix and lay down on the bed with it.

People talk about Hendrix in the same breath with Joplin, as if he'd died with a needle in his arm. The truth is he had one too many sleeping pills after a couple of long days. He wasn't depressed, he didn't mean to kill himself, he didn't even want to get high. He just wanted to get some sleep. The actual cause of death on the certificate is "inhalation of vomit," same as my father. If the old bastard had a grave he'd be spinning in it.

Hendrix was a black musician with an almost exclusively white audience. He grew up with the blues and did the chitlin circuit of southern R&B clubs in his late teens, backing the Isleys and Little Richard. From there he went to New York and fronted his own band, sometimes called the Rainflowers, sometimes Jimmy James and the Blue Flames, at the Cafe Wha? in Greenwich Village. They played rock standards, "Hey Joe" and "Like a Rolling Stone" and "Wild Thing" and "Shotgun," and Hendrix took everything he'd learned into a new dimension of feedback and echo and sustain and sheer volume. This was the summer of 1966.

That's where Chas Chandler, newly ex-bassist of the Animals, discovered him and took him to England. There he found him a couple of English boys with the right haircuts: Mitch Mitchell, a brilliant jazz drummer, and Noel Redding, an out-of-work guitarist on bass by default. In 1967 they demolished the Monterey Pop Festival and in '68 they were tearing up the charts. By '69 Hendrix was head-lining pop festivals, with or without the Experience, including Wood-stock. On Friday, September 18, 1970, he was dead.

There was a sound in his head that he was never able to get out. He told *Rolling Stone*, "I just lay around daydreaming and hearing all this music." And he said, "I just can't play guitar that well to get all this music together." With his third album, *Electric Ladyland*, he began to produce himself, spending endless hours and days and weeks in the studio. The studio bills were so high that it seemed like a good idea to build his own. The idea became Electric Lady studios in Greenwich Village, where he slowly accumulated pieces of a new double album, *First Rays of the New Rising Sun*. It was to be his farewell to conventional electric rock and roll. He'd talked about various new directions, especially moving deeper into jazz with Miles Davis and Gil Evans.

First Rays was to be the ultimate fusion music: rock, jazz, blues, R&B. Healing music, unifying music. Only Jimi couldn't seem to get it together. Chas Chandler says that the night before he died, Jimi called and asked him to come back and produce the new record, like he had the first two.

I went upstairs and listened to *Cry of Love* and *Rainbow Bridge*, the records Reprise cobbled together from the pieces Jimi left behind. Yes, there is something here. You can feel Hendrix's urgency and frustration, and it gives the music, some of it anyway, a fearsome power. There is also an incredible diversity of music tangled together.

What finally did it for me were the pictures of Jimi in his final days. No more processed hair, just a short Afro showing signs of gray. He was tired of the stage show, of playing with his teeth, of setting the guitar on fire. He wanted people to listen to the music, and you can see the fatigue in his face.

He's never alone. The people around him all want something. Young women, black activists, promoters, musicians, all basking in the glow. There's this one picture in particular by Erika Hanover, the German photographer who took so many classic rock photos. Jimi is in a restaurant with a half-eaten plate of food in front of him. Hanging on to his arm is some unidentified woman with long black hair, looking at him with both adoration and anticipation. In his left hand is a cigarette which has burned down to the filter. His eyes are puffy and tired, but you can see that he wants very badly not to disappoint anyone. He smiles bravely for the camera.

I got two packages from UPS. One was from Graham, with videotapes of Hendrix and audiotapes of a radio show called *Live & Unreleased* from Labor Day of 1988. The other, from Mike Autrey, had a type-written manuscript called *Crosstown Traffic* by an English music jour-nalist named Charles Shaar Murray. There were also two Xeroxed pages in Hendrix's handwriting. The first was titled "Songs for Strate Ahead," with ten of the *First Rays* songs, enough for a single album. The second, according to Autrey's note, was later, a list for *First Rays* itself. It was broken down into four sides, though Jimi had obviously quit before he had anything but "Angel" figured out for side four. Bruce Gary, who put together the radio show, had found it in a box of quarter-inch stereo mixes for the album at Al Hendrix's house.

I broke down and said yes to enough repair work to keep my hands busy, to help fill the hours. I took walks again in the morning, three and four miles a day. I went to book and record stores a couple of times a week and came home with a stack of books on Hendrix and England in the sixties. And finally I bought a new TV and VCR with some of Graham's money, as much as anything so there would be voices in the house again. I was tired of days where I didn't hear another human voice.

I followed the news about the Chinese students in Tiananmen Square. For a while it seemed like the sixties all over again, only better, where unarmed kids faced down tanks, soldiers threw down their guns to join the protesters, working people gave the students food and money to survive on. Later I watched the first reports of the massacre come in. It had the horrifying inevitability of the National Guard opening fire at Kent State, or the Chicago police moving through Lincoln Park.

I couldn't watch the news after that. I retreated to the past, watch-ing and listening to Jimi Hendrix on tape, or reading about him, thinking about *First Rays*. I memorized the song lists, could almost hear the finished albums in my head.

I talked to Elizabeth maybe five or six times. A month after she moved out, we had dinner at the Lone Star Cafe, a chicken-fried-steak place down the street from me. Neither of us ate much. She talked mostly about Dude, and about summer school.

Eventually Elizabeth said, "I've gone out a couple of times with this new teacher that transferred in. It's a little weird. I mean, I don't know what I'm doing with him because I don't know where the marriage is. Is this like a trial separation? Are we going to get divorced? Are we waiting for something? If so, what is it exactly that we're waiting for?"

My stomach clenched and I wanted nothing more in the world than for the conversation to be over. I was trying to second-guess her again. Did she want to be set free so she could start over? Did she want things left open?

I thought of that Hanover picture of Hendrix, trying to make everybody happy.

"I really don't see," I said, "any reason to go on. If you're ready, then, I guess I'll go ahead and file." I got my breath and said, "For divorce."

She sat back in her chair. She's always been good at hiding what she feels. Most of the time I think she has it hidden from herself. "I'm ready," she said. "Let's get on with it."

When I got home I called Graham. "I'm not saying yes. But fly me to London and I'll take a look."

———

I went to see a lawyer the next day and she gave me a bored account of the process. Texas is a no-fault divorce state. She would file a petition on my behalf alleging that the marriage had "become insupportable" and there was no "reasonable expectation of reconciliation." Elizabeth's lawyer would respond with a meaningless formal denial, we'd work out a property settlement, wait sixty days, then I would go before a judge who would sign off on the whole thing. All very simple, all very cut-and-dried. I didn't know whether to be relieved or depressed by the simplicity of it. Weren't marriages supposed to last forever?

I came home and took my wedding ring off and put it in a drawer. Then I sat in a lawn chair and watched the sun crawl down the sky. Okay, I thought. You wanted it, you got it. Now what?

———

Two weeks later I was on a plane for England. It was June 27, blistering hot in Austin. I hadn't been to London since I was a kid and I was genuinely excited about it. I'd spent six months in the Sudan with my parents in the early sixties, turned thirteen while I was over there. My father was doing salvage archeology for the Aswan Dam, early human settlements, not pyramids or anything glamorous. We saw Europe on the way over and the way back. What I remember most about Africa is trading Pepsi bottle caps to native kids for dried dates, which I ate constantly, and them throwing rocks at me for going around without a shirt. Nobody had told me that it broke some kind of religious taboo.

What I remember about England is the gleaming tile cities of the Underground, and the sweetish smell of Penguin paperbacks. I vaguely remember our first hotel in Soho, this in 1963, and my mother's shocked reaction to the strip joint next door, the photos on display in a glass case outside that she wouldn't let me look at, though I could see enough from a distance to feel a sudden new and powerful interest. I remember some of the tourist stuff, Parliament and Big Ben. Mostly it was just another move, another dislocation.

At six in the morning London time, which was only one A.M. in Austin, the attendants came through with coffee and rolls and everybody opened their window shades to the daylight. The sunshine fooled me sufficiently into thinking I was awake and I watched the soft green hills of England unroll below me.

On Graham's instructions I took the express train from Gatwick to Victoria Station, where I had my picture taken in a coin-operated booth and bought myself a one-week travel card for the Underground. Then I had a cup of coffee and watched the crowds, getting used to the vast, echoing station, getting used to the idea of being in another country.

Elizabeth and I had always talked about Europe and never been able to afford it. She loves everything English, got up before dawn to watch Charles and Di get married in 1981. I was conscious of how alone I was, prickly from being awake too long, full of second thoughts about getting involved in another album.

I wondered what it would be like to be there with Lori. She's such a world traveler. She would know how to find the best restaurants, how much things are supposed to cost, how many stamps to put on her postcards home. It was three in the morning in Cozumel. Calling was not the thing to do.

I'd left a life behind me in Austin that felt like a dark room full of somebody else's furniture. I couldn't seem to move without running into something that hurt me. In England I was free of that. If not a clean start, it was at least a reprieve.

I took the Victoria Line to Green Park and the Piccadilly Line to Russell Square, where Graham had reserved a room for me at the Russell Hotel. From there I called Charlie Murray, who wrote the *Crosstown Traffic* manuscript and was supposedly a friend of Graham's. Charlie said he would take me around and show me the Hendrix sights.

I met him in a literary hangout called the Cafe Munchen. It's off New Oxford Street at the beginning of the West End. There's a big office building maybe a block away that says Centre Point on it. To the south is the theater district, to the southwest is Soho and Wardour Street, to the north is the British Museum, and due west are the shops along Oxford, Bond, and Carnaby Streets.

There are metal tables on the patio of the cafe. The inside has a few ferns, a glass display case of boiled pub food, and a bar. Charlie was inside, near the door. He's medium height, dark, with wiry hair and a crooked grin. He shook my hand and asked after Mike Autrey and Graham. Then he went to the bar and got a fat bottle of European beer for himself and a glass of lemonade for me, which in England is carbonated and tastes like 7-Up.

"Graham told me I should help you," Charlie said. "And I get the feeling this has something to do with those two CDs he sent me. The *Smile* and the *Celebration of the Lizard*. The Doors is some really scary shit, man."

I shrugged. I wasn't crazy about this. Graham hadn't told me that Charlie knew about the bootlegs.

"So," Charlie said. "Naturally I'm dying to know where they came from."

"I can't tell you," I said. "It's not that I don't want to, it's that I can't."

"Is it Hendrix next?"

I tried to think of a way not to answer, then nodded.

"Fantastic!" He slapped the table. "You've got some kind of line on unreleased stuff from *First Rays*, then, have you?" He had a slight stammer, which I hadn't noticed until he got excited. "This is fucking great. What can I do?"

I shifted my glass around on the tabletop, still uncomfortable. "I need information. About everything. What the album would have been like, about Hendrix, about London in 1970."

We went through my *London* A-Z and he showed me some of the crucial places: where Hendrix had played, where he had died. I wrote the addresses down. "What was the city like? How was it different from now?"

He leaned back in his chair and thought for a second. "Soho—where the Marquee club was—is very different now. Basically they closed down most of the sex industry and moved the boutiques and designer restaurants in instead. It was definitely much wilder and woollier in those days. In 1970 I would come up to hang out with the underground press and then I would go home. I was basically an eighteen-year-old kid with a major Jewish afro.

"By then it was clear that the world was not just going to turn Day-Glo and solve everything. What I came into in seventy was just about the end of the party. There was still a bit of food and drink left, but there were more empty cans than full ones and a lot of the bottles had roaches in them.

"It was basically the slow deflation of hippie. It receded, and what was left in its wake was very big colors and flared trousers. It was like hippie with all the style and creativity taken out. If you want to use music as a reference point, the death of Hendrix and the breakup of the Beatles essentially put the kibosh on the sixties."

"Or maybe earlier," I said. "Brian Jones dying, and then Alta-mont."

"Yeah. Could be."

"I just can't seem to get a handle on it. Why it had to happen. Even how it happened."

"The late sixties were about the notion of an infinite expansion of possibilities. By the end of the sixties it was a sense of the contracting of possibilities again."

"Was it the drugs?"

"The drugs went with the times. In the Mod era in London it was pills and a bit of pot. In the hippie era it was pot and a bit of acid. By about seventy, serious powders were beginning to get fashionable. There was a bit of this, y'know, doomed young poets and romantic squalor kind of chic going on."

"The Jim Morrison thing."

"Yeah, like on *Celebration of the Lizard*. Morrison was just ahead of his time. By seventy it was everywhere. It was like the moment had come and gone."

"Where did *First Rays* fit into all that?"

"It was a millennial concept. Hendrix was a millennial optimist. But I think his belief in the power of music to heal was really damaged by the fact that he finally realized how fucked-up his own situation was, and how little control he had over his own life. Because that last tour, things had been intensely mismanaged, he had these immense bills to pay for the construction of Electric Lady studio, and his record royalties were frozen because of lawsuits. The only way to pay his bills was to do a tour he didn't want to do, where an audience insisted that he did his old act, which he didn't want to do. When you see him in the Isle of Wight film, you spend an hour looking at a man who is really not enjoying himself. I mean, he only smiles about two or three times in the whole show.

"Hendrix knew that he had to regain control. He'd started to get his own lawyers and accountants. He wanted to wrap everything up with *First Rays of the New Rising Sun* and make that like the absolute peak of his rock and roll or pop career. What he was intending to do when he died was to go to New York, get all the tapes of the *First Rays* stuff, and bring them back to London and get together with Chas Chandler to finish them. To overdub and mix and edit them with Chandler. He was looking to tidy up all loose ends, get everything cleaned up, and go forward from there. And that's the precise point at which he died.

"He died because he was sloppy with prescription drugs." There was pain in Charlie's voice suddenly, and this vast wistfulness. "I mean, in the universe next door he woke up with a shocking hangover and, y'know, slept it off and carried on. Or he woke up in a puddle of his own puke and thought, 'Oh shit, man,' went and had a shower and probably didn't drink any more alcohol or take any more drugs for a couple of days. Or if they'd sat him up, or laid him on his side in the ambulance, he'd have got to hospital, they'd have pumped his stomach, told him he was a very silly boy, and sent him home. Then he would have gone to the studio with Chandler and *First Rays of the New Rising Sun* would have come out in late seventy or early seventy-one. There you go. It would have been a different world. And frankly a preferable one."

We sat there for a while watching the black taxis queue up on St. Giles High Street. With great British delicacy Charlie said, "So, then, what are your plans?"

I looked at my watch and told him I knew he had to be going. I thanked him for his time and we both stood up. "If you want to walk with me," he said, "the Experience's original rehearsal room was just up there on Denmark Street."

We walked toward Charing Cross Road. The streets feel uniquely London: the tall, charcoal-business-suit-colored buildings, the red double-decker buses, the arrows painted on the crosswalks advising pedestrians which way to look for oncoming traffic. Denmark Street is livelier, with a few trees and window boxes, a mystery bookshop, cafes, and a row of music shops with overpriced American guitars in the windows. The buildings are three stories, different shades of brick and stone, all shoved up against each other.

Charlie stopped and pointed to a restaurant on the south side of the street. The sign says BARINO TAVOLA COFFEE BAR. Above it are two stories of red-brick flats. "There, I think. Apparently he got a bit loud, enough to annoy the neighbors. And after a particularly hard night he'd have a bit of trouble tuning in the morning, y'know. He'd be tuning up at three hundred watts. Shaking the street.

"It's funny. A decade later the Sex Pistols would have their own rehearsal space just down the street. It's all there somehow, in this street, over those few years. Two groups that had so much to say about the times they lived in. Taking something as far as it can go, until it simply snaps."

We shook hands and I thanked him again, and he hurried off toward the Tottenham Court Road tube stop. I stayed for a few minutes to picture Hendrix rehearsing above my head, full of excitement, feeling everything was just starting for him. It would have been winter, of course, but 1966 always seems like summer to me.

———

Denmark Street empties into Charing Cross Road, which looks new and is full of bookshops and nightclubs. The Marquee Club moved here only a few years ago. It's a punk and alternative venue now. The chalkboard outside advertised bands like Thin White Rope and the Alarm. I bought a T-shirt anyway, in memory of the Stones and Yardbirds and all the other brilliant bands that started there.

I followed Charlie's directions west to Wardour Street, where the Marquee used to be. The address matches a gap in the solid wall of buildings. Black streaks of soot from a fire have left stains all over the surrounding brick. Across the street is a pub called the Intrepid Fox, from which Hendrix was supposedly ejected late one night. It's been freshly painted red, with hanging plants inside and posters from American crime films.

I turned right and walked up to Oxford Street, with its boutiques and record stores and mobs of foreign tourists. Two blocks north is Margaret Street, where the Speakeasy had been at number 48. Now it's just a pair of glass doors, locked, with a directory inside listing a couple of foreign-sounding businesses. The stairs lead up now instead of down and there's no trace of the club that used to be in the basement.

For a while it had been the center of fashionable London. People would go to the Marquee to see a show—Hendrix, say—and then go to the Speak afterward for spaghetti bolognese and a few rum and cokes. Hendrix would likely show up there too, and jam until dawn. He was supposed to meet Sly Stone there the night before he died.

I took the Underground to Notting Hill Gate. In the sixties, Charlie said, it was the nearest thing to a genuinely integrated neighborhood in London. It was the home of the Free School and black activist Michael X; boutiques and vegetarian restaurants lined Portobello Road; West Indians and hippies and Marxist radicals lived cheek to jowl. All the underground papers were published here, and everybody came here to score. "A liberated zone," Charlie called it.

Now it seems to be endless rows of white-columned town houses, half with scaffolding across them as they're cleaned and pressed for new, upwardly mobile tenants. I thought of Van Dyke Parks and "columnated ruins domino." I thought of Los Angeles devouring itself, and Austin doing the same thing, driving dozens of poor families out to make room for one rich one, carting its history to the dump.

I walked down to Ladbroke Grove, immortalized in Van Morrison's *Astral Weeks*. On Lansdowne Crescent the neighborhood turns into walled gardens and trees, balconies with hanging baskets. No cabs, no traffic at all, just private cars parked along the street. Birds clucked quietly and even the sunlight seemed muted.

Number 22 is one of dozens of identical white-stone row houses. It used to be the Samarkand Hotel and there is still a brass Buddha on the door at street level. Black wrought-iron steps lead down past a couple of trees to the flat where Hendrix stayed. A window with Venetian blinds opens onto the stairs.

Hendrix had stood where I was standing, but I still didn't have the picture. It was like in L.A., seeing the bulldozer where Brian's house used to be. The past felt out of reach.

I ate and took a train to Russell Square. It was nearly ten o'clock and the sun was just going down. There were clubs and shops and bars and theaters, an entire city full of things to do. What I wanted was to go to the Speakeasy, or the Bag O'Nails, and watch Mick Jagger walk in with Marianne Faithfull, or see McCartney with Jane Asher at the table across the way. I wanted Jimi Hendrix to come onto the tiny stage and jam with Sly Stone. I wanted Brian Jones not to be dead and George Bush not to be president. I want to feel like my life is happening right now. Not in some vague possible future time where Lori manages to leave Tom, and not in some inaccessible past where I'm still in love with Elizabeth. Now. Right this minute.

I'm not afraid that saving Hendrix's life would be hard to imagine. Like Charlie said, he could wake up with a hangover. They could have put him on his side in the ambulance. I'm afraid that I'll go back, that I'll wind up physically there, the way I did with Brian. Not because there's no other way to get the album.

Because I want to.

———

I woke up at four in the morning. It was eleven P.M. in Austin, time to think about going to bed. I should have been deeply asleep and instead I was thinking about Jimi.

His final night has already passed into legend. Everybody has their own version of it, usually that Jimi called them up or came by sometime during the night to talk about his future. If you believe all the stories, he struck new management deals with two or three different people, hired numerous musicians for sessions, set up club dates and tours and recording sessions, wrote lyrics and made sketches for paintings.

Some things seem pretty certain. He was hanging with a German woman, a beautiful blonde skating instructor named Monika Danneman. The room at the Samarkand Hotel was hers. The night of the seventeenth he went without her to a party at the flat of a young rich guy on the scene. He had a few drinks, maybe a joint, maybe retired to a back bedroom with one of the women. There was some of the Lizard King in Jimi, flesh to balance the spirit. He didn't care much about drugs or booze, but women seemed so beautiful to him.

Monika came to pick him up and for some reason Jimi kept her waiting in the street. Finally they left and drove around for a while, getting back to Lansdowne Crescent before dawn.

Jimi'd had trouble sleeping. His ulcers were acting up, partly because he was in such a quandary about his career. Later that day, Friday, a trial would get under way to settle the U.K. end of an old contract with Capitol Records. Then there was his bass player and old Army buddy, Billy Cox, who'd been given his first hit of acid in Holland and had freaked out in a major way. He was holed up in a hotel, trying to cool out enough for Jimi to ship him back to the States. All on top of the usual hassles of too much travel, too many people who wanted things from him.

He asked Monika for some sleeping pills. He took a few and couldn't get to sleep so he took a few more. By this time the sun was up. During the morning he vomited in his sleep. At ten-thirty Monika got scared when she couldn't wake him and called for help.

I can see his face. Tired and yearning at the same time. I can see him in the ambulance choking. Feeling his life slipping away from him and unable to stop it. It's what Lori meant when she said my father's mask was full of vomit. Even if my father wanted to die, there was a part of him that wouldn't let go, that knew there's nothing after this, that fought for life to the end. And Jimi didn't want to die. He must have felt so helpless and afraid.

Once I took three different kinds of pain pills after surgery on my gums, a half hour apart, trying to get something to work, and they'd all come on at once. I felt myself slip backward into darkness. I was sweaty, sick to my stomach, dizzy and scared. I thought at the time it was how Jimi must have felt.

I didn't want him to die. I had a feeling about him. He was like Brian Wilson, somebody really special. Like he was meant to be my friend.

I got up and took a leak and washed my face. Sleep seemed unlikely. Okay, I thought. We'll do this plain and simple and logical. The same way I did the Beatles song, the way I did *Celebration of the Lizard.* I got out my little hand-held cassette recorder and put on a work tape I'd made for *First Rays,* cuts from *Cry of Love* and *Rainbow Bridge,* from *Loose Ends* and *War Heroes,* bits and pieces from the *Live & Unreleased* radio show, finishing up with the instrumental jam he'd played at Woodstock. If I stumbled onto the real thing it could go right on that tape.

Plain and simple. Hendrix lives. He goes to New York. He gets the tapes and brings them to London. He and Chas work up the album. I would listen in and the music would come out of my little recorder.

So. Step one. Put him on his side in the ambulance.

I closed my eyes. Lansdowne Crescent. The trees are still green, the sky is gray. An ambulance pulls up to the curb, not an American EMS wagon but an old-fashioned British ambulance with the high, rounded back.

It wasn't happening. I felt myself pull away from the image, afraid to let go. I had Lori on my mind instead of Jimi, and that blue hole off Palancar Reef where the bottom falls away forever.

I got up, went to the closet. I put on jeans, a tattersall shirt and a sweater, socks and Converse All-Stars. I opened the blinds and let the lights of the sleeping city into the room. Then I sat on the bed with my head in my hands and closed my eyes.

Start again. Lansdowne Crescent. The white columns, the trees, the potted plants on the balconies. The bronze Buddha on the door of the Samarkand Hotel. Hendrix is downstairs, his body in spasms, his eyelids too heavy to lift, dizzy and sick and scared. Needing somebody to know what to do.

The ambulance pulls up . . .

I opened my eyes. It was gray and cool, close to rain. The ambulance had its lights flashing but no siren on as it rounded the curve of the street and pulled up in front of number 22. I was across the street on the curb, dressed in jeans and a sweater and tennis shoes.

I wondered what I'd been so afraid of. I felt like I was underwater: weightless, exhilarated, powerful, and free. I watched two young guys in white coats go down the stairs to Monika's apartment. One was dark, maybe East Indian, with heavy beard stubble, and the other was blond with steel-rimmed National Health glasses. I crossed the street, letting a big, square Mercedes sedan pass in front of me. As I got to the top of the stairs the blond medic ran up.

"Best clear off, mate. We've got a bit of trouble here."

"Is something wrong with Hendrix? He's a friend of mine."

"I wasn't introduced. D'ye mind?" He pushed past me and I went on down the stairs.

I came in through the kitchen, then into the living room where there was a long white couch, a bar, a TV set, various cushions on the hardwood floor. A gas fire burned in the fireplace. A maple-neck black Stratocaster, the one he'd used at the Isle of Wight, lay on top of its case on a table in the corner. There was a dining area and beyond that French doors that led into the garden.

Around the corner was the bedroom. The sour smell of vomit hit me as soon as I was through the door. Jimi lay on his back on the far side of the bed, covered to the waist. His bare chest moved up and down as he struggled to breathe. There were vomit stains on the pillows and sheets. Next to him was a chest of drawers with a sheet of paper on top. From across the room all I saw was handwriting, maybe a poem or lyrics.

Monika stood near me, wearing bell-bottoms and a red sweater. Her hair was light blonde, nearly white. She had a strong nose and heavy-lidded eyes, and her mascara was badly smeared from sleep and tears. She was smaller than I'd pictured her, more vulnerable. The dark-haired medic was feeling for a pulse in Jimi's wrist. He and Monika both turned to look at me.

"I'm a friend of Jimi's," I said. "This happened before. You have to be careful he doesn't choke."

"I don't need any bloody advice," the medic said. "Mind you stand clear of the door, he'll be bringing a litter through."

I moved into the room. Hendrix was an unbelievably powerful presence, even unconscious. His huge hands lay on the outside of the sheet, dug into the mattress, and his face contorted in pain and confusion.

You're going to be all right, I thought. Just hang in there, man. I'm going to take care of this.

The other medic came with the stretcher and they loaded Jimi onto it with practiced timing. I followed them out to the ambulance and when they had him inside I said, "Make sure he's sitting up. If you lay him down he'll choke."

"We know what we're about," the blond said. "We always sit them up."

Not always, I thought. The blond got in back with Jimi and as I watched he sat Jimi up against the rear wall and strapped him in. The black-haired guy shut the rear doors and waved me away.

"Where are you taking him?" Monika asked him.

"St. Mary Abbots Hospital, Kensington."

She looked at me. "Do you know where it is?"

I nodded. I'd looked it up on the map the day before.

"What is your name, anyway?" she said. "Who are you?"

"My name's Ray. I'm a friend of Jimi's. Where's your car? We should follow them."

Monika nodded and we ran to a blue sports car parked down the street. The ambulance pulled out, the two-note European siren keening at last, and we swung in behind them. Monika drove like an expert, keeping on their bumper in spite of the traffic.

"It's going to be okay," I told her.

"He would not wake up," she said, staring at the road. Her German accent was fairly thick, and she seemed uncertain of her words. "I am very frightened."

"As long as they keep him upright he'll be okay. I promise you."

We took Campden Hill Road to Kensington High Street, then turned on Wright's Lane. The hospital is on Marloes Road, only a few blocks from where we were. They would pump his stomach, I figured, and keep him overnight for observation. Jimi believed in flying saucers and spirit beings. I didn't think he'd have a problem with me being from the future. I would wait around until Monika and I could get in to see him, then he and I would talk.

The ambulance pulled up to the emergency entrance and Monika stopped in the driveway with the engine running. The place looked dingy and dark, red bricks and soot instead of the American pretense of sterility. I realized that Monika was freaked out badly. "It's okay," I said again. "Turn off the car, we'll go inside."

I helped her out of the car. She still seemed pretty dazed so I took hold of one arm. She smelled of expensive perfume and nervous sweat. There were deep circles under the mascara and I remembered she hadn't slept much the night before. I left her in the waiting room and talked to the nurses, who promised to find me as soon as they had word.

I sat down with Monika. She had a piece of sketchbook paper in one hand and she was crying. I took the paper away from her and saw a drawing of nine nines, each larger than the last, with the circle parts concentric.

"What is this?"

"Jimi was drawing that yesterday. He said it was very important. Over and over he was telling me. Very important."

I gave it back to her. "If Six Was Nine" was the cut on his second album where he said, "I'm the one that's got to die when it's time for me to die." Now nine nines. I had no idea what it meant.

We sat there for an hour. Every few minutes I asked for an update and the desk nurse shook her head. Monika sat with her eyes closed and didn't seem to want to talk.

I was nervous.

It was just before noon when a doctor came out and one of the nurses pointed at me. I was out of my chair in a flash with Monika right behind me.

"I'm sorry," the doctor said. "There was nothing we could do."

======

They'd put Jimi in some kind of head restraint in the ambulance. He was sitting up, but unable to lean forward. When he threw up, the vomit ran into his lungs and all he could do was sit there and strangle to death.

Monika went hysterical just as another of Jimi's girlfriends, Alvenia Bridges, showed up. She'd stayed with Eric Burdon the night before, and she was the one Monika called when she couldn't wake Jimi up. I left Monika with her and went into the men's toilet.

I was dizzy, unable to concentrate. Jimi was dead. Again. My being there had made no difference at all.

I couldn't believe it.

I splashed water on my face and looked at myself in the mirror. It was not supposed to happen this way. I was supposed to be in control. I could not accept it. I turned toward the door and then my balance went out. The floor rushed up at me.

I never felt myself hit. The next thing I knew I was on my face on the bed in my hotel, back in 1989.

CHAPTER 7
CHAPTER 7

Jimi

I was back in Austin for two days before I could make myself call Graham. "I tried," I told him. "I didn't get it."

"Are you okay? What happened?"

"I'm all right. Jimi died." I told him the story.

"We gave it a shot. Let it go."

"I want to try again."

"Ray, leave it, man. You did your best. I thought you could do it without, you know. Things getting weird. It's not worth it. We've got *Smile*. Which, by the way, I'm going to send you some more money for. We just went gold! I've shipped fifty thousand units. Part of it is, I got to feeling guilty and scaled the price way back. Still. Fifty thousand units of a bootleg! This is absolutely incredible."

"Graham, I . . ."

"You don't sound good."

"I'll tell you the truth, I feel like shit. Everything is a blur. It's like a hangover and being drunk at the same time."

"Jet lag. It's going to take you a couple three days. Just rest up, okay, partner? We'll talk some more."

"Okay," I said. "Later."

I finished up the last of the paperwork on my repair jobs and put my tools away. Unless I changed the message on my machine the shelves would stay empty. I took down all the posters and photos and wiring diagrams on the north wall, all but the one Hendrix poster that was already there. Then I went through my books and cut out photos of Jimi and everybody else who was part of the London scene then: the Boyd sisters, Pattie and Jenny, blonde fashion models who were married to George Harrison and Mick Fleetwood respectively; Marianne Faithfull, with her ties to both the Stones and the art world; John Mayall, whose bands had turned out one brilliant guitarist after another. Shots of the young and trendy on King's Road, of fans lined up outside the Roundhouse or sprawled around Hyde Park at a free concert. A couple of Michael English's psychedelic posters from OZ magazine. A great photo of Erika Hanover and Linda Eastman taking each other's picture, Erika in a crouch as Linda shot down at her, European nobility meets American plutocracy.

I played my *First Rays* work tape and I played other music from the late summer of 1970: *Eric Burdon Declares War*, Fleetwood Mac's *Then Play On*, Dave Mason's *Alone Together*, Santana's *Abraxas*, the Stone's *Get Yer Ya-Ya's Out*, PG&E's *Are You Ready* with the blistering vocals of Charlie Allen. I made a tape with singles on it like "Love or Let Me Be Lonely" and "Tighter Tighter," "Ride Captain Ride" and the Joe Cocker version of "The Letter." I turned up a British singles chart from September of 1970 but virtually everything on it was American: Smokey and the Miracles, Elvis, Three Dog Night, the Chairmen of the Board, Bread.

I remember hearing all those songs in 1970 as I drove around Austin looking for work. Every ad I answered turned out to be a door-to-door sales job. I was so desperate I spent a day pushing Cutco knives with a borrowed sample case. My one sales pitch was to a stoned college girl who didn't even have a piece of bread for me to demonstrate the knives on.

Meanwhile Jimi toured Europe and played the Isle of Wight. He came home to London to jam at the Speak and hang out with Monika, and with Devon Wilson, his old girlfriend from Harlem, immortalized in "Dolly Dagger," a song that would have been on *First Rays of the New Rising Sun.*

Peace and love were not only losing ground, they weren't paying the bills either. Jackson State and Kent State and the days after, when Nixon and Agnew declared open season on student protest, had left everybody I knew full of helpless anger. A lot of my friends talked about moving out to the country to start a commune or a co-op, and a few of them eventually did. I joined a new band that didn't last a month. To go back to college for a liberal arts degree sounded like a bad joke. My love life was nonexistent.

Which is how I ended up in Dallas, going to DeVry on money borrowed from my parents, living in an efficiency in Oaklawn, working Sundays on my father's fishpond. That was the year I started to drink seriously, even though I was still underage. There was a guy in some of my classes at DeVry who was in his thirties. We would play tennis on Saturday afternoon and he would buy a couple of cases for me afterward.

It's hard to remember what it feels like to be that young. I could drink all night and it didn't make any difference the next day. My relationships would last a month or two before I would get bored or she would get nervous and one or the other of us would stop calling or start to make excuses. No matter who broke it off, when it was over I always felt relief. Free again.

Freedom seemed important to me at the time.

Jimi had a couple of regular girlfriends—Kathy Etchingham in London, Devon Wilson in the States—but there were no strings. He had women on the road, women at parties. He was a guy who couldn't say no. I wonder if that didn't start to wear on him, the way it finally started to wear on me. In the spring of 1970 he found out Kathy had gotten married without telling him, to some guy from the Eric Clapton organization. She'd been married since November. Jimi flew to London to try to talk her out of it and after a couple of days he saw she was happy without him. Then he called Monika in Germany, who was sick and wouldn't see him. For the first time he seemed tired of being footloose, seemed to think seriously of marriage.

Jimi was twenty-seven when he died. For that matter, so was Jim Morrison, and so were Janis Joplin and Brian Jones. When Brian Wilson was twenty-seven, his father sold the rights to all his music behind his back. After that Brian took to his bed, and that, more or less, was the end of his career.

At twenty-seven I worked nine to five in the Printed Circuit Design department of Warrex Computer Corporation, bored out of my mind. The PC draftsman, a guy from Plano named Charles Lane, helped me work on my car and took me fishing now and again. We'd become friends the year before because we were the only two people in the company who gave a damn when Elvis died. Charles told me how he got married when he was just my age. "It's that kind of time in your life. Things start to catch up to you."

I told him I didn't have anybody to even think about marrying.

"That don't matter. When the time comes it'll happen, that's all."

A week or so later Elizabeth brought me a prime rib at the Lemmon Avenue Bar and Grille and I felt it happen, just like Charles said. An urgent need to move or be left behind, a sense that this was my last chance to beat the endless pattern of love and loss, the roller coaster of emotions. So I jumped, and never imagined it might one day become insupportable, without expectation of reconciliation.

It's all so tangled together. Seeing Jimi in concert in February of 1968 and again that summer, with Alex both times. This black, long-sleeved shirt with green polka dots that I would sometimes wear when I went out with Alex, but was mostly my rock-and-roll shirt, that I wore with the band, playing Jimi's music, that I wore until it was literally rags. My first stereo, a cheap fold-out portable from Columbia Masterworks, that my parents bought me so they wouldn't have to listen to me play Jimi's albums on their hi-fi anymore. My best friend Les Michaels stuck a blue-and-green vinyl flower on the top of it after we went off to Vanderbilt together, you know the ones, a blue circle with five smaller green circles around the edge to represent the petals, you used to see them everywhere and now they're just one more example of how naïve we all used to be, to believe you could change the basic nature of something by putting a flower on it.

Was it that way for everybody, music and sex and politics and love all inextricably part of each other, or is it just me? How can you ever know how much is true for everyone and how much is only true for you?

It took me a week to feel like I was ready to try again.

I put on the same clothes I'd worn in London, as if they were part of the magic. I'd bought some pre-1970 pounds from a coin dealer, enough to get around for a day or so, and I had a few hundred U.S. dollars in my wallet. I was cold and deliberate, like somebody laying out the implements for suicide. It was 3:10 in the afternoon. I went up to my workshop and put on my *First Rays* work tape, and then I sat on my leather couch and closed my eyes.

Charlie Murray had described the Speakeasy to me and I tried to make the images come alive in my head. You went downstairs at 48 Margaret Street and through a set of double doors. On the left as you come in is a cigarette machine and a couple of what Charlie called "fruit machines," slot machines. He said there's always somebody there risking the last of their coins in hopes of paying off their dinner bill. Straight ahead, at the far end of the club, is a tiny stage with a tinier dressing room behind it. There are booths along the walls, a few tables and chairs. Everything very dark and moody. On the right is the restaurant area, walled off, with windows so you can still see the stage, but where the volume of the music—I mean, think about Hendrix playing in a nightclub—is cut down enough that people can actually talk. The cuisine is basic Italian, so you can probably smell the garlic, even over the smoke and beer residue of the club.

Things are going to hell in England just like they are in the States. The underground paper OZ has been busted for obscenity; investors have figured out there's real money to be made, everywhere from the Roundhouse to Carnaby Street; the cops have hounded Brian Jones into alcoholism and death; the Isle of Wight festival is inundated by half a million kids, driven by a desperate longing to be part of the scene, the moment, to at least brush against it or maybe rip a tiny piece of it loose for themselves before it's gone.

Hendrix could turn it around. I could make him see. Instead of going with Monika that Thursday night he could come to my hotel and talk, crash in the spare bed, get up in plenty of time for his court date. After the hearings we could go to the Speak to celebrate.

It felt real, more real than my empty house and the endless Texas afternoon outside. Somewhere that was how it really happened. Somewhere it was the truth. I let the music take me and I was there.

I crossed Margaret Street in the last of the early September daylight. I heard music by the time I hit the stairs and it made me light-headed. It was like every Saturday night party I'd ever been to in high school, every major gig I'd ever played. Anything could happen: romance or enlightenment, friendship or heartbreak.

Inside it was smaller than I'd expected, low-ceilinged and English and old-fashioned. There was a strange heart-shaped pattern on the wallpaper and a framed poster of the 1920s vintage nude woman. Near the stage several of the little three-foot-square tables had been pushed together and abandoned. The booths were full and a few of the other tables too, everyone talking, the men all with thick sideburns, their hair parted low and combed straight across their foreheads, the women with long straight hair parted in the middle. Everyone had flared trousers and squared-off shoes, and they were all smoking. Nobody paid attention to the guy with the acoustic guitar on stage, who I thought might be Long John Baldry. I didn't see Jimi.

I found a table in a dark corner and ordered a lemonade when the waitress came by. I counted on Jimi to show up, to let me get next to him. I didn't have the right to count on anything, not since I sat in that hospital waiting room and let him die, but I couldn't help it. I felt lucky.

I took a longer look around and this time I hesitated at a tall, graceful woman with long red hair who sat in a booth by the stage. I knew her from somewhere. The guy she was with had black wavy hair past his collar, bangs, and sunglasses. He wore a black shirt and striped tie and white pointed shoes, like a gangster. He seemed to be arguing with her. When the couple in the next booth left, I took over their empty table.

". . . killing yourself, Erika," the man said. "I love you and I'm not going to help."

Christ, I thought. It's Erika Hanover.

"It's my life," Erika said, "and it's not worth a damn to me right now." Her voice was low and husky, her accent strictly British upper-class, no trace of the Continent left. "For God's sake, Tony. Please."

"No," the man said, and stood up. I glanced over and saw him kiss the top of her head. "I have to get back to the tour. Mick is bonking some beauty queen from Texas and I've got to get him to Paris for the Olympia on Sunday. It's going to be a madhouse."

"If you loved me . . ."

"I do love you. And that's why I'm not going to be an accomplice to this." He let out a long sigh. "Take care of yourself. Please. Get some help." He passed my table, headed for the door.

I sat for a while and listened to Erika cry. I thought about Jimi, and about lost opportunities. Then I moved to the seat across from her.

"Go away," she said. She had her face in her hands and didn't look up at me.

"I don't want anything from you. I want to help."

Now she did look at me. "Are you holding?" I hadn't heard that expression in so long it confused me for a second. "Have you got any drugs?" she said.

"No." She was recognizable as Erika Hanover: high forehead and brilliant dark red hair, penetrating gray eyes. Tonight her broad face was puffy and her eyes had dark circles underneath. She would be close to forty at this point, at the height of her notoriety. She was almost as tall as me, languid and sensual, full-bodied but not heavy. She wore jeans, a white T-shirt, and a denim jacket. There were streaks of grime on the shirt.

"Then you can't help me and you should please go away."

After a long minute I said, "I really admire your work."

"You can't possibly know me."

"There's a picture of Mick Jagger at Hyde Park, at the free concert that was supposed to be a memorial for Brian Jones. He's covered with dozens of dying butterflies." She nodded slowly, as if it was somebody else's work. "John Lennon, with Yoko reflected in his round mirrored sunglasses, she's in black, he's in white. Hendrix, with this half-eaten meal and a cigarette . . ."

"You surprise me. Most people never look to see who took the picture."

"If I like something, I want to know who's responsible."

"What's your name?"

"Ray."

"I'm Erika." She held out her hand, palm down, and I gave it a gentle squeeze. "Where in America are you from, Ray?"

"Texas. Austin."

"I've been to Austin. It was lovely. Not what you'd think Texas would be like, is it? With the trees and lakes and such."

"No, I guess not."

"Would you be a love and get me a drink? Anything, I don't really care."

At the bar I ordered her a rum and coke. When I took the drink back to the booth I half expected her to be gone. Instead she'd calmed down and lit a cigarette. Baldry finished his set to a quick flurry of applause as I sat down. Erika left the drink by her right hand, untouched.

An unseen DJ put Pink Floyd's *Atom Heart Mother* over the PA. I learned forward and said, "Look, I couldn't help overhearing earlier. What was that guy saying about you trying to kill yourself?"

Her eyes were really very beautiful, alert and intense, despite the strain they showed. "I don't wish to be rude, but why should you care?"

"I do care. I care about your pictures, and . . . I just care, that's all."

"You don't know me. I'm not a very nice person."

They were almost the exact words Lori had said to me. The thought of Lori hurt more than I thought possible.

"What's wrong?" Erika asked.

I shook my head. "Nothing. I was going to say you should let me decide whether you're nice or not for myself."

"I'm looking for heroin, Ray. Junkies are seldom nice people. I was hoping to score from Tony, and failing that, I thought perhaps Marianne might be here." Tony, I realized, must have been Spanish Tony, Tony Sanchez, purveyor of drugs to the Stones and Marianne Faithfull's sometime lover.

"Marianne Faithfull," I said.

"Yes, Ray. She's a junkie too. And a friend. It's very liberating, in a way, heroin is. You're just one more junkie. No one cares if you're a pop star or a photographer or on the dole. We're all the same." She stubbed out her cigarette and, in a swift movement, drank off half the rum and coke. "Do you think we could get out of here?"

"I . . . I don't know," I said.

"You were waiting for someone, weren't you?"

"No, I mean . . . I was hoping to see Jimi Hendrix. I know he comes here to jam."

"Not tonight, love, not that I've heard of. Do you know Jimi?"

"I've never met him. I just . . . feel like I know him."

"Yes, he affects people that way, doesn't he? He's a wonderful man. A true gentleman in the old-fashioned sense of the word. And a fantastic fuck, of course."

I suddenly remembered an interview I'd read. They asked her if she ever slept with any of her glamorous subjects and she replied, "Most of them, actually." I found that suddenly intimidating.

She looked at me expectantly, with heavy-lidded eyes. I held up my hands. "I guess I don't really have any plans, then." Erika was part of the London inner circle, the hundred or so people who went to the same parties and took the same drugs, set trends and made headlines, joined each other's bands and fell in and out of each other's beds. If she couldn't get me to Hendrix, no one could.

As I followed her up the stairs I thought, to hell with Lori. She was twenty years and thousands of miles away, in another reality, a reality where she was still with Tom. Why should I be alone? Erika might not have been in the shape she once was, but she was still powerfully sensual, totally desirable.

I caught up to her and let one hand rest in the small of her back, feeling her heat through the jacket. She smiled at me, amused, I think, that I'd ended up wanting her like everyone else did. As we came out onto Margaret Street I tried to remember what lay in her future. I didn't know if she'd died at the end of the sixties or simply faded into obscurity. It was an eerie feeling.

"Do you have someplace?" she asked.

I wanted to tell her that I was out of my league, playing way over my head. She had to already know that. "I just got here, I don't even have a hotel yet."

"Yes, well. I'm afraid I'm of no fixed abode myself at the moment." She lifted her hand and a cab squealed to a stop. "I need to run one errand," she said as we got in, "then we can find you a hotel." To the driver she said, "Bag O'Nails, please, on Kingly Street."

The streets of London looked like they'd been hand-painted in psychedelic colors. There were posters on the walls, exotic clothes, fresh paint on new businesses. The ragged spirit of underground culture had turned into the hard gloss of commercial enterprise, but it was exciting just the same. It was like a big-budget Hollywood movie, with lots of flash and glitter so you don't notice the lack of soul.

As the cab pulled up outside the Bag O'Nails Erika said, "You couldn't lend a girl a fiver, could you?" I peeled off a five-pound note and she kissed me, unexpectedly, on the cheek. "Wait here," she said, "I'll be right back." She walked slowly, not quite steadily, to the door of the club.

The cabbie caught my eye in the mirror and grinned. "Nice night, eh, gov'nor?"

I nodded and looked away. He didn't have to recognize Erika specifically to know she was special. She was what everybody else aspired to, and it showed in the way she dressed and talked and moved. I didn't think she'd be back. It was only a question of how long I was obligated to wait for her.

"What time is it?" I asked the driver.

"Half eleven, sir."

I reset my watch. Almost midnight, and people thronged the sidewalks. Street vendors sold everything from homemade clothes and jewelry to underground papers like *IT* and *Frendz*. Tourists and older Londoners stared at the parade of finery. If Jimi and Erika were the royalty, the kids were their subjects, brightly dressed, hung with chains and medallions, eyes darting nervously ahead, voices slightly too loud, too high-pitched.

There was a rattle at the door and Erika climbed in next to me, smiling. "Everything is now wonderful," she said.

———

I had the driver take us through Soho to the Russell Hotel. It was the only place I could think of. I quickly lost my sense of direction and when we turned one corner I saw the ruins of a building overgrown with weeds and grass. Erika caught my stare.

"It's a bomb site. You Yanks are always so surprised. You should see Germany. Most of them here are gone now. It's only the forgotten places like Soho where you still find them. They give everything such a *Wasteland* quality, don't you think?"

Erika waited discreetly in the lobby while I checked in. I wanted to put Erika's name next to mine on the registration card to make it seem more real. It was only when I handed the card back that the date on it hit home: 15/9/70. I had only Wednesday and Thursday to make contact with Jimi and get my message across. Then I turned and saw Erika and knew I'd have to risk it.

By the time we got to our floor, Erika was chewing her lower lip and rubbing at her cuticles. She left one newly lighted cigarette in the ashtray of the lift while she lit another. As soon as I got the door open she pushed ahead of me and shut herself in the bathroom.

The room was much the same as the one I had in 1989. The wallpaper was a little more drab and the bed was slightly larger, a bit bigger than a twin bed in the States. There was only the one, plus a chest of drawers, a desk, and a bentwood chair. I pulled the bedspread down and stacked the pillows against the headboard. I kicked off my shoes and lay down, knowing Erika was using my bathroom to shoot up. She was famous and powerful and spoiled, and there was nothing I could do to stop her.

On the other hand, I was also pretty sure that my cooperation would be rewarded with her body. It had been two months since Mexico and Lori, two months since a woman had touched me with kindness in her hands. I felt withered and dry.

After a while I heard the bath run. She was in there for a long time, and took a long time to dry off afterward. My mind veered back and forth between thoughts of her damp nakedness and wondering what she thought of me, expected of me.

She came out with her hair wrapped in one towel and her body in another. The towel around her body left cleavage at the top and impossibly long thighs at the bottom. She wobbled slightly as she walked. She lay down next to me and kissed me lightly on the lips. Her eyelids seemed too heavy to stay open on their own.

She rested her head lightly on my chest and said, "Thank you. I'd been without a decent bath for a while." Her voice was both sleepy and coy. "I don't know how I could ever repay you." She rolled slightly away from me, onto her back, and somehow the towel around her body came undone. I was acutely conscious of the overhead light, the brightness of the room. I could see one breast, large and soft, the skin white as milk. I turned her face toward me and kissed her, to see what it would be like. Her mouth was soft and she kissed me with impersonal intensity. It felt good, sensual and sweet, and at the same time I was disconnected from it. I was concerned about how narrow the bed was, whether she could actually feel any sexual desire behind the heroin, that this was Erika Hanover, for Christ's sake, of the royal Hanover line, who had slept with Hendrix and Jagger and God knew who else. And that I was here in bed with her when I should have been trying to find Jimi.

She pulled the towel loose from her hair. I pushed the other towel aside as well and kissed her nipples while she ran her hands lazily through my hair. "Mmmmmm," she said. "That's lovely."

I took my clothes off and lay down again. I was still not erect. I kissed her some more and ran my hands over the soft, warm skin of her body but it didn't help. She touched me and saw the situation and tried to massage some life into me. "Is everything all right?" she asked after a while.

"I don't know," I said. "It feels wonderful. It's just not, I don't know. Not happening."

She touched my cheek. "Was it something I did? Is there something you want me to do?"

"No, nothing like that."

"Then don't worry about it," she said. "I'm pretty stoned anyway. Can you turn out the light?"

I got up to turn out the light. I couldn't believe it. I'd actually wound up in bed with Erika Hanover, one of the most desired women of the decade, and I couldn't get it up. I grabbed the useless piece of meat between my legs and choked it. Bastard, I thought. Useless bastard.

When I got back in bed I thought at first that Erika had nodded off. Instead, in a very slow, dreamy voice she said, "It's so difficult, the whole sex thing, isn't it? I mean, it's got so it's simply expected. Whether you actually fancy someone or not, one still feels as though one ought to. From gratitude or politeness or perhaps just on principle."

"Do you even want to?" I asked her. "I mean, when you're . . ."

"On heroin? Oh yes, it's a very sensual drug, heroin is. Not sexual perhaps, but sensual. Everything feels so good." In the faint light from the window I watched her stroke the pillow in a slow, rhythmic motion. Her voice seemed to come from nowhere, the words distinct, soft and very, very slow. "The truth? I don't suppose I really care if I actually pull someone or not. It's so lovely to lie quietly afterward . . ."

She was quiet for long enough that I thought once again she'd nodded out. Then she said, "It feels so good. I hate to waste it in sleep. Do you mind talking?"

"No."

"Are you afraid of death?"

"I don't know. I guess so." I thought about swimming into the abyss. Afterward, in my room, I'd been terrified. "What brought that up?"

"Heroin is like a little taste of death for me. So peaceful. But men are so afraid of death. It's not like that for women, I don't think. Why should that be?"

"I don't know."

Her sentences had become simple and short, with long pauses in between. "I think maybe life is such a struggle for women. So much blood and pain. Death is a release from all that. Did you know Marianne actually died? In Australia, last year. She was so upset over Mick. She took a hundred and fifty Tuinal. She had the most amazing vision. She saw Brian there, Brian Jones. He'd only been dead a few days. She told me about it. She was walking along this plain. There was no wind or heat or shade. Just this rocky, vast plain. Like something out of the *Inferno*. Suddenly Brian was there. He was so pleased to see her. He'd been so frightened and lonely. The first thing he asked her for was a Valium.

"They started to walk together, just talking. She knew somehow they were on an adventure. The walk took days. They talked about life and death and God. They took a lot of comfort in each other. And then they came to this vast chasm. Brian said, 'I have to go now. Thanks for coming with me.' And he went over the edge. Marianne says she stood there for years. Then she heard voices, calling her back. She found herself in this place like an airport. It was a place where you wait. And then she said her name must have been called. Because she woke up.

"She'd been unconscious for six days. Can you imagine? It sounds like heaven. To sleep like that. When she got out of hospital she went traveling around Australia. All over the country. And she came to this place that was just like the one in her dream. It's called Piggery, in Byron Bay. I wrote down the name. It's along a beach, by the sea. Marianne said it looked like the moon. It was like the place in her dream, and she'd never been there before.

"There's so much we'll never understand, isn't there? So many things we can never explain away. I believe that, don't you?"

"Yes," I said. "I do."

I shifted around, got more comfortable. I could smell the soap on her skin and I felt the first tentative prickling of renewed desire. "Erika?" I said. She was asleep.

I lay there for a long time, my face hot with shame and frustration. It had happened a few times before, most notably on my first sexual experience, with Annette Shipley from my high school drama club. She'd been to bed with a lot of guys that I knew, but she'd always stopped short of actual sex with me. "You're different," she would say. "I *love* you." Then one summer afternoon I came over to her mother's apartment to swim. Her mother was gone and Annette took me to bed. She was very businesslike. I guess I'd expected romance. I'd never touched an entirely naked woman before and I didn't really know what I was supposed to do or say. Like Erika said, it was the sixties, we were liberated, it was something you did.

We tried for a while and then she smiled and went into the kitchen for a Coke. I remember the radio in the kitchen was tuned to the classical station. I was ready then, but it was too late, my mother was due to pick me up. I saw Annette again a couple of times that summer and she never gave me another chance.

There's something inside me that gets confused, that loses track of who this other person is here in bed with me, that is suddenly naked and afraid, that feels her expectations more strongly than desire. Sometimes all I need is to hear the other person's voice to get my perspective, to feel connected again.

I wanted to wake Erika up and talk to her, or maybe try again. Jim Morrison was inside me, telling me to prove my manhood. Brian Wilson told me to be cool. I touched Erika's cheek and saw she was deep into her drugged sleep. It had all gone wrong. I remembered the party when I felt so lost and Brian found me outside. I felt more lost right then, with nobody even to look for me.

For a second, on the edge of sleep, I saw the road I'd been on since my father died. Morrison first, the starting place, the selfish sensual being inside all the men I know. Then there was Brian, the child, generous and playful, not strong enough to make it on his own. Then Jimi, who tried so hard to put it all together, the flesh and the spirit, only he's weak and struggling too. So where does that leave me?

I slept badly. I woke up tired and still hating myself at ten in the morning, to find Erika gathering up her clothes. She looked at me oddly so I said, "Ray. Ray Shackleford. I met you at the Speakeasy—"

"Don't be silly. Of course I remember you." I wasn't at all sure that she did. She was wearing panties and nothing else, untangling her T-shirt. She made a face at the way it smelled. I was of course stiff as a baseball bat but I didn't see a chance to make up for the night before.

Erika said, "You told me you wanted to meet Hendrix, but you never said why."

"He's in danger. I can't tell you how I know. If I could talk to him, I could warn him. It's literally life and death."

She sat in the bentwood chair, jeans forgotten in her hands. "What sort of danger? Is this some CIA plot? King and the Kennedys and now Jimi?"

"No, it's . . . you remember talking about Marianne last night, and you said there are all these things we'll never understand? This is one of them. There's this accident waiting to happen, and I think I can save Jimi from it."

I felt like she wanted to believe me. "You understand that I have to be careful. Jimi is one of God's innocents. He has no discrimination with people, and he's so vulnerable. Right now he's being devoured by all these negative forces around him, negative people. He doesn't need another person who simply wants something from him."

"It's the other way around. I want to help him."

"I seem to remember your saying something like that to me yesterday. It would be nice to think that in some other life you could perhaps help me. You seem a very kind person. I would love to photograph you, but—" She made a vague gesture with her free hand. "I seem to have misplaced all of my cameras. Sad, really. I don't even know if I could do it anymore. One needs a certain hunger, and I seem to have misplaced that as well."

"You don't take any pictures at all?"

"I haven't for almost a year. But don't let's go on about me." She pulled her jeans on, suddenly very brisk. "We were talking of Jimi. There's still hope for Jimi, after all." She got into her shoes, picked up her jacket, and stopped by the door. "Every human will hit moments of absolute truth. I would like to think I've done it a time or two, maybe the picture with the butterflies. Jimi is so special because he has trained and refined himself to do this more than anyone I've ever known. There's really nothing else for him, you see, but this struggle to break through the wall, to get to this truth."

She opened the door, then turned back. "Eric Burdon's playing Ronnie Scott's club tonight, in Frith Street. I expect Jimi will be there. Come late, perhaps one or two. If he's there, I'll introduce you."

"Wait. Can't you stay—"

"No, love, I must go." She blew me a kiss from the doorway. "I'll see you tonight."

———

I went back to sleep and dreamed again about my father. It's night and I'm sitting in the yard on a wooden table, reading *Rolling Stone*. My father is sitting next to me and he keeps rocking the table with his foot. I swat at him with the magazine, very playfully, and he picks up a big chunk of concrete and playfully begins to bash me with it. I ask him twice to stop but he seems to think it's all a joke. I lose my temper and attack him, trying to pinch his nose shut to suffocate him. When that doesn't work I put a pillow over his face and try to smother him. That's when my mother comes out and tells us it's time for dinner.

———

In 1989 London is one step further into the future than the United States, a little more toxic, more hostile. There's less employment and fewer resources to go around. The third world is on every corner, East and West Indians, Africans, Asians: their shops, their newspapers, their music. Entire squatter cultures thrive in the council flats of Brixton. Public utilities are starved to the breaking point by the Conservative Party, then privatized. The rich protect themselves with insanely high property values and a heartless prime minister named Thatcher.

In 1970 London leads the way too. The newspapers complain of "stagflation," a combination of stagnant consumer demand and run-away wage and price inflation. Underground fares have doubled and auto parts workers and miners have been on strike all summer long, while Prime Minister Heath sailed his sloop around the Isle of Wight, the same island where Jimi just played. Meanwhile, on Carnaby Street, fashion has already turned into a parody of itself, all huge collars and lapels and monstrous ties. They play rock and roll in all the shops, not out of love of the music but because, as Erika would say, "it's simply expected." American music, of course; English music seems as much a victim of stagflation as everything else.

I wandered into a record store on Carnaby Street where, between the stacks of *Let It Be* and *Led Zeppelin II*, I found dozens of forgotten bands: the Fourmost, Judas Jump, the Equals, Love Affair, Blue Mink, all of them with top ten hits, none of them able to make it last. The bins held only jackets and the records themselves were in paper sleeves behind the counter. I had nothing to play them on, no way to take them back to Austin except in my head.

I ended up in Hyde Park. It was a decent autumn afternoon, cool, with the sun breaking through now and again. There were a lot of kids there in the grass with long hair and patched jeans and guitars.

Keep this, I thought, keep the kids and the park and the weather. Lose the guys in the dark suits with the bowlers and umbrellas and red carnations who stared at them with open hatred. Lose the pollution and the cars, keep the trains and the buskers in the tube stops, with their music echoing through the long tiled halls. And keep Jimi. Most of all keep Jimi.

———

I got to Ronnie Scott's club at midnight to see the show. It was a jazz venue, guys in suits and turtlenecks, guys in goatees and berets. The tables were all taken and I had to stand by the bar. I ordered a lemonade and checked the setup: Lonnie Jordan's Hammond B-3 and the drums and congas and the stacks of amps completely filled the stage. A roadie made a last pass to duct-tape anything that moved, and then the lights went down.

War had been gigging for ten years in San Pedro, now they suddenly had a gold record and a European tour. It didn't matter that front man Eric Burdon had been in the spotlight forever. They were hot. I saw the excitement and longing and bravado roll off them like sweat.

And tonight, for me, there was something extra. A chance to see Jimi perform again, and the knowledge that, in another world, this was the last time he would ever play in public.

The band tore into "They Can't Take Away Our Music." There's a sound a well-miked snare drum makes on stage that you can never get on record, like an ax splitting wood. That sound alone was reason enough to be there. Burdon had shag-cut hair past his shoulders, looking younger than I would have thought, rejuvenated by the band's energy. A spotlight hit Howard Scot for his guitar solo and the notes he played cut through the rhythm section like lasers. He fired them out of a blond-neck, sunburst Telecaster, looking fierce in sideburns that came down to meet the ends of his mustache.

As the spotlight tracked him I saw Jimi in the audience down front. Monika was with him, and a woman I thought was Devon Wilson, and five or six others crowded around. Jimi had on a shirt that looked like it was made out of peacock feathers.

I didn't see Erika. I wouldn't have a chance to talk to Jimi until after the show anyway. I stayed where I was and listened to the band. They did about half their album, standards like "Midnight Hour" and a couple of Animals tunes. They finished off with "Spill the Wine" and by this point the jazz crowd was on its feet.

Burdon gestured to Jimi and he got up on stage. He already has his black Strat up there, and he strapped it on and they went into "Tobacco Road." It was awkward at first. Jimi seemed to expect to run things and the rest of the band wasn't interested. When the time came they gave him a solo and Jimi cranked up and played hard.

Once Jimi started to play the personality clashes didn't matter. It was loud enough that I thought my eardrums might bleed. His feedback went inside me and left me ringing like expensive crystal.

When he was done he built up to a big finish. The band played right over him and took their own solos. Jimi looked pissed off. He took his guitar off and started to walk away but Burdon grabbed him by the shoulder and yelled in his ear. Jimi shook his head resignedly and put the guitar back on and comped rhythm chords. He had a look on his face like "why am I doing this" but he stayed out the song. Burdon introduced him and he got a big round of applause, which seemed to cheer him up.

They went into "Mother Earth," a traditional blues from the album, and things really caught fire. Howard Scot traded licks with Jimi and they both played blistering solos. People stood on their chairs and shouted and drank everything in sight. About this time some guy, either the manager or Ronnie Scott himself, came out and made frantic throat-cutting signals. It was the same thing I'd seen in my club days, managers terrified that somebody might have too good a time.

The band wound the song up and said their thank-yous and split. The house lights came up and the magic disappeared, leaving spilled drinks and cigarette butts, the knowledge that the last train had already run and there would be long queues for a taxi. For me it was worse, it was the sudden fear that this would after all be Jimi's last show. There was no sign of Erika, and I started to panic. What if Jimi went out the back door and disappeared? A heavyset guy in leathers refused to let me backstage.

I was contemplating an all-night vigil on Lansdowne Crescent when Erika finally showed up. She was breathtaking in a strapless cream-colored dress. I had seen that body naked, had spent the night next to her, and never really touched her. I knew I wouldn't get another chance. She had a young guy with her in leather pants and a white shirt and a ponytail like mine. She saw me as I stood up and the two of them made their way over. "Have they already finished then?" Erika asked.

I nodded. I wanted to apologize for the night before, but it wasn't the time or place, even if she'd wanted to hear it. She introduced me to the guy, whose name I immediately forgot.

This time there was no problem getting backstage. The dressing room was mobbed, and a line of young women stood against the wall, like they were there for an audition. Monika and Devon guarded Jimi from either side. Now that he was through playing he looked drained. His eyes were narrow and lined and there was no light behind his smile.

After all the hours I'd tried to imagine this moment, I was speechless. I knew Jimi was lost by looking at him. I was an idiot to think I could change that.

Then he saw Erika. He came to life and hurried over to hug her. He was not quite as tall as me and there was a shyness in the way he moved that was the opposite of the way he was on stage. He kissed Erika on the lips and said, "Baby, you look so *tired*. I'm not trying to put you down, I'm just worried, you know, I want to be sure you're okay and everything."

"I'm fine. Listen, this is a friend of mine, Ray, from the States. He needs to talk to you and I think you should listen."

I tried to swallow what felt like a ball bearing, stuck halfway down to my stomach. Jimi shook my hand and said, "Hey, Ray, brother, what's happening?" The grip was familiar, large and dry and powerful, like his father's. Everything about him was familiar. It was like I had known him all my life. "So did you like see the show and everything?"

"Yeah, it was really good. I saw you in Dallas, too, the first two times."

"Oh yeah, Dallas, wow, man, that place is a real hassle sometimes. That first show everybody got real uptight over a little lighter fuel, you know?" He turned to Erika to bring her in. "They wouldn't let me burn my guitar or anything so I kind of put out this row of footlights."

"With the head of his guitar," I said.

"See? The man was there."

Erika touched Jimi's cheek. Over her shoulder I saw the young guy in leather pants talking with Eric Burdon. She said, "Jimi, I really think you're pushing yourself too hard."

"Well, you know how it is, this and that, I got that trial thing coming up Friday. And there's always somebody wants you to be somewhere, you know, it's hard to get away."

"Could you get away with me?" I said, finding my nerve again. "Just for a couple of minutes?"

Jimi looked at Erika and she said, "Go ahead, Jimi, I'll wait here."

We went through a fire door into an alley behind the club. It was red-brick and dark and the night had turned chilly. "Wooo, man," Jimi said. "I don't know if I'll ever get used to the weather over here. This is supposed to be September, can you dig?"

I nodded. "Look, this is going to sound weird to you however I say it. I don't know any way to do this except just blurt it out, okay?"

"Yeah, okay, whatever."

I squatted down and Jimi squatted next to me, his huge hands tucked into his armpits. I looked at the bricks at my feet and said, "I know you're open to things that most people aren't. UFOs and magic and spiritual things. So if I sound crazy maybe you'll give me a chance to, I don't know, a chance to convince you."

I knew I had to go ahead and say it or I would lose him. "I'm from the future and I can prove it."

"Oh, man."

"I know things nobody could possibly know. I know you want to get with Chas Chandler again. I know you're planning to fly to New York after court on Friday, to get the tapes for *First Rays of the New Rising Sun*, and bring them back here for you and Chas to work on, to finish the record, so you can go play with Miles Davis."

Jimi looked genuinely terrified. I hated to scare him, hated to look like some obsessed lunatic. "Who are you?" he said.

"My name is Ray Shackleford. I'm from 1989. I want to save your life."

"Mike Jeffery sent you, right? Oh God, I knew this was gonna happen."

"I'm not from Jeffery, I swear to you. I want you to finish the record. I saw a list you wrote out for it. Side one: 'Dolly Dagger,' 'Night Bird Flying,' 'Room Full of Mirrors,' 'Belly Button Window,' 'Freedom'; side two: 'Ezy Rider,' 'Astro Man,' 'Drifting,' 'Straight Ahead'; side three: you started out with 'Night Bird Flying' again—how could I know all this?"

"I don't know."

"Because I'm who I say I am. And in the world I come from, you die Friday morning because you take a few too many of Monika's sleeping pills and choke to death in your sleep."

"Oh, man." He looked at me sideways, like half of him wanted to laugh and the other half wanted to run away. "Oh, man."

I rubbed my hands over my face, tried to relax. "Don't make up your mind yet. Just listen. I know your rooms at the Cumberland are a cover and you're staying with Monika at 22 Lansdowne Crescent. I know you just sent Billy Cox home because of an acid freak-out. I know you can't trust any of these people who are all over you because they all want something."

Jimi balanced himself with one hand and turned until his back rested against the wall of the club. "Man, it's like, I just don't know anymore, you understand? There's all these people and there's this new thing, like peace and love, right, and maybe these people really do love me, but . . ."

"Maybe they just need what you have. They see you on stage and they see how that music makes you so alive, and they all want that. Even if they have to take it away from you to get it."

Jimi didn't say anything.

"That's not what I want. I want to save your life. I want to see *First Rays* finished."

Jimi shook his head. "So tell me again what's supposed to happen? I mean tell me exactly."

I told him. I told him what the inside of Monika's flat looked like, I told him the pills were called Vesperax and he shouldn't take more than two, I described the attendants who picked him up.

"Man," he said, "you're really not bullshitting me are you? You really know something. You're from when?"

"1989."

"And I never finished *First Rays* or *Straight Ahead* or anything?"

"No. They did a single album called *Cry of Love* and a soundtrack for this really stupid movie called *Rainbow Bridge*, from that concert you did in Maui. Reprise threw them together from whatever was lying around. But everybody still knows who you are. You still win guitar magazine polls as favorite guitarist. They put music on these computer discs now, they call them compact discs, and they've reissued all your stuff, plus live albums and interviews and studio jams, everything they could find."

"So I guess they've got computers playing everything, right? Is that what the music is like?"

"It's like Led Zeppelin, mostly, only heavier. Heavy metal, they call it. That's what most kids listen to."

"Man."

"The Beatles never get back together, but the Stones are still touring. And the Who."

"I don't know, man, this all sounds so weird and everything, all these old guys playing rock and roll. Did everything just like stop after I died?"

"Pretty much. There was something called punk at the end of the seventies, that was pretty exciting, only it got commercialized too fast. Now there's rap, which is drum machines and chanting, not much music in it at all. But if you live, see, you can change it. With *First Rays*, by playing with Miles—"

The back door of the club swung open. Monika and Devon were

there, and a black man in an expensive suit and a neatly trimmed beard. "Jimi," Monika said, "shouldn't we be maybe going home now?"

For a minute I'd had him. Now Monika had brought him back to earth, the real world of food and bed and court cases. He stood up and dusted at his velvet trousers. "Yeah, okay, whatever."

I stood up too. "Listen," I said. "I want to come see you. Thursday night, at Monika's place. To make sure nothing happens, okay?"

"Sure, man, come over about twelve or something, all right? We can talk some more, that'll be real nice."

As they went inside I heard Monika ask, "Who was that funny man? What was he wanting?"

I stayed in the alley for a minute or two to get my breath. Okay, I thought. I can't miss this time. Everything is going to be okay. I went back in. Jimi was gone, and so were Erika and her new boyfriend. That was okay too. Everything was going to be okay.

———

I was at Lansdowne Crescent at midnight sharp Thursday night. I knocked on the door downstairs and when nobody answered I tried to see in the darkened window, and finally sat on the steps to wait. It hadn't rained all day but the air was damp and the chill got into my bones. I was wearing new clothes that I'd bought on Oxford Street and I'd been to see Sly Stone at the Lyceum. I'd seen Eric Clapton in one of the box seats, but Jimi didn't show.

When he wasn't at Monika's flat by two I started to worry. He might have decided I was crazy and gone to the Cumberland Hotel to avoid me. He could take the same Vesperax at the Cumberland as he could at Monika's and wind up just as dead.

I heard Monika's sports car a little before three. A minute or so later the two of them came down the metal stairs, Monika in the lead. "Jimi," she said, "that strange man is again coming around."

Jimi looked disappointed to see me. "I'm really sorry," he said, "there was this thing at this rich cat's flat I had to go to."

"You just have to promise me one thing and I'll get out of here. Promise me you won't take more than two of Monika's sleeping pills. They're stronger than anything you're used to."

"If I don't sleep tonight I swear I'll go out of my mind."

"Just take one or two, and if they don't put you out right away, give them another few minutes. I promise you they'll knock you out. And you'll still be alive tomorrow."

Monika had only been half listening. "Is this man making threats to you?" she asked.

"No, be cool, baby, he wants to help me."

"Everybody is wanting to help you."

"I just want him to promise," I said to her. "If he takes any of your Vesperax, he shouldn't have more than two."

"Okay, all right, already, I promise." He laughed with no feeling in it. "I promise."

I shook his hand and said good-night. Monika watched me suspiciously all the way up the stairs, but that was okay. Watch over him, Monika, he needs a guardian angel tonight.

I stood outside in the cold knowing there was nothing more I could do. Finally I caught a cab on Ladbroke Grove and went back to my hotel.

———

I was outside the flat at ten the next morning. My heart was in my mouth. I hadn't fallen asleep until after sunup and it seemed like only seconds later that I got my wake-up call. I felt like a knife that had been sharpened over and over for a single job, and now the job was nearly done but I was worn away to nothing. I sat and stared at my watch, and every few seconds my eyes would flick back to the wrought-iron gate at number 22.

At 10:13 Monika came up the stairs, looking rumpled. She headed down the street toward the local market. It took all I had not to bolt down the stairs to see if Jimi was okay.

Monika was back at 10:24. I was wound so tight that I jumped to my feet when I saw her. I hadn't meant to say anything to her but now it was too late. She froze and stared at me as I ran across the street to her.

"You again," she said.

"When you go back to bed, please, please make sure Jimi's okay. If it looks like he's been throwing up, come get me. I know what to do."

"I only gave him the two pills. Like you said."

"He might have gotten up in the night and taken some more. Just check him, please."

"I will check him. Now please go."

I nodded and walked away so she wouldn't call the cops. She went downstairs, I circled the block, and sat on the curb again. Worst case, the ambulance would be here at 11:30. It was a long wait. I spent it in weird, violent fantasies in which I fought the ambulance attendants for Jimi's life.

Eleven-thirty came and went, and I started to breathe easier. By 11:45 I was light-headed, ecstatic. By noon the fatigue caught up to me. I walked back to Notting Hill Gate and found a bakery with sweet rolls and orange juice and lingered over them as long as I could stand it.

At one P.M. I made a last pass by the flat. All was quiet. No ambulances, no police, Monika's car parked where it had been.

Jimi was alive.

========

I had a long, deep sleep, then went down to the lobby, where there was a television. There was nothing on the news about Hendrix, just train strikes and the ongoing hostage crisis in Jordan, where three hijacked airliners had been blown up. A newsreader asked if we had entered the Age of Terrorism and I didn't want to be the one to tell him yes, we had. The *fedayeen*, the men of sacrifice, were sharing their sense of helplessness with the world. Just like the rest of the starved and desperate people picking up guns and knives in Southeast Asia and Latin America. Could Jimi Hendrix change that?

I walked down Southampton to a nice Italian place I'd found. It was a beautiful evening, too beautiful to spend giving myself the third degree. Hendrix could do as much good as anyone, and I'd given him some time to do it in. It might take him weeks to come up with a final mix of the album, and I would hang around until he did.

I lingered over dinner and took a cab to the Speak after midnight. There was always the chance that Erika would show up, or somebody else that I might want to meet. I was ready for something. The room was crowded, and Rod Stewart and the Faces were playing loud enough to rattle the glasses on the bar. I got a lemonade and let the movement of the crowd take me toward the stage.

I wasn't too surprised when I saw Jimi holding court at a row of tables down front. He saw me on the sidelines and beckoned me over. "Heyyy," he said, shaking my hand. "My man. Future man. What did you say your name was?"

"Ray. Ray Shackleford."

"Ray. Cat that knows his drugs. That shit of Monika's, like, I took a couple and I was laying there, thinking, 'Man, this is not happening,' and I was gonna get up and take some more and then remembered what you said so I just lay there awhile longer and then pow, it just laid me *out*. Hey, you got to meet my people. This is Mitch, and Sly Stone, you know Monika, this is Devon and this is Eric Clapton. Next to Eric there is the Queen of Sheba. Yes, the Queen of Sheba, thank you very much." Actually it was Pattie Boyd, still married to George Harrison. Clapton would write "Layla" for her next year in Miami.

I shook hands all around and somebody brought me a chair. I'll never forget the next two hours. Part of it was the glamour, of course. They were all beautiful and rich, talented and famous. None of that was as important as the way music mattered to all of them. The conversations were hard to follow, three or four of them going at once, Eric earnest and adamant, Sly full of revolutionary fervor, Jimi laid-back, saying, "Well, you know, like, dig, brother," while the music blasted all around us. Like in a song, the words didn't matter as much as the feeling, the community, the warmth. Jimi seemed renewed. Maybe things had gone well in court, maybe on some level he knew he'd cheated death. Maybe all he'd needed was a good night's sleep.

After the Faces finished, Jimi and Eric got up to jam. Jimi wanted to play "Sunshine of Your Love" and Eric didn't. Jimi started it anyway, laughing and saying, "Oh come on, don't act like you don't know it, it goes just like this here," and they ended up trading solos for ten minutes while Ron Wood and Kenny Jones backed them up. They did "Key to the Highway" and then Sly got up and sang "Land of a Thousand Dances." A part of me knew that it would never have happened without me, and it was all the thanks I needed.

The jam broke up a little after two. It could have gone on forever and been all right with me. Monika and Devon, still jockeying for position, went backstage. I stayed and talked with Pattie Boyd, mostly about her sister and Mick Fleetwood. She was surprised I knew so much about the band, since they hadn't really broken in America yet.

Jimi and the others came out carrying guitar cases. I stood around with them and when I had a chance I asked Jimi about New York and the tapes.

"Oh yeah, for sure, man, I talked to Chas this afternoon. He's got me a flight over on Monday and then I'm going to come back and we're going to see if we can do a thing with them. He's really groovy about it, I think it's going to happen. Listen, when I get back, you should really come down with us and hear what we've got."

"I'd like that," I said.

I guess I wanted him to give me addresses and phone numbers on the spot, and it took me a second to realize he was only being polite. "Sure, man, you can like come by the studio or something, it'll be real nice."

"Okay," I said. "Thanks." I shook his hand. I didn't want to leave, but the time had clearly come.

Jimi felt it and let me off the hook. "If you're not doing anything, you could come along over to this party. Probably be some, I don't know, like free booze or food or girls or something."

It's the kind of thing he must have done all the time, one more little act of kindness, like all the others that had eaten him up, chipped away pieces of him until there was nothing left. At that moment I didn't care. I was grateful for the piece he'd offered me. "Yeah. I'd like that."

The group moved slowly toward the stairs. Jimi handed me his guitar case while he put on a trench coat. One more thing to make me feel like I belonged. Monika kissed him quickly and went ahead to get her car. We went upstairs into the cold light of Margaret Street. There were only a few people left on the sidewalks.

"Christ, we'll never get a cab," Eric said.

"I'll go ring one up, shall I?" Pattie said. She moved in close to him and he put his arm around her. It made me lonely to look at them.

"Give it a minute," Eric said. "Something will turn up."

Some kid with shaggy hair over his ears and collar came up to talk to Jimi. I couldn't hear any actual words, but the rhythm was American and sounded harsh and unpleasant. Jimi stood there with his hands in the pockets of his trench coat, but guitar at his feet, smiling and answering the kid's questions. I looked away for a second, trying to spot Monika or a cab.

When I looked back the kid had a gun.

"Look out!" I yelled.

I started to run toward him. Jimi was looking at the gun. He didn't try to run or knock it away. There wasn't time. The kid fired five times, point-blank, into Jimi's chest.

CHAPTER 8
CHAPTER 8
CHAPTER 8

Voodoo Child
(Slight Return)

I was on the floor of my workshop. My jeans had dried stiff where I'd pissed in them. I hurt all over, mostly in my head and my stomach. I tried to stand up and took a chair over with me when I didn't make it. Mostly I was embarrassed. I didn't want anybody to see me this way. I didn't want to end up in the hospital again and have to explain what it was that put me there.

I crawled downstairs, headfirst, on hands and knees. I realized it was a bad idea when the blood rushed to my head. I lost all feeling in my hands and feet, and I slid the last dozen steps on my chest.

The linoleum at the foot of the stairs felt cool on my face. I thought if I put something in my stomach I would be okay. I pulled myself into the kitchen on my elbows, like when I was a kid playing army.

I got a half gallon of milk out of the refrigerator. I hoped it was still fresh. My brain couldn't process the information from my nose. If I knew what day it was it would help. I held the milk carton to my chest with one hand and scooted into the living room on my ass. There's only a secondhand armchair where the sofa used to be. I dragged the cushion off the seat and leaned against it and turned the TV on with the remote. According to the preview channel it was two in the afternoon on Sunday, July 16. I'd been unconscious just under two days.

I drank a little of the milk. My hands shook enough to make it hard. Then I put the milk down and thought, this is not so bad. I'm lying here, watching TV, like anybody else. Then I threw the milk up all over myself.

I was freezing. It didn't occur to me to turn off the air-conditioning. Instead I took off my shoes and emptied my pockets and crawled into a tub full of very hot water, clothes and all. I rested there for an hour, adding hot water every few minutes. After a while I was able to get out of my clothes, which I heaped in the sink.

Drowning began to seem a greater danger than the chills. I scrubbed myself down and got out and wrapped myself in towels. I found that I could walk, provided I held on to something. I staggered to the kitchen for a Coke and that gave me enough energy to put on dry clothes. I rested for a while and then drank another Coke and ate some peanut butter on toast.

Then I got into bed in my clothes and slept for fourteen hours.

———

There were messages on the machine from Elizabeth and my mother and a couple of customers. I called my mother and told her I was in L.A., that I was with Graham, and asked her to call Elizabeth for me. I'd cast off all lines and headed for the open sea.

I drank a lot of juice and ate whenever I felt like it—cereal, frozen dinners, cookies and ice cream. The rest of the time I lay on pillows on the living room floor, under an afghan that my grandmother had knitted, surrounded by Hendrix books, which I read again front to back.

Charlie Murray's book says they put Hendrix on his back in the ambulance. David Henderson's says he was sitting up. I read somewhere that Hendrix and Joplin were both killed by the CIA, because of their anarchistic influence, but now I can't find it. The kid who shot Jimi was American. Could he have been with the CIA? The mob? The Klan?

There was a mention of Erika in Norm N. Nite's *Rock on Almanac*, under "Deaths in 1971." "Erika Hanover (photographer), Wednesday, February 10 (drug overdose; 41)." It was so final. I thought about what she'd said to me in the hotel room. That it was too late for her, that there was still hope for Jimi. I thought, I'll save you too if I can.

I watched my Hendrix videotapes over and over. I replayed the jam session at the Speakeasy in my mind until I couldn't tell whether I was remembering details or making them up. When I least expected it something would slip sideways into my consciousness: the warm, dry touch of Jimi's hand, the husky sound of Erika's voice.

Mostly I replayed that final scene on Margaret Street, with tiny changes. Maybe one of the bouncers walks us out, heads the kid off, maybe even frisks him and takes the gun.

Maybe Jimi stays downstairs in the club long enough to put a coin in one of the slot machines. He hits the jackpot. He leaves all but one of the coins on the bar, laughing. "It's like I really don't care about the money, you know. It's the luck I need some of." When he goes up into the street Monika is already there with the car. He brushes past the kid fan who doesn't have time to say anything, and he gets in the car and drives away.

Maybe Jimi flies on to New York that night instead of going to the Speak. Once he's there he decides he wants to finish the album at Electric Lady. Maybe Chas flies with him. New York feels safer to me somehow. In London and California the dream is dying, in New York it isn't quite as obvious. I can imagine Chas and Jimi there, in the cool, subterranean darkness of the studio, as they bring everything together.

I couldn't hear it.

I was too weak, I couldn't throw myself into the vision. I needed to rest somewhere, maybe lie in the sun for a few weeks.

Yeah, great idea. How about Cozumel?

I couldn't even face the sunlight that came in the windows. The blinds had been drawn for days. I'd finished all the frozen dinners and the canned soup and the bread. For dinner I had plain spaghetti and the last of the olives and a can of pork and beans and a glass of water. The refrigerator was empty except for the cans of Budweiser, all ten of them, which I would not touch. To relapse into alcohol at this point would be crazy.

The only food left is a can of tomato paste and some rice and flour. I don't want to go to the store. I might run into somebody I know. Maybe even Elizabeth. What would I say then?

If it was 1970 in New York, though, I could be there with Jimi. We could finish the album. There are lots of good places to eat in New York. I could eat there. The longer I think about it, the more sense it makes.

To go to the grocery store I would have to shower and shave and dress. I would have to go outside, and I would have to take my father's pickup truck. I haven't used it in weeks and it might not start. And then drive all that way, and have to deal with all those people. My leg doesn't even feel strong enough to work the clutch.

It's easier to go to New York. I don't have to get up. New York is here in my mind, here in front of me.

Right here on Fourth Avenue, outside the curved brick entrance to Electric Lady Studios.

I knew Jimi would come out any minute. I wished I'd had a chance to shave. I must have looked a little shabby, hair not brushed, jeans not especially new or clean, white T-shirt with a couple of holes in it, navy blue blazer from high school. Jimi wouldn't mind. Appearances were never that important to him. He was like Brian that way, he knew it's what's inside you that counts.

I'd never been to Greenwich Village before, never been to New York other than a few hours at Idlewild, before it was JFK, on my way to Africa with my parents. I'd seen it in movies and TV shows enough to know what it looked like. It was late afternoon, the sun just going down, not quite dark enough for the cars to put their lights on. The weather felt timeless, warm enough to walk around in shirtsleeves, cool enough not to break a sweat. The street was full of bright yellow cabs and there were people on the sidewalk across the street, but there was nobody within a hundred yards of me. It seemed only natural and expected.

Jimi came up the stairs from the studio. Chas Chandler was with him, and a couple of the studio's guards, huge black men in full motorcycle regalia. Jimi stopped when he saw me. "Hey, Ray," he said. "I didn't know you were in New York."

Jimi was wearing glasses, round ones, with wire frames. I knew he'd always needed them but he was too vain to wear them. It was why he was such a terrible driver, because he couldn't see.

"I didn't know I was going to be here," I said.

"Hey, you know Chas, Chas Chandler?"

"Pleasure," he said, his Newcastle accent more Scots than English.

"So like what are you up for, Ray? Maybe a hamburger or a pizza or something?"

"Yeah," I said. "I'd like that."

Chas said, "I best get back to the hotel. It feels like midnight to me already. I don't know how I used to manage this all the bloody time."

We said good-bye to him and walked down Eighth Street into the heart of the West Village. The sky was deep blue, laced with pink from the setting sun. It was the most beautiful, heartbreaking color.

"How's the album going?" I said.

"I don't know," Jimi said. "It's like I can't see the shape of it yet or whatever. Was it Michelangelo or maybe Bob Dylan who said there's this thing already inside the marble and all you have to do is get rid of all the other that isn't supposed to be there? So I've got all these marbles and I'm not sure which ones I should shoot and then sometimes I just think what it is is I'm losing my marbles altogether."

Jimi stopped and said, "Listen, Ray, man, I got an idea. Let's go on up to Harlem, we can get some real soul food. Go to the Palm Cafe up on 125th Street. Check out the band, see what's going down. You ever eat any real soul food?"

I shook my head.

"Man, you like all those colored singers, but you never lived the life. You got to see where it is all that music comes from."

"When did I tell you about the kind of singers I like?"

"In London, man, I don't know, sometime. You like Marvin Gaye and Sam Cooke and Otis Redding and all like that, right? That's what you told me."

"Yeah, but . . ."

"But what, Ray? Come on, brother, spit it out."

"I can't go to Harlem with you. I'm white."

Jimi looked at me over the tops of his glasses, like he'd never noticed before. "You don't have to worry, you'll be with me and everything. These are my people up there, they'll take care of us. Hey, man, it's not even dark outside."

We got on the A train, like in the Ellington song. Once past Columbus Circle I was the only white face on the train. Maybe I should have been scared, but I never felt like I was on the outside of anything. There was the same distance between all of us. All the faces

I looked into seemed to have stories to tell. A middle-aged man in a dark suit, wiping his face with a red bandanna, a tiny teenaged girl with a crying baby. Nobody recognized Jimi in spite of his flashy clothes, the necktie knotted around his head and his weird patchwork jacket.

The train car made a sharp turn, the lights flickered, and Jimi said, "So, you feel like you're getting anywhere?"

"What do you mean?"

"You know. With your father and all."

"My father?"

"You know. Trying to work out all this about your father dying and everything."

"This isn't about my father. This is about *First Rays of the New Rising Sun.*"

Jimi didn't answer. The motion of the train made his head bob up and down. He smiled slightly and looked away.

When we came up on 125th Street it was still light. The sky was the same pink and purple and blue, the air was late-summer warm. Only now the air was full of smells: cabbage and roast pork, burning leaves and perfume. The streets were more crowded than in the Village and the clothes were even brighter, from leopard skin to gold lamé. Every different kind of music, from jazz to gospel, from Arab wailing to rock and roll, clashed in the air and made something brand-new, and voices shouted and laughed and chanted over it all.

I read somewhere that in Africa white is the color of death. I felt like a ghost then, not quite real, as I floated down the street. I didn't think anyone but Jimi could see me, let alone touch me. Jimi sucked all those smells deep into his lungs. "This is where it all really started for me, you know. I had this old lady back then, Fayne Pridgeon. She really loved me, took care of me, made sure I had enough to eat and all. I was playing down in the Village, you know, or out on the road with like Joey Dee and the Starlighters or something, but this was home."

Jimi stopped in front of a plate-glass window that said PALM CAFE. It had a few tables, a bar, a tiny stage at the back. A middle-aged guy at the bar said, "Jimmy James, blood! What you know?"

I ended up at a table with Jimi and five of his old friends. Three were men and two were women, the youngest around thirty and the oldest close to fifty. The cook brought out ham hocks and collard greens and mustard greens, hog jowls and pigs' feet and chitterlings, fried chicken and mashed potatoes and sweet potato pie. There was red wine and Jim Beam to drink, though I stuck to Nehi. Everybody ordered more and more food and seemed to get a kick out of watching me try it. I was able to eat enough to satisfy them. In fact I could hardly taste it and it didn't seem to fill me up at all.

It was hard to follow the conversation. It was mostly reminiscences about people I'd never heard of and places I'd never been, but I understood the drift of it, the sense of loss and inevitable change, and Jimi was there beside me with a shy smile or a touch on the arm or a reassuring nod.

There was a square-faced clock on the wall over the bar. It read six o'clock when we left, the same as when we came in. It was still light outside, but the streets had emptied. Everyone had gone home for dinner, I thought.

"Where you off to now, Ray?" Jimi asked me.

"I don't know. I guess I hadn't really thought about it."

"Man, you better start to think about it. I got to let you go now, there's someplace I got to be."

"Sure," I said. "I understand."

"If you get back on that A train, you'll go right downtown. Everything will be fine."

"Okay," I said. I still felt empty. It wasn't hunger, it was something else. "Listen, can I come by the studio tomorrow? Hear some of what you're doing?"

Jimi's face was full of pain and sorrow. I didn't understand it, but I knew it meant no. I felt like he wanted to say good-bye.

There was no traffic on 125th Street except one white panel truck, roaring toward us much too fast. Jimi shook my hand and turned to cross the street.

I saw what was about to happen. "Jimi!" I yelled. "Look out!"

He turned to face me. The truck was still coming. He looked at me sadly and said, "Ray. I'm the one that's got to die when it's time for me to die."

And then he turned and stepped out into the street in front of the truck.

I stood there for what seemed like forever, not questioning, really, letting the moment rise up around me and take hold of me.

Then I walked off the curb after him as the truck's brakes started to scream. There was a horrible wet thud as the flat front of the truck hit me, a weightlessness as I flew through the air, and another crunching sound as I landed on my shoulder and neck. There wasn't any real pain, just a deep sense of something terribly wrong, something that could never be repaired, something absolute and final.

CHAPTER 9
CHAPTER 9

Heaven

I was walking through a summer forest. Everything was very green. The trees stood well apart, with high grass in between. I heard birds and squirrels and what might have been human voices. I stopped to listen but I didn't call out. I was calm and happy and full of energy.

I walked for an endless time, maybe for days. Eventually I came to a park bench under a tree. Jimi sat there in the military jacket he'd bought when he first came to England, the one with the gold braid down the front.

I sat down next to him. "Hey, Jimi."

"Hey, Ray."

"Where are we? What is this place?"

"We're dead, Ray."

"Both of us?"

"Both of us."

I let that sink in. It made sense. There had been the business with the drop-off in Cozumel. Then I'd let myself run out of food in Austin, and gone after Jimi again in spite of how weak I was. Still it seemed unfair. "Why didn't you let me save you?"

Jimi seemed to listen to the forest for a while. Finally he said, "I had my thing, you know, which was music. I wanted to be able to move people in a higher way and everything, to move them spiritually and maybe show them something that I might think at that particular time was the truth. But it's so hard, man, it's so hard to get their attention. So I would make love to my guitar or play with my teeth or set my hair on fire or something else and people would say, 'Ooooh, there's the Wild Man of Borneo,' or whatever, but they listened, at least for a while. And that was what I had it together to do, that one little thing, you know? It wasn't up to me to save the world, single-handed with just me and my guitar. Why did you think I could?"

"Because you're like me," I said. The words surprised me. "You did want to save the world, no matter what you say. That's what *First Rays of the New Rising Sun* was all about. Music to save the world, to heal all the broken places between men and women, between black and white, between mothers and daughters and fathers and sons. Because music is the only thing that can do it, because music doesn't have a country or a language except itself."

"No, man. I mean, that is a very beautiful idea and everything, but you got to understand that that is you talking, that is what you wanted that record to be. You can't expect me to go saving the world for you. Dig. I couldn't save the world if I wanted to. Not with no album and not by making love to every pretty woman who wanted me and not by giving money to every brother that came to me with a good line.

"And you couldn't save me, either, man. Some things you can't have. You got to figure that out, figure out what you can have and what you can't, you got to learn the difference."

"It's a little late now, isn't it? If I'm really dead?"

"You're really dead. But you're here too, which means there must be some things you haven't let go of yet." He stood up and stretched.

"Where are you going?"

"I got to move on, Ray. You understand."

"No. No, I don't understand."

"You rest here a while. Maybe your head will quiet down or something and it'll all make sense."

"Am I going to see you again?"

"I don't think so, man. But that's okay. Everything be everything. Just lay back and get into something real nice right here."

———

It was really beautiful under that tree. My thoughts wandered where they wanted. I thought about making love to Lori, and laughing with Brian, and seeing Jimi play at the Speak. I remembered how I used to feel after two or three sets of good tennis, tired and peaceful, like all the jumbled pieces inside me had been polished up and laid back where they belonged. I remembered nights when the Duotones had torn the place up, when all the voices in my head had been turned into music and set free. I remembered a patch of sweet peas next to the porch of our house in Santa Fe, the rich, deep colors and the thick cloud of perfume that hung over them in the late spring. I remembered running down a hillside in Arizona on the first day of summer with a cloudless sky overhead. I remembered sitting on the porch with Boy Baby in Tucson, eating a grape Popsicle that my mother had made in our freezer with Kool-Aid and a red rubber mold. I remembered a crib and a white blanket, and soft light and comforting voices in another room.

After a while I'd thought about those things long enough. I got up and followed the path deeper into the forest.

The trees gradually got thicker, cutting off the light. After a long time I came to another bench, on the other side of the path. Jim Morrison sat next to an old man in clothes the color of dusty concrete. Morrison was instantly recognizable from the videos: black leather pants and concho belt, loose white shirt, hair to his shoulders.

"Say hey, brother Ray," he said. "How you doing?"

"You know me?"

"Sure I know you. If it wasn't for you I would never have made *Celebration of the Lizard*. Hendrix was through here a while ago, told us to watch out for you."

I had to walk slightly uphill to get to where they were. "What happened after the album? Did you keep it together and stay sober?"

Morrison shrugged. "It was pretty good for a while. My lawyers took care of that accident business, we did a tour." His voice came from the center of his body, hoarse and full of dramatic pauses. His eyes were nearly black and his stillness was the stillness of a coiled snake. "But after a while you think you really are on top of it, you know? I'd have a couple of drinks and then another couple, and pretty soon there I was, back on the floor."

"So," I said. "You got busted in Miami?"

"Yeah. Busted in Miami. Went to Paris with Pam, let her talk me into something stupid, wound up dead in a bathtub."

The old guy next to him followed the conversation back and forth, and didn't seem to have anything to add. "That's all there was to it?" I asked Morrison. "No mystery, no faked death? With the closed coffin and no witnesses and everything?"

"Drug trouble, Ray. Everybody covered their asses. I died, man. People want dreams, not reality. They want to hang on. They want me to be alive. They don't like consequences. Consequences, Ray. You know what I'm talking about." His voice was calm, modulated, soothing. "Don't you?" His eyes burned holes in me. "Don't you?" he said again, and I saw he wasn't going to let it go.

"What do you mean?"

"Ray, I want you to meet a friend of mine. This is Billy Joe Powers."

The old guy held out his hand and I shook it. I could smell his dingy clothes and the cheap wine on his breath. "Hi," I said.

"Billy Joe was born in 1918, on Armistice Day. Isn't that right, Billy?" Billy nodded. "He came to California during the Depression to pick citrus."

"Met that Woody Guthrie, the singer," Billy said. "Nice fella he was, too. Come and picked oranges right next to me. Told him my story and he said he'd put it in a song one day. Don't know if he ever did 'cause I didn't get to hear too much music, you know?"

"Woody Guthrie," I said. "That's really something."

"Got married when I was sixteen. She died the week after my fortieth birthday. Never had no other woman, before, during, or after."

"Remember?" Morrison said. "Remember when you set me up to make *Celebration?* Remember the accident my lawyers had to get me out of? Well Billy Joe here is the man you threw under the wheels of my car."

My legs wouldn't hold me up. I sat down against the trunk of an oak and stared at the old wino. "You're not real," I said. "I made you up."

"I'm real, all right," he said. "From the look on your face I expect you can smell me well enough. You didn't make me up, buster, you found me, that was all. Everything you can think of exists somewhere. I existed once, and now I'm dead. It wasn't no great life, sleeping in washaterias, riding that Night Train, but it was my life and you took it from me."

Morrison got up. He was still grinning. "Okay, Ray, you get the point. You can have the bench now, me and Billy Joe are going to walk on for a while. Pam's waiting for us down the way. You rest up now, okay?"

═════

I sat on the bench and said, "I didn't know." Except it wasn't true. Part of me had known all along that if the music was real then so was the dead man.

I felt bad for Billy Joe Powers. Not the racking guilt I would have felt if I was alive, the icy fist in my guts. It was too late for that, like it was too late for Hendrix's advice.

I was dead.

I don't know how long I sat on that bench, in a reverie. At some point I saw a shadow through the trees, a big man, maybe six and a half feet tall, carrying a lot of weight. I tried over and over to tell myself it wasn't Brian Wilson, but of course it was.

When he saw me, the confused, childish look on his face gave way to a huge smile. "Ray. What in the hell are you doing here?"

I stood up as he came over and hugged me. "No, man," I said, "what are *you* doing here? You're not dead."

He looked sheepish. "I think maybe I am, Ray."

We sat down on the bench and looked at the trees. After a while I said, very softly, "What happened?"

"It was *Smile*, man. The music was right, you heard it, you know it was. But all it did was screw up my life. Mike Love quit over it and Al went with him. That was the end of the Beach Boys. I played it for my dad and he hated it. Capitol hated it and didn't promote it so it only sold forty thousand. I kind of took to my bed, and Marilyn got fed up and split.

"I mean, I just wanted to do an album that would make people happy. And I lost everything."

"Christ, Brian, you didn't kill yourself . . ."

"It's a fine line, you know? I mean, you can take a lot of pills or drive off a cliff, that's the sure way. Or you can get really stoned when you're all alone in a big house and fall off your stupid slide, onto the edge of your swimming pool. Knock yourself out and fall in the pool and . . ."

"Drown."

"Yeah. Like your dad. I didn't want to have to tell you that."

Once I was past the first shock, his being there didn't seem like such a surprise. Like with Billy Joe Powers, a part of me had known what I was doing, the chance I was taking, when I pushed him to finish *Smile.*

"So what happened to you?" Brian asked. He made his goofy face. "This is like one of those prison movies. 'What are you in for, kid?'"

I felt totally off guard. What was I supposed to say, I got run over in a dream? "I don't exactly know."

"Yeah. See? See what I'm saying? In the prison movie, everybody in prison is innocent. And here, everybody died by accident. Only, come on. All those accidents?"

"If you hadn't finished *Smile* you'd still be alive. This is my fault."

"If I hadn't finished *Smile* I would have gone crazy. Crazy or dead, that isn't much of a choice. At least this way I left a hell of a good album behind. Don't work yourself up over it. We have to go on, you know?"

"Go on? It's over, Brian. We're dead."

"No, man. I mean, go *on.*" He pointed to the path, and stood up. "It was really good seeing you, Ray. Be nice to yourself, will you?"

"Wait," I said. "Can't I go with you?"

"Sorry, Ray." He was already walking away. I could have run after him. It was all right, though, just to sit a while longer. My thoughts had been a jumble at first but slowly, like Jimi said, they were quieting down. I could sit for a long time watching a branch move in the breeze and not think at all.

Finally I got up and walked some more. I took it easy. Brian was long gone, and there was nowhere I needed to be. I noticed tiny variations in the shape of the oak leaves, found familiar shapes in the patterns the breeze made in the tall grass.

Some time later I heard a noise like barking and I stopped to listen. It *was* barking, deep and relentless, that turned into a baying sound at the end. I would have recognized it anywhere. It was Lady, my basset hound, who died the week before I met Elizabeth in 1978.

I crouched and clapped my hands and she ran up the path toward me. When she saw me she got so excited she squatted to pee, then rolled on her back and kicked her stubby legs in the air. I rubbed the stiff white fur on her stomach and said, "Hey, Lady, how you been?"

It was the usual story. I was twelve when I got her and I promised to feed her and bathe her and take care of her, the way a kid will. I went away to Vanderbilt and I couldn't take her with me, any more than I could keep her in the succession of ratty apartments I lived in before my marriage. By then my parents were so used to her, and vice versa, that she wasn't really my dog anymore.

When her kidneys finally gave out my mother put her to sleep and didn't tell me until it was done. She couldn't understand why I was so angry at not getting to say good-bye. She had no idea what it was like to sit in my drafty garage apartment and watch snow fall yet again in a Dallas winter that had been constant snow, to drink Jack Daniel's straight out of the bottle and know that the one creature on the planet that had ever loved me without reservation was dead.

It seemed a long time ago. "Hey, Lady," I said to her. "You want to go outside?" She jumped up and down and barked, her long brown ears flapping in the air. The very word "outside" had always been magic to her, even if she'd just been out, even if she was outside at the time. It was the eternal promise of something better.

We went up the path together, Lady's chest practically dragging the ground as she waddled along. I had figured out by then what had to happen next. I still hadn't decided how to handle it when the path turned around a particularly thick old oak and I came to another park bench. Sitting in the middle of it, like I knew he would be, was my father.

———

I sat down. "Hey, Pop."

"Hey there, Junior."

He looked about fifty. His hair was completely dark, even at the temples, and cut fairly short. He wore a flannel shirt with a brown-checked pattern, buttoned to the neck, and khaki pants. Benny Goodman's "Please Don't Be That Way" played in the distance. It brought back countless Saturday mornings when I would wake up to the sound of the big bands. Music meant my father was in a good mood. I would put on my bathrobe and find him in the front room with his stamp collection, or maybe just listening.

No wonder I'd grown up loving music. I remembered Maynard Ferguson's "Hot Canary" and Perez Prado's "Cherry Pink," my first two records, which I used to listen to over and over. They went back to before I was in school, before I could even work the record player by myself.

"What are you doing here?" he said.

"I'm dead, Pop. Just like you."

"Figures. What did you do, walk in front of a truck?"

"Funny," I said. "Very funny." Lady sprawled at my feet and panted happily. The song ended and Helen Forest sang "Bei Mir Bist Du Shön."

"Did you ever amount to anything?" my father asked. "Or were you still farting around fixing record players?"

"Fixing record players is not so bad. This music sounds really good, Dad. I haven't heard it in years. I miss it."

"You have all of my old records. You could listen to them if you want."

"Mom has them."

"Unh." He stared off into the distance. The impression he gave was that he was listening to the music first and the conversation was a distant second. One ankle rested on the other knee. There were worn vinyl house shoes on his feet.

I saw then that he was exactly the same as he'd ever been. I saw that jokes and arguments were the only language we'd ever had. There were no words for anything personal. Just because we were both dead was no reason for that to change.

Except that we were both going to be dead forever and forever was too long to keep it all closed off inside me. "You have to talk to me," I said.

"Have to?"

"I want to know what happened to you. At the end. When you went over the edge. I need to know what you were thinking."

"You want the truth? I don't really remember."

"But what about me? Were you thinking of me at all?"

"No, not really."

"Did you ever think of me?"

"Sure I did."

"What? What did you think of me?"

"I don't know. I suppose you were all right, for a kid."

I remembered dream after dream where I would hit him and kick him, stalk him with weapons, bash him with rocks. This would be the point, I thought, where the violence would start. Instead I said, "There's things I never got to tell you when you were alive. Like when you had your heart attack, back when I was in high school. For months before it happened I had dreams about you, about you dying. Usually in a car wreck." I looked down at the grass, at Lady lying there, at the black underside of her tongue. "The dreams made me feel good. I felt guilty for it, but they made me feel good. I liked the idea of you dying. I liked the idea because I hated you. I never got to say that to you."

I half expected him to pull back into one of his sulks. Instead he said, "So what do you want, a medal?"

"I . . ." I felt like I was on the edge of something, but I didn't know how to break through. "I . . ."

"Ay yi yi yi yi," my father said. "You were always one for noises. When you were a little kid you were always going 'but but but but but.' "

" 'Just like a motorboat,' " I said, finishing it for him. "Remember the kee birds? You always used to say, 'It's so cold the kee birds are out.' "

"Kee," my father said. "Kee, kee, kee, kee-rist it's cold."

"So why did you have to be like you were? Why didn't we ever play catch, or go down to the playground and shoot some baskets, like other kids did with their fathers?"

"You didn't want to. You were always a weird kid."

"No," I said. "No, I'm sorry, but I don't believe you. I don't believe that if you came to me and said, 'Let's go play some catch,' that I wouldn't have crawled on my knees through broken glass to do it. I don't believe you."

"Believe what you want."

"It didn't have to be that way, goddamnit! I was just a little kid!" I reached in my back pocket and took out the photograph that I knew would be there. It was the picture of the three of us, my father, me, my mother, sitting on that bench in Laredo. "I was just a sweet little kid who didn't know any better. Look at me, I'm right here in this picture. Why couldn't you play catch with me?" I held it up to his face. "With this sweet little kid, right here in this picture? Why did everything have to be a competition? Why did you try to run all my friends off? Why couldn't you ever tell me you were proud of me? Why couldn't you have put my goddamned doll in the trunk, and not driven away and left it there on the side of the goddamned road?"

He looked down at Lady and wrinkled his nose. "Jesus, that dog still stinks. It's not even a real dog, it's some kind of goddamn phantom dog, and it still smells like hell."

"Listen to me, goddamn you! We're not talking about the dog! We're talking about you and me, understand? You and me."

"Oh, grow up."

I got up, my legs trembling so hard I could barely stand. "No," I said. I grabbed him by the shoulders and shook him. All I wanted was for him to put his arms around me, but I was not going to ask him for it. "*You* grow up," I said. "*You* grow up."

Finally he looked at me. He looked me right in the face and I saw nothing there but fear and loneliness.

"Let go," he said.

He didn't mean my hands. "I can't," I said, and finally the tears came. "I can't let go."

"Then don't," he said. "Suit yourself. But don't come crying to me if it doesn't work out."

He looked away again. I dropped to my knees. Something tore loose inside me. The music was suddenly louder. I couldn't think for the music that filled my head. It came from down the path, back the way I'd come. Everything that had seemed so distant and painless exploded in my head. Lori, Elizabeth, Jimi. Vomiting milk up onto my shirt, Boy Baby abandoned beside the road, the Duotones in the band shell without me. Lady sat up and howled from deep inside her chest.

"And do something with your goddamn dog, will you?" my father said.

I sank into the earth and the trees arched over me into a dark green tunnel. I was falling then, and I felt the wind on my face. Then I felt nothing at all.

CHAPTER 10
CHAPTER 10

Ray

I opened my eyes. I was in a hospital. My mother sat in a chair in the corner, working a puzzle in a crossword magazine.

"Mom?" I said.

She hurried over to put her arms around me. "Oh thank God," she said. "Thank God."

I was in bad shape. It was hard to lift my arms and the air whistled as it went in and out of my lungs. I had bruises and IV tracks on my arms. I was calm, though. I had no desire to get out of bed or do anything but lie and look at the trees outside my window.

"What happened?" I asked.

"You've been in a coma for over a week." The word "again" was implied. "You had a heart attack in the ambulance that brought you here. Your heart stopped and you were legally dead for a minute and a half. It's a miracle you're alive at all."

"I remember dying," I said.

"I'd better ring for the doctor."

"Fine. Whatever."

That night I tried to go back again. Sort of. It's hard to explain. I put it together in my mind, London in 1970 first, then L.A. in 1966 when that didn't work. Not that I wanted to go, exactly. I wanted to open the door, to see if those places were still on the other side. I had to know if I could still do it.

I couldn't. Or maybe I didn't want to go badly enough, or I was too scared. In any case it didn't happen, and when it didn't I felt only relief.

———

It was Elizabeth who found me, it turned out. She got concerned when I never answered any of her messages. Mom told her I was in California, so she called Graham and found out I wasn't. She came over and pounded on my door for a while and then let herself in. She found me on the living room floor, unconscious, and called EMS, then my mother. I was on my way to St. David's when I died on them. They gave me CPR and a shot of adrenaline and that got me started again. Which was a good thing, I learned, because they don't have electric defib machines on ambulances, there's no way to ground them.

Elizabeth bowed out when my mother got there. They kept me in ICU overnight, then moved me to a private room. I lay in a coma for a week and then, with no warning, simply woke up.

———

They let me walk around after a couple of days. I didn't want to talk to anybody about what had happened. They hadn't been there, they couldn't possibly understand. All I had to know was whether or not Brian Wilson was still alive. I called a local radio station and they said yes, he was alive and more or less well. So I don't have that to feel guilty about, not in this world, anyway.

I didn't talk and I wasn't interested in TV. I ate what I could. The food tasted good, it was just that I filled up so quickly.

Mom had a jam box there that used to be my father's. One of the tapes she brought was the Goodman Carnegie Hall concert, recorded off those same old green-label Columbia LPs my father used to listen to. She told me she'd played it her first day there, but not since. I let her think I was humoring her when I asked her to play it again.

On Wednesday, my third day out of the coma, Elizabeth called my mother and had her ask if it was okay to come by. I said it would be fine. She showed up an hour later, with flowers. She kissed me on the cheek and then sat down across the room. My mother went to the cafeteria and left us alone.

"I guess you saved my life," I said. "Pretty weird, huh?"

"When I told Frances about it, she said I should have let you die. That that's what she would have done." She smiled to show she meant no harm. "I don't hate you, Ray. You know that. Whatever else has happened between us, you know I don't hate you."

"No," I said.

"And I hope one day you can stop hating me."

"I don't hate you."

Elizabeth made a sound.

"Look," I said, "I won't pretend I wasn't hard to live with. I was pretty boxed up. But that Ray died. Now I'm here, and I don't know what I feel. I don't feel a lot, if you want to know the truth. But I don't hate anybody, and I for sure don't hate you."

We talked about school and she told me her lawyer had worked up a preliminary draft of a property settlement. Whenever I felt up to it. I told her to go ahead and send it to the house.

"There's one more thing," she said. "This is hard. Maybe I should do it another time."

"Just tell me," I said.

"Well. It's that guy I've been seeing. It looks pretty serious." I nodded encouragement. "It happened so fast, I'm scared to trust it. But it seems really . . . really good."

"I'm happy for you," I said. "Really."

"I'll probably give up my apartment at the end of this month. I mean, we're already pretty much living together. There's no point in . . . anyway." She got out a notebook and wrote a few lines and tore out the page. "Here's the address and phone number. You can call me, you know. Whenever. Any time."

She touched my hand, told me to say good-bye to my mother for her, and left. I had this nagging sense that I had disappointed her again. That she would have liked to see it hurt me at least a little. It did hurt: partly the lost years, mostly that Elizabeth had somebody and I didn't. I just didn't want to show it.

By the time my mother got back the hurt had faded and the conversation felt like no more than a period after a sentence. Marking, finally, the end.

———

When I was in Nashville I tried for a month to sleep on a split shift, three to seven, A.M. and P.M. both. It was the only way to get eight hours' sleep when band practice lasted until two every night and I had an eight o'clock class every morning. I began to dream in intense, vivid detail. I started a journal and the first thing I noticed was that I died at the end of every dream.

In one dream I'm sitting in a bar when I start choking to death. I woke up in my dorm room, in my bed, where I should have been. Only I was still choking. I fell out of bed and crawled toward the door, and as soon as I touched the door handle I woke up again, back in my dorm room, back in my bed.

I never completely got over the feeling that I'd woken up too many times, that the world where I ended up was not the same as the one where I'd started. That's how it was with dying. I've seen worlds where Brian Wilson finished *Smile* and Jimi Hendrix woke up on September 18. I've been dead and seen an afterlife. What does "reality" mean to me?

When they let me out of the hospital it was conditional on my seeing a therapist twice a week. My mother asked if I wanted her to stay on for a few days and I said yes. I assumed it was what she needed to hear. Once it was said, though, I realized it was true. I wasn't ready to be alone.

My first night back in the house I called Lori. It was ten o'clock and my mother had already gone to bed. It wasn't something I thought about for a long time, I just needed to hear her voice. My luck was good and she was there alone.

"I miss you," I said.

"I've been thinking about you too."

"What were you thinking?"

"I was worried. I had this feeling something was wrong."

"Yeah, well, there was. There is." I told her I'd tried to rescue another album, that I'd had a heart attack, that it had nearly killed me.

She said, "Oh God."

"Lori?"

"This is so scary." She was crying. "Are you going to be okay?"

"They say I'll be fine. I have to take it easy. They've got me on some drugs and I have a diet and an exercise program and all that. There's nothing to be worried about."

"I want to be with you."

It was what I'd been waiting to hear. I took a breath and said, "Then come."

"You know it's not that easy. If I came up there it would be . . . there would be no way to go back."

"Exactly."

"This is not a good week. Tom got into some fire coral and I've been taking the tour out. If I left he'd have to refund their money and it would probably wipe him out."

At the same time that her words cut me, the sound of her voice made me dizzy. I could see her mouth and deep blue eyes, the crisscross tan lines on her back. I wanted to hold her and smell the coconut oil on her skin. "There's never going to be a good time to leave him. You can always find a reason to stay. You're going to have to just decide and do it."

The silence went on and on.

"What?" I said. "What are you thinking?"

"There's only one reason I'll ever leave him, and that's because I'm ready to go. Just like there's only one reason to stay, which is that I'm not ready yet."

"When will you? Be ready?"

"I don't know that. I can't tell you. You want hard-and-fast answers, and I haven't got them."

"Do you love me? Because if you love me it seems like you would want to be with me."

"I do want to be with you. I already told you that. And yes, okay, I do love you. But if you're going to take the gloves off, then there's a couple of things I have to ask you. Are you so sure you know what you want? Do you love me or are you just in love with the idea of me? Have you seized on me to replace Elizabeth because you have to have a woman in your life at all times? How long ago did she leave?"

"Almost three months."

"Three months. That's not a hell of a long time. And it sounds like you haven't stopped long enough to think. So tell me. How long have you ever gone without being involved with somebody?"

There was another long silence, mine this time.

"Ray, that wasn't a rhetorical question. I'd like an answer."

"Six months."

"So if I don't show up in six months, maybe you'll have found somebody else."

"No," I said. "I don't want anybody else. But that's not the point, is it? Look what you're asking me. You want me to just wait here for you, on the off chance that you might leave Tom. Meanwhile you've got him and I'm up here all alone."

"You think I don't care about you, but I do. More than you realize. There are a lot of people that care for you. You don't want to hear this, but your father talked about you when he was down here. He was proud of you, he thought it was great that you hung up your corporation job to start your own business. He couldn't say it to your face, but he talked about you to everybody else."

"Could we leave my father out of this? We're talking about you and me."

"I don't think we *can* leave your father out of it. And I think maybe being alone might be the best thing you could do right now. Not for my sake. For yours."

I should have cried. I mean, that's been my reaction lately when I feel persecuted. It always used to get me what I want. But this time I was too mad. Mad and bitter and scared of something, though I couldn't say what.

The silence went on for at least a minute, maybe two. I wanted her to offer some kind of hope or consolation. She made me ask for it. "Will you call me sometime? Collect?"

"Yes. I will."

"Promise?"

"I promise." Then, "I love you, Ray. You have to believe that."

"I love you too. But I don't know what I believe anymore."

"I have to go. Will you promise to take care of yourself?"

"Yes. I promise. Tell me you love me, one more time, and I'll let you go."

"I love you, Ray. Go to sleep."

My therapist's name is Georgene. She's in her late forties, maybe. It's hard to tell. She has good skin and doesn't wear makeup. She has a kind of stern look about her which is good because it makes me afraid to bullshit her.

After the first couple of sessions I thought to hell with it and told her about Brian and Jimi. I said they were elaborate hallucinations. She said if the experience was real to me, then we would treat it as real. She didn't seem alarmed and she didn't want to put me in an institution. I offered to bring in one of the tapes, but she said it wouldn't mean much to her.

Mostly I talk and she listens. She asks me how I feel a lot. If I ask, she'll tell me what she's thinking. It's not quick or efficient, but whatever this process is, speed and efficiency don't seem to be the point.

Graham called the first week I was home. "Two things," he said. "First I was worried. I heard from Elizabeth but not from you, so I wanted to make sure you're okay."

I told Graham the whole story, including the near-death-experience part. "So it's not going to happen," I said. "No *First Rays*. I guess we, I don't know. It's like we don't deserve it."

"I wish I'd never sent you after it."

"You tried to call me off after the first time. There was nothing you could do to stop me, once I had it in my head. It wasn't just about the album, it was about my father and a lot of other stuff too. But it's over now."

"Well, Carnival Dog is paying your hospital bills. No argument on that one."

"Okay, I won't argue. You said there were two things. What was the other?"

"Hang on to your hat. Capitol Records is buying the master for *Smile*. They played it for Brian, and he supposedly said, 'I don't know where it came from, but that's my album.' He thinks it's great. There's a clause in the contract that's airtight immunity for me and everybody else involved. They've got this massive reissue series planned for next year, every Beach Boys album in the Capitol catalog, most of them two albums per CD. They were planning to wind up with *Pet Sounds* as the climax. Now it's *Smile*. There's more money, of course, but the main thing is it's going to be out there, in record stores. They might even release singles off of it."

"Graham, that's fantastic. What about *Celebration?*"

"Well, I probably should have talked to you first, but I don't feel good about that record anymore. I've let it go out of print. If somebody else wants to bootleg our bootleg, they can have it."

"I think that's fine. What about you? Are you okay? You don't sound right."

"Well, hey. I've got a couple of medical problems myself. My kidneys, you know, are not that great. Being in a chair like this is not the best thing for you."

"How bad is it?"

"It's not bad, I just get stones sometimes. They have to fly me out to this special clinic. They put me in this swimming pool and then break them up with sound waves. Sounds crazy but it works."

"Nothing sounds crazy to me anymore. Listen, will you promise me, if things are not okay, will you promise to tell me?"

"Sure, man, I'll be straight with you. There's nothing anybody else can do for me. I need to take better care of myself. Maybe have a couple less beers."

I hung up feeling there was something else I should have done, but I didn't know what it was.

———

My mother stayed for two weeks. She did her best to stay out of the way: went to bed early, spent a lot of time in her room reading. I had to give her the white room, of course, but it didn't seem like that big a deal. She cooked and cleaned for me and at night we would play Yahtzee or cribbage. It went against all my conditioning to let her wait on me, even though I knew it was necessary, even though it made her feel more useful than anything had since my father died.

I called the *Chronicle* and had them run my ad again. I knew it would take a while to get my clientele back up to where they'd been, but I was ready to start. I needed something to do with my hands, something that looked toward the future instead of the past.

I worked every afternoon for a few hours. I slept a lot, eight or nine hours a night, plus a nap after work. We played games, and we talked.

She told me about the first year and a half of my life. Some of it I knew and some I didn't. "You were a breech birth. You stood up the entire pregnancy. Sometimes you would kick me so hard you would knock the magazine off my lap. You were two weeks late, but when you were ready, you came right out."

This was in Oregon, in the dead of winter. I came home to a one-bedroom apartment. "There weren't any other kids in the building, so we were afraid to let you cry. We never let you cry. I wanted to breast-feed you but I didn't have any milk. I bled when I tried to nurse you. We even tried to use a pump but there was nothing there."

We moved for the first time when I was three months old. The place we moved to was cinder block and very damp. My mother said her asthma got worse and worse until she couldn't take care of me. She started leaving me with a neighbor during the day, then for supper as well, then after a while I would only come home to sleep. Finally I was at the neighbors' full-time for a couple of weeks while my mother was in the hospital and then in the desert recuperating.

"The doctor said no more kids," my mother said. "If we'd had another child the asthma would have killed me."

I was ten months old when we moved out of the cinder block house, and we moved twice more in the next eight months, ending up in Tucson so my father could get his Ph.D. "I tried to make up to you for what I felt was neglect when I was so ill. I remember that winter when you turned one was a very happy one. We read. We listened to music. We had coffee breaks. If you hate the *Peer Gynt Suite* today it's because you wanted to listen to it every day."

The morning after she left, the house felt empty and lifeless. I had weirdly conflicted emotions. As grateful as I was to have her there, she still drove me crazy. She still called me Jack and my father Ray. Most of what she talked about was completely trivial. And she has the same unyielding quality my father did. She's never satisfied, not with other people or her physical surroundings or her health. I guess he had to die before I could see how much it's a part of her.

Alex's number was on the notepad by the phone. I looked it up when I got home from the hospital and tried to decide ever since if I was ready to call her. I made myself a sandwich and ate it standing up in the kitchen, by the phone, while I tried to work up my nerve.

In a way this all started with Alex, with her and "The Long and Winding Road," with fantasies about what we could have been. Now I had fantasies of a different sort. What if her marriage was in trouble too? What if they'd split up, even? It could happen. I wondered what she would look like after twenty years. Her mother had been thin and wiry, but it was hard for me to picture Alex like that. I wondered if she ever thought of me, if she remembered the romantic summer afternoons at the park and the botanical gardens, the long, sex-drenched weekends when my parents were out of town, or if she just remembered the jealousies and tears and countless teenage acts of cruelty that passed between us.

On impulse I went to the garage and found a box of papers that went back to high school, saturated with the smell of incense. There were letters from Alex, paycheck stubs, old driver's licenses, chords and lyrics for songs I wrote in the winter of 1970 in one of my sporadic attempts to learn the guitar again. Two black-and-white photos of Alex in capri pants and a halter top, circa 1968, coy, flirting with the camera. I can't remember what making love to her felt like. We were just kids, after all, barely knew what we were doing.

It was two in the afternoon. She might not even be home. What the hell. If I thought too long I wouldn't go through with it. I picked up the phone and dialed.

It rang twice before she answered. I recognized her voice from the way she said hello, high-pitched but with this throaty purr inside it. "Alex, it's Ray Shackleford. I don't know if you—"

"Hi, Ray. I was just thinking about you."

My heart lurched. "You were?"

"Of course. That's why you called."

I remembered all her claims of psychic powers. "I did?"

"Just because it's been twenty years doesn't mean I haven't kept track of you."

"I've thought about you a lot too."

"So, are you ready to talk to me?"

"I guess that's why I called."

"You should probably come out here, then. That way you can see the place. I'll give you directions."

I took 183 south of town, almost to Lockhart. I turned off on a county road and drove 3.2 miles to a mailbox that had a rural route box number on it but no name. The land was flat, with a few scrub oaks and mesquite trees. This late in the summer the grass was parched and yellow, except close to the house where it had been watered. The house was small and square, finished in those big white asbestos shingles. Behind it was a corral and a corrugated-metal barn.

I could see Alex as I drove up. She was on the back of a huge, muscular horse, and a girl of seven or eight rode a large pony next to her.

Alex waved as I got out of the truck. "Do you want to ride?"

"I don't think so," I said.

"Okay. I need to brush this guy out and feed him. Come on in."

I climbed over the rail fence as she got down from the horse. My imagination had failed me. She hasn't changed that much since high school. Reddish-brown hair, parted in the middle, hanging past her shoulders; large, light brown eyes, a small, bent nose like the beak of a tiny hawk, full lips. She was wearing jeans and a loose, long-sleeved white shirt. She's older now, of course, heavier in the waist and hips, and motherhood has changed the coy look to something more confident and a trifle stern. She has small, square, wire-rimmed glasses that emphasize the maturity over the glamour that's still there.

"I'm a little horsey," she said. "You may not want to hug me."

"I'll live dangerously." She did smell of horses, but also of perfume, strong and floral, as always. She squeezed me and then kissed me for just a second, her lips very soft and barely touching mine. It was an effort not to lean into her for more.

"Mmmmmm," she said. "I remember that."

So did I. Deep, cellular memories recognized Alex and claimed her as fair game. We were still standing very close and there might have been another kiss if her little girl hadn't said, "Mommy?"

Alex snapped to and went to help her down from her horse. "Ray, this is Jennifer." Jennifer is clear-eyed and beautiful and that afternoon she was wearing shorts and a plain brown T-shirt. With a bit of urging she came forward to shake my hand, one firm pump. She stared at me pretty hard, as if she'd picked up some kind of vibe between her mother and me.

We led the horses into the sweltering heat of the barn. I sat on a hay bale and watched the two of them rub the horses down, using metal brushes strapped to both hands. "Isn't he beautiful?" she asked me. "He's a Morgan, we just got him this year. This winter, if everything goes right, we get him a mare and start breeding them."

"It sounds like what you always wanted," I said. "House in the country, horses, family . . ."

"It's exactly what I've always wanted. I love it. I just wish you could meet the rest of them. David's at work and D.J.'s off on a camping trip."

"Maybe next time," I said. My fantasies melted in the August heat.

"D.J.'s going to be a senior this fall." She stopped combing long enough to look over the horse's shoulder at me. "He's the same age you and I were when we went around together. I've thought about that a lot."

The kiss had opened me to a flood of emotions. In another world I might have been D.J.'s father. The thought filled me with wonder and vertigo. I didn't feel old enough for fatherhood, let alone for the idea of us as potential grandparents. I had a sudden memory of Alex and me at a party the night I graduated, all of our closest friends together in one place for what we already suspected was—and in fact would turn out to be—the last time. Candles, rosé wine, a couple of joints.

"That's enough, sweetheart," Alex said. I realized she was talking to Jennifer. They shook the combs off their hands and we walked to the house.

It smelled a little musty inside, the way old houses do. The linoleum was warped here and there, and the walls were cheap paneling painted white. We walked through the kitchen past a dusty TV and VCR, a shelf of books with titles like *Drawing Down the Moon* and *Pagan Meditations*. I sat at a wooden drop-leaf table while Alex washed her hands and arms at the sink. Jennifer tugged at Alex's blouse and whispered a question in her ear when she bent down. "Okay," Alex said, "but stay close by." Jennifer flashed me a shy smile and ran out of the room.

"I saw your ad in the *Chronicle*, years ago," Alex said. "I thought about calling but I didn't know if you'd want to hear from me or not."

"Sure I would have."

"And your wife's picture was in the *Statesman* last year. Some kind of teacher's award."

"We're separated. The divorce'll be final in a few weeks."

She nodded. "I had a real funny feeling from that picture. I thought, 'Ray's *not* married to her.'"

She got a couple of Cokes out of the refrigerator and told me about David. He runs a printing company, is finally making enough money that she was able to quit her legal secretary job two years ago, when they moved out to the country. She showed me a picture of the four of them out by the corral, Alex leaning her head back in laughter, David next to her, dark and bearded, with a glint in his eye, Jennifer huddled against her mother's skirts. And then there was D.J., off to one side, in a white T-shirt and jeans, his long brown hair tied in a ponytail.

"Yes," she said, as if she really could read my mind. "It was the first thing I thought of when I saw you. How much D.J. looks like you. But it's not biologically possible. He was conceived in Seattle, and I hadn't been near you for two years at that point."

"You and David have been together for what, almost twenty years now?"

"It was a bit off-and-on at first. I never doubted he was the one. I just had a little trouble convincing him of that."

"You knew it from the time we broke up." I'd found the letter that afternoon, out in the garage. It had arrived early in the spring of my sophomore year at Vanderbilt, the spring I dropped out. I remember reading it before English class. It talked about David, how he was the love of her life. She had finally found the one, she said. My friend Les snatched it from me and started to read it out loud. "Jesus," he laughed, "how corny can you get?" I wanted to kill him.

"It wasn't just David," Alex said, reaching across the kitchen table to take my hand. "I couldn't have gone on with you, in any case. You had me on such a pedestal. You wanted me to be too perfect. I couldn't keep from disappointing you. It finally got to where I couldn't stand to see that disappointment in your eyes."

I thought of my father, and now my mother, so disappointed in everyone. "I still think about those times, wonder how much of a jerk I really was."

"No," she said, and slapped the table. She seemed genuinely angry. "You weren't a jerk. You were wonderful. I loved you then, and I loved you when we broke up. I never stopped thinking about you. I just couldn't be the person you wanted me to be. The two of us weren't cut out to be lovers, partners, soul mates, whatever you want to call it, not the way David and I are. That doesn't make anything wrong with either of us. It doesn't mean we can't still care for each other."

She got up and walked across the room, then turned and faced me with her arms folded. "Or still be attracted to each other. I *am* still attracted to you. But it's a dead end, and I'm not going to risk what I have here for that. Even if it might be a pretty damned exciting dead end."

I held up my hands. "Hey. I didn't even ask."

She smiled. "Sorry."

"That's okay. I was thinking it."

She came back and sat down. "Maybe it's our generation. We seem to have a hard time growing up. Maybe because when we were in high school we thought we'd never have to. The music told us we would live forever, everything would be love and peace and harmony. It took me a long time to let go of that. Even having D.J. didn't do it. But I've finally started to get there."

"And I haven't."

"I can't tell you that, Ray. You'll have to answer it for yourself."

"You can't read my mind?"

"Of course I can. You're easy. But that's not the point and you know it."

"I guess. You're still into all that occult stuff?"

"Of course," she said. "I always told you I was a witch. Did you think I was kidding?"

Back then I guess we all believed in magic. Alex was just a bit more literal. Over the years she's gotten more serious. She's part of a coven that meets on full moons and pagan holidays and does a few simple rituals, helping the crops along, guaranteeing a safe birth for one of her foals.

"Out here you're closer to the natural cycles," she said. "You feel the connections more."

"I met some witches in Cozumel. I liked them."

"It's growing. People are tired of technology, they don't believe it has all the answers anymore. They want to feel connected to the earth, to each other, not like they're caught up in some 3D video game. I'm preaching, aren't I?"

"To the converted. Listen, I should go." I was truly happy for her. But there was no place in her life for me, not as horny and sad and out of place as I felt then.

"Can't you stay for dinner? It's no trouble, I promise. David would love to meet you."

"Next time," I said. I hugged her good-bye and held her for a good long time, horsey smell and all.

―――――

I used a couple of sessions with Georgene to talk about my mother. She listened to the story of my first months and said, "If I were into body work—which I'm not, especially—I would find your mother's asthma pretty significant. The inability to breathe as the inability to feel secure, to feel supported. Having a child is exhausting, but in a good marriage, if one partner has a hard time the other partner is there to pick up the slack."

"And you don't think my parents' marriage was like that."

"What do you think it was like?"

"Yeah, okay, probably not real supportive. And I could have picked that up?"

"You tell me."

"And this business of the asthma killing her?"

"It must have felt that way to her."

"But would a doctor tell her that?"

"People with asthma have babies every day."

"And what about being a bottle baby, and being left with the neighbor, what would that do to me?"

"The question is not what it could do to you, but what it *did* do to you. And you have to tell me that."

"Isn't that first six or eight months when the child is supposed to bond with the mother?"

"Generally, yes."

When I didn't say anything she asked, as she usually does, "What are you feeling?"

I said, "Like she's not my mother at all. Like she's some stranger that I'm supposed to feel something for and I can't."

=====

August turned into September and we finally got some rain. Tuesdays and Thursdays I had therapy with Georgene. Friday afternoons I would go for a movie and a pizza with one of my customers, a woman named Joan. She was in the middle of a separation too, but she was still in love with her husband and not looking for anyone else. We found each other easy to talk to and it was nice not to have to go to movies alone. Saturdays I would see one or another of my friends, maybe go to Sixth Street and hear a band.

An impulse took me into Strait Music one afternoon and I fell in love with a guitar. It was a beautiful left-handed Strat, maple neck, black body, white pick guard. It seemed to me as I held it that if I'd always wanted to play guitar, then that was what I should do. I had the money and the time to learn, so I bought it on the spot, and some books and a Princeton practice amp to go with it. I took them home and set them up in the white room.

Inside two weeks I could work my way through a few simple songs. It was a feeling of power, not the drunken kind of power I'd felt going after Hendrix, but like the power I felt when I put an amp back together on my workbench and music came out of it. Music out of nothing at all—it was the same small miracle. I got out the songs I'd found in the garage and decide I could live with about half of them. I worked on the chords, wrote some new lyrics.

I had the TV on for company every once in a while, mostly MTV or music shows like *Austin City Limits*. Still I couldn't miss the fact that as I was changing, so was the world around me. The twentieth anniversary of Woodstock came and went virtually unnoticed. If the sixties were finally dead, the nineties had begun. In Poland, Lech Walesa's Solidarity Party legally and quietly took over. Gorbachev pushed harder for reform in the Soviet Union and suddenly everybody talked about Eastern Europe in a way they hadn't since the Prague spring of 1968.

By the end of September I was bored and restless and my days had blurred together. I let Graham talk me into a trip to L.A. We did a couple of days at the beach and a day of crawling through record stores all over the city. On Friday he told me he had a surprise. He took me to a warehouse in West L.A. with a sign over the door that said BRAINS AND GENIUS. For some reason I twigged immediately that it's a near anagram for "Brian's and Eugene's." As in Wilson and Landy.

A guy in a pink tank top and white shorts answered the door. He had blond hair in a surfer cut and a slight sunburn. "Hey, Graham," he said.

"Mike, this is Ray."

He crushed my hand briefly. "Come on back and meet Brian."

Brian was restlessly pacing a carpeted office with lots of windows. He looked trim and fit, his hair nearly blond and cut conservatively, his face more lined than I'd imagined it. Landy, in a black silk shirt and jeans, shook my hand and said, "We can only spare you a few minutes." In the corner another surfer type recorded us on videotape.

Landy introduced me to Brian, who said, "Ray Shackleford. I feel like I know you. Why is that?" His voice was slurred and the right side of his face seemed numb, as if he'd had a stroke. He was visibly nervous, turning his head constantly, even while he talked.

"I can't say. But I do know you. Through your music, I mean." I tried to project calmness. "That's all I wanted to say, really. To thank you for letting me get to know you that way."

"Hey. That's really nice. Thanks."

To be honest I don't remember a lot of the conversation. There were long, awkward pauses. I told him how much I loved his solo record, especially "Love and Mercy." Brian reminded me that Landy had co-written the song, which made Landy smile like a proud father. He told me that he and Landy were hard at work on a follow-up. Nobody mentioned *Smile.* After a few minutes we shook hands all around and Mike walked us back outside.

I sat in the car while Graham got himself in and the wheelchair stowed. He started the engine and said, "Sorry."

"For what?"

"I wanted it to be a nice surprise."

"No, man, it was great. I mean, this is the real world, the world I have to live in. To know him here, to have really—"

"It was a disappointment."

"No, it was . . . yeah, okay, it was a bit of a letdown. I mean, I smoked hash with the guy. We were friends. But that all happened, I don't know, somewhere else. Still. You can see it in him. All those songs, that fragility."

"Yeah. Let's get a beer."

If Graham had cut down, I hadn't noticed. He drank half a case a day. He stopped at a 7-Eleven and bought a case of Bud, then took the Santa Monica Freeway to the beach. He parked on the street where he could see the waves come in and reached for a can. Instead of opening it he set it up on the dashboard and looked at it. "Shit, Ray," he said. "You quit this stuff cold. How did you do that?"

"I don't know. The going up wasn't worth the coming down anymore. Then there was a while there in Mexico where I was really happy."

"Lori."

"Yeah."

"Whatever happened to her?"

"She wouldn't leave her boyfriend. I guess it's just one of those fucked-up dependency things." I leaned out the window and breathed the ocean air for a while. The smell reminded me of Lori too. Finally I settled back in the car and said, "I miss her."

"But you didn't start drinking again."

"After I'd been sober a week things looked different. I hated to lose whatever it was I had. Momentum, maybe."

Graham was still looking at that beer can. "The docs want me to quit. They want it pretty bad."

"Come to Austin with me. We'll get on a plane tomorrow. You can see my house, see my shop. The change'll do you good."

"No way," Graham said. "I couldn't do that to you."

"I'm asking you. It's a big house. It's been empty for a long time now." I took the can of beer off the dash and put it back in the box. "Don't think about it. Just say you'll come."

"What about all this beer?"

"It'll keep," I said.

―――――――

The stairs were a problem. I pulled his chair up once, so he could see where I work. He went through my tapes and records and CDs and didn't find anything he didn't already have, of course. So we went back down and that was where we stayed.

Graham wheeled along with me on my morning walks. I put a basketball hoop over the garage door and we shot baskets in the afternoons. At night we rented movies or watched MTV or sat around and read. Graham worked his way through my stack of old guitar magazines and I tried to read Proust. It wasn't so bad, really. On Fridays he went to the movies with Joan and me, and Saturdays to Sixth Street.

We talked a lot. I told him what I'd learned about my mother. We traded drinking stories and band stories. And one night, finally, I said, "You don't have to do this if you don't want to. But we've never really talked about sex. I mean there's times I don't know what to say to you, because I don't know what your situation is, I mean, what you're able to do, you know . . ." I let it trail off because I saw I'd made him uncomfortable.

"Look," I said, "I'm sorry. It's not really any of my business. Can we forget I said anything?"

"No, no, man, it's okay. I mean, it's okay for you to ask, you just have to understand that I don't have to answer. The thing is that I never talk with anybody except my doctor about sexual things. Other than women, of course, that I'm in bed with. The reason is that I want to be as near normal as I can be. So everything about me that is different I have to play down. Do you understand what I'm saying here?"

"Sure, of course."

"For one thing, spinal cord injuries are not just one way or another. You might say the spinal cord is like a telephone cable. If somebody comes along near New York and partially cuts the cable, it may knock out Pittsburgh, and it may knock out Austin, but the rest of the places aren't affected. And that's what happened with me. Now, obviously, if the entire cable is cut through, then everybody's cut off. And a lot of times that happens. So people—even doctors—tend to stereotype people that way. If they hear something about one person in a wheelchair, then everybody is that way. So when you try to date somebody, you have to fight all these stereotypes. I mean, if a woman just assumes that the whole country is not getting phone service, so to speak, then you're not going to have a chance. The pool of people that you're able to approach is already pretty small, because they have to accept the fact that you can't walk.

"People can be so fucking thoughtless, you just wouldn't believe it. Okay, I will tell you this one story. I have to wear a catheter to take care of my urinary functions. I've never told anybody else that, any other nonmedical person. So I was in the hospital one time and there was a close friend of mine and his wife in the room visiting me. This nurse walks in and says, 'Hey, we're going to have to change your catheter.' Right there in front of them. I told her later, I said, 'I was so shocked when you did that, I didn't know whether I wanted to shoot you, or my friends, or myself.' I said, 'You just don't realize, you're around these things so much it becomes second nature to you. You don't realize that people have a life outside the hospital.' "

"I feel like a real jerk now," I said.

"Don't. You wanted an honest answer, right? So I gave you one. This is just my attitude, remember. I've known a lot of other disabled veterans who were totally open. And I tried to stay away from them because I always thought—whether it was true or not—that one of the reasons they were so open was because they wanted pity. And that's the last thing I want. I want to be totally normal. Except for the fact that I'm sitting in a wheelchair.

"My doctor, she's always saying, 'You're just too damned independent.' And I say, 'I know, I know I am.' But the only thing bad I can see about it is how it's going to affect me in the future, when I can't be independent anymore, when my health starts failing and I'm not strong enough to do it."

We sat quietly for a long time. Finally Graham said, "Man. I thought you were supposed to be helping me through this shit. Here you're making me want a drink something awful."

"Look on the bright side," I said. "If you can get through this without drinking, you got it made."

━━━━━

He stayed three weeks, through most of October. It was cold and raining when I put him on the plane. By that time we both knew he was going to make it.

I came home and tried to work for a while. The house was too quiet but there was nothing I wanted to listen to. What I heard in my head was Benny Goodman's "Let's Dance" and Glenn Miller's "Moonlight Serenade." I could have gone out and gotten them on newly remastered CDs, but that wasn't what I wanted. I called my mother and told her I was coming up for my father's albums.

"They're not in very good shape, you know."

"I don't care. I just want them. I think he would have wanted me to have them."

"Well, I guess it's all right. I don't listen to them all that often."

"You never listen to the actual records. You've got them all on tape. I'll be up sometime tomorrow afternoon."

"Well, that will be fine. I'll look forward to seeing you."

I took her out to a Mexican restaurant the next night. When we got back to the house I said, "What did you do with Dad's ashes?"

She looked at me like I'd cracked up. "They're in my bedroom. They're on top of the dresser, in a sandalwood box that your father brought back from Burma."

"I want to take some home with me."

"Well, yes, of course, dear, I always meant for you to have some, when you were ready."

"I think I'm ready now."

She bustled around, finding a small bottle for me to put them in. Then she got very ill at ease. "Would you . . . I mean, I don't think I could actually . . . Can you do it without my being there?"

"Sure."

I went into the bedroom and there it was, a foot long and five inches wide and maybe three inches deep, with carvings of plants and animals all around the sides. I sat on the bed and opened it up. The ashes were inside, in a round bottle nested in tissue paper. I took the lid off and spilled a few of them into my hand. They aren't ground up nice and fine like an American creamatorium would do them. There are a few black cinders, and some little chunks of bone, oddly shaped, a lighter shade of gray against the fine dark gray powder. They left a stain on my palm. They are my father.

I put them in my bottle, along with another small handful. Then I closed up both bottles and put the box back on the dresser. I packed my bottle in my overnight bag and went into the living room.

"I've never seen you cry for him," my mother said. It sounded like an accusation.

Maybe you would have, I thought, if you'd come in there with me. But I saw then that her suffering was private, not something she knew how to share with me, that she would always be alone. The way my father was alone when he went over the edge in Cozumel. What I had to do was fight with all my strength and all my heart to make sure that I didn't end up the same way.

"Not yet," I said. "Soon."

⸻

I drove back to Austin the next day. I have a wooden box that my parents brought me from Europe years ago, and I set the bottle of my father's ashes inside it and put it on top of the bookshelves in the white room.

My life reverted to routine. It was hard to get up a lot of mornings. If I went back to sleep there was nobody to notice except me, and what I noticed was a headache and grogginess for the rest of the day. I would schedule customer pickups at ten in the morning to give me a reason to get up and get my walk and shower and breakfast over with.

The house was especially empty at night. I would lie in bed and idly hold my penis as I thought about Lori or Erika or Alex, remembering women I'd slept with before I was married, women I'd lusted after since. Half the time I didn't manage enough enthusiasm to get erect, let alone to masturbate.

It was the loneliness as much as the lack of sex. I wanted somebody to wake up next to. Somebody to say, "I love you" to, somebody to say it back. I felt winter coming on, and with it the urge to curl up in front of the fireplace in a pile of blankets. But not alone. Fall is everything dying and it triggers a longing in me, not the romantic, expansive lust of spring but something more primal and intense, the need to fuck death away.

That was when Annette Shipley called, the last Saturday in October. I hadn't seen her since my senior year of high school, when she was in Dallas briefly, ejected from VISTA and recuperating from an abortion. I'd heard about her occasionally from mutual friends, same as with Alex. I knew she'd worked as a stripper at the Yellow Rose here in Austin, and more than once I'd thought about going down to see if she was there.

"I saw your ad in the *Chronicle*," she said. "Do you make house calls?"

She had a small, run-down house off Airport and Fifty-first, and a Panasonic all-in-one stereo that just needed some cleanup and a new fuse. She worked at Penney's in Highland Mall, her dancing days long over because of arthritis in her back. She looks good, better than I'd imagined, her hair still long and blonde, her body in great shape. What I'd forgotten was the downward twist to her mouth and her sardonic amusement with the world. "Not bad" is her favorite expression. It was what she said after our failed sex more than twenty years ago.

It was also what she said when, after a few tentative and somewhat brusque dates, we went to bed together. It wasn't exactly like making love. She was very businesslike, with her own condoms in a drawer by the bed, her clothes neatly folded over a chair as she took them off. At that point I was just grateful. My presexual jitters passed pretty quickly and when I came it seemed to take an enormous pressure off my chest.

We lasted two weeks. Some desperate part of me wanted to fall in love and wasn't succeeding. Some desperate part of her knew I wasn't able to give her what she wanted: romance, tenderness, some kind of hedge against a long, solitary old age. It made her quarrelsome and me sullen. She kept asking me, "What the hell is it you want?" I couldn't tell her.

One morning I woke up and realized the answer was Lori, or if it wasn't Lori it was somebody who could make me forget her. I had a date that night with Annette and I spent all day trying to think of a way out of it. I showed up late and Annette let me in with a perfunctory kiss, then headed to the refrigerator for a glass of wine. I followed her into the kitchen and said, "I was thinking we could go on to dinner or whatever, but maybe I shouldn't spend the night."

"Are we breaking up?"

"I think maybe yes."

"This pisses me off a little. I was going to break up with you, and now you've gone and done it first."

It didn't exactly call for an apology so I didn't say anything at all.

"I don't know what you're looking for, Ray. But I've got the feeling I haven't really been there in bed as far as you're concerned. Not who I am now. Just some nineteen-year-old Annette Shipley that you want to prove yourself with. You're not fucking me, you're trying to fuck your own past."

"I feel shitty about this. I feel like I've let you down."

"Of course you do. You were the same way in high school. You wanted everybody to like you. Well, Ray, I'm going to let you in on a secret. We all like you anyway. You can quit trying so hard. So go do what you have to do. I'll skip dinner, if it's all the same. Call me up sometime if you want to get to know me. We don't have to fuck or anything."

"Okay," I said. I tried to kiss her good-bye but she pushed me away.

"Just go," she said. "You've been real good about not playing games or trying to bullshit me, so don't start now."

———

I drove to Dallas for Thanksgiving, went up there a week early so I would be with my mother on the night of the sixteenth, the anniversary of my father's death. "I'm fine," she assured me. "Yesterday was rough, dreading it, you know, but today is fine."

In other words, I thought, you've handled it. These bad times will always happen some time or some place when I'm not around to see them. She didn't ask about me and I didn't have anything to offer. As I lay in my familiar bed in the guest room that night I waited for some kind of emotion to come, but it didn't.

I had my guitar with me that week and when I felt claustrophobic I would take it to my room and practice. I also spent a few hours every day knocking down the rest of the fishpond.

Thanksgiving dinner was chicken and rice and canned green beans, cooked to death just like my father liked them. Donna from next door and her husband ate with us, and my mother was her usual brave and slightly overcheerful self. She had a little wine and seemed happy to be the center of everyone's attention and concern.

She knew I was in therapy. I had a few questions, and my mother's answers were apologetic, even defensive. There was nothing they could do about all the moves; it was bad luck that landlords had broken lease after lease. My father, she said, had quit the Park Service so he wouldn't have to spend another summer in the field. I had to understand that they'd done everything they could.

I saw her with new eyes. For the first time I knew that I could live through her disapproval, that I could give as good as I got. It kept me from being quite as angry, and when I did get mad there was always the sledgehammer and the fishpond. She cried when I left and I reminded her that Christmas was only a month away, that I would see her then.

Christmas came before I was ready. I bought a tree the day before my mother arrived, which took all my willpower. It was something Elizabeth and I had always done together, on her birthday. It was seventy degrees outside and I was devoid of goodwill and charity. I remembered again all those Christmas vacations and birthdays on the road.

We had Christmas dinner with Pete and his wife, Cindy. My mother had a couple of glasses of wine with dinner and decided to tell the story of me at Indian Bible School. This was the summer when I was ten, at Chaco Canyon National Park. I guess it's the thing I'm most ashamed of in my life. My parents decided to send me to the Vacation Bible School with the Navajo kids. On the first day, in church, I announced in a loud voice that the pew I was sitting in was reserved for white people.

Pete and Cindy looked at their plates, embarrassed for me, and I saw red. "And where the hell do you think I learned that?" I said. "I wasn't an adult, no matter how hard you worked to turn me into one, to never let me have a childhood. I was a mirror of you two. You taught me how I was supposed to feel about Indians. You taught me to sit off by myself. You made me into that scared, lonely, knotted-up little kid. You and nobody else. And if you want to brag about it, you can do it somewhere else."

We didn't stay long after dinner. On the drive home my mother said, "I think I should see if I can get a flight out in the morning. I just remembered I was supposed to look after Donna's mail, and I'm worried about this leak in the back outside faucet."

"No," I said. "I don't want you to run away. We've been running from things in this family as long as I can remember. You fucked up, okay? You embarrassed me in front of my friends, for no good reason. So I embarrassed you back, and now it's over. And we're going to go on."

She stayed through the twenty-ninth. We played games and watched TV and she even came up one afternoon to learn a little about what I do for a living.

The day after she left was my thirty-ninth birthday. I spent it at the movies, four of them in a row. It took all day. I got home about ten o'clock. There were a lot of birthday messages on the machine, from Joan and a couple other customers, from Pete and my mother and even Elizabeth. I was listening to them when the phone rang.

"Will you accept a collect call from Lori?"

"Yes." I was instantly wound up. "Yes, please."

"Hi," Lori said.

"Hi yourself."

"I thought I'd say Merry Christmas and see if you were okay."

"You sound so close."

"No, I'm not in Austin." There was a short pause. "I kind of wish I was."

"Is Tom there?"

"No."

"Then you can wish me happy birthday, too."

"I knew it was your birthday. I just didn't know if I should say anything. Are you okay?"

"Yeah, pretty much. I think so."

"Are you . . . did you have to spend the day alone?"

"I don't guess I had to. But I did."

"So you're not . . ."

"Seeing anybody? No. I . . . I was for a couple weeks last month. It didn't work out. There's not much to say."

"Yes there is. There's lots to say. Because your relationships with women have a lot to do with anything that might happen between you and me."

"I didn't think anything was *going* to happen between you and me."

"Nobody ever said that. I have to get my life sorted out. And I have to know you're sorting yours out too."

So I told her about Annette, everything I could think of. I can't imagine she got any pleasure from details of my sex with another woman. I was as honest as I could manage. "I was lonely," I said. "I need a relationship. I need to be touched. You said it yourself, how you get weird living alone."

"How do you think that makes me feel? Is that all you want from me? To plug me into some slot labeled 'Relationship' in your life? Am I that interchangeable?"

"No," I said. "But you're taken."

There was a long silence. "I've left Tom. Finally."

"Jesus Christ. Where are you?"

"I'm in Mexico City right now, but I'm coming to the States."

"I want to see you."

"No."

"Lori—"

"I mean it, Ray. I'm not ready. I need some time to put myself back together."

"Are you hurt? Did that son of a bitch—"

"No, there's no physical damage. It's all on the inside. Right now I don't feel like there's a real person for you to see."

"I can help."

"You're doing it again. Stop trying to rescue the world and work on yourself." A second later she said, "You're sighing again."

"Breathing. I'm breathing. Will you let me know where you end up? Write me or call or send a telegram? You have my address with you?"

"Yes."

"I love you."

"We'll see," she said.

———

New Year's Eve, 1989/90. I went to a party at Pete's and danced with a number of women and collected a few kisses and then came home for a good night's sleep. The Berlin Wall was down, Lori was free, it was the nineties. It was something to get up for in the morning.

———

Take a broken stereo, where only one channel comes through, or where the sound cuts out without any warning except a tiny click, or where there's all bass and the speakers just hum and fuzz. You take it apart and you isolate the circuits and you track the problem down. Sometimes it seems hopeless, that there is no possible explanation. Then you figure out that you've taken something for granted that you shouldn't have, that there's one more question you should have asked. And there's your answer. Maybe you have to order a part, maybe you can rig a fix there in the shop. Either way, you end up with a stereo that plays again, the music as clear and clean and pure as you can make it, and it's there whenever you ask for it.

That's what I did through January and February and the first half of March.

There were times when I thought about making a pass at Joan, about calling Annette again, about trying to lure Alex away from her family. I learned that impulses go away if you ignore them long enough, at least the stupid ones do.

One Tuesday in February I found myself finally telling Georgene about my near-death experience. When I came to the part about what my father said, the part where he said, "Let go," it made me cry pretty hard.

She thought it was important. She said I'd started to grieve for him. I don't know if it's true, but that Thursday I took the box and the bottle of ashes into her office. That was where I finally dumped them out into the box. We made a little ceremony out of it, I guess the way I would like to have done with my mother.

I've heard it's possible to go your whole life with, say, the muscles in your back completely tense. It's only if somebody tries to massage them that you start to feel the pain. And then, slowly, gradually, maybe you can get them to relax. To let go.

I got Lori's letter on March sixteenth.

It said she was in Houston, taking a Master's in Social Work at Rice. She wasn't sure what she would do with it. There were hospitals, there was family counseling, she didn't know. The work was hard and she was long out of practice at being a student. She thought of me a lot but she wasn't ready to see me yet.

There was a return address on the envelope.

I was in Houston by late afternoon. The address matched an apartment in a slightly run-down neighborhood east of River Oaks. A beat-up yellow Chevy Nova was parked in front of her door.

My hands shook as I got out of the car. I walked across the street and rang her doorbell. After a few seconds I heard footsteps. My throat swelled shut. I knew she was looking at me through the peephole in the door. A muffled voice said, "Oh shit."

"Lori, it's me. Are you going to let me in?"

"I'm thinking."

"You put your address on the envelope. What did you think I'd do?"

"Respect my wishes and leave me alone."

"Okay," I said. I turned around and walked toward the car. Part of me had known this would happen and was saying I told you so. I had this masochistic image of myself going home and closing all the blinds and licking my wounds in the darkness. Better off alone, it said.

I heard the door open behind me. "Ray," she said. "Wait."

I turned around. She was wearing an Aztec calendar T-shirt that came to her knees, and she had fuzzy pink socks on her feet. Her hair was darker than I remembered it, her tan faded. Her eyes were just the same.

There was a lot we had to talk about. We didn't talk. I kissed her there on the doorstep and we backed into the apartment without letting go of each other. I didn't see the furniture or the color of the walls. All I saw was her, her eyes, her mouth. She pulled at my shirt and then we were both naked, and I was inside her there on the cheap shag carpet.

Eventually we made it to the bedroom and we didn't come out until the next morning. During the night we finally talked.

"You should have told me you were here," I said.

"I wasn't ready," she said. She lay in my arms, her head on my chest.

"I just think about the weeks we lost."

"We've got time. We've got years. If that's what you want."

"You know it is. Why don't you come to Austin? You can transfer to UT. I've got the house, you wouldn't have to worry about rent . . ."

"No. I'm sorry, but there's no way. Austin doesn't have a teaching hospital, and I think that's where I want to work. I'm already halfway through the semester here. It's not fair to ask me to drop that."

"No," I said. "You're right." I saw where we were headed and felt a moment of panic in my guts. "Whereas I can do what I do anywhere. I can fix stereos in Houston as well as in Austin."

"I can't ask you to do that either. To leave your house . . ."

"You didn't ask." I took a deep breath, and in that long second let myself feel everything that was tied up in that house. The house where

I'd lived longer—by a factor of two or three—than anywhere else in my life. Where my father had stayed and Elizabeth and I had spent most of our marriage. Where I'd planted shrubs and mowed the lawn and raked the leaves, where I'd finally started my own business.

None of that mattered as much as the woman that lay next to me.

"You didn't ask," I said. "I offered."

For the rest of March and all of April I spent two days a week in Austin, finishing the repairs I was committed to there, making arrangements to rent out the house, packing. Lori and I found a four-bedroom house a few blocks from her apartment and signed a year's lease. I put our new phone number in my first ad in the Houston *Press*.

Lori was not that crazy about moving so quickly from one long-term relationship to another. I was prickly, despite all my best intentions, about leaving Austin. Sometimes we're up until two or three arguing it out. It's so different from the long, lonely silences of my marriage to Elizabeth. The fights are part of something alive and growing, something the two of us are building together, using the pieces of our broken lives as material.

I tried to get Georgene to continue our sessions by phone, but it wasn't her way. She gave me a list of people in Houston. I wasn't prepared for how much it hurt to say good-bye to her.

I was still there in Austin, loading the last of my possessions into a U-Haul, when the phone rang. It was unnaturally loud in the empty house.

"This is Dr. Ling in Dallas," the voice said, and I knew it meant my mother.

"How bad?" I said.

"Your mother's had a stroke. We don't know how serious it's going to be yet."

"What hospital?"

"St. Paul's."

"I'm on my way."

Lori was in class the first time I called. I called again from Dallas and this time she was in. She made sure I was all right before she asked about my mother.

"She's asleep," I told her. It was dusk and the blinds were closed in the hospital room. My mother's breath was ragged from asthma.

"She was awake when I got here and she recognized me and everything. She's numb all down her right side and she has trouble talking. They think she's going to be okay."

"Good."

"Well. It means she can't go back to living alone. She's going to have to go into some kind of nursing home."

There was a long silence, and then Lori said, "No. She's staying with us."

═════

And so it came to be that I live in Houston in a big house with my mother and the woman I love. Lori works at M. D. Anderson Hospital as part of her degree, counseling female cancer patients and their families. Most of her patients die. She tells people it's okay, that she's always been good at short-term relationships. Behind the humor something else is working itself out. Her job is healing her, and she is healing me.

My mother is another story. When she gets Lori alone she talks endlessly about my father, about what a great sex life they had, about how he was as warm and expressive in private as he was cold in public. She's staked out her own personal, private memories, memories that exclude me. Someday I'll accept that, and I'll grieve for my father, and for the wasted years of my marriage, and the childhood I never had. I get closer to it every day, and one day it will simply happen.

Life is quiet. My mother is teaching me to play bridge. Sometimes it's hard for her to hold her cards, but her mind remains sharp. Her memories, real or imagined, seem to get more vivid every day as the present recedes. We have a cat named Herbert and some beautiful art deco furniture from the antique shops along Westheimer. Graham says he's tired of L.A. and thinks it's time to move Carnival Dog to Texas. He wants to get away from oldies and give some new young bands a start. I wouldn't be surprised to see him here by New Year's.

We listen to *Smile* now and then, even though it makes me lonesome for Brian. I tried *Celebration of the Lizard* the other night and enjoyed it, but what can I say. It's not me.

It's still too painful to listen to Hendrix.

Last night I dreamed about my father again. It wasn't much of a dream. He and my mother and I are staying in some kind of beach house, maybe in the Caribbean. We have lunch together and my father tells the halibut joke. I take a towel and go down to the ocean by myself to swim. The water is clear and beautiful.

When I woke up Lori was nestled behind me, with her arms around my chest.

═══════

I guess that's about it. Business is great, and I like to think that it's because of the quality of the work I do, that it's because I really care how the music sounds. If you're ever in Houston and need your stereo fixed, you should give me a call. I'm in the book.